The Gunny Sack

About Apollo Africa

The original Heinemann African Writers Series was launched in 1962 with the publication of Chinua Achebe's *Things Fall Apart*, Cyprian Ekwensi's *Burning Grass* and Kenneth Kaunda's *Zambia Shall Be Free*, with Achebe himself acting as an editorial advisor. Over the next 40 years, the series continued to publish the best writing from across the African continent.

One of the founding aims of the Heinemann series was to make books by African writers available to as wide a readership as possible. Apollo Africa – a collaboration between Black Star Books and Head of Zeus – is proud to continue this work, ensuring novels, essays, poetry and plays from the original series are once again made available to readers all over the world.

The Gunny Sack

M.G. Vassanji

Black Star Books and Head of Zeus would like to thank the following organisations: The Miles Morland Foundation, The Ford Foundation, and Africa No Filter. This publication was made possible through their support.

First published in the Heinemann African Writers Series in 1989 by Heinemann Educational Publishers

This edition first published in the UK in 2024 by Head of Zeus Ltd, part of Bloomsbury Publishing Plc.

Copyright © M.G. Vassanji, 1989

The moral right of M.G. Vassanji to be identified as the author of this work has been asserted in accordance with the Copyright, Designs and Patents Act of 1988.

All rights reserved. No part of this publication may be reproduced, stored in a retrieval system, or transmitted in any form or by any means, electronic, mechanical, photocopying, recording, or otherwise, without the prior permission of both the copyright owner and the above publisher of this book.

This reprint is published by arrangement with Pearson Education Limited.

This is a work of fiction. All characters, organizations, and events portrayed in this novel are either products of the author's imagination or are used fictitiously.

9 7 5 3 1 2 4 6 8

A catalogue record for this book is available from the British Library.

ISBN (PB): 9781035900794
ISBN (E): 9781837930425

Excerpt from 'Vacillation' reprinted with permission of Macmillan Publishing Company and A. P. Watt Ltd. on behalf of Michael B. Yeats and Macmillan London Ltd. from *The Poems of W. B. Yeats*, edited by Richard J. Finneran, Copyright © 1933, Macmillan Publishing Company renewed 1961 by Bertha Georgie Yeats.

Excerpt from 'Utendi wa Inkishafi' in *Anthology of Swahili Poetry*, edited by Ali A. Jahadhmy, Heinemann Educational Books (East Africa), Nairobi, 1975.

Typeset by Siliconchips Services Ltd UK

Printed and bound in Great Britain by
CPI Group (UK) Ltd, Croydon CR0 4YY

Head of Zeus Ltd
First Floor East
5–8 Hardwick Street
London EC1R 4RG

WWW.HEADOFZEUS.COM

for Nuru,
With gratitude

From man's blood-sodden heart are sprung
Those branches of the night and day
Where the gaudy moon is hung.
What's the meaning of all song?
'Let all things pass away.'
                                W. B. YEATS

enga taa katika pepo
haiziwiliki izimikapo sasa mi
huona izimishiye

[Behold the lantern in the wind
now beyond help
you see it extinguished]

Contents

About Apollo Africa	*i*
Author's Note	*xiii*
Part One: *Ji Bai*	**1**
1. Shehrbanoo	3
2. The Two Jewels	16
3. As Strong as Bhima	31
4. The Spirits of Times Past	47
5. The Sin of One Man	56
6. The Suffering Mukhi	68
Part Two: *Kulsum*	**71**
7. View from the Birij	73
8. How I Killed My Father	83
9. Dar es Salaam	104
10. Habib Mansion	123
11. God, Two Queens and the Famous Five	141
12. Forbidden Fruit	158
13. Cricket and Elections	180
14. Boyschool and Independence	198
15. Red Skies and Western Eyes	218
16. These Dreams, Ready Made and Gone	237

Part Three: *Amina* — **245**

17. Big Black Trunk — 247
18. Dar, Massachusetts, New York, and the Moon — 283
19. Britannia's Children — 294
20. Deluge and a New Saviour — 302
21. Marriage of Minds: Alliances — 316
22. And the Final Night — 336

Glossary — *341*
Acknowledgements — *349*
About the Author — *351*

Author's Note

The non-English words – which are mostly in Swahili or Cutchi-Gujarati – are intended to be integral to the text. In most cases their meanings are obvious in context, or explicit. The Glossary provided should be useful, but I hope it is not so necessary as to become an impediment. In using it the reader should bear in mind that the meanings given are particular to a place, time, and group of people and might not agree with dictionaries. I have also taken liberties with language, using 'Swahili' for 'Kiswahili' and English plural forms for Swahili words. Thus: Mshenzis, Mdachis. These usages have not been entirely uncommon. The map should make some places more concrete but I hope, like the Glossary, it is ultimately dispensable. This is a work of fiction, with some historical events and characters as background. The Shamsi community is fictitious, as are the towns Kaboya and Matamu and much else.

Part One

Ji Bai

1 | *Shehrbanoo*

Memory, Ji Bai would say, is this old sack here, this poor dear that nobody has any use for any more. Stroking the sagging brown shape with affection she would drag it closer, to sit at her feet like a favourite child. In would plunge her hand through the gaping hole of a mouth, and she would rummage inside. Now you feel this thing here, you fondle that one, you bring out this naughty little nut and everything else in it rearranges itself. Out would come from the dusty depths some knick-knack of yesteryear: a bead necklace shorn of its polish; a rolled-up torn photograph; a cowrie shell; a brass incense holder; a Swahili cap so softened by age that it folded neatly into a small square; a broken rosary tied up crudely to save the remaining beads; a bloodstained muslin shirt; a little book. There were three books in that old gunny that never left her bedside, four-by-six-inch, green, tablet-like, the front cover folding over into a flap fastened with a tiny padlock! On the cover of each, neatly carved, two faded inscriptions in gold, wriggling in opposite directions: one in an Arabic-looking hand, the other indecipherable, supposedly in a secret script. 'He who opens it will suffer the consequences,' she, who did not read, would gravely pronounce to her awed listener.

We buried Ji Bai a few weeks ago on a cold November afternoon...

From near and far, young and old, they came to see her go, in this small overseas community. Not that many here knew her or had even heard of her; she was only passing through, a traveller. But they would go away the wiser, about her and themselves and the common links between them. Such are the merits of a funeral. The converted supermarket was half full. The old, the exiled old, sitting on chairs on one side, visible but unobtrusive, outwardly implacable and unperturbed, watching the funeral ceremony proceeding with clockwork precision in the hands of the Westernised funeral committee. What thoughts behind those stony masks? The rest of the congregation, the younger members, sat on the floor, facing the ceremony. With practised precision, with appropriate gravity of speech and bearing, the head of the committee led formations of select relatives and friends to partake in the more intimate rituals. She lay inside a raised open coffin, a younger, doll-like Ji Bai, face flushed pink but hideous and grim. What have they done to you, Ji Bai? Someone had taken the pains to iron out every wrinkle on her face, to clean out the grey, to stretch the skin taut like a cellophane wrapper. Once, when time was plenty and the hourglass slow, every man, woman and child present would come and kneel before the dead and beg forgiveness and pay their last respects. Now, in collective homage the congregation filed past the pink face in the coffin; the women took their seats, the men formed two closely spaced rows. A sob stifled, a wail choked (practised wailers, some of these), the coffin was closed.

'Stand back,' said the leader, gruffly. 'Stand back!'

'Praise the Prophet!' The coffin was slowly if shakily lifted on to the shoulders of the male relatives and the committee members. Then it took purchase and at shoulder height bobbed away easily like a boat in a slight current, between the two rows of males, as anyone who could gave it a shoulder or even a slight shove on its way to be rolled into the black funeral car outside. An older, experienced voice, rich with feeling, took away the chant:

> There is none but Him
> There is none but Him
> There is none but Him
> – and Muhammad is His Prophet...

(Once, a rickety yellow and green truck with men sitting on both sides of the coffin at the back chanting the shahada, at the sight of which pedestrians would stop and fold their hands in respect.)

Afterwards, I watched from a distance the last clod of earth thrown perfunctorily on the grave, the last of the congregation – how can I call them mourners? – leave. Someone made a gesture in my direction but then thought the better of it. I was left alone. Trees rustled in the wind, dead leaves scraped the ground. In the distance another burial was in progress, this one more opulent, its mourners in black, with bigger and better wreaths, bigger and better cars. Traffic zipped along the highway. What cold comfort, Ji Bai, I thought. Even worms couldn't survive in such a grave. I had a vision of her small frail body under six feet of cold earth that would soon freeze. I could see the body shrink, under icy pressure, the skin dry and peel off and fly away like a kite, the skeleton rattle and fold and rearrange itself to form a neat square heap like the firewood that was once sold outside her store in Dar.

A week later Aziz her grand nephew stumbled in to see me with a large blue vinyl suitcase.

'With the compliments of Ji Bai!' he announced cheerfully.

'What? A suitcase?'

A vinyl legacy from a vinyl-faced Ji Bai? No... The twinkle in his eyes recalled the mischief in Ji Bai's, as with a flourish he proceeded to lay it on its side, and like a salesman swung it open as if to display its capacity and interior. A ball of kapok glided out and sailed away.

'The gunny sack,' he spoke, the same instant I saw it, brown and dusty, looking threatened and helpless in the brand-new interior. It was drawn loosely shut with a sisal string. 'You used to sit before it so long, she thought it should be yours.'

'Isn't it rightfully yours?' I asked.

'No. It's yours. She wanted you to have it.'

'Come, come… what if she had died there? Would you have posted it?'

'But she died here.'

Young Aziz, he knew more than he let on. He was Ji Bai's companion during the last few years of her life. She had said she would travel, and Aziz accompanied her, first to India then here. Wherever she went, her gunny went with her. Did she know she would die in this foreign place, then? With Ji Bai there was no telling.

He said, 'If my family had had their way they would have burnt it long ago. It's brought nothing but bad luck, they say. They want you to burn it, once and for all to bury the past.'

'And you – do you want me to burn it?'

'Look at it first – it's what she wanted, after all. Then, maybe burn it. To tell you the truth, I almost burnt it instead of bringing it here.'

Now Ji Bai's bones clatter in my sack.

It sits beside me, seductive companion, a Shehrazade postponing her eventual demise, spinning out yarns, telling tales that have no beginning or end, keeping me awake night after night, imprisoned in this basement to which I thought I had escaped.

(There should be no misunderstanding. This drab gunny is no more Shehrazade than I am Prince Shehriyar. She is more your home-grown type, a local version, good at heart but devoid of grace – yet irresistible – whom I name this instant Shehrbanoo, Shehru for short. Shehrbanoo, Shehrazade, how close in sound, yet worlds apart.)

Light drifts in through the only window, and I have already discovered a pastime for the daylight hours. I follow footsteps. What can feet reveal? Old worn-out shoes on large unwieldy feet, casual wallabees, businessmen's polished leathers, pretty little feet in sandals, an occasional chappal trailed by the inevitable sari border. Feet that I see only once and others that I see every day relentlessly punishing the pavement, following the same course. But even here there is no respite. You, says my drab Shehrbanoo, addressing the feet, you who walk by in this flurry of activity, hurrying here and there, seemingly getting somewhere but really nowhere: listen, step aside from the tedium, enter, there are worlds here and worlds...

Images like confetti, like cotton lint in Ji Bai's mattress shop, drift through my mind haphazardly, each one a clue to a story, a person. A world. Sounds knock in my brain demanding entrance, rude gatecrashers jostling for right of way, until I in a dizzy spell say, All right, now what, Shehrbanoo? Leave this magic.

Listen, the sound of feet outside: clip clop, clip clop, clip-clip-clop, clip-clip-clop clip clop, clip-clip-clop clip clop...

Miss Penny Mrs Gaunt, Miss Penny Mrs Gaunt, Miss Penny Mrs Gaunt...

Miss Penny returned one morning, presumably from her honeymoon, as Mrs Gaunt, headmistress of our primary school. Every morning at seven-thirty sharp, before the bell rang for assembly, he came to drop her in his car. And gave her a lingering, passionate kiss goodbye as a circle of curious wide-eyed faces formed around them. My first exposure to European passion. (Years later, one would hear of the cars parked at Oyster Bay at night, inside which if you peeped you could see even more compromising postures.)

It was Miss Penny who first asked me the question, 'Where do you come from?' and later would say, 'Begin at the beginning.'

At the beginning, then.

(Sometimes I think of you, Miss Penny Mrs Gaunt, I wonder where you are. Perhaps in an English village teaching a class of noisy youngsters? And he who so passionately used to kiss you: does he still kiss you?... Has time been kind to you, Miss Penny Mrs Gaunt?... Can you imagine, Miss Penny Mrs Gaunt, prim proper perfect in a chair in the shade of a mango tree, the impact you had on a seven-year-old so many years ago? Every time I think of you, I search for the beginning, every time I utter 'beginning' I recall you, Madam.)

The beginning.

One quiet night they sat outside their doorways in little groups, gurgling hookahs and talking in murmurs. The babies were sleeping and the women were inside with them. From somewhere there rang out an occasional sound from the older children playing. The night was starry, and a cool wind rustled the leaves of the mango and almond trees. Around them the crickets chirped. Moths and other insects weaved dances around the solitary lamp hanging from a tree. A tall, bearded man came in sight, in a long white robe and a white skull cap. Pausing in the distance, his long wide shadow merging with the darkness of the trees and forest, he began clapping his hands in rhythm and dancing the rasa. He went one full circle, singing of hope. They listened. Then like a ghost he disappeared, as he had come. The next night again he came and did one full circle of the rasa; and sang. The sound was sweet, the message enticing with promise and hope. Slowly they got up, one by one, from where they were watching and started walking towards him. They formed a circle around him. Then, clapping hands and clicking fingers, together they danced the garba, a circle of singing men in motion around the white figure. A little later the women came out from the huts and joined them. Then came the older children from where they were playing. The whole village danced the garba and sang. Then the man initiated them into the secret. He taught them new prayers and he taught them songs. One day the sun would rise from the west, he said. They must wait for a saviour.

His name was Shamas, and they called themselves Shamsis. Thus was the village of Junapur in India converted to an esoteric sect of Islam that considered thundering Allah as simply a form of reposing Vishnu.

And so much for mythology, says Shehru. Now for some history.

But that was the puff that grew into a wind. India was only beginning to feel its seams. It was due to community conflicts, with origins in that conversion some three centuries before, that my young great-grandfather Dhanji Govindji, sporting an umbrella, a new turban and new leather shoes, but otherwise quite undistinguished, left Junapur early one morning on a bullock cart on the road to the harbour town of Porbander. For the saviour had failed to arrive. Villagers had sung and prayed for the missing avatar. In their prayers and hopes they climbed up mountains and trees, scanned the horizons westwards for he who was destined to march in triumph to their village on a white horse, leading a troop of elephants and soldiers bearing shiny weapons in a blare of trumpets, to be welcomed by women dressed in white with a shower of pearls and champeli flowers. Times were still difficult. In Junapur the rains were missed for the second year. The community was breaking up, proselytisers hung about like vultures, waiting to pick up the pieces as this community that was both Hindu and Muslim broke up in confusion. Tempers were short, daggers glinted at secret meetings.

In Porbander, Dhanji Govindji waited two weeks at the home of a relative until the dhow for Zanzibar was ready to leave.

Zanzibar! The Jewel of Africa, isle of enchantment. There are those who still weep tears for the Zanzibar that was. Dhanji Govindji had heard of Zanzibar, had dreamt of Zanzibar as a boy. Men returned from Zanzibar invariably rich; and when a bullock cart entered a village carrying its exotic passenger from abroad, gangs of boys would usher it in, with cries of, 'Africa se aya hai! Africa se aya hai!' He comes from Africa, a hat wearer: in Africa they doffed their turbans and put on hats, these pioneers. If one of these boys got into trouble, 'Go to Africa,' they told him. 'Go to Jangbar. See what Amarsi Makan did for himself. And he was no better than you.' Amarsi Makan was the example. From a loafer, to stowaway, to the Sultan's customs master and the richest man on the island: now there was a man!

From Porbander to Zanzibar was a sail of two tedious and monotonous months, with one break at Muscat, where the already crowded boat was packed further with Arabs with their harems and their slaves and more Indians. The first sign that the island was in sight was only an excessive shouting and a bustle of activity on board as the crew impatiently began preparations and found confused passengers getting in the way. What emotions stirred in Dhanji Govindji's breast as the low-lying island came into view eastwards, a dream city suddenly risen from the ocean, with its brilliant, luxuriant verdure, the shimmering white of the Arab houses in the foreground, the numerous dhows, boats, steamers and naval vessels of different flags in its harbour? As he stepped off the boat pushing aside Arab and Swahili guides babbling in Swahili, English and Cutchi? As he walked among the throngs that crowded its narrow streets, black, white and brown, slaves, masters and freedmen, businessmen, hustlers, beggars and prostitutes, sailors, diplomats and explorers?

Zanzibar… here Indians had lived and traded for centuries. There had been others before Amarsi Makan… there was Babu

Goss the Cutchi pirate, after whom boys had fashioned games and legends and dreams… who plied the seas between Mandavi and Mombasa, the Comoros and Zanzibar. In the open market of Junapur would often be heard the cry, 'I am Babu Goss, surrender your ship!' as a gang of urchins bearing twigs and branches followed their leader across a gutter…

Dhanji Govindji worked as a clerk in Zanzibar at one of the stores of no less a personage than Amarsi Makan. But there was only one Sultan's customs collector; and the competition to get to the top was cut-throat. There were scores of apprentices like himself, from all the villages in Gujarat, Kathiawad, and Cutch it seemed, all lured to the island by dreams of becoming like Amarsi Makan or Jairam Shivji or Ladha Damji – owners of chain stores, underwriters to Arab, Indian and Swahili entrepreneurs, to whom stranded explorers came for credit. The wise and enterprising sought other frontiers; the rest stayed on, enchanted by the island's perfume and musk and spice… the soft rustling movements behind silky veils, the giggles behind lattice screens… the mysterious look of two eyes through the slit in a veil, chilling you to the heart and then with a movement of the lashes commanding you, 'Come,' and you follow the trace of the halud through the teeming streets to wherever it will lead you, ready to lay down your life for its bearer… On a clear morning you could just about see in a distant haze the land mass that was the continent of Africa. In the evenings some saw the fires that slavers made as signals to incoming dhows. Every morning the harbour was abustle, with dhows setting off for the mainland. Traders, hunters, guides, explorers, porters, immigrants and civil servants left every day for that sleeping, beckoning land mass, waved off by well-wishers and onlookers. A year after his arrival at Zanzibar, Dhanji Govindji landed at Bagamoyo. While the Europeans, the hunters and porters, the seasoned Swahili traders, went inwards to seek greater fame or fortune, my forebear joined a small caravan going southwards on the slave route. Thirty-six miles on foot and donkey later, he unloaded his stuff at the village of Matamu. The caravan marched on towards Kilwa, and Dhanji Govindji walked into the nearest store and asked: 'Where is the mukhi's store?'

Dhanji Govindji. How much lies buried in a name... Dhan, wealth; Govind, the cowherd butter-thief gopi-seducer, dark Krishna. A name as Banya in its aspiration for wealth as Hindu; yet gloriously, unabashedly, Muslim. For the esoteric sect of the Shamsis there was no difference. But Govindji, the elders will now tell you, is not a family name — where is the attak, the last name, that can pin you down to your caste, your village, your trade? Absent, dropped by those to whom neither caste nor ancestral village mattered any longer. Later this irksome Govindji too was dropped by one branch of the family and replaced with Hasham. Whence Hasham, an Arab clan name? Thus the past gets buried, but for my drab, my sagging ugly Shehrbanoo, from which the dust of Kariakoo has not been shaken yet.

You can place the names of succeeding generations in a column and visualise the crazy dance of history; the logic behind the mad parade of names, from Dhanji and Samji to Aisha and Faruq, with a hundred years jingling between them — each new variation and fashion in name signalling a new era, a new beginning. In astronomical terms it was Samvat 1942 when Dhanji Govindji first set foot in Matamu. 1885 AD. And he asked for the shop of the mukhi.

There was a mukhi wherever there were a few Shamsis. And the mukhi would put you up; he would introduce you to the others of the community and he would show you the ropes.

There is still a mukhi wherever there are a few Shamsis. There is a mukhi in London, in Singapore, in Toronto. There is still a mukhi in Matamu, but there is no longer a mukhi in

Junapur (history has seen to that). You could land in Singapore and call up the local mukhi. 'Mukhi Saheb,' you say, 'I am new here and I need a little help.' 'Where are you staying?' the mukhi would ask. He doesn't let you finish. 'No no no, that simply won't do. Aré, listen to me, you come here first, then we'll see.'

Which is exactly what young Dhanji Govindji did. Mukhi Ragavji Devraj, formerly of Jamnagar, welcomed him to Matamu. And after a suitable interval a small handwritten sign went up outside an empty store: Dhanji Govindji of Junapur, and Matamu's only street boasted another Indian dukan. The mukhi found him some brokendown furniture and gave him merchandise on credit to start up with. And for good measure, he threw in a servant at a cheap price: 'She knows how to cook, she'll take care of you.' And with the sly smile of the elderly setting up a youngster, added: 'And who knows, it's warm enough here, but it can get quite cold at night. The ocean, you know.'

She was called Bibi Taratibu, Gentle One; a slave, discarded to an Indian on the slave route from Kilwa. The slave trade was over, but the keeping of slaves, especially women, still persisted on the coast.

In Matamu, Dhanji Govindji became an agent to an agent. Tribesmen from the surrounding areas, still carrying bows, arrows and spears, would come into town heaving basketfuls of gum copal to barter for cloth, beads, wire – and the occasional rusty flint-lock Zanzibari gun. Bargaining went on for hours, round after round with several customers at once, sometimes into the following day. In the end a product of Cutch, Hamburg, Philadelphia or Versailles found its way into the hinterland of Africa; which in turn yielded up the sticky translucent substance dug from its earth or tapped from its trees.

Dhanji Govindji obtained goods from Mukhi Ragavji Devraj, the local agent for the firm of Amarsi Makan. He sold the copal to the mukhi at a commission. From this commission he paid back the mukhi for the goods and for his own groceries, and put aside a little savings kept in his name by the mukhi.

In time a son was born to him and Bibi Taratibu, whom they named Huseni.

Tell me, Shehrbanoo, would the world be different if that trend had continued, if there had been more Husenis, and if these chocolate Husenis with curly hair had grown up unhindered, playing barefoot in kanzus and kofias, clutching Arabic readers...

But no. In Junapur and other towns in Cutch, Kathiawad and Gujarat a cry went up. Our sons are keeping golis, black slaves in Africa. And there are *children*, half-castes littering the coast from Mozambique to Karachi. Do something! It was claimed that a group of young preachers, called 'missionaries', had set out from Bombay to help keep the community in line. They never made it past the allures of Zanzibar, for no one saw them in the coastal towns.

When Huseni was five years old, Dhanji Govindji duly received a summons from home. May the Merciful God grant dear son Dhanji abiding contentment and happiness; increase in income and wealth; a long and healthy life; and an ever-growing faith. Amen. This is to write... and so on. He was to go and get married.

There is a story of how Dhanji got married. He took a dhow to Zanzibar, where he had to wait a week to catch the next one to Porbander. In Zanzibar he stayed with a widow to whom he brought a letter from Ragavji Mukhi. The widow had a daughter. When the week had passed, Dhanji was not on the Porbander boat; he had married. There are those who see the hand of the mukhi behind all this. It is the mukhis' job, after all, to see the congregations settled; they are still at it, from Dar es Salaam to Manhattan, Singapore to London. But that is not all. How can a young man simply marry a girl from a family he doesn't know, without a formal proposal and the negotiation of mohor, without his family's permission?

The widow, Ji Bai would swear, had put something in the boy's food, had cast a spell on the poor innocent. Trapped him like a spider. A widow in Zanzibar! What tricks would she not know? And how did she earn a living... yes, yes, that's it. But surely, if the mukhi went to her... Why not?

My scholarly brother, who studies old manuscripts, writes from the University.

Kala, I am thrilled that you now have possession of the three padlocked books. The script is known. It is a form of Devanagari (of which the Gujarati script is only one example), an old form, with modifications (extra curves, characters turned sideways, Arabic-looking additions, etc) to confuse outsiders. Isn't that exciting! Our own script! I'm not asking much (yet). Could you just make a photocopy of the cover inscription and send it to me? If it doesn't copy well, you could try to copy it by hand. Just that, for God's sake! Yours, Sona.

I hate to make a copy of the books, even the cover, to play the tourist to my Shehru; to rob her of her personality, as some tribesman might say. I can't say no either. I think, as the Masai used to do, I'll ask for payment. After all, we have to pay rent here, Shehru and I.

The reply from Sona comes two weeks later:

Kala, The Jinn Abdul testifies that he who opens the book takes the full weight of the consequences on his own head.

The same thing in Swahili (that's what the Arabic script said – they used Arabic in those days.) Jinn Abdul be damned! I say let's open these books and find out what the old man was up to!

Sona and Kala: our nicknames. Gold and black. The colours of Africa.

2 | *The Two Jewels*

While Dhanji Govindji worked as an apprentice in Zanzibar – and even later as the caravan he had joined went its leisurely pace southwards along the coast, making elaborate rest stops on the way, stared at by curious or enterprising villagers, as his donkey plodded on the way to Matamu and the porters sang to keep their minds off the loads on their heads – movements were afoot that would change the face of East Africa for ever after. Later the villagers of Matamu would take credit for having hosted the Herr Doktor Karl Peters as he went about from tribe to tribe making treaties that only he and his interpreter understood. We gave him water, they'd say, he bought some chickens from us; he bought wire and cloth on credit. The truth is that perhaps there were more Germans in the area at the time; and later, when there were many and strong and fierce, when they had come to stay and suspected treachery, some flattery was seen to be in order.

By the time Dhanji Govindji brought his bride Fatima out of Zanzibar five years later, Matamu and much of the coast were under German rule, bought from the Sultan; the mainland behind it was simply annexed in the name of the Herr Doktor's treaties. Drab, grass-grown Dar es Salaam, Sultan Seyyid Majid's aborted dream, his 'haven of peace', became the seat of the German dream in East Africa. This time Dhanji landed in the booming capital, its streets neat and already lined with new whitewashed government buildings, with its sedate European quarter, its bustling Indian bazaar. From Dar es Salaam, Dhanji on foot and Fatima in a hammock carried by two bearers, accompanied by a gang of porters, they came to Matamu.

The gentle Bibi Taratibu, of course, had to go. She moved to a house at the further end of the village, bordering the forest, where she sold tea and sweets to the transient Mshenzis from the interior. The boy Huseni stayed on. The Zanzibari widow's daughter, Fatima, was a tall, stately woman, with large and luscious hips, hefty breasts, extremely fair. When she stood on the store threshold, haughtily looking out, arms on her hips, veil covering her head but not that body, not a passing man could resist a glance at her impressive proportions. Except for one flaw, she would have done proud any Zanzibari harem. It was said that with one look, and without looking at anybody, she could unsettle a roomful of people. She was squint-eyed. When she first came to Matamu, protective mothers kept their children well hidden from her, from fear of that malevolent look that could strike from any direction. Fatima bore one daughter who died in her first year. Then was born Gulam. Gulam was a gentle boy, Ji Bai said. Gentle, and as fair as his mother. He became Ji Bai's husband.

They called the half-caste Huseni 'Simba': lion. He was the kind of boy who unerringly senses all that is forbidden or feared in the home, and proceeds to do them one by one; whose single-minded purpose in life is a relentless enmity towards his father, whose every move he tries to thwart, every rise in esteem he tries to bring down. Huseni's friends were not townspeople but the Mshenzis. Even now, a 'mshenzi' is a barbarian. In those days, when the coastal folk regarded themselves as the epitome of civilisation and urbanity, a Mshenzi was anyone who was not from within walking distance of the coast. Huseni and his Mshenzis spent their time romping around the towns debauching; in the afternoons they would laze under a shade, gambling and drinking. Sometimes in a great flurry of excitement and talking in tell-tale hushed tones, they would bring into town a tusk, undoubtedly picked off a straggling porter from some caravan in the area, which would then be dispatched posthaste and cheaply into some risk-taking Bania hands.

German justice was harsh, swift and arbitrary. In return, you could leave your store unattended without fear of robbery. Thieves had their hands chopped; insubordination was rewarded with the dreaded khamsa ishrin, twenty-five lashes from a whip of hippo hide dipped in salt, which would never break however much blood it drew. It was said that the streets of Dar es Salaam were clean because even the donkeys feared to litter them – you only had to whisper those words 'khamsa ishrin' into a donkey's ears and it would straightaway race to its stable to empty its bowels.

Outside Matamu were two German farms, a coconut plantation belonging to Herr Graff and a cotton farm to Herr Weiss. Early every morning these two gentlemen, the Bwanas Guu Refu (Long Leg) and Wasi, would walk into town in their khakis and sun hats, slinging rifles, accompanied by their foremen. Twenty job cards for each farm were dropped with great ceremony outside Mzee Guaro's house by the respective foremen in the manner of playing a winning hand, and then the party waited with arms folded for the return play. Mzee Guaro was the former jemadari of the village, the Sultan's representative, now a German agent. A few minutes later, perhaps sensing the expectant air outside, Mzee Guaro would emerge from his rooms and, drawing in his kanzu like a woman does her skirts, patiently pick up the passes from the ground and start distributing them to the first twenty able-bodied men he could find. Work on the German farms was hated, and Mzee Guaro as the harbinger of that fate was hated like the angel of death, Azrail, his other nickname. There were many stories of cruelty in the farms; of beatings and lashings, of a hanging, of insults to age and traditional rank. And one unnecessary death at which shrieks rang out for many nights.

One day, Guu Refu instructed his young water-carrier Yusufu not to move from a certain spot, whatever. Guu Refu was the more terrible of the two Germans. Everything he ordered was always followed to the letter. So that when a rain of coconuts cut from the trees around him started falling with great thumps as the men atop let them drop, the frightened Yusufu shouted, too late, but did not move from his spot. The battered body, of which all that bystanders saw was a bloodied boy's kanzu, was brought into town with great ceremony. It was paraded in .the lanes, the women wept and ululated and the men threw curses at the Germans.

Sometimes Guu Refu's arrival was preceded by news that he was on the lookout for more men for a special project; and as soon as the lanky figure with the sunhat and the rifle was sighted, towering over his askaris, men and boys scurried towards the forest, at which sight the German and his mercenaries stomped after them in their heavy boots, cutting off their paths to safety.

It was as if a man-eating lion had taken up residence in the area, with every now and then a new victim.

When the Germans had marched out of the village with their sulking recruits, exhorting them to sing, Huseni and his Mshenzis would appear under their tree.

One morning, news arrived of trouble in the interior. A mchawi had appeared who had found a medicine to drive away the Germans. All you had to do, it was said, was to go to a meeting and drink the medicine, take an oath and the German would be powerless against you. You could spit on his cat-eyes that shone in the dark, burn his big white house, drive a spear into his white belly, and he could not touch you. As soon as you chanted the words 'Maji maji maji maji...' his bullets would turn into water.

The men of Matamu were not fighters. And though they were familiar with many medicines, this one they had never heard of. Late one afternoon a rumour spread that the mchawi's followers were in the vicinity to recruit and at nightfall a nervous silence spread over the village like a blanket. Stores closed early, shutters were fastened carefully and lamps burned low. The medicine men were dreaded as much as the Germans. If you refused to take the medicine, it was said, straightaway you would receive a spear in your belly. And if you took the oath and went about chanting 'Maji maji maji maji...' and were caught, straightaway you would be strung up from the nearest mango or mbuyu tree. Your farm would be razed, your family sent away. The Germans employed barbarous askaris, the Nubians, who had no qualms opening up the bellies of women with child. The Masai, the rumours said, were already on their way from the north. And a ship full of German soldiers and more guns had docked in Dar es Salaam.

That night the village did not sleep. And when in the early hours of the morning, just as the brave muezzin began his 'Allahu Akbar Allahu Akbar Allahu Akbar...', a frantic knocking sounded on the courtyard door and a chill went through Dhanji Govindji's household as it prepared for prayer. On tiptoes Dhanji Govindji went outside to see or hear what was up. 'Baba, it's I,' came the half-caste's urgent voice, 'quickly, let me in, upesi!'

The lion of Matamu was admitted home nervous and trembling. 'They are after me,' he said. 'The Mdachis.'

'And what did you do that the Germans are after you?'

'I was watching the Maji Maji with my friends.'

Dhanji Govindji hastened his son inside and tried to abate Fatima's fury.

'So,' began Dhanji Govindji. 'What was it like, this Maji Maji?'

'It's like they say. The men, and even women, were drinking from gourds. Then they put leaves on their heads and began chanting. We joined them. All those who were hiding in the bushes came to join. "Maji maji maji maji," we were shouting. "The Mdachis? Kill them! The Mdachis? Spear them, spear them!" Then the Mdachis came with their askaris. They began shooting peu, peu, and some men fell. Then all started running, scattering everywhere, and the Mdachis started shooting with this gun that throws bullets like water – pye-pye-pye-pye-pye, like this, and aiii, many fell. Many will hang, I tell you. Guu Refu was there.'

Dhanji Govindji looked at his son. 'And do you think it is right that for the sake of your games and to show your cleverness you endanger the lives of these children? And the water on your back, you think that's the German bullets turned to water, do you? You fool, if a bullet had touched you, you would be meat for the hyenas.'

Huseni looked hurt. He was hidden for three days in the loft in the store, behind gunnies of produce. The next morning the Germans made a show of strength in Matamu and nearby areas, appearing with their askaris, and the villagers had their look at the notorious Nubians. Thus the Maji Maji revolt, which spread like a bush fire in the night across more than a quarter of the country, bypassed Matamu.

One day when Gulam, the other son, was fourteen he was sent to neighbouring Kitmangau on an errand. He came back on a stretcher carried by two Mshenzis from a nearby village. He had been attacked on the way, and the servant who accompanied him had run away. The first people to see the stretcher come in were Huseni and his gang under the tree.

'Wey! Who is sick?' shouted Huseni to the bearers.

'Bwana Dhanji's son has been attacked by bandits,' came the obsequious reply.

'Move-move-move, pisha!' cried the half-caste, up on his feet, pushing aside the bearers. 'I am also his son. Do you think I'll simply sit while you carry my brother home?'

To this incident is traced the first transformation of my grandfather Huseni. The Maji Maji incident had already sobered him somewhat. Now he saw himself as the oldest son, the protector of Fatima's children. So complete did his transformation seem, and so great was Dhanji Govindji's relief, that to make sure the boy did not revert to his old ways he took a proposal of marriage to a local family who had in their home a girl who was of age.

My grandmother was an orphan of fifteen and the proposal was quickly accepted. Her name was Moti, pearl, and she was the first jewel in Dhanji Govindji's life. The other was Ji Bai.

Ji Bai's actual name was Mongi, precious. She was called Ji Bai because to every command from her father she promptly answered, 'Ji, ha,' yes, sir. If her mother or father called her – Mongiiiii! – or whenever anyone else called her – Eh, Mongi! – promptly would come the reply, 'Ji!' Such politeness in a child, so often desired, so rarely fulfilled! Ji Bai was the darling of Bajupur.

In Bajupur, Ji Bai at thirteen liked to play bandits. Like many girls of her age she had no plans for getting married, but imagined herself always in her father's village. One day, she and her friends went to the local Brahmin to have their palms read. 'I see a successful marriage in this hand,' droned the pandit, holding her hand, 'you will be married to a *second*-timer, and your hand shows *many-many* children...'

'Go, go,' said Ji Bai, pulling back her hand. 'You have teeth in your head. Like *this* I will marry a second-timer.' She showed him a derisive thumb and skipped away.

'Remember,' called out the pandit, with a red, liquidy paan-filled grin, holding up his forefinger, '*many-many* children...'

She woke up one day two months later to the sounds and smells of a wedding in preparation. The air was laden with the sweet, rich smells of hot ghee and saffron, cloves and cinnamon, as the mithai-makers got under way. In a compound outside her father's house women were cleaning the rice and pulse was being pounded. And the most tell-tale sign of all: the women, all women, had on their lips the joyful, teasing songs of marriage. Her mother and father were not to be seen. She went to her sister-in-law and asked, 'Aré, Bhabhi, *whose* wedding is this?' And the bright-eyed Bhabhi looked up, joyfully teasing, 'Oh, my! Haven't you heard? Yours!'

Ji Bai found that it was three days since she had been formally engaged. A troupe of men had come to their house with the mukhi and taken away her father's consent in a register. Now a whole section of Bajupur was closed off to her because that was where the groom's party had camped.

That was the first time she remembered saying 'Na' to her father.

The boy was Gulam, sent to Junapur by his father in the company of Ragavji Devraj, when his first wife from Kitmangau died three months after the wedding. The girl Mongi was sighted playing with her friends as they stopped over on their way inland from Porbander. Enquiries were made, and two weeks later Ragavji Devraj returned with the boy and the proposal.

For her remaining days in the village Ji Bai sent constant word to her father to change his mind.

'Are you crazy?' came the reply. 'Do you want me to break my word?'

For those remaining days, as the village celebrated her

supposed joy, she wept alone in a dark room and refused to touch food. On the last day, the day of the wedding, her father came to see her.

'What is it, my grandmother?' For she was, to him, his own grandmother returned.

'Where are you sending me, Bapa?' she cried. 'Where is Africa? I know no-one in those parts, I'll never see you again.'

'I am your father, na? Trust me,' he said, patting her head. 'You'll never be unhappy. Now be good and make me proud.' He embraced her and she relented.

One last gesture of love for her father, one last gift to make him happy. For truly she would never see him again. She sat on his lap, and from the plate he had brought with him he fed his darling daughter with his hands as he gave her advice on conduct.

'Don't let me down, Ji Bai. Do nothing to bring shame upon yourself. Never walk out alone. Don't speak of your home outside the four walls. Always cover your family's shame. Don't come back without your husband's permission…' And he bade the female members of the family to come and bathe the bride, to anoint her with saffron, to await the puro, the procession of singing females of the opposite side bringing in the bridal clothes and henna.

So the pandit's prophecy came true. And Mongi overnight became a woman. She came to Africa with her husband in a steamer. Disembarking in Dar es Salaam, the two respectfully touched the feet of Dhanji Govindji and his wife who had come to meet them.

By this time the Indians of Matamu and neighbouring towns had acquired a sheth in Dar es Salaam, their agent Karmali Samji, who bought their produce and supplied them with goods. Karmali Samji's dhows plied the sea between Dar es Salaam and Kilwa; his team of porters went a hundred miles into the interior along the old caravan route. Zanzibar, which had ruled the coast for centuries, finally lost its grip on the mainland. Amarsi Makan's millions had been squandered, as were Jairam Shivji's and Ladha Damji's. In their place, new 'uncrowned kings' of business were setting up along the coast from Kilwa to Mombasa, with empires stretching all the way up to Kampala in the interior.

Ji Bai and Gulam stayed a month in the newly-constructed rest house of Dar es Salaam, after which they travelled in one of Sheth Karmali Samji's dhows to Matamu. The dhow anchored in shallow water, and Ji Bai was carried ashore on the back of an African as Gulam followed with rolled trousers, instructing the porters. They were welcomed by a band playing an Indian wedding tune on reed flutes, and the procession left for Dhanji Govindji's shop, stopping at the mosque on the way, for the bride and groom to bow their thanks. As they crossed the threshold of their home a shower of rice grain greeted them, waiting women broke into a geet, and the crunch of clay saucers under their feet wished them good luck.

One of her first acts when she reached Matamu, Ji Bai would say, was to engage in a childish squabble with one of Fatima's children. Growing up in such a short time was not easy.

With two jewels in his breast, Dhanji Govindji's luck seemed to have blossomed. What past acts come now to reward me like this? he would say with a satisfied sigh. The sounds of their pleasant voices, their laughter, their singing and games rang joyfully through the house and filled him with pleasure. Like all respectable women they did not meet his eyes, of course, and they hid their faces behind their pachedis. Nevertheless there grew a communication between them, an understanding. Whenever their laughter and singing desisted for long, when prolonged silences were punctuated by mutterings and whispers and sighs, he would call Fatima and ask what was the matter.

Instantly matters would return to normal. In turn the two girls pampered him. When he praised some food one of them had prepared, it would be repeated after a suitable interval. A severe mood on his part would be placated by a favourite sweet, a mithai. A more lax atmosphere was taken advantage of by more extravagance. He was like a god to them, whom they daily propitiated, whose attributes they sang to each other, whose idiosyncrasies gave them joy to recall.

A few months after she arrived, Ji Bai, pushing aside the gunny curtain, entered the outhouse late one night before going to bed. Her kerosene lamp, raised in front of her, revealed a black face, wide-eyed, frightened and looking drunk. Herself frightened out of her wits, she asked, 'What do you want?' Back came an incoherent reply. There was a rustle in the shadows, and when she raised the lamp higher she saw two more men.

'We're hiding from the Mdachis,' a voice said. 'Don't call out.'

Here Ji Bai used the remaining wits she had left with the sense of humour she never lost. 'Well, I have a need,' she spoke with determination.

'It's all right, mama,' came the unruffled reply. 'We can't see in the dark.' A man came and took the lamp away, lowered the wick, and left it burning in a corner, and Ji Bai sat on the pit and relieved herself in the darkness.

When a man hides inside a house, the first place to look for him is the lavatory. Dhanji Govindji, presented with the *fait accompli*, hid the three men in his loft inside the store. The next morning Guu Refu's head was found on a pole on the road leading to his farm. Askaris appeared and began combing the area, but Indian shops were spared. Mzee Guaro came with the message, 'The Mdachi commander requests that you check your lavatories at night.' The three men left at dusk, pretending to be three grateful customers, just before Dhanji Govindji closed for the day and went to pray. Ji Bai never knew if the men later hanged for the crime were any of these.

Dhanji Govindji and Sons, said the new sign outside the shop. Business was flourishing. But then, with two Lakshmis resident in his home, what else could he expect? His two eldest sons were in harness, and there seemed no danger of them breaking loose. Moti gave birth to a boy, who was born on a Friday and thus called Juma. Ji Bai's son was born six months later and named Husein. With increased wealth and family came respect and influence. His unwitting deed in hiding three men from the Germans was known about and hinted at in respectable and prudent Swahili company, although he wished it were forgotten, lest inquisitive German ears came to know about it and destroy all he had built up. The pinnacle of Dhanji Govindji's success came when he was made mukhi of Matamu after Ragavji Devraj retired.

It is not good to be too happy, anyone can tell you, just as it is not good to be too beautiful or handsome. Children who laugh too much go to bed crying, and it is always prudent to administer the bitter with the sweet. The jealous, evil eye lurks not very far off.

Ji Bai said that it was exactly during this happy interlude that Fatima's mother, the Zanzibari widow, showed up to visit her daughter. Mother and daughter held long huddled talks. Mother and husband did not speak. Things were never the same again.

A few weeks after the widow left, Moti, hidden behind a veil, had a long chat with her father-in-law. That night Dhanji Govindji summoned Huseni. 'Why were you not at the mosque today?' he asked. 'I was visiting,' was the reply. 'You have been seeing Bibi Taratibu behind my back, you have been consorting with the Mshenzis again.' There was no answer. 'You fool,' said the father in uncontrolled rage, 'you are descended from the Solar Race! What do you have to consort with slaves for?'

The sullen Huseni, eyes red, shifted on his feet. He raised his head.

Then he simply spat at his father's feet and walked out. He never returned, he was never heard from again. There were reports that he had become a bandit, that he had gone to Zanzibar, that he had stowed away on a ship to Bombay. But nothing was confirmed. Every time he welcomed a traveller into his shop, or bid one goodbye, or wrote a letter, Dhanji Govindji would sense a message from the restless Moti. Ask. Please ask. Enquire about him. Discomfited, sad, remorseful, he would begin: 'Ah, yes. I would like to enquire about my son, a big black man with a large, round head, tall like a tower, like Bhima in strength. If you have seen him or hear of someone like him…'

Moti was always a little fickle; but she waited two years for her man. Then she asked for permission to remarry.

Moti and Mongi, the two jewels in the house. One lost its place and fell. It is her turn to cook today and she returns from the market holding Juma by the hand. Baruti the servant walks behind with a basket of produce on his shoulder. The shop of Nanji Kara and Sons comes up and son Rajan in white singlet and red loincloth leans out to spit. Aaaahk!-thuck! She draws her veil shyly and averts her eyes, too late. Eye has met eye, and heart found heart. She walks on with thudding heart and he draws back, but the old woman his mother, sitting on the doorstep, feet planted solidly on the street, making paan in her lap, sees all and remains quiet.

Some days later Nanji Kara and wife and eldest daughter-in-law came with the proposal.

'What widow?' cried Dhanji Govindji in anger. 'Henh? What widow, there are no widows here. What, you have already buried him, you have said the rites for him? I don't remember.'

'But Mukhi,' said the dutiful bahu, and here came the barb,

'how long will you keep another's daughter in your home against her will?'

Mukhi Dhanji Govindji, who had not seen deep enough into Moti's heart, fell into the trap. 'Of course, it is up to her. I will ask her. That is all I can do.'

'That is all we ask for,' said Nanji Kara. 'The girl has no parents.' And the troupe stepped out.

Dhanji Govindji quickly went inside to reassure his daughter-in-law. 'Moti,' he said. 'Moti, no one asks you to go. This is your home. You are my daughter. We will look after you and your son. The matter is closed.' He patted her head.

'Bapa, I would like to accept, with your permission,' she said, still looking down.

'Well, if this is your wish—'

That night he pleaded with her, he begged her not to go. But Moti was adamant.

First Moti had to be declared a widow. A witness was quickly found who claimed to have seen Huseni hanged. Then as mukhi, Dhanji Govindji gave his daughter-in-law in marriage to Rajan Nanji Kara. Rajan and Moti left the next day for Voi in Kenya. 'The British have built a railroad,' said the elder Nanji Kara, 'and business is booming there.'

'I had two eyes once,' Dhanji Govindji would say wistfully until the day he died. 'Now I have only one.'

Tell me, you who would know all... What was she like, this gentle one, this Bibi Taratibu given to my ancestor for comfort on lonely, breezy African nights when mango and coconut trees rustled and crickets chirped and the roaring ocean echoed with reminders of a distant homeland? From what ravaged tribe, gutted village, was she brought to the coast, and did she not also think of her home, her slaughtered father and uncles, her brothers and sisters also taken away...

She demurs, my gunny sack. Slave women, she says, wore a colourful cloth round their bodies, under the shoulders. She must have been dark dark, because she came from the interior. And technically she was not a slave, because the British Government of India had forbidden its subjects to keep slaves. Other than that? Surely there must have been something between this slave woman and her son Huseni, for he kept on seeing her against his father's wishes, against respectability. Did she know where he went? Did Dhanji Govindji seek her help? No, most likely he had her house watched.

One day she too left Matamu and was never heard from again.

3 | *As Strong as Bhima*

They were the days of magic and spells. Of Bantu medicines, Arab djinns and Indian bhuts… you could find them all on trees, in graveyards, or under one roof running their nocturnal rounds, doing good or evil at their masters' bidding … It is still a world of magic and spells. Everyone remembers that afternoon, a few years ago, when African Stars played Young Albion at Dar's Illala Stadium. An old, undernourished white cock left the sidestands at half time and ambled to the edge of the field, waited uncertainly like an old veteran at a road crossing, then began to cross it, to the tumultuous encouraging roars of one side and hopeless finger-wagging pleas by the other. 'Jamani…' said the announcer on radio. 'Jamani!' screamed the announcer, the pitch in his voice rising to a fever… 'kuna ajabu linatokelea hapo!' There's a wonder at work here. The following day the Albion players anxiously searched the alleys of Dar for medicine that would reverse the jinx. The verdict? Change the name. Thus was born the Azania Football Club of Dar es Salaam.

And now… even here… this gaping hole in the gunny that has me mesmerised, this brown pouch that holds me spellbound, holed away in a basement listening to endless tales… Ji Bai was not innocent of magic and spells, and I realise that I sit here obedient to her charm, watched over by this watchdog Shehrbanoo of the gaping mouth, who holds many secrets...

Dhanji Govindji was in contact with a number of people, in different towns across the land, who had been asked to help look for his son. A chocolate-coloured young man, Huseni by name; with hair like an Arab's, not completely kinky, he wrote, and if you look into his eyes you will see that they are not coal black but a shade of brown. He is big, tall and muscular, a bull of a man, strong as Bhima ... A network of mukhis was working on his behalf – in Portuguese East Africa, Kilwa, Dar es Salaam, and Zanzibar on the coast; in Mpwapwa, Kilosa, Dodoma and Tabora in the interior; in Mombasa up north – and these mukhis kept an eye open for half-castes in their congregations, employed agents to search the brothels where such types reputedly loitered, to enquire in work gangs and prisons and comb the African tenements. Even after Moti had given up and left, Dhanji Govindji had no doubt his son would be found and could be persuaded to come home. To assist him on the home front he enlisted the help of Bwana Khalfaan.

This Bwana Khalfaan had moved into Matamu from the Kilosa area a few years before, during the Maji Maji troubles, and was a mchawi of renown. It was said that he had predicted the arrival of the Europeans, and had talked of an iron boat which would run on land from the coast all the way up to Ujiji, well before the Central Railway Line came into existence. Bwana Khalfaan had a cure for any ailment, and to protect a village from attack he had the medicine that would make its huts appear as ant hills.

One morning Dhanji Govindji strode into his shop accompanied by the mchawi. Bwana Khalfaan was a short, wiry African of about thirty-five who wore a black, embroidered waistcoat over a white kanzu; evidently a man of substance.

With him was a boy, also in a kanzu, bearing a sickly-looking white cock. The first thing the mchawi did was to check if there was an adverse effect at work in the household that kept Huseni away. To this end he proceeded to line up the members of Dhanji Govindji's household, including the old man himself, the young children and servants. They stood before him like obedient pupils waiting expectantly, not sure what the master's next move would be, and he eyed them one by one, as if trying to guess which of them was the evil influence, before his own tests revealed the conclusive answer. He picked up the cock and thrust it roughly into the arms of each one of them. This was originally the test for ascertaining if a claimant to the power was genuine; if the cock crowed, not recognising the power, immediately the pile of kuni on which the impostor stood was put to flame. Bwana Khalfaan's cock did not see anything unusual in any of the people lined up there, in Dhanji Govindji's shop. It protested angrily at every pair of nervous hands that tried to smooth its feathers, until it landed in Fatima's arms: here it came up with only a small squawk. The mchawi picked it up and handed it to the boy, then rubbed his chin, eyeing Dhanji Govindji's haughty wife. 'A wonder, this,' he said. 'This woman has the powers, yet she does not have the powers.'

He was answered by an oblique stare and a 'Hmph' as she thrust out her chest and stalked away inside.

'Meaning?' asked Dhanji Govindji.

'There's some power behind her, that is certain.'

'Her mother!'

'We'll have to proceed slowly. Then we'll see what we'll see.' His eyes gleamed with excitement, he began pacing the floor in short, springy steps, with his hands clasped tightly behind his back. Then he stopped to put a question to Dhanji Govindji. 'Now listen. What taste did your son prefer – salt or sugar?'

'Salt.'

'Then bring me some salt.'

Ji Bai went inside and brought a heap of salt on a plate. The mchawi took it from her, turned away and whispered prayers over it, finishing by blowing three circles over it.

'Take it. Every night take a handful and sprinkle it outside. If you need more, call me.'

Someone was to make a pile of sticks outside the town on the road to Guu Refu's farm, with a rock of salt in the centre, and check every morning that it had not been disturbed. Having given these instructions, Bwana Khalfaan strode out, followed by his acolyte. He looked on the ground as he walked, and people moved out of his way. It was not advisable to cross his path.

Every morning the pile of sticks and branches would be found in disarray, the rock of salt missing, white flour sprinkled on the ground, and Ji Bai would reassemble the pile over a new piece of salt.

Huseni did not come. Early one morning the captain of a dhow delivered with much ceremony a letter for Dhanji Govindji from Zanzibar.

'A man answering your description has been sighted. Come soon before he begins to suspect.'

Dhanji Govindji packed a trunk and set off with the dhow on its return leg. Thus began the first of Ji Bai's viraha, the long anxious waiting of a woman for her journeyman beloved: every morning she peeps out of the door to see if he's coming, all day long her eyes fix with hope on a returning traveller, every night she looks out wearily one last time before finally closing the last panel of the door, pulling the stopper shut, fastening the bar, hanging noisy metal objects behind it to keep out intruders in the night.

And what did the gentle Gulam think of his wife's silent though somewhat unusual vigil? The gentle Gulam was appreciative of Ji Bai's solicitousness after his father's welfare. Father and son never exchanged an angry word. Neither did mother and son. The haughty Fatima simply said, 'Let him go to jhannam with his slave's son!' Ji Bai and Fatima had never quarrelled either. During Ji Bai's early days in Matamu, while she and her mother-in-law would enter pregnancy together, wondering who would make it to the end, Fatima would confide to her. 'Tell me, what is my sin, that I should inherit this slave's son with my marriage... this junglee who stands out like a wart in this family, a bad influence on my children, ruining their good name...' And young Moti outside making a racket with pots and pans, pretending not to hear, speaking loudly as she came in, to give ample warning... Fatima came from a family of slave owners. 'See,' she would say, 'Arab blood runs through my veins, I have Shirazi ancestors, look at my skin, see how different it is from yours...'

Dhanji Govindji returned one month later, empty-handed. 'A waste of time,' he told Ji Bai. 'The man's name was Abdulla Bombay, short and thin, selling ices at the harbour... simply because he has brown skin, with some Arab blood, or Indian blood, or some weird mixture, the mukhi thinks it's Huseni! A proper swindler, a thief, just after the money. Did he look at the description I wrote him? "Big and strong," I said. "Muscular," I wrote in clear handwriting. "Strong as Bhima!"' Here his voice rose and he thumped his chest. 'And this man, this seller of ices to tourists? Short and thin, an Adam's apple large as a khungu, a squeaky voice like an old woman's... ah! a shoga, a fag, wagging his bottom as he walks. I thought perhaps if he had seen our Huseni... so I asked him. And where does he take me, this shoga?... Ah, my dear, you should go to sleep.'

Dhanji Govindji, sitting at the store threshold at night, a panel open, feeling the cool salty air from the ocean, hearing the occasional voice or shuffle of feet on the road, the roar of the ocean in the background. Sometimes he shelled peanuts as he talked, sometimes he soaked his feet in water. Dhanji Govindji on the threshold, looking out, Ji Bai inside on a stool some feet behind him, head appropriately covered, listening respectfully, venturing a word here and there. He received several letters, asking him to go and check out some half-caste sighted, and he would go. Sometimes he simply took it upon himself to go and search some city, investigate some new route that had opened up. Every time he returned, he would talk to Ji Bai.

'Bai,' he would say, 'when I came, Dar es Salaam was not fit even to spit on... grass growing in the streets, a few Arab and Banya shops, but mostly empty, crumbling houses with snakes and scorpions, bats and chameleons for tenants... and every now and then junglees would raid the town. Seyyid Bargash who followed Seyyid Majid, Bai, simply left it to ruin. Now what wonders these Germans have achieved. As you approach it from the sea, as you enter the harbour, you see to the right all those beautiful, white buildings of the Europeans... there is already a church there – a big, tall building with a spire, to which the Germans go on Sunday – and there is the Governor's house, an alishaan building fit for a king truly... the government buildings... the dainty houses with red roofs, all laid out cleanly with gardens, and servants looking out. Behind this beautiful, white European face of the town is our modest Indian district, every community in its own separate area, and behind that the African quarter going right into the forest. Sheth Karmali Samji's shop, if you remember, is on Ring Strasse near Bagamoyo Strasse – strasse is "road", by the way – this Bagamoyo Road goes right into the jungle and if you take the road north from Matamu, past Guu Refu's farm, you will hit this same Bagamoyo Strasse. It goes up to Bagamoyo village, and from there you can go all the way up to Tabora and further. On this road the slaves and ivory used to come, and the great traders of old used to travel, with hundreds of porters in file. Because of this road the likes of Jairam Shivji and

Amarsi Makan made their crores. Now, of course, there is the railway train. I took this train all the way to Kilosa. And everywhere it stopped you had these hustlers coming to sell you eggs, chicken, carvings, and to anyone who seemed to have a little sense in his head, I would ask: "Have you seen my son?" I asked conductors, askaris, akidas, and jumbes, thieves and prostitutes... Don't think I haven't been fooled; I have been taken to see men who were only caricatures of my son, I have been presented with shogas of all colours, and I have been taken into alleys and robbed. The District Officer at Kilosa took me to the prison and showed me a lame man. "But my son had two legs," I protested. "Maybe he lost one," the swine answered. I have been alone with women, beautiful, alluring, Arab and half-caste, I have been lonely and disheartened, but I have never wavered. Tell that to the mother of my children.

'Now Mombasa, Bai, there is a place to tempt a man, to draw young men to it like flies to a sweet shop. When I walked ashore in that Bombay of Africa, saw the multitude of people from all the corners of the world, I thought here, surely, must I find him. It is an old city, Bai. Here the Portuguese and Arabs have had their raj, now the British have theirs. And in what style they move. Every saheb has his own trolley, like his own rail gadi, and it moves on two metal rails just like one, only it is being pushed by two barefoot Africans in kofias and short trousers. It has a roof and awnings and screeches along at full speed on four heavy, iron wheels... inside sits a stiff memsaheb fanning herself or a moustachioed saheb nervously looking up and down the street, smacking himself with his stick. Now hear this. From every house in the beautiful European quarter, a pair of rails leads like two iron threads from the front door to the street! The houses are called "villas" there. The sahebs visit each other and go to their offices in their trolleys.

'At night, the streets are dark with strange shapes and shadows, alleys that lead into pitch blackness, the road feeling slimy under the feet, appearing truly fearsome to the stranger. It seems as if behind every shadow lurks a daku, a robber or a ghost, every strange-looking shape you pass could turn and spring behind you with a dagger, every sheikh you see carrying a lantern returns having thrust a child inside a well, behind every giggle is a nest of prostitutes and shogas. The imagination can run wild in such instances, and only with a prayer on your lips could you feel safe. The windows are shut tightly in the houses, and the doors are heavy. And the sahebs also feel afraid at night, for you rarely see them venture out after sunset. One evening a trolley trundled past me at full speed, as if the saheb inside was late for something; but when he saw me from behind the gadi, immediately he called for a stop. "Ao," he said in Hindustani. "Where are you going?" "Nowhere in particular, saheb," I told him. "Oho, badmaash," he said. "Catch him," he told one of the boys, and the saheb and one boy, who was called Shomari, held me while the other went to fetch an askari. "What are you?" he asked. "Madrasi, Panjabi, Memon? Speak!" "Shamsi, saheb," I said. "Oho. Juth bolte ho! Then tell me the name of the mukhi." The name of Mukhi Lalji Jetha saved me that night. Some Madrasis and Panjabis from the railway gangs never went home, the mukhi told me, and the police tried to deport them.

'The railway goes from Mombasa all the way to the lake in the interior, and everywhere the train stops there is an Indian settlement. The line was built by our Indians, every stationmaster is an Indian, and every conductor is also one of us. Our people are doing well under the British, Bai. But in Mombasa I inquired about our Moti, and I learnt from the mukhi that Moti had gone to Kibwezi with her husband Raj an Nanji Kara, and had become a widow, her husband having died of the black fever. This Kibwezi is an old town, much used by travellers in the past. So I had this hunch, Bai, a premonition like I sometimes get, that Huseni had followed his wife to

Kibwezi. Early in the morning I set off on this train... there were besides people of every shade in the station, also ostriches and deer, and cubs of lion, leopard, and every animal you could think of save the elephant, in boxes bound for Europe. From Mombasa the train climbs up; first the dense, rich forest of the coast is passed, then comes a poor land with red, dusty soil and hungry-looking plants and grass; it is called Taru. Many a caravan has perished in this desert, they say. Then comes the forest once more. Kibwezi was reached in the middle of the night. I waited at the station until dawn, when the stationmaster directed me to the shop of the mukhi, Nanji Lalji. From Nanji Lalji I heard the sad news that Moti had married once more. Her children by her two previous marriages she was forced to give away to a relative further inland. Then she herself died of childbirth at the nearby town of Voi. So we have lost my grandson Juma, too... where to find him? In which of the small towns littered along the railway? In Voi station where there is a big dining-room the train stops for some hours, and the Europeans have a long and leisurely meal. On the return journey I went and stood by her grave.'

Mombasa kept him for four months. Every time the old man returned, disappointed and tired, more of the business was in the hands of Gulam and his two brothers, all in the control of Fatima. Dhanji Govindji ignored her, she despised him. What savings he had not spent in his quest disappeared, and of the earnings in his absence he was not informed. Slowly he became a guest in his own house. He would come to cool his heels, as it were, biding his time, collecting himself, and then, at a letter or a hunch, take off. Dhow captains knew of his quest, and so did caravan leaders and porters. It was the captain of a dhow called *Mariamu* who convinced him that he should see Mozambique.

'We have the British to the north and east of us, the Germans are in our midst, and to the south, Bai, are the Portuguese. These gentlemen are different because they take to themselves women of the land; as a result there are numerous half-castes down south – Arab and Black, Indian and Black, Portuguese and Black. The town is old like Mombasa, but with many churches and Portuguese soldiers and priests. The Portuguese are carried in a machela, an open box with curtains slung on a pole covered with some animal skin, borne by black men at a trot… On the day I arrived, on a narrow street I came across a donkey laden with bales, driven with sticks, kicks and curses. I moved into a doorway to let it by, but as it passed, one of the bales pushed me quite roughly straight into the arms of a tall Swahili sheikh sitting on a stool. This sheikh, called Yakub, was of considerable age, dressed in immaculate white right to his beard. He spoke a little Gujarati, and it seemed he had been to these parts. He heard me out and offered to show me around. Together we went through the Arab quarter, then the Indian and the African quarters. In the Indian quarter I sought out the mukhi, asked him a few questions, and stayed for a meal. In the African quarter I saw Makonde women with lines drawn on their faces, and there were other black women with gold and jewellery, who Yakub said belonged to Portuguese chiefs. We met prisoners and their askaris working on the roads, and we questioned them.'

Dhanji Govindji returned by the same dhow, the *Mariamu*. He never left Matamu again. He was still the mukhi and resumed his duties. But he was resigned and wistful. 'Africa has swallowed him up, Bai, taken him back into her womb… My only regret is that I have not taken the rail gadi to Tabora and further, or the gadi from Mombasa further, up to the lake and into the land they call Uganda… Perhaps there… But how far can one go… this land has no end.'

Africa was not as small as he had once confidently thought. It was more than the towns and the markets and the caravan routes. One could go deeper and deeper into it and perhaps never return. Perhaps that's what happened to his son Huseni. When anyone asked him now: 'What news of Huseni?', 'He died,' he would answer. But the strangest thing was that when he saw someone from his community off at the door, he would often murmur, 'Forgive me,' as though absentmindedly. 'What?' would come the reply; then an embarrassed laugh, an ambiguous turn of phrase, and the guest would hastily depart with an apologetic but knowing look at whoever else was present. It seemed that Dhanji Govindji's grief and his fruitless journeys had affected his mind.

One day with much commotion, and preceded well in advance by rumour and speculation in the street and expectation of business in the dukas and hastily constructed stalls, a detachment of askaris under a district officer from the interior arrived at Matamu on their way to the capital. It was noontime with its glaring, sticky heat, and the company broke up for rest. One of the askaris eating an orange at a stall caught sight of Bwana Khalfaan, eyes on the ground, hurrying to his house. The askari – his name turned out to be Daudi Amin – quietly got up from his stool, spat out a seed, and trotted off to the tent of Herr Lambrecht, his district officer. From there he picked up two other askaris and together they pounced on Bwana Khalfaan outside his house as he was hurrying off to another destination. Bwana Khalfaan, it seemed, had been recognised as one of the ringleaders inciting villagers to take the Maji Maji oath in the uprising around Iringa. A hearing was set for late that afternoon, and Bwana Wasi, as the local district officer, was asked to preside.

A table was set under the mango tree at the end of the village; behind it on chairs of local manufacture sat Bwana Wasi and Herr Lambrecht – or Rambureshi as he was locally called.

To one side sat Bwana Khalfaan, guarded by Daudi Amin. On the same side, a little further away, sat the twenty-odd askaris. Facing the table were the villagers. Except for the Europeans everyone sat on the cool ground. The rainy season was at hand and before the hearing the ground had to be cleared of its carpet of caterpillars.

Bwana Wasi began by summoning Daudi Amin before him. Amin was a huge, fair-skinned askari, a dumé of a man, as the crowd observed audibly, with the blood of many races in him.

'Askari Amin,' said Bwana Wasi. 'You have identified Bwana Khalfaan, a resident of Matamu, as one of those you saw inciting people to take the Maji Maji oath in Mafinga. Tell us the particulars.'

'Yes, Bwana. On the night in question, I and my fellow askaris were on guard at the boma outside Mafinga under Herr Lambrecht. We had heard of the disturbances in other areas. Lately we had heard that a group of men was on its way bringing with them the medicine. So we were prepared. On this night we were woken up by heavy footsteps and dogs barking outside. A man cried out in pain and there was a scuffle outside. Then my men brought in this fellow Abdurehman, an Arab. He had been bitten by a dog as he was trying to enter the boma, and he was crying and swearing in Arabic. "Wé Abdurehman, what are you doing here at this time of night? Do you also steal, koni?" we asked him in some anger because he had woken us up. He said that a group of men had arrived quietly that evening and were going around the houses ordering people to take the oath. His neighbour Shaban Mrisho had refused, saying Herr Lambrecht knew him and would surely find out and hang him. This Shaban Mrisho was a Swahili businessman who supplied our boma and was on good terms with us. "Well," said Abdurehman, "as soon as Shaban Mrisho refused, someone angrily thrust a spear in his stomach, and he fell, saying Aiiiiii... now why did you do that?" It turned out that Abdurehman, as soon as he heard that the Maji Maji men had come, went to Shaban's house to hide, because being an Arab he thought he would be molested. From behind a curtain, hiding in the women's quarter, he saw and heard all this.

'When he had heard this, Herr Lambrecht sent me and three other askaris to assess the situation. We started towards the village, but on our way we heard voices and we saw a lamp burning in a clearing to our right. We went and hid behind some bushes. From there we saw this man Khalfaan making a speech.'

Daudi Amin, standing at ease with his hands behind his back, indicated the mchawi with a nod. The crowd, all this time silent as attendant pupils, sent forth a murmur. 'This Bwana Khalfaan kumbe is more than we thought.'

All this while Bwana Khalfaan had been looking intently at the askari.

'Watch him carefully,' said a voice. 'He'll transform the yellow dumé into an ant.'

'A swine.'

'He'll transform this whole baraza into an ant's market.'

'The whole town into an ant hill.'

'Aah, quit joking.'

'This Rambureshi, eti. He is a quiet one.'

'Like a snake. He controls the whole thing. He's instructing Bwana Wasi.'

'Silence!' spoke Bwana Wasi.

Two askaris made a threatening gesture and quiet returned.

'What was Bwana Khalfaan saying?' asked Bwana Wasi.

'He was saying, "First they ask us to pay taxes in mhogo; then they ask for goats; now they want rupees. Where can we get rupees? Who is going to buy goats and mhogo when everyone has goats and mhogo? And what is this rupee but a piece of metal to make us go and work on their cotton farms?" And so on. The crowd was saying "Yes! Kweli!" Then this man said, "This here medicine is given to us by a renowned mchawi called Hongo. Drink it and you will become invincible." So they drank the water one by one, and they were shouting "Maji maji! Homa homa! The Mdachis? Cut their stomachs open!" and they were dancing up and down with their spears. Then they ate meat and were told not to touch their wives. And not to call things by their names but by certain other names that he gave them. We did not wait longer but returned to report to Herr Lambrecht. There at the boma we loaded our rifles and waited for them. Early in the morning they came, shouting "Maji maji! Homa homa!" and waving their spears up and down. They were carrying twigs and branches and wearing mhogo leaves on their heads. We came out with our rifles but still they kept coming, screaming, "Homa homa!" We were not frightened because we had seen some action in Kilosa and Mpwapwa. We fired in the air, but they kept coming. Then we fired at them, and some died. Others kept coming. We fired again, and many died. Then Herr Lambrecht shouted, "Leave this foolishness. It will only cause more death. Throw down your spears." And they threw down their spears and we hanged many of them. But this man Khalfaan was not to be seen. We heard from the village that he was not from those parts but was a stranger.'

Daudi Amin had commanded complete attention. When he finished, the crowd released a sigh or two but remained otherwise silent, their heads raised expectantly at the spectacle before them. Bwana Wasi consulted with Rambureshi and then spoke.

'Bwana Khalfaan!'

'Naam?' came the reply.

Immediately three askaris were on their feet and had pulled the mchawi on his feet. 'Stand up, you!'

'You have heard the askari. Are there any lies in what he said?'

'Yes.'

'And any truth?'

'Yes, some.'

'Were you in the village of Mafinga at the time he speaks of?'

'I don't know what time he speaks of.'

'Heh. Just look at him!' spoke a voice in the crowd. Two askaris pounced on the speaker and removed him to one side.

'Khamsa ishrin,' nodded one sage to another.

'Ai, khamsa ishrin,' came the reply.

Meanwhile the questioning went on. 'Were you ever in that village, then?'

'That, I was.'

'And did you make people take the Maji Maji oath?'

Silence. A murmur in the crowd. 'He should start something now. Watch his eyes. The Mdachi has met his match!'

'Speak!' said Bwana Wasi.

Bwana Khalfaan shifted his weight to his left leg and made as if to move. Then he spoke. 'I asked them to take the medicine that a great mchawi had discovered.'

'And so took them to their deaths with bullets that did not melt.'

'And so took them to their deaths at the hands of mnyamas like this one who shot them and hanged them and cut open their women and burnt their farms.'

Bwana Khalfaan's eyes were fixed on Daudi Amin. The crowd stirred, a murmur of 'Salaaaale!' went up, and the askaris stood up.

'Enough!' said Bwana Wasi and consulted with Rambureshi again. Then he thrust his chest out and spoke.

'Bwana Khalfaan, you have done a great wrong. I am going to hang you.'

'Get on with it, then.'

The crowd stood up and moved back. What will he do now? they wondered. What magic will he invoke? His tricks are many, but his enemy is powerful too. A thick sisal rope was produced, a noose formed at one end and passed around a thick branch of the tree. Another, thinner, rope was brought and Bwana Khalfaan's hands tied behind his back. The askaris looked at the two Germans. Bwana Wasi looked at Rambureshi, and the crowd said that the latter nodded with his eyes. Bwana Wasi nodded more visibly at the askaris. A tall askari picked up Bwana Khalfaan with great ease, another one slipped the noose past the small head and around the neck. The tall askari with a signal let go of the mchawi and at that instant the hefty Daudi Amin pulled the rope around the branch, and Bwana Khalfaan was left hanging and strangled. 'Allah!' went a cry.

They watched the mchawi hanging from the old scarred mango tree, opposite the house where Bibi Taratibu used to live, under which Huseni and his gang used to loiter. 'Truly,' they said, 'these Mdachis are powerful, to vanquish a mchawi like that one. But perhaps some day they will meet one to match their strength. Then we shall see.'

4 | *The Spirits of Times Past*

How I came to see Matamu.
The green lorry races southwards along the coast. On the left, the early morning sun bearing down, already hot, the ocean pounding heavily on the shore in an early tide. Coconut trees, mango, mbuyu flash by on the right, a sparse population of giants, each with its own peculiarity of shape and location, lending an occasional shade to the green and brown landscape; man-sized plots of banana, cassava, cashew; a man chewing on a mswaki, a woman wrapped in colourful khanga, a child running around in circles, nowhere. The road, a thin grey ribbon hugging the coastline at this point, is devoid of life save for the occasional cyclist pedalling away patiently in droll sisyphian rhythm, and this noisy lorry filling the air with its rattling, backfiring and excited voices.

'When she comes, when she comes…'

At the back of the lorry – whose sides are marked boldly in white by the proprietors' name: DEVRAJ BROTHERS LTD – stand the thirty-odd members of Form III B of the Shamsi Boys' Secondary School, BOSS for short, with some teachers, bound for a Sunday picnic at the plot owned by the Devraj brothers outside the village of Matamu. Voices hoarse with prior singing and excited shouting improvise on an imported tune.

'She will be dancing with Mr Gregory when she comes, when she comes…'

The subject of the song – other than the unnamed but forthcoming lady – sits on a dusty tyre with a look of mild boredom on his face, his unlit pipe hanging from his mouth, his Somerset Maugham and Graham Greene pressed down under one knee, protected from the ravages of the wind. Our sanyasi from the West, purveyor of Shakespeare, Macaulay, Dickens to this outpost of the Empire, bringer of light. And an eccentric, even amongst his own kind. His is the eccentricity not of a type, born from a differentness, a mere quaintness, or the nonchalance that comes of a superior station in life. It is the genuine stuff, a rarity anywhere: it is what he is. And the result is his supreme indifference to one and all, to everything around him.

His appearance, each time encountered, sends an immediate ripple to the brain, a minor shockwave: it does not fit into the order of things. His speech is a low drawl, almost a growl; and he walks slowly, lazily, shuffling along corridors as though under pressure. His khaki shorts come up to his ample middle, and the sleeves of his oversized shirt – white or light blue, old and certainly not recently washed – come down to his elbows, from where two thick, hairy arms dangle at his sides. Sometimes a button missing from his shirt reveals a red patch of skin he is not loathe to scratch, and when he does so, with an intensity that startles by its sudden appearance, he sends a positive tickle down the spines of the Gregory watchers at BOSS. There are those who will swear, as a result, that he never washes. And when, very rarely, he wears an ill-fitting suit, they wonder to what or whom the honour is due. Did you see Gregory? – this visitor must be something, eh? The occasion is the visit of some lord or lady, some highness. So he is not completely free after all, our Gregory, he too feels the occasional pull of invisible chains.

'She will be wearing pink pyjamas when she comes, when she comes, she will be wearing pink pyjamas when she comes…'

The lorry swerves to the left, away from the tarmac and on to a grassy trail leading towards the ocean; the occupants at the back are thrown to the right in one motion; after a short distance it stops at the gate. The caretaker is shown a note from the proprietors, the lorry goes in through the gate and stops under a shady tree. The driver gets out and disappears into the bushes, presumably headed for the village and its pleasures; the boys race to the water and let it lap their feet; Mr Gregory shuffles out, books in hand, beating his clothes to shake off the sand.

Matamu. Sweet; but what? Opinions vary; it is now part of the character of this town, this question asked only half seriously. Sweet, but what? It's the water, some will say, from the nearby Mnene, the fat stream; others will point to one of the numerous fruits you can find here. Ma-tamu. The name always had a tart sound to it, an aftertaste to the sweetness, a far off echo that spoke of a distant, primeval time, the year zero. An epoch that cast a dim but sombre shadow on the present. It is the town where my forebear unloaded his donkey one day and made his home. Where Africa opened its womb to India and produced a being who forever stalks the forest in search of himself. It is where Bibi Taratibu, given as a gift for cold nights, was so used and discarded, and then disappeared. Only traces of that past are visible here. It is almost a ghost town, barely hanging together, where one stops for a drink of cold water on a hot day, but not for too long, and buys some fruit if it's not too softened from lying all day in the sun.

As you approach it along the beach, the first sight that strikes your eye is that of some ngalawas bobbing on the water or pulled on to the beach; one or two nets stretched out, and perhaps a couple of fishermen mending them. The beach gives way to a swamp, at the head of which lies the village. You can reach the village by skirting the swamp and walking a few hundred yards through the bushes. On the way comes an old house, or rather a broken-down wall, some mounds of red mud, and broken sticks that once were poles. A large house once, an ugly sight now, with old yellow newspaper scraps blowing about, Coke bottles, milk cans, banana peels, coconut husks. Beyond it is the inhabited village. An unpaved street two hundred yards long, lined on both sides with houses and stores, at most three deep. The street ends in a small ground bordered on one side by the paved road – the local football ground. Small alleys lead into the houses behind. There could be nothing sleepier than this village on this hot Sunday afternoon. Perhaps the home team is away. Perhaps there is no home team. The only sign of life is the barber practising his trade on an old customer on the far side under a mbuyu tree.

The village gets roused. A coconut seller appears magically, then a peanut seller suggestively hissing. A game of bao gets under way on the stone bench outside a large stone house, a coffee seller appears, clinking his vessels. The villagers have decided they might as well do something now that the visitors are here.

There are three Indian stores and one Arab. The largest is two stores in one, selling cloth on one side, general produce on the other. The cloth store appears dark from the brilliant, sunny outside. Inside – rolls and rolls of cloth standing upright or lying on shelves; khangas of all colours hang neatly, partly folded, from wooden beams and pipes hanging horizontally from the ceiling; khaki and black shorts clipped to a board in two rows for display; frocks hanging from a rack; a clump of baby knickers and bras hand-sewn and brought in from the city. P.T. Somji, says the Coca Cola board outside. P.T. Somji brings water in Coke bottles, from a refrigerator inside, which he normally sells at five cents apiece, and distributes it around. A thin, middle-aged figure in a fishnet singlet and a red and black khanga wrapped round his waist. Two hairy jungles under his arms. What news from the city, hein? Has there been a funeral recently? No – only that of – Hein? – Who? Oh yes, a sad event, that. Silence. Thus he measures the passage of time, keeping tabs on his generation. He is all hospitality. As the Swahilis say, mgeni siku ya kwanza ... on the first day treat your guest like a king; to rice and meat. Of course, on the tenth day, when he's overstayed his welcome, with kicks and blows chuck him out. It is our first day, and he'd love to feed us. We've had lunch. The invitation is politely refused, with a profusion of thanks.

At one time, there used to live and trade here nine Shamsi and seven Bhatia families, the two rival communities on either side of the swamp. Diwali and Idd were celebrated jointly and with great pomp, with processions, dances and feasts; surely a sign, as any, of prosperity and stability. The trade in gum and hides was brisk. To the south, about fifteen miles away at Kitmangau, was another similarly prosperous settlement of Asians. The caravans from Kilwa stopped for rest at either of these two stations, transforming the already busy scene into a bustling one...

Perhaps the only visible signs of that period are the ruins of a building, away from the main village. The roof is gone, as are most of the walls. Close by is a huge mbuyu tree, and behind, an old grass-grown cemetery with a few rounded remains of headstones. It is the part of the village no one ever goes to; there is at least one ghost resident there. An eerie feeling descends upon the whole town as grey twilight, grim maghrab, approaches. Then the sun is behind the trees and the sea is dark – but not silent. It is a time that invokes fear in the young and inspires prayer from the old. Mbuyu trees abound in that area. And who doesn't know the mbuyu, the huge mbuyu with its shade like a cool room under the burning sun, but alas picked by solitary djinns, especially of the variety who like to pray, for their special abode? You would not dare to pass under it at maghrab, lest you step on the sensitive shadow of the ethereal one and are turned into an albino, if nothing worse. And only the most ignorant or the most obtuse would stop to urinate in its inviting shade and risk letting loose a stream on that stern soul as it kneels in pious obeisance. The wrath of such a defiled djinn is terrible. Sometimes at night, at exactly midnight, it was said that you could hear the footsteps of someone walking on the road in that village. No mortal is around at that ungodly hour. My young grandmother Moti, sleepless in her lonely bed, would quietly lower one hand from the sheets, pick up a chappal and smack the floor once, twice with it. The footsteps would recede, hurrying away. I have often wondered: did she ever stop to enquire, before giving up hope, if the approaching footsteps were those of her husband's ghost returning?

The building used to be the Shamsi mosque. In 1912, one December morning at five-thirty, Mukhi Dhanji Govindji left the mosque and set out for his house. He took a diversion to walk by the beach, as was his custom, lingered at the water for a while, looking out into the ocean: waves beat on the shore, the sun was rising on the horizon, the fishermen were preparing to set out. Having cast his customary glance at the elemental vastness, as though his earlier meditations at the mosque were not quite enough, he turned inland, walking along the street. It was still dark in the village. As he approached the house, men leapt out from an alley, carrying curved Arab daggers and, going behind him and in front of him, stabbed him in the stomach, in the arms, the chest, the back. He did not have time to call out. A little later he was found by a vendor of breakfast delicacies who was preparing to set out from house to house, calling out her first 'Eeeeeeeeeh vitumbuaaaaaaa!' Seeing the man crumpled up at the side of the road, blood and all, she ran up and down the street in panic, crying, 'Aaiiiii! Sharriffu has been killed!'

The murderers were not found. The crime was attributed to three men who, it was said, had camped outside the village, or at a neighbouring village, committed their deed at dawn and gone back to Dar.

A few years before, the Shamsi community in India had been torn apart by strife. Various parties had sprung up, with diverging fundamentalist positions, each taking some thread of the complex and sometimes contradictory set of traditional beliefs, hitherto untainted by theologian hands, to some extreme conclusion and claiming to represent the entire community. The bone of contention among these Shia, Sunni, Sufi and Vedantic factions became the funds collected in the small centres and mosques. Faced with this situation, Dhanji Govindji had simply stopped sending the money on to any of the big centres and kept it in trust for the Matamu community. The strife had resulted in murders in Bombay and Zanzibar. And now, it seemed, in Matamu. But why unimportant Matamu, why Dhanji Govindji, no one could say. This was one year after his return from Mozambique in the *Mariamu*.

Mukhi Dhanji Govindji, Sharriffu to the Swahilis, was buried with full honours by the village of Matamu, carried in a procession of males headed by Shamsi, Bhatia and Swahili elders to the grave, grieved for by women ululating along the way.

A few days later, the widow's daughter started disposing of

her husband's belongings. Ji Bai was entrusted with burning the bloodstained clothes. Which she did, except for the muslin shirt she would keep the rest of her life. And before the widow's daughter or anyone else could discover them, she took Dhanji Govindji's three padlocked books from behind a shelf in the store and hid them with the possessions she had brought from her parents' home.

Kala. Thank you so much for the copy of Book I (as I have designated it). God make you live a full hundred and one years! Unfortunately, it is rather a disappointment. It looks like a ledger, with entries for debits and credits. A typical entry: 20 rupees to Bhai Rehemtulla Sharif for potatoes! This one, my dear chronicler-brother, is the most atypical *entry and should interest you: 30 rupees to Ragavji Devraj bai na mate, for the woman! A cut-rate price, I should think. But then of course the slave trade was over. Considering that both you and I are the result of that one purchase, not a bad deal, don't you think? There are also two pages with only numbers on them, which he was using presumably for rough calculations. It's a mystery, this need for the padlock. A theory I am working on is that in those days people liked to keep their business dealings secret. Perhaps the old man was afraid some djinn would read them – not as far-fetched as it sounds, why do you think children's given names were not used? Sona.*

Dear Sona, you and your djinn theory! If you had looked carefully at the two pages with 'only numbers' on them, you would have seen that they are not calculations, but entries – anonymous. I am willing to wager anything that they are secret records of community funds, which Dhanji Govindji held in trust, unwilling to send on to Zanzibar. Remember that community accounts have always been kept secret, sometimes with the aid of codes. What you call rough calculations are actually columns of entries – each column for a family, perhaps, each entry for a donation. I wonder where the money went. Your brother Kala.

Kala. Touché. *Sona.*

5 | *The Sin of One Man*

One bullet, they say, lime liliya, throughout Ulaya. The wits of Matamu. Every afternoon they emerge having said their prayer at the public mosque, a pair playing bao outside a house, a line of elders sitting on the stone bench outside the mosque, a group playing cards under a tree, in their immaculate kanzus and caps, sipping coffee or ginger tea, chewing tobacco or counting the tasbih; and discussing siasa: politics. Now it's the war in Europe that's on their minds. Close by, in an open room, an elementary Quran-reading class is under way, and the chorus of boys begins, 'an-fata-ha-tin in-kisira-tin un-zamu-tin…'

One bullet, they repeat, has reverberated throughout the length and breadth of the land where the Mdachi and the British are neighbours. It has killed a prince and Ulaya is burning. It has exploded like a keg of powder to which a mischievous hand has applied a match. No, it's burning like dry leaves in a forest. And even we can feel the heat. Yes, times are a-changing. Did you hear what this one here said? – Eti, the times are a-changing: the times *have* changed, my brother. Did your grandfather ever trade in paper money? Ah, I have no use for paper money… since when has paper any value? But this one is guaranteed by the Government. It has the signature of the Governor himself, Herr Bwana Von Soden. The Indians like it, they are raking it in, they can fill their pillowcases with it. You can rake it in too if you go to M'logoro or Dar – Eti, is it true there is work – So it is. You can make bullets or sew boots – You can carry for the askaris – travel to Korogwe or Moshi or Tanga – Ah, I'm too old for that… but the young are going. They are fools; they go looking for excitement, but soon they'll cry for their mothers.

In the class the chanting stops, and the old men raise their heads expectantly. The teacher is heard telling off a boy; a cane whistles thinly in the air, the sound of weeping starts and the boy emerges pathetically from the doorway clutching his kanzu, his nose running, as the class resumes, 'Kan-fata-ha-tin…'

'What happened, my son?' asks an elder. 'The mwalimu cane you?'

The boy, clutching his kanzu even tighter, nods forcefully and sobs like a grief-stricken woman.

'You wet your pants?'

Before he has quite nodded assent, he narrowly misses a cuff on the head ('Mpumbavu weh, shame on you!') and escapes, wailing even more loudly than before.

He has to learn, the wise men nod to themselves. Times are a-changing, says the man who said it before. Times are a-changing, mimics his companion.

Old Man, did you go to see the *Koniki* on the Rufiji? Ah, I have no time to walk forty miles just to view a ship and rub my face against an insolent askari. You have no strength, you mean. That, too. They say the *Koniki* lies mouth open like a dead fish. A crowd goes there every day to watch; from Kitmangau, and Kisiju, even Kilwa. They say that the British manuari chased the *Koniki* on the ocean like a cat chases a mouse. The *Koniki* entered the mouth of the Rufiji, pye! and raced in. But then it went kwama: khon! and it got stuck! There it lies in the river, for all to see. The shame of the Mdachis. If you ask the askaris what happened, they threaten to shoot you. What worries me is that now there is no manuari to defend us... how long before the British cannonballs go flying through our roofs? The Mdachis have had it, you think? The Mdachis are trembling. To the north are the British, to the west the Belgians, and to the south are also the British. And in Zanzibar, and on the ocean...Yes, the Mdachis have cause for trembling. But what about us, Old Man? Ah, when two elephants fight, it is the grass that is injured... But the grass is persistent... when the elephants are gone the grass keeps on growing and proliferating...

It was August 1915. Gulam at twenty-four was mukhi of Matamu in place of his father, now dead more than two years. He and Ji Bai had a crop of five children, the youngest, Mongi, just over a year old. With them lived his younger unmarried siblings and the squint-eyed matron Fatima. News of the war reached them through word of mouth and gossip in the village, and dispatches from Sheth Samji in Dar es Salaam. Exports to India and Britain had stopped, there were shortages of food and stockpiles were being depleted, and the government had introduced the one-rupee note to conserve metal. Villagers had heard of the *Konigsberg* – or *Koniki* – how it was destroyed in the Rufiji, and they watched fearfully the grey silhouettes that were the British man o' wars, manuari, patrolling the ocean like wild animals on the prowl. The prevailing mood among the Indian duka wallahs of Tanganyika was that of uncertainty; of being alien subjects in a time of war. India, Zanzibar and Mombasa had become out of bounds, and families were not heard from. Cash and jewellery were at hand and ready to be moved; the rest was hidden away.

The closest German farm was that of Bwana Wasi. This gentleman had now lived in the area for twenty-seven years. One day he had gone north to the Usambara region, to the

German town called Wilhelmstahl, and brought back with him a wife. Bibi Wasi was a schoolteacher, a laughing redhead in long skirts, with two pigtails and brown eyes. As soon as she arrived her husband set aside a banda and they opened a German school. Early every morning a file of boys in kanzus, ranging in age from eight to fifteen, snaked its way in and among the bushes outside Matamu to the school of Bibi Wasi. Bringing up the rear were Gulam's brothers Nasser and Abdulla. For several years Bwana Wasi had done business at the store of Dhanji Govindji. An order was left punctually on the first and fifteenth of every month, which was then forwarded to Sheth Samji. When the goods arrived they were carried by porters to the farm; and Bwana Wasi who had previously paid only in produce now paid in cash.

A few weeks after the *Konigsberg* was destroyed the stocky German came to the store with his retainer Kasoro Mbili. The retainer, as the German would explain, was born in 1903 and technically was still a slave. Slaves born after 1905 had been declared free under German rule; Kasoro Mbili's loss of freedom by two years was reflected in his cumbersome name, which he bore stoically along with his status. To the villagers he was simply Kasoro, or Mtumwa: slave.

'Karibu, Bwana Wasi,' one of Ji Bai's sons greeted him as he entered and shook the dust and mud from his boots. Bwana Wasi still carried a rifle when he came to town. 'Thank you,' he replied, and taking off his sunhat sat on a three-legged stool, wiping his face and neck with a handkerchief. Kasoro Mbili had also come in and sat on the floor.

'Call Bwana Gulam,' commanded the German.

After much whispered discussion inside, and several peeks through the curtain, Gulam appeared in his best obsequious manner wiping his hands on his shirt: 'Welcome, Bwana Wasi. Welcome. You do me an honour. Was the last order all right? Nothing missing? Nothing damaged?' Abdulla came scurrying from inside, bearing a rattling cup and saucer slopping over with tea.

'No,' said Bwana Wasi, holding up his hand as if to push the boy back. 'No tea at this time. Bring me water, in a clean glass.' The boy turned back.

'Bwana Gulam,' said Bwana Wasi. 'This is going to be a fierce war.'

'So we hear, Bwana.'

'The British surround us from the land and the sea.'

Gulam was all attention. Not only was Bwana Wasi a white man and a valued customer, he was also the Government representative in the area. His words had to be sifted for all possible meanings like those of a mystic.

'I am giving you advice, Bwana Gulam. Take your family a few kilometres inland, move to some town there until the war is over, or danger from the sea is past.'

'Will the British manuari attack Matamu?'

'They could attack Matamu from the sea, or they could land troops here and march to Dar es Salaam. Tell the other Indians what I have said. If the British attack, the Africans can run to the bushes, but where will you run?'

'Thank you, Bwana Wasi. I will talk to the others. But what about you?'

'I am going to fight for my King. Tomorrow Bibi Wasi goes to Dar es Salaam to live with her family. The day after I travel to Iringa to join the troops.'

'We are sorry to hear this, Bwana. And the boys will miss your teacher-wife.'

'Yes. My watchman has agreed to join me as an askari in the army, and my two servants will come as porters. And this mtumwa, Kasoro Mbili – stand up! – I want you to have him.'

The boy obediently stood up. Gulam eyed him and waited for the German to continue.

'In return,' said Bwana Wasi, 'I would like to have some supplies from you.'

And so, in one hour of bush diplomacy, one of the last slaves in the country changed hands, and the wishes of the Government were made known to an alien minority. As one of his last gestures of kindness to the Indians of Matamu, Bwana Wasi brought several sacks of paper money which he used to buy stock and even offered to exchange for coins. 'Paper, Bwana Gulam, is lighter, and German money does not rot.'

They thanked Bwana Wasi profusely. They waved his wife-teacher goodbye, and the day following saw the man himself off accompanied by his retainers. Then they proceeded to do as he had instructed, and diverged to separate towns inland so as not to overcrowd any particular village.

The community in Matamu, fifty years old and more, vanished overnight. The traces they left behind were the boarded-up stores, with some possessions in them, the empty mosque where Ragavji Devraj and Dhanji Govindji had once presided, the cemetery where they buried their dead, the platform behind the mosque where they assembled for festivities. Retainers had been kept to watch over the homes; but there was a sense of finality in this parting, as there was in the events around them. The men had their wives and children with them, they had their money, one-rupee notes stuffed in gunnies, and their wives' jewellery tied around their waists; and they took whatever else they could carry. If they did not return they could start again, elsewhere. A long caravan left in the morning and headed inland through the grassy bush trails, every member loaded with two packages. There were no animals, a few porters, and two guides. At every junction where two trails crossed, two families would leave the caravan and take the cross-trail to the nearest village. They used a simple device to select the two families whose turn had come. A woman would sing a line from a song; the next one would sing one from another song, beginning with the last word sung. And so the game was played as the singing caravan proceeded deeper inland, until at a junction one of the guides called a halt, selecting the woman with a song on her lips, and her predecessor. The two families would then start their farewells to the rest of the caravan.

The one whose name is called last wins. Ji Bai had always been good at the game, and she often won. The trick, she would say, was to take the cue quickly, without a moment's hesitation, and to pick a short line to sing – no matter how silly it sounded. This time it was important she should win, and perhaps they let her win because the mukhi's wife should be the last, the mukhi should see everyone else settled before settling himself. Forty-five miles from Matamu and three days later, the sole remaining family of the caravan trudged into Rukanga behind Gulam. And found that they had walked into a crossfire.

Rukanga was more a market than a place for habitation. It was an artificial village, put there by Swahili, Arab and Indian foreigners from the coast for the mere purpose of trading. There were no streets; ten shops sat at the perimeter of a large clearing, which was the central square where people from the countryside came to sit with their wares; until recently Sheth Samji's porters would come bearing ready-made and imported goods from the capital, and take away local produce. But not any more. A path led from the village to the top of a hill, where stood a German boma. Behind the hill a small German force had set up to defend itself against a British attack from the northeast. The day Sheth Samji's porters did not arrive from the east, and no further word was forthcoming, the people of Rukanga braced themselves for the impending battle. This was when Gulam walked in, followed by Ji Bai carrying Mongi in the heat of fever, and Fatima and the boys, Nasser and Abdulla and the other children, and Mtumwa. And they went to the Rukanga mukhi's store and asked for water.

'I have lived through hell,' Ji Bai would say, 'and this was hell. First the long walk in the hot sun, followed always by hungry hyenas who never left sight of us, looking out for snakes, fearing lions, afraid the guides and porters would murder and rob us. We told Mtumwa always to listen to what they were saying at night when they made the fire and ate, so we would have advance warning of their intentions. When we got to Rukanga we had blisters the size of boils just from mosquito bites, and feet covered with blood from killing the giant mosquitoes… and flies covered our bloody feet until they looked black. I cursed my husband for having decided on the journey, and I cursed my poor father for having sent me to Africa. In India we travelled by bullocks, we could talk to people in the villages, they were our own kind… and even the Europeans talked our language. But in this jungle the merest sound in the night would send our hearts aflutter… and the men would call out to the guides, seeking reassurance.'

In Rukanga, sugar and flour went for the price of gold, and this is what the visitors from the coast brought with them and what got them through the ensuing months. General trade had stopped. Only specific shortage items were bartered. The staple food was maizemeal; bird and deer meat were sometimes available; milk was scarce, but local beehives supplied honey.

A few miles away, two strange and foreign armies had met in an uncaring jungle to fight a minor round of a World War. The Germans used African askaris led by white settlers, and the British, so the reports went, had all kinds of strange askaris – Indians, coloureds, and Africans who spoke no local language. Reports were brought in by natives of the area, and smuggling between the village and the two forces had begun. At night Rukanga lived in fear. Sometimes, lone rifle shots and what were believed to be human cries were heard in the distance.

In the village there was total blackout. Sometimes running footsteps were heard: not ghosts but deserters. The presence of deserters was established when a house was robbed and a girl raped. During those nights, immediately before the first direct encounter between the two enemies, when silence and darkness were the first priority for fear of raiders, Ji Bai would gag little Mongi whose fever had recurred. Sitting on the floor beside the hammock, she would rock the child, give salt-water compresses, and silently weep. Only when the child started breathing deeply did she herself breathe easy. One morning she woke with a start and went on her knees to undo the child's gag. But the child was still, her eyes open. That afternoon Gulam and a few other men buried Mongi in the local grave half-way up to the boma.

Early one morning the whole village was woken by a tremendous racket: there were the sounds of rifle-shots and the continuous rat-tat-tat of machine guns; there were shouts and screams in the vicinity, the thumps of booted feet outside, desperate knocks on doors, that went unanswered. The two forces had finally met; or so the villagers thought. Some time later there was complete silence. Then the natives started coming in and familiar, reassuring sounds returned. Front doors were opened and enquiries rang out. The people of Rukanga heard about the ignominious defeat of the British force. The smaller German force, it was said, had used the aid of bees; and there are no fighters more ferocious than bees. The British troops with their inexperienced foreigners had simply walked into a forest of beehives, was the other interpretation. Whatever the case, the bees had routed the British, who had fled in terror in all four directions firing guns and screaming and banging on doors. By sunrise most of the British force had disappeared into the bushes or been captured. Foreigners always learn the hard way, people would later say. With such weapons are battles won in Africa. The Germans have learnt well.

But German triumph was short-lived. The routed British force was only a tip of a protracted British advance on eastern Tanganyika. One month later, as the family finished supper, a knock came on the door. As usual, nobody in the house stirred. Then a tired voice came: 'Gulam Bhai, it's me. My father has called a meeting of all heads of households. Come now.' It was the Rukanga mukhi's son.

Gulam was let in through the side door into the mukhi's courtyard. A lamp was burning in a corner. A group of men were sitting on the floor in a loose circle; in the middle was an Indian soldier in khaki drill, drinking tea from a saucer.

'This man brings a message from the British commander,' said the mukhi. 'His name is Hari. He says Dar es Salaam is taken by the British. We must proceed and report there.'

'But it's not safe to travel,' argued one of the men.

'Aré, yar,' said Hari, 'if you don't hasten, there will be no place to go. Listen, you are my brothers. Please. I beg you. You must go. Besides, it's the commander's order. You are British subjects, you must obey. There is going to be fierce fighting here.'

'Like last time,' grinned the mukhi.

'Yes, yes, what fierce fighting!'

With one of their own, the men felt braver than usual.

'No jokes,' said Hari sharply. 'This is the commander's order. If you don't go, we are not responsible for your safety. Tomorrow we attack. This town has supplies and shelter, which the Germans might go for. And don't take your shops with you; if you are seen not carrying anything, you might not be attacked.'

He stood up, gave a fierce look around, and left.

Among the trading immigrant peoples, loyalty to a land or a government, always loudly professed, is a trait one can normally look for in vain. Governments may come and go, but the immigrants' only concern is the security of their families, their trade and savings. Deviants to this code come to be regarded and dismissed as not altogether sound of mind. Of the ten store-owning families in Rukanga, seven were Indian; six packed up and were ready to leave by dawn. Again, the gunnies stuffed with one-rupee notes, the jewellery tied around their waists; once more the promises of returning, the hiring of men to watch over what was left behind. But in the mukhi, the Germans had a friend; he had supplied the boma while it was in use and it turned out that he still supplied its former inhabitant, the German captain, in the bush. The mukhi stayed; and so did Gulam's brother Abdulla, who had learnt German in Bibi Wasi's classroom in Matamu and become Germany's lifelong friend.

The road to Dar es Salaam was uneventful. They stayed close to the railway line and after some time saw a train. They also saw motor vehicles and troops moving west and hailed, 'Biritish, zindabad! Rani Victoria, zindabad!' At the end of the second day, the sun behind them, they finally came upon the famous Bagamoyo Strasse. It was just as Dhanji Govindji had described to Ji Bai in Matamu. They passed several miles of African huts, before finally reaching the first Indian shops at Sultan Strasse and Sheth Samji's busy depot at Ring Strasse. They stayed at Sheth Samji's for the night. The next day they toured the entire Indian quarter and met friends and acquaintances, they gaped at the houses with parts of roofs blown away by British guns. The town was crowded and noisy, like a big market. The streets were packed with lorries and troops, horses and mules, and the air was filled with exhaust fumes and dust and rank odours. Tents filled the open spaces between buildings. They went to the seashore and admired the church and the white government buildings. They held their breath as they watched from a distance the governor's palace, now fallen, being bombed by a British ship, and they gaped at the imposing statue of von

Wissman who had long ago quelled one of the first revolts against the Germans. And when they returned in the afternoon and sat down with the sheth to discuss their future, they found themselves to have become penniless.

'Haven't you heard?' the sheth said. 'They are making fires out of it. It's useless, this Deutsch Ost Afrika eine-rupee. The new Government and the banks will not honour it. What *goods* do you have?'

'None,' she said.

We had to start from scratch, borrowing and buying on credit, and we opened a small duka in the African section, selling kerosene by the jigger and packets of spice, and our fortunes never rose again, we were mukhis once, people called us Sharriffu, Germans called us Bwana, but for forty years and more we stayed poor, changing trades, trying this and trying that, moving from here to there. Collectors would shout and wave their hands, making sure the neighbours heard, and we would pay out of shame even if we had to borrow more money to do it. We blamed it on the sin of the old man, my father-in-law, but how can you blame an entire war on the sin of one man?

6 | *The Suffering Mukhi*

Before he died Dhanji Govindji probably asked everyone for forgiveness but they laughed. What was his sin, Shehrbanoo, that could be equated to the ravages of war? Only now she begins to tell, to explicate the crime that Ji Bai herself would only hint at… now that the secrets of one green book are unlocked and the accounts of the past lie open…

From Dhanji Govindji Africa exacted a price, she says, nothing but his soul. Listen.

One morning (it is related) a pir and his murid went walking the hills together. The terrain was rocky, the day was hot, but the pir appeared tireless, taking his follower higher and farther as if to some pre-chosen destination. Presently they came upon a snake on a stone. It had been hit by a rock or a stick. It was writhing in agony, beating its head upon the stone first on one side and then the other, and crawling all over its wounded broken head was a swarm of black ants.

The pir and the murid stopped at the sight.

'What poor soul can this be, for what sin could he be punished like this?' the murid was moved to remark with pity.

'For the sin of stealing the wealth of the community entrusted to him,' replied the pir. 'The snake is a former mukhi and the ants are his community come to torment him. He has been punished enough, I have come to release him.' So saying, the pir picked up a stone and put the snake out of its misery.

There is no sin greater, there is no shame deeper. But Dhanji Govindji, for the sake of his half-African son, committed it; dipped into community funds when his own savings had run dry, to pay his numerous informants and agents, to finance his quest. This was the sin Ji Bai mentioned, the guilt which they carried silently in their breasts, with the knowledge that there were people, there were families, who knew of it and could point their fingers at them. And perhaps… perhaps it was not the outsiders who had murdered him after all and there were people in Matamu who had sought revenge, or for the safety of their remaining funds had seen fit to act… and put the suffering mukhi out of his misery.

No wonder then, the mistrust of the past by Ji Bai's family, the sons and grandsons of Gulam and his brothers. But Ji Bai knew better. There was more to the past than just the sin.

Part Two

Kulsum

7 | *View from the Birij*

Meet Kulsum: haemorrhoid sufferer, a TV commercial might dub her, with a suitable close-up of a woeful expression on an otherwise sprightly face. She will relate her sufferings in the most graphic detail to any stranger who shows the slightest interest. 'These headaches,' she will start… 'Once I get one it just doesn't leave, simply incapacitates me.' 'A couple of Aspros, perhaps,' the stranger might venture, not wanting to be drawn in but already in the net. 'Oh, they have no effect,' she says, 'too weak. I've had headaches since I was wee high. I've had glasses since then, too. I used to sew. Did Singer embroidery, you know; and was clever at it too, won prizes. And we used to do caps, decorate them until late at night, stitching sequins one after another until the eyes seemed to pop with the tension and the pain. And what did we get after all that work – two cents for a cap. Of course, our parents kept the money … we were poor, hardly had enough to eat, we all had to pitch in – why, chapatis were a luxury and we would jump for joy…' Our stranger gets impatient: 'What do you take, then?' 'Oh, nothing helps,' she answers. 'But I take Panadol. And when I take Panadol, I constipate, and then my haemorrhoids start up.' The stranger is squirming now. He would do anything to get away from this imposed intimacy. 'Indeed,' he ventures. 'Oh, yes, I've had haemorrhoids since Salim here stayed in the stomach. They were so painful, his father brought a tube – you know, the tube of a tyre, Dunlop – for me to sit on. And when I'd been to the lavatory my mother would fan me. My mother always came for my deliveries. After he was born, I could have had an operation to have them removed, but the doctor said it was risky.' 'Eat vegetables,' the stranger finally ventures, hoping he's out of the worst. 'Oh, you think I don't? I even don't eat very much. Can't.' The stranger starts breathing again.

She's graduated from laxatives and purges, of which she's tried all – milk of magnesia, epsom salts, senna, liquid mixtures, tablets, leaves, powders and chocolatey concoctions. Now she's on to bran and fibre supplements. And in the belief that soft, refined foods will give her smoother motions, she avoids meat until she's tempted by a plate of samosas or kebabs, and eats marmalade by the spoonful, has cake for lunch and – although she denies it – dislikes vegetables.

Kulsum. In our catalogue of names, where history moves in a noisy parade wearing faces like masks, Kulsum comes along with the generation of Sheru, Zera, Daulat, Rehmat… The generation that to the present age represents age, decay, death. A generation that embarrasses, which does not speak English, whose personal manners make us flinch… Men and women physically shapeless and retarded, old and dying at sixty.

Yet Kulsum was a flower once. And while still unplucked though in full blossom at sixteen, she stood behind the birij of her father's shop one Mombasa morning and watched with curious eyes the conference of four adults in the front of the store. The birij was a wall-length wooden shelving that partitioned the store from the rest of the house, leaving room for a narrow, curtained doorway. Her nose stuck first inside one opening and then another in the birij, between piles of bright Indian-made kikoi and msuri, white Marikani no longer from America, and colourful khanga and black kaniki, catching whiffs of newly unpacked and still-unpaid-for cotton and feeling the fine dust over it. She strained her neck and ears to catch a trace of the solemn conversation now in progress in the shop. Below her, among the lower shelves, young Zarina did the same.

'Do you think it's for Daulat?' asked Zarina, looking up.

Such lengthy discussions conducted with such quiet formality, such straining civility, between her parents and two strangers, so that the one or two customers who stepped in took heed of it and quietly stepped back into the street, could only be about one thing. Marriage.

Mitha 'Diwano' Kanji had a problem on his hands; actually, he had seven problems. He had seven daughters (besides four sons), only one of whom, the eldest, Fatu, was married. After Fatu came Daulat, and then Kulsum. The proposal should have been for Daulat. But Kulsum with beating heart knew better.

One of the two women talking with her mother and father was Zera 'Sopari' (betel-nut chewer) from the store across the road. The other was a tall, thin woman with a long nose and a serious face. Kulsum had seen them the previous day; that is why she knew. Fate had come to call. The future beckoned with all it held ready for her, and she would have to go. Yesterday morning, her mother had called her into the shop. 'Kulsa, these women want to see your embroidery; go and bring something to show.' 'Come here in the sun, beta, where we can see better,' Zera beckoned. But it was not her embroidery they wanted to see. Across the street in the shadows of Zera Sopari's shop there was a movement; across the street a man got up from a bench, moved casually to the threshold and threw a glance across. A young woman of medium height, fair, and with spectacles on her round face. That's all he saw. It was enough. Now they had come to bring the proposal.

'Kulsa,' her mother called as before. Kulsum walked in past the rag curtain and stood in front of the birij. At that moment there was a movement across the street and this time the man was framed by the sunlight. Instinctively Kulsum pulled her pachedi across her face, but not before giving one deep and curious look at what had been decided for her. Then she looked at her mother and went inside.

'But he's so dark,' observed young Zarina from the floor, having watched through the birij.

My grandfather Mitha Diwano, Mad Mitha, was a deeply religious man of the unusual kind: one who practises simply and consistently what the rest profess. Often he would take his blanket and steal away into the night to spend the rest of it in the bosom of his true mistress. With great reverence he would emerge from the mosque walking backwards, so as not to show his back to it, taking twelve springy steps before turning around. And then, with his close-cropped white head stuck forwards, his white suit crumpled, he would stride home, bobbing up and down and muttering a prayer or singing a bhajan. At this time no emergency – no robber, policeman or fire – could have drawn a word from his mouth, until he had reached home and deposited his acquired merits on the household. He was taken by the rest of the people in Membeni in a light-hearted fashion. Beginning with his nickname, which they turned into Mitho Diwano for Sweet Madman, he was treated as a joke, a local phenomenon good for a few laughs. A devotee of his intensity they had only heard of in legends, and obviously could never take seriously in their midst. Businessmen delighted in enticing him with new stock, which he bought on the basis of a hundi signed to a bank; and when the maturation date approached and the stock languished on the shelves and behind the birij, his wife Hirbai would go around giving it away at discount to raise the money.

The Sweet Madman left Jamnagar in Gujarat with his

brother and their wives a few years before the First World War. The two wives were also sisters. Mitha got off at British-protected Zanzibar, and his brother continued on to German-ruled Dar es Salaam. A few years after the war, with one daughter married and three others in line and with two sons, when life was hard and Zanzibar was too small a place to hold everybody, Mitha received a vision. And when Mitha had a vision, people listened, even those who normally ridiculed him. The vision told him that Zanzibar was doomed, that he should go to the mainland. When Mitha and his family took the boat to Mombasa, several other families went with them. They all set up shop in the bustling Indian quarter at Membeni.

My grandfather Mitha had a simple strategy for getting his daughters married. He accepted the first proposal that came. 'We will not accept abuse,' he would tell his wife. This was because the proposal always said something like, 'We would like your daughter to be our son so-and-so's wife.' Having called his precious daughter 'wife' and so put a smudge on her, my grandfather figured, they would have to accept her as a wife. Which they had come to do anyway. Thus my mother Kulsum almost instantly got engaged to my father Juma.

'But he is so dark,' said little Zarina at Kulsum's side. Yes, he was dark. Not the dark of charcoal, the mweusi of the African from the interior, the Hehe, the Ngoni, the Haya; or the light dark mweupe of the Chagga; or the red-dark of the half-naked Masai, his arse showing firm and proud as he walked; but the dark of the Indian, the persistent brown-dark of sedimented coffee that refuses to whiten with any amount of milk. My father Juma was wearing white trousers and a white shirt in the European style, when Kulsum first saw him, and he had on shiny brown leather shoes. His hair was glistening black and he sported a red scarf at the open shirt neck. 'But he is smart,' said Kulsum, 'and he is strong. He will pick you up and throw you away.'

It was 1938, and my father was thirty years old. He was, like his father Huseni many years before in Matamu, in the process of getting tamed.

Moti, the orphan bride, the fallen jewel of Matamu, my father's mother: she had waited two years for her vanished husband Huseni, before marrying again and setting off to make family and fortune in Kenya. My father Juma was four years old and went with her. When she died in Voi a few years later, she was on her third marriage. Her husband packed off all her children – three daughters and Juma – to her sister, Awal, further up along the railway line in Nairobi and disappeared. Had Dhanji Govindji, who came looking for Huseni not long after, stuck around longer in Voi or even Mombasa, he might have traced his grandson Juma and perhaps taken him home; and the world would have been different.

Awal was the wife of Hassam Pirbhai, one of the pioneers who had left the Indian Community behind in Mombasa, packed closely in their shacks around the mosque in the narrow streets of Membeni and Kuze, and struck out in the wilderness in the wake of the railway, shopkeepers to their compatriot coolies, artisans, stationmasters and infantrymen, before finally making their homes in the new capital Nairobi. Now the firm of Hassam Pirbhai and Co Ltd, Pioneering Trading Company, the famous PTC, clothed the police and the King's African Rifles, supplied safari needs from matches to tents, and exported ivory and hides. The two sons of Hassam Pirbhai walked tall and proud in town, in the company of – if not always equal to – the most influential men in Nairobi. The old man and his wife stayed with their own kind, the new rich incapable of shedding their origins; he, shrewd and reticent, accepting homage from fawning relatives with the air of a gentle prince; she, haughty, humble only before God; the two of them driven around by a black chauffeur, from home to shop, to other homes, to mosque, and on Sundays along the avenues of Nairobi to the hills around it where new suburbs were springing up with their neat bungalows and pretty gardens and khakied servants.

Awal was the proverbial stepmother. Most stepmothers at the time, when children came in packs and often unwanted, were of that proverbial kind. Knowledge of Juma's pedigree followed him to the capital. And so Juma, because even the big house was packed, and to avoid his associating with her sons, was given a room in the courtyard, next to the servants' quarters and the outhouse. There he grew up, a second-class citizen, nothing more than a glorified servant; whom the family sent away on pretexts when important guests arrived; who never sat in the family car except with the chauffeur; who to earn money ran errands for Awal's sons; who more often ate in the kitchen than at the table. When the boys went on safaris, Juma went with them to skin the deer and clean the meat; when the family went on picnics or the Muslim servant was absent, Juma was the slaughterer. My father would tell of how his cousins would play jokes on him. 'Oh, he is only the driver,' they would say when a guest raised an enquiring eyebrow. 'Oh, he is the cook.'

One afternoon when a Kikuyu vegetable-seller arrived, they told her: 'Mama, your lost son is looking for you,' and directed her to Juma's quarter, where he was taking a rest. And when the poor, innocent woman actually went, and saw an angry young man ready to throw her out, she said, 'Oh, my unfortunate son, they are making fun of you!' From that time, whenever she came around she would greet him, 'Ah, mwanangu, how are you?' She called herself, simply, Mary. And she attached herself to his fife.

In Juma, his cousins thought they had the family sidekick, the cowering poor relative always dependent and always at their service; but Juma was made of stronger stuff. By the time he was sixteen he had grown away from the family and had a life of his own unknown to them. When he was seventeen he committed a terrible crime, for which they made him reckon. But by that reckoning they admitted that their old ways with their poor relative were over. 'In those days,' Kulsum would say, 'they gave terrible punishments to their sons.' But what did he do? 'Oh, something.' As if it were nothing; but then why the terrible punishment?

Outside the family, information flows freely. One day in mosque, Hassam Pirbhai presiding, the congregation standing up for prayer – 'Oh Lord, grant us increase in our progeny' – when, houuuk! a loud hiccup from Juma, and those around him stir uncomfortably. 'Oh Lord, Oh Merciful Giver, grant us increase in our earnings.' Again, houuuk! This time there are giggles from the children's section and muffled grunts elsewhere, and one or two young men walk out grinding their teeth in agonies of controlled laughter. Meanwhile, looks like light-beams have gone back and forth, from Awal to Juma, from Awal to her sons, from the sons to the attendants manning the pillars. 'Oh Merciful and Kind Lord grant us increase in our lives.' And houuuuk-uk! as two attendants converge on the drunk Juma and escort him outside.

At home, when the hearing was over, he was handed over for punishment to the dreaded Raju Master. It was only fitting that when the crime was against God, the man who had taught him, or tried to teach him, religion should punish him. Juma was hanged by his feet at a doorway and whipped with a cane. The family watched, the two stepbrothers urging the master on, the women to keep pity or remorse at bay reminding each other of the crime. And when his howls drew an enquiry from a cruising police car, they said, 'Oh, the dog is sick.'

Juma for some years afterwards lived a life of his own in and around Nairobi and then altogether disappeared for three years. Of these three years, as of any of his wild exploits before marriage, Kulsum does not have much to say. Apparently he travelled a lot; and operated a taxi somewhere. But Kulsum, who likes to bring in associations of prestige, does remember that he went to Mwanza, to seek out Amir Merchant who, my father had heard in Nairobi, was a relation of his mother. Amir Merchant later went to India and subsequently became the head of one of the twenty-two families or so that reportedly at one time owned all the wealth of Pakistan; at whose daughter's wedding no less a personage than the Shah of Iran was a guest. Of this far try on the part of my mother there is no need to say further.

One day Hassam Pirbhai received a call from the agent of the British Castle Lines in Nairobi. He apparently had received a telephone message from Mombasa. Juma had stowed away on one of its steamers to India and had been apprehended trying to disembark in Bombay. My father saw Bombay only from the porthole of the cabin he was locked up in. The agent informed Hassam Pirbhai that if his family did not pay the boy's fare, the company would turn him over to the police. Hassam Pirbhai did the only honourable thing: hid his family's shame. He agreed to pay the fare. In Juma's absence his three fair half-sisters had rediscovered their ties with him. To appease these three young women, Hassam Pirbhai himself went to Mombasa, offered Juma a job, and brought him home. The marriage followed in due course, for which project Awal was assigned the job of looking for a fair beauty from a humble but respectable home. Mombasa was the natural choice as the home of the humble where, moreover, Juma's reputation was unknown. The fair beauty was spotted by Awal in a Membeni street, returning from school.

Running away. Wanderlust. Having come to this theme yet once again, memory plays a trick on me. From her corner

Shehru throws a wink at me… and do I imagine that the gaping mouth with its sisal moustache has a silent laugh on its thin old lips…

The question that comes to mind is: in coming here, have I followed a destiny? Satisfied a wanderlust that runs in the blood? Or do I seek in genes merely an excuse for weakness, an inability to resolve situations? Perhaps it is this weakness that's in the blood: can you distinguish such weakness from wanderlust? When does a situation become impossible enough to justify escape?

I too have run away, absconded. And reaching this grim basement, I stopped to examine the collective memory – this spongy, disconnected, often incoherent accretion of stories over generations. Like the karma a soul acquires, over many incarnations, the sins and merits, until in its final stages it lumbers along top-heavy with its accumulations, desperately seeking absolution.

I, like my forefathers before me, have run away. But what a price they paid. Dhanji Govindji, his self-respect and his sanity. His son, the joys of family life, the security of community life. My father Juma, I don't know what price he paid for running away – it was Hassam Pirbhai who paid the cash price – but he did pay a price for coming back. He joined his tormentors. And in joining them he lost his compassion for those of whom he was also a part – if only a quarter.

Perhaps I judge too harshly.

8 | *How I Killed My Father*

When they married, my mother was sixteen and my father a cynical, rough man of thirty who had seen quite a bit of the world and was now a salesman at the firm of Hassam Pirbhai in Nairobi. Kulsum had studied up to Standard Six in Gujarati, and always stood second in class, but her father had seen no use in education for his girls and did not let her finish school. But for one more year, she could have been a graduate, become a teacher… married well. She did not resent the marriage but the way in which she was given away. My father had been in and out of school and had learnt English on the streets and later at work. After the wedding at the Membeni mosque, they spent the night in a room at the home of an acquaintance of Hassam Pirbhai. The next morning, weeping, Kulsum said goodbye to her family and friends, and with her husband took the train for Nairobi. When she stopped crying, they had reached Voi. She looked up at her husband, seeking comfort, but the irate Juma who had spent the day watching the scenery turned around from the window and sarcastically said, 'Bas? Is that all you're going to cry? We're not even half-way there.'

There was a pitch-black, palpable darkness outside, the air was humid, and in the stillness – perhaps caused by the sudden cessation of the din of the iron wheels on the rails, the steam puffing and compartments rattling – the shouts of people in the distance sounded strangely hollow. They were alone, together, the two of them, and they looked at each other across the compartment in the dim light that had already attracted clinging insects. They reached some resolution, for she got up and set out the dinner her mother had packed for the journey, and he rang the bell and ordered tea. Sometime later the train let off a belch of steam, gave a lurch, and proceeded warily into the darkness. The way ahead was uphill, and there were elephants and giraffes about.

'They said, "We have quarter-and-lac-shilling bungalas in Nairobi,"' Kulsum would later say, 'and what did they give us? This,' she would show her thumb. Awal had also failed to mention, when she haughtily brought the proposal to Membeni and proceeded to inspect the girl as if buying her, that the boy had certain bad habits, kept a haunt at the New Salisbury and often came home late in the night. He also had debts. During their first months of marriage, when he would return in the evenings to breathe spirits down her neck, the naive daughter of the Mombasa mystic, not sure at this point which she dreaded more, his return or his absence, who wanted to push the brute away but knew she mustn't, would ask him about the strange smell of his breath. 'It's only lemonade,' would come the passionate reply.

In those first years of marriage they lived in Juma's old room, now converted into an apartment. There were in the household then Awal's two sons, now married, and her three nieces, my aunts. Over the six young women the tall, thin-lipped, long-nosed puritan Awal ruled with an iron hand. 'If your pachedis keep slipping off your heads, use a nail,' she would rail, in her constant efforts to preserve her home's khandaa-nity: that snobbish form of respectability which every family, however crooked, lays claim to. Daughters-in-law, responsible for the khandaa-nity of their fathers' names, occupied the lowest rungs in the family hierarchy. Kulsum was the wife of the orphan, the half-caste, and herself of humble origin: there was no one lowlier than her at the home of Hassam Pirbhai. The women took turns cooking, and inevitably the unsophisticated Kulsum, bringing with her a crude and limited cuisine from the dukas of Membeni, earned the ire of the old woman. My mother was told to assist the others and learn from them. And in this role she made mistakes that spoke sadly of her breeding and background and brought her the contemptuous taunts of her sisters-in-law. When the months passed and she put on weight – but she was robust, not weak, her belly round, not sagging, her periods regular – her chores increased, the sarcasm was more biting. Hassam Pirbhai at dinner: 'Why no mangoes yet?' His wife Awal drawing blood: 'They say that in Mombasa the trees are barren this year.' What irked my practical mother more, however, was the fact that three-quarters of her husband's salary went towards their upkeep in that house.

From time to time her 'other mother-in-law' Mary would turn up with a companion, a basket full of produce slung on her back, hanging by its long leather strap fastened tightly round the forehead. Calling Kulsum over the back gate and shouting for someone to hold back the barking dog, Mary would give my mother a head of lettuce, a cabbage, a bunch of carrots.

The year following their wedding, war was declared in Europe, and Kulsum's father promptly closed shop in Mombasa, packed, and set forth with his family to Dar es Salaam, where their son Hassan had gone to seek his fortune. In the previous European war, Mitho Diwano in Zanzibar and his brother in Dar had been separated, without a word exchanged for more than two years. In this war, he decided, he was not going to take any chances. Mad Mitha was not one to draw fine distinctions between the Europeans, especially when they made war.

It was about this time that Kulsum effected her release from the domination of her in-laws. One evening, while the rest of the family drove off to mosque, my mother, smelling of sweet perfume and makeup, her lips red, her cheeks flushed, her contours round and soft in the frock-pachedi, smiled shyly at my father and told him to take her to the cinema. My father did not say a word as he locked the door to their apartment and reminded the servant Karanja to watch the house. Then he looked at her again, and in the best European fashion offered her his arm, and the two walked to the Odeon a few blocks away.

In such circumstances there is no time to confess, to plead extenuating circumstances: a mischievous whim, a romantic mood. The crime is discovered and judgement follows irrevocably. When my parents returned, the sinful couple, the entire family was waiting for them. The matriarch and patriarch on the big sofa, one pair of eyes glowering, the other twinkling. At their flanks the heavenly host: the three pert sisters, the two furious brothers-in-law with their two wives affecting a damaged, suffering look, quieting down with excessive vigour and unnecessary smacks the three cherubim. The family khandaan had been betrayed. First, they had gone together (when she should have waited for the zanana show on Wednesday afternoon); then, they had violated the sacred hour. My father and mother had made the mistake of going to the theatre which the family partly owned. As soon as the manager had counted the show's takings, he had headed straight for the mosque.

The wrath was delivered to my father, the barbs aimed at my mother.

'Going to picture during maghrab,' the matron began. 'With pimps and prostitutes and Bhadalas. Does that suit our reputation—'

'But Ma,' said the Sweet Madman's sweet daughter. 'Even Europeans go, all the communities go—'

'Keep quiet!'

There followed a torrent of abuse such as my mother had

never heard; during which Hassam Pirbhai, seeking refuge in an argument with his servant Karanja about his medication, wisely withdrew. My father remained standing, silent – men did not defend their wives from their families – and Kulsum sat on the floor, sobbing.

'Eat, now,' my father would beg her for the next two days. But my mother pushed the plate aside and intermittently sobbed.

The first guerrilla was surely a woman. The ways of a woman are softer but surer. The timing is precise and the target just right. When she strikes, with a force not overly strong, the whole machinery threatens to come to a riotous stop. Scandal and public embarrassment looms not far ahead, while panic takes over. At such a moment whatever she demands, she can walk away with. I talk of course of the traditional, extended family household. There are those – and I can name one – who will maintain that, nevertheless, the war was always lost; only isolated battles were won. In this one my mother carried the day.

My father, of course, had been softened and was no longer the bully who had scoffed at her grief once. He, who could have put a stop to her show, if only by increasing her suffering, therefore simply ignored the suggestions of his sisters and the sarcasm of Awal ('If men would only slap their wives once in a while…'). Saturday turned to Sunday, and when at lunch time my mother's hunger strike showed no sign of abating, the old man intervened.

'Come, Beta. You must eat. Forget this quarrel.'

'Just because I have no one here… (sob)… they bully me all the time… (sob)… they talk about my family… (sob)…'

My father stood at the door, discomfited, Kulsum talked behind her veil, Hassam Pirbhai sat beside her, solicitous as a physician.

'So you won't eat, then?'

'No.' Sob. Sob-sob-sob.

'Now... if you feel that badly... that we've mistreated you... if you want to live by yourselves...'

'Yes (sob) we want to live by ourselves...'

'Well, Juma, is that what you want?'

'If that's what she wants,' said my father.

Kulsum, in triumph.

Those were the war years. What they saw of the war were the soldiers in transit to and from the Ethiopian campaign, the shortages of food, the weekly broadcasts, the blackouts. They had a room in Ngara, not far from their previous home. My father had acquired considerable influence through his job. He came to know commissioners, police inspectors and heads of government departments. And the more people he knew, the more indispensable he became in his job.

Still Kulsum failed to conceive a child. Now all of his salary came to her, and what he spent were his commissions. The girl from Mombasa had been taught to save. 'Eggs were 33 for a shilling; yet I would not eat one, saving it for him to eat the next day. Chappatis were a luxury. We had no table and chairs, but sat on the kitchen floor across from each other.' At the end of their first year alone she sprang a surprise on him by showing him a sum of money she had saved to pay towards his debt. 'His eyes opened.'

In the absence of a child, she took to her old hobby of sewing. And she profited from the war. He would bring in orders for mosquito nets for the army which she would sew during the day, and in the evenings he would help her to put on the cotton top and border.

Seven years passed; seven years of childless marriage, in which joshis, pandits, sheikhs and pirs were consulted, stars, tea leaves, palm and archaica read, predictions made and proved false. Then came Suleiman Pir. He was a holy man from Bombay who had a strong following in East Africa. Whenever Suleiman Pir came from Bombay, a mela was held. Families gathered in clusters in a big festive field and he, accompanied by attendants bearing his chair and an umbrella, would come and sit in their midst, asking after their health and wealth, blessing their offerings of food and newly announced marriages. Suleiman Pir was short and thin, fair like a Parsee, with a long nose, and he wore a white suit and a topee. Hassam Pirbhai's clan had gathered with five married children plus my three aunts, now married, and my father, and a horde of grandchildren. Suleiman Pir, having blessed collectively one and all, having blessed the vast trays of fruit and nuts brought before him, was seated, wiping his face, suffering the attentions of the old man and his sons, ready to go to the next family waiting for him. Then he saw my father and mother, sitting together by themselves, and he asked for their children. 'Where is the aulaad?'

'No aulaad, Pir Saheb,' said my father.

'No aulaad at all?'

'None at all, Pir Saheb.'

My father did not think it proper to ask, but the pir heard the plea in his voice, he read and understood the beseeching eyes of my mother. He picked up an apple from a nearby fruit tray, whispered a prayer over it, and handed it to my mother. 'You will have aulaad,' he said, and left.

In the commotion of attendants rushing after him, the men and women looking with awe as he passed (it was said that you could not meet his eyes), forgetting their restless children meanwhile, and then preparing to leave, the apple was picked up by one of the wives and put away with the other fruit.

There followed a ruckus. My mother imputed bad faith to Hassam Pirbhai's family and rushed to gouge out the eyes of

Shiri, one of the daughters-in-law. 'You bastard-bitch, you born of a pig—' The mela turned into a mêlée.

The females of Hassam Pirbhai's family converged around the towering Awal, in a show of sisterly solidarity. My father called helplessly from the side, while the other males of the family looked on, confident of their wives. Kulsum had some of Shiri's skin in her nails and was perhaps in for a good clobbering.

Enter Gula, Kulsum's sister. Gula was three years my mother's junior and had moved to Nairobi with her husband. She was big, fat, strong and quarrelsome, and came to stand beside my mother like a bodyguard, putting her hands on her hips, throwing a challenge. 'Come,' she called hoarsely.

A war of words followed.

The high culture these ladies had picked up in this most European of East African cities, their new snobbishness, was cast aside, and they were back in their elemental form. Here was not Parklands and Ngara anymore but the alleys of Mombasa and Zanzibar, the villages of Cutch and Kathiawad.

'Just look at her, all blubber.'

'Yes, just look. How her husband finds her hole, God only knows.'

'Probably wide like a cup.'

'Like a sack.'

'That's none of your business, you bitch—' my aunt Gula screamed. 'You button-holed bone-pie! Yes, he sips milk and honey from this cup, do you hear? Milk and honey!' (Here she danced a small jig.) 'He sees Mairaj every night—'

'What, that sissy—'

'Oh, yes? Come and play with his tanpura one night and hear his sweet music—'

'Enough!' shouted Hassam Pirbhai with the twinkling eyes, now that there was cheering from the spectators. The mud-wrestlers retired.

Meanwhile the children, like voracious army ants, were all over the food trays and one lonely apple caught Juma's eye, and he pocketed it before it too got devoured. 'Eat it,' he told Kulsum. 'If you have faith it will do just as well.'

Nine months later, on 7 May 1945, when the clash and clamour and the boom and thunder in distant Europe seemed finally to show signs of subsiding, as King George was addressing his subjects over the radio and talking of peace, Kulsum went into labour. My grandmother Hirbai was present, flown in by my father from Dar. And as Jenabai Midwife put the little girl in my exultant father's arms, he slipped her a hundred shilling note as gift. Thus was born my sister Begum, King George's daughter. Kulsum had gone without meat for the nine months, and not until every girl in the girls' school had been fed pilau and sweets, not until Kulsum had been to the mosque, placing coconut and shilling, coconut and shilling, on every step as she descended and came home, did she touch meat.

The rest of us came easily.

Kulsum's theory of creation.

When God was well and ready after all his exertions finally to create mankind, he sat himself beside a red-hot oven with a plate of dough. From this he fashioned three identical dolls. He put the first doll into the oven to finish it, but, alas, brought it out too soon: it came out white and undone. In this way was born the white race. With this lesson learnt, the Almighty put the second doll into the oven, but this time he kept it in for too long. It came out burnt and black. Thus the black race. Finally the One and Only put the last doll inside the oven, and brought it out at just the right time. It came out golden brown, the Asian, simply perfect.

(Thus our nicknames: Sona for the golden boy, the youngest

and favourite, my brother Jamal; Kala for the one who came between, Salim, Salum in Swahili, the overdone.)

There followed the years of contentment, the Eden of our later dreams. We would remember them by the tins of Black Magic and Trebor, Kit-Kats and candyfloss and Pez; school ties, blazers and cardigans; toy trains that ran on steel tracks, prizes won at baby shows. There is a Black Magic box full of old photos in my gunny. A picture of my father shows him drinking a toast with his friends: Juka Chacha and Ali Chacha and Babu Chacha and Mithoo Chacha, and two Europeans who could be District Officers, all jovially raising their glasses. A family picture shows my father and mother seated at two extremes, five children in between. Standing between them, three girls in identical pinafores of a dotted material and a bow in front, King George's daughter Begum with our cousins Mehroon and Yasmin. Sitting in front of the girls, Sona and Kala.

Sunday afternoons, having visited uncles and aunts first, we would drive to City Park in T8016, our black Prefect, for the 'band-waja'. Juma would park the car, and we would stroll towards the bandstand and stop some distance away. There would be European couples, and white nannies sitting primly on the few chairs, their knitting on their laps, chatting with each other, and African ayahs sitting on the grass, their bare feet pointing upwards. Surrounding the bandstand would be a wreath of white children playing, running after each other with spades and buckets, bows and arrows and guns, shouting and laughing. The bandsmen, black except for the leader, were in khaki shorts and shirts, red sashes round their middles, red fezzes on their heads. The drummer wore a splendid leopard skin over his front, and he would twirl his sticks round and round on his fingers and catch them at just the right time and thwack his drum. In the centre of the semicircle, conducting, was the white bandleader in a white uniform. At six o'clock sharp there would be a long roll on the drum: the scurrying

European children froze, the nannies climbed stiffly to their feet, arranging their frocks, and closer at hand Kulsum's sharp eyes kept her children in reasonable control (her perpetual complaint: 'How well the European children are behaved! Did you see anyone asking *them* to keep still?'), and with beating hearts we heard the bars of God Save the King announcing the end of our Sunday fun.

Beautiful, beautiful Nairobi. But all was not well in this Eden; there were rumours, rumours in Government offices and the big stores that supplied them, rumours in the bars and the clubs… of an evil secret society… and a fear rustled ever so slightly in the background, rearing its head sporadically like a devil toying with children, with a murder here and a fire there. The dreaded words were Mau Mau.

On the evening of 20 October 1952, when my father Juma came home, we all waited expectantly in bed for the clap of his hands to bring us jumping out of our beds, for the drive out to Icelands for ice-cream. But the door was firmly shut, all the bolts fastened and checked, the windows locked, the curtains drawn.

'What's up?' asked Kulsum anxiously.

'Something is going on,' he replied. 'I don't know what. There are rumours. We'll stay indoors and wait.' He turned on the radio. A talk show was on, discussing farming techniques in Kenya.

Early the next morning we were woken by the sound of lorries – not one or two, but a military convoy carrying white soldiers.

'Is this a new war or something?' asked my mother.

'How should I know?' came the impatient reply. 'Keep the children at home. Tell Abdulla to stay out—' Playing tough, he pretended he would go to work, going behind a door, draped in khanga at the waist, to change – until, as expected, Kulsum expressed alarm and absolutely refused him permission to go out. Shortly afterwards, at breakfast, the funereal tones of the Hindustani Service announced that the Governor was going on air. The Emergency was declared; Mau Mau was an acknowledged word.

The First Battalion of the Lancashire Fusiliers had arrived the previous evening and was now making its appearance on the streets of Nairobi in a flag march, driving around in the backs of military lorries, bayonets fixed, meaning business. In Mombasa the cruiser HMS *Kenya* had docked, and the Royal Marines were giving a similar show of British might. The Europeans waved, Asians heaved sighs of relief. 'Peace at last,' said my father when he heard the Governor.

But peace did not truly come, and violence hovered nearby.

At about this time my Aunt Gula died. Unfortunately, she had been too accurate about what she described as her husband's musical prowess. One day she doused herself with kerosene and set herself aflame. The forty days of mourning had not passed when her husband announced his marriage to a young nurse. They went to Mombasa, taking his two boys with them; my cousins Mehroon and Yasmin came to stay with us permanently.

At the firm of Hassam Pirbhai, Pioneer Trader, European farmers from the Highlands would stop by, Government servants of all races would check in. Close by were the Rendezvous, where they could have cakes and English tea, the Ismailia, from where they could order samosas and brewed Indian tea, and the New Stanley, where they could sip Martinis under bright canopies in the sun and watch the traffic on Delamere Avenue directed into neat lanes by a traffic policeman in starched whites. Woolworths, the first Nairobi supermarket, agents for *Reader's Digest*, and vendors of the London *Times*, the *Illustrated London News*, and much else besides, was a stone's throw away. From this European and Asian hub, my father would come home at lunch and dinner time, bringing news of the Mau Mau.

The Bucks were a young English couple with a farm in Kinangop, and a seven-year-old son. Mrs Buck was a doctor who ran a part-time clinic on the farm. The Bucks were regular customers at Hassam Pirbhai's. They bought their safari clothes and their servants' khakis from the store. They had bought a tent. Recently they had installed a siren. One evening at dinnertime, the servant walked in from the kitchen bringing with him an armed gang. The bodies of the man and wife were found horribly mutilated in the dining room. The boy's body was found in bed, in what was said to be a worse condition. Civilised Nairobi was sickened. 'No worse horror can be imagined, no worse butchery described,' wrote the *Nairobi Herald*. The settler community was up in arms. At the dinner table my father expressed profound shock. 'Their own servant,' he would say. 'This, our Abdulla, suppose he turned around tomorrow and betrayed us—' 'Don't say such things,' Kulsum said. 'Besides, he's not a Kikuyu. He's a Muslim.'

A few weeks later there occurred the Lari massacre, right under the nose of the Uplands police station. Lari housed a large number of Kikuyu loyalists, including the Kikuyu Home Guard. That morning the local detachment of the King's African Rifles had been called away; that night the Kikuyu Home Guard were patrolling the forest; so when the Mau Mau arrived there were plenty of women and children... when the huts were set on fire on the Lari plain, there were enough women and children. When the Home Guard returned to charred and mutilated bodies, all the strength in the world could not have stifled their howls of anguish.

Feelings ran high the following weeks, fear was at an intense pitch. 'What are the British good for, anyway? "About turn, left-right," parading on Delamere Avenue, but no action.'

'Aré, what we need are the Gurkhas. These Fusiliers are just dandies – boys from England. One platoon of Gurkhas could chase these Kukus up Mount Kenya—'

On a Sunday my Chachas had gathered at our home, playing bridge. In the courtyard Abdulla had grilled meat for supper. When the men had finished their meal, the servant brought water in a jug for them to wash their hands. He would go to each one at a time and pour water on the fingers held over the plate. Some water fell on Ali Chacha's lap; our favourite Chacha who wore dark glasses and had brought my father a set of Kashmiri daggers. Ali Chacha got up in a fury and gave poor Abdulla a slap on the face and a kick. 'Blaady basket! Blaady Kikuyu Mau Mau—'

'But he's not Kikuyu,' insisted the girl from Mombasa, 'he's a Muslim.'

Poor Abdulla ran sobbing to his room.

A few days after the Lari incident, my father brought home a pistol. It stayed in the thief-proof compartment of his wardrobe. Every night for a few weeks, before retiring, he would take the key from Kulsum, and get the gun out. Then, as my anxious mother watched with prayers on her lips, he would open the front door and, taking steady aim, fire twice into the pitch darkness that was the shrubs, trees and refuse dump of the unused lot across the road.

There once was an incident, or non-incident, that we would all like to forget. It conflicts too much with our image of our father: Juma, who consorted with police inspectors and DOs, who had once been served a drink at the Norfolk Hotel, whom people came to call in the middle of the night seeking help and influence.

Operation Anvil was under way to wipe out the Mau Mau and there were regular spot-checks by what we called the military police. The military police were British soldiers, the police, and the police reserves, including local vigilantes. The pass book was introduced and the city was being searched sector by sector for Mau Mau sympathisers. Cars were stopped, trunks searched, and passengers scrutinised. In residential areas servants were questioned, often with slaps and kicks. In all cases, suspicious-looking Kikuyus were taken away in caged trucks like wild animals to a zoo.

One evening while returning from the mosque, my father was waved to a stop at the bridge on Nairobi River, just before the road climbs up to Ngara and Parklands. It was here that the incident or non-incident occurred. Two European men, almost boys, one questioning my father outside, the other leering inside, the car packed with Kulsum and five children. The road was dark but the two men had torches and there was light from other cars. Just that. An exclamation from my mother, my father getting into the car and snapping at her question. A hushed ride home. Begum would say later that the military policeman slapped my father. 'Don't be silly,' Kulsum would answer, 'he was only flipping the pages of his book. Did your father look like a Kikuyu? And anyway he complained.'

The gunny would like to throw out one more bad memory. Spit out a pang of conscience that's been eating away at the insides, like a particularly thorny pip that's been swallowed. Operation Anvil again. Hundreds of Kikuyus, guilty and not guilty, were sent away every day to await further screening; thousands waited at Langata. One night fearful Mary, Mary with the long, bony head and big, white teeth, this time wearing an old dress of Kulsum who had become bigger, knocked on the door. With her was a man. My father went outside to talk to them, and Kulsum was in a panic. Whenever my mother was agitated, her eyes would widen, she would turn pale and look in front of her, sometimes picking her chin. You could tell she was praying, some mantra was being invoked;

My father came in and said, 'She wants us to keep her son.'

'And you said yes?'

'How could I refuse? Anyway, let's wait till tomorrow. Give me the key, I'll hide him in the store room.'

'Jambo, mama!' Mary peeped in from outside.

'Jambo,' my mother replied woodenly.

Actually, Mary had begged my father to employ her son and get him a pass book. All night my father and mother sat up in bed looking at each other, frightened, waiting for the night to pass. Stories of Mau Mau murders, of trusted servants taking grisly oaths and betraying their employers to grisly deaths, went through their minds. Every rustle outside acquired menace, even the crickets sounded eerie, and every motor vehicle that sounded as if it might stop at any moment could have been the military police.

At daybreak, my father took us all to the neighbour's house, then he walked to the road and hailed a passing police car and said that there was a man hiding in his store room. Mary's son was found among sacks of rice, potatoes, and onions, hiding in an empty sack, and taken away.

'The police would have found him anyway,' said my father.

We never saw Mary again. Perhaps she too was taken away, to be screened, detained even. Was she a Mau Mau sympathiser? What did we know of her – a friend from another world who came periodically and then once at night in an hour of need – whose memory we now carry branded forever in our conscience…

The Mau Mau years did not tarnish our memories of Eden.

'Just when we had established ourselves, when the future lay open before us, he went away,' Kulsum would say. And I, who took it all away, would look down in shame.

Four gallons of milk were spilt one day and all her happiness was washed away with it…

Four gallons of milk, boiled once in the morning and skimmed for the malai, now carried back to the fire by Yasmin to be heated. The pan is large and shiny, used only for the milk, and wide and heavy, and she walks in small jerky steps, grimy feet on a grimy floor, face twisted in a grimace, shouting, 'Move... move, basi – oh Mother!' Kulsum is sending Abdulla on an errand, I fail to move out of Yasmin's way and bang into her, she stumbles back and four gallons of milk come pouring down my dark little body.

We all stared at the marriage of white and black on the floor, the white milk spreading out and breaking up into sickly little islands on a black sea – from which a frantic Kulsum divined disaster.

'Oh Mother!' cried my mother. 'You bastard, you motherfucker...' A rain of blows kept pouring on my milk-washed body. The wet slaps smarted but not a tear I shed. Thump, slap, slipper, smack... I bore on back, face, buttocks, arm... thump, slap, slipper, smack... how can I forget?... until finally I whispered, 'Forgive me, Mother.'

'Leave him, Auntie,' said Yasmin. 'Leave him, Mummy,' said Begum. 'Please leave him,' they all begged.

How could she forgive me, my crime was murder.

The milk was wiped off the floor, my mother went off to her room, and I was bathed, tears falling freely now. Not at the pain but at having hurt my mother. Fifteen minutes later, she came back, tearful, her tasbih in her hand. 'Put him to bed,' she told the girls.

My father was not told of the incident.

There followed seven days of intense expiation, seven days of intense prayer on one leg; seven days of sweet offerings to the mosque; and the following Sunday a niani. Seven clean maidens put a clove in their mouths before going to bed the previous night and arrived to lunch with sore tongues, wet mouths and the soft clove. They sat in a circle, on a mat in the dining-room, and waited shyly to be served. Kulsum served each one of them herself; no child was allowed to help, Abdulla was sent away. First she gave each girl a glass of yogurt to swallow the wet clove with. Then on each plate she put portions of sweet rice steaming in cinnamon and saffron, and chick peas. And when they had eaten of my mother's hands, they trooped off to the tap outside to wash their hands and returned to where she sat, on a low stool, a pan of water and a bowl beside her and a cup in her hand. Each girl raised her right foot over the bowl and Kulsum poured a little water on the big toe and washed it. And the water that had collected when all of them had passed her was solemnly drunk. Then each girl took a sweet and a handkerchief as gift, and my father returned them all to their homes. Thus were the gods and goddesses, orthodox and unorthodox, placated on my behalf.

But the gods are not always heedful.

A few nights later my father woke up with a pain and asked Kulsum to call Dr Joshi. All his usual bravado was gone. 'I think there's something wrong with me.' Abdulla was woken up and quickly dispatched with a note. But this was still the Emergency and Abdulla (although a Muslim, as Kulsum said) did not return for a few days. Day was breaking, a delicious cool breeze brought the smell of earth and dew and wet leaves through the window with the first golden rays of the sun, when I was woken up by a heart-rending scream from my mother.

We stayed in our bedroom all day, my brother and I. We tried playing ludo first, then snakes and ladders. We brought out the train set and the doctor set. But the sombre mood of the house was over us too, and we felt miserable. We cried a little and we slept a little. We held on to our natural urges until it hurt. Then my brother wet himself. I watched a trickle slowly move down his legs, the smell filled the air, and the front of his shorts gradually acquired an ever-widening wet patch. Then I too let go and relieved myself.

By opening the door a crack we could watch the proceedings

in the rest of the house. The dining room table had been moved to a side and the floor was laid with mats and sheets. The sitting room furniture was hooded with ghostly white sheets. In the early afternoon the people trickled in. First the women, in twos and threes, talking in hushed, important tones, advising my sister and cousins and ordering the servant. They sat on the floor counting beads, some with eyes half-closed, others staring blankly in front of them, lips moving; and when something occurred to one, she would turn and mutter in a husky voice to a neighbour; and then go back, to counting, staring, meditating.

Then came the men, when the sitting and dining rooms were almost full of women, standing behind with a respectfulness I'd never seen in any of them before. Drinking companions, gambling companions, men he'd had released from arrest, men he'd lent money to, policemen, civil servants. Babu Chacha, Lai Chacha, John Chacha, Mr Stephens; there were Sikhs, Goans, Patels, Shahs and Manjis; and they stood respectfully at the back, dressed modestly in trousers and jackets, hands in front of them, heads lowered, waiting.

Finally came the elders, pushing gently through the group of men, and the mukhi among them enquired of the women in front with a gesture that said: 'Where?' And the bedroom door was thrown open as they went in, and remained wide open. Inside, on a long, low table, was a figure draped in red cloth, and I saw Kulsum for the first time that day, sitting beside the all-covered figure, her own head covered with a white pachedi.

A murmur filled the outer two rooms where the men and women were congregated and, suddenly, a woman's voice started in a wavering voice that slowly picked up:

O fickle mind, you desire…

The murmur subsided, a loud sob was heard, and the chorus went relentlessly, unmercifully on, drawing tears in its wake:

> How flowers wither
> And Kings pass on…

The red cloth had been partly lifted to show my father's face. The mukhi sat on one side of him and Kulsum on the other. Then, at a signal, she got up and knelt before my father, and the mukhi with a sprinkle of water on the stony face forgave him on behalf of her.

I saw death but I did not know it. I saw my father stretched out stonily on a low, wooden table, I heard my mother sob, I heard the singing that induced tears among the women, yet I did not know it was death. But a gloom descended over my brother and me, and we started to cry, the two of us, not knowing what was happening around us. Our sister and cousins opened the door and strode in, saw two wet pants, sniffed the air, and got to work. Soon my brother was fresh and ready, rubbing his wet eyes and sniffing, and was taken out of the room. Then he returned with Mehroon, and she took my hand. At that moment my mother walked in. She looked at me and said, 'It's not necessary to take him. He's too young.'

The two of us sat in the room, alone again. We were told to go to sleep, but we sat there on the bed in bewildered silence. Presently there was a commotion outside, voices, movement. Then we heard repeated sobs and we dared not open the door to look. There were people on the other side of our door, we could hear men, and heavy footsteps. Then, some sharp calls, by men. It was as if the men had taken over from the women.

'Babu! Here.'

'Is it over?'

'Yes, soon now. Where is—'

Then a man's slow, resounding cry, the Shahada, and a woman's sob broke out into a long long wail. Kulsum.

The hair at the back of my neck stood on end. A shiver ran down my spine. We stared at each other with wide-open eyes, our hands hanging in front of us at our crotches, our legs stretched out on the bed, and, simultaneously, we too began to wail loudly and hoarsely.

After what had transpired between her and the Hassam Pirbhai females, Kulsum found herself in a hostile city without an ally. Two months later we had visitors. Two elderly-looking women came, hugged my mother, and the three of them sat down on a mat and cried in grief, as custom required. They were Kulsum's elder sisters Fatu and Daulat, and they had come to convince her that it was best for her to move to Dar es Salaam, where most of her family now lived.

Six months after my father Juma died we took the train to Mombasa, stayed with Kulsum's cousin Zainab, and then sailed on the SS *Kampala* to Dar.

9 | *Dar es Salaam*

There lived in this town, then called Mzizima, at the place where Sea View now enters like an eagle's beak into the side of the Indian Ocean, a rich Indian merchant called Majigo, whose son Badula was caught in the act with Mwatatu the daughter of Kitembe, an elder of the town. The girl's brother Mwanashehe, who surprised the young lovers, was a big dumé of a man, who took Badula and twisted his neck like it was a chicken's. When Majigo the Indian discovered his son's murder, he went to Said bin Abdalla, another elder of the town and a good friend of Sultan Majid of Zanzibar. 'Mwanashehe bin Kitembe has strangled my son,' he complained. 'Why did you do this?' asked Said bin Abdalla of the son of Kitembe. To which proud Mwanashehe, without looking up, replied: 'I know nothing of the crime.' Said bin Abdalla was angered. 'There is no law in this country,' he said. 'I shall go to Zanzibar and speak with the Sultan.'

When Said bin Abdalla reached the presence of Sultan Said Majid of Zanzibar, he was welcomed and duly fed. After dinner, as they sat relaxing over halvah and coffee, catching the sea breeze and watching the stars, Said bin Abdalla, as if beginning a riddle, said, 'There is a beautiful country, but it has no law.'

The Sultan remained silent, immersed in thought. A minute,

two minutes, passed. Then he sighed, and shifted his weight. 'Which country?' he asked.

'It is called Mzizima.'

'Who lives there?'

'The Shomvi live there and they pay tribute to the Pazi.'

'Who lives there?' asked Said Majid again.

'Kitembe and his family. Gungulungwa and Tambaza. Shomvilali. Palalugwe, Zalala and Abdullah Usisana. These are the chief men of Mzizima.'

'I will come and see this country,' said Said Majid.

When the Sultan in his sailing ship reached Mzizima, he anchored outside the channel and sent a letter to the elders of Mzizima. 'Sultan Said Majid of Zanzibar is here and wishes to see you and all your male relations.'

The elders of Mzizima, Kitembe and Tambaza and others complied, and when they were assembled before the Sultan, Said Majid spoke to them. 'I have called you all here because I wish to settle in your land.' The elders of Mzizima were all not of one mind on hearing this, and they began arguing, so the Sultan told them to go home and think about it, but to return together when they brought the answer. The next day they gave their answer. 'Come in peace and live with us.' Said Majid returned to Zanzibar and came back with Arab soldiers, a carpenter and many other retainers. This time he sailed right into the harbour. He stayed several months and he brought many gifts. And he built houses of stone. His people cultivated the soil. And like the illustrious Caliph Haroun al Rashid, who took Baghdad by peace, Said Majid, who took Mzizima by peace, also called it Dar es Salaam, the haven of peace.

Thus is the origin of the name Dar es Salaam, as told by one Edward bin Hadith, tailor and fundi in Kichwele.

Mzizima, Prosperous Town. There was talk, much later, of

changing the name back to Mzizima. There is not much difference in the two names, really: Prosperous Town or Haven of Peace – dreams, both of them, dreams and hopes.

There was still hope when we disembarked from the SS *Kampala*, and were rowed ashore to Dar es Salaam harbour with our trunks rattling with memories...

A hope that was stalwartly being defended in a letter by a local pawnbroker to the *Tanganyika Herald*. Tanganyika will become like America one day, and Dar es Salaam will be its New York! This was in reply to a quip by an American visitor, that the town was half the size of a New York cemetery and twice as dead. 'Perhaps our Yankee visitor,' wrote our enraged citizen A.A. Raghavji, also known as Nuru Poni to the locals, 'has not ventured too far from Sea View, where he has presumably put up with European friends, and mistaken the cemeteries and crematorium in that area for the town itself. Let him walk the streets of Kariakoo (if that is not too much for his dainty constitution) and he will see life. Let him knock on our doors, and we will show him life!' The letter then entered into a discussion of the meaning of the word *life*, which digression the esteemed editor wisely suppressed.

That year, double-decker buses had been introduced in the streets and, in some areas, were running into electric wires not strung high enough. And there were those who objected that the passengers in the upper deck could see over the stockades into the compounds of their huts. Eti, if a woman is bathing... a woman out of buibui... a girl in her period... the anxiety of the invasion of privacy. Nuru Poni was right, as he was right about many things. Perhaps the American should have taken a ride in a double-decker bus.

There were three dreams in this town that aspired to Baghdad once and New York afterwards. The European dream stayed near the seashore. Everything beyond Ingles Street up to the ocean in the north and east was Uzunguni, 'where the

Europeans live'. Whitewashed, tree-lined, breezy: dreamlike. Huddled behind the Europeans, crowded, came the Indian quarter, with its dukas of groceries, produce and cloth: gutters overflowing and smelling at street corners, rotten potatoes and onions smelling outside the produce shops, open garbage smelling in the alleys. Then came a breathing space from the European and Asian... the Mnazi Moja ground, uninhabited, uncultivated, a sandy desert: beyond this, in the interior, was Kariakoo, formerly home of the German Carrier Corps, the beginning of the African quarter. Only a few streets ventured, from the Indian quarter, into the African quarter, but once inside, got lost in the maze of criss-crossing, unpaved streets lined with African huts.

One of the streets that actually braved into Kariakoo was Kichwele, carried by the poorer Indian dukas, themselves of mud and wattle, a respectable distance up to Msimbazi Street, along which they turned right, with a little loop around the market, then past it and back almost up to No Man's Land again. A long entrepreneurial, exploratory and tentative U-turn into the interior, barely thicker than a line.

My grandmother Hirbai's shop was one half of a dwelling on busy Msimbazi Street, rented from A.A. Sagaf the Arab butcher. The other half was occupied by my uncle Hassan and his family.

The thousand faces of Kariakoo... From the quiet and cool, shady and dark inside of the shop you could see them through the rectangular doorframe as on a wide, silent cinema screen: vendors, hawkers, peddlers, askaris, thieves, beggars and other more ordinary pedestrians making their way in the dust and the blinding glare and the heat, in kanzus, msuris, cutoffs, shorts, khaki or white uniforms, khangas, frocks, buibuis, frock-pachedis... African, Asian, Arab; Hindu, Khoja,

Memon, Shamsi; Masai, Makonde, Swahili... men and women of different shades and hues and beliefs. The image of quiet, leafy suburbia impressed on the mind, of Nairobi's Desai Road, cracked in the heat of Dar into a myriad refracting fragments, each a world unto its own. One of which was grotesque and mysterious, always threatening, that never failed to leave a chill in your heart every time you encountered it... Of Abdalla the beggar, a mere torso of a man, a foot-and-a-half high, a baby's body with an adult moustachioed face always looking up, making conversation that sounded serious and earnest but never seemed to make sense to anybody... of Bibi Fatuma, thin and old and so weak it took her ages to go from shop to shop, tottering into sight leaning on a staff taller than herself and with much difficulty coming to a trembling halt and putting out a hand: expecting not a penny or two like any other beggar but a ten-cent copper, and she would throw back at you anything smaller you offered and totter away... of the beggar, perfectly healthy if you did not count his head, a full two-and-a-half times any normal head and hopelessly lopsided, who would take his penny and walk away with a sinister grin...

The shop was cleaner than the two rooms behind it, or the courtyard; the floor was spotless and swept from time to time, everything was neatly folded and in place or displayed on a rack or a board. Khangas of the most recent fashions, judging by the print and the proverb on it, hung folded lengthwise from beams suspended parallel to the ceiling. Then would follow a row of kikoi hanging likewise, and lastly the lowly loincloth, the msuri with assorted checks. There was always the smell of new cloth in the air. Whenever Grandmother or the servant Hamisi flapped open a piece of folded khanga or some other cloth, with a brisk phat! a faint powder would fly in the air, which I eagerly sniffed. I would watch the mamas in buibuis step in from the street, in twos and threes, and wait hesitantly at the threshold, when Grandmother would call out, 'Karibu!

Welcome, Mama, welcome! Come in, Shoga!' And the mamas would all say, 'Thank you, starehe, don't trouble yourself, Bi Mkubwa.' And they would come in and proceed to examine the khangas, or buibuis, or kaniki. Grandmother would then hobble up and down, concerned not to let the customers slip away, ordering Hamisi, bargaining the prices to the narrowest possible profit margin.

Nguvumali was in town and every day people flocked in their thousands – clerks, messengers, thieves, policemen and the occasional shopkeeper – to see him and be cured and bring back charms. There was one khanga, much in demand, that punned: 'Nguvumali husema akili ndiyo mali,' Your mind truly is the important thing, or: Use your heads. But all turned a deaf ear to this proselytiser for reason against magic, wearing the khanga only to laugh at its killjoy message.

Shoplifters were called 420, or char so wis. Once, when Grandmother was not looking and Hamisi was away, one 420 stretched out a long stick and picked up a child's dress hanging at the door frame. My uncle Rehman was about and seeing the theft, shouted at the thief and called out to my other uncle: 'Come on, Hassan! Let's show him!' The two uncles ran out of the shop and soon the 420 was on the ground, and a fight ensued in the dust, Grandmother frantically trying to get the bystanders to stop it. But a large crowd had gathered, people happily calling out to each other to watch the two Indians struggling against the African. When, finally, they separated, the thief disappeared into the crowd and my sore uncles limped in, Rehman clutching in his hand the battered dress, crumpled and dusty, the hanger broken. That night they both received intensive massages and went to bed early.

The nights were warm. Dim lights inside the house threw long shadows against the walls, leaving parts of it in permanent darkness. Outside was a thick darkness, a black, menacing universe, with faces occasionally illuminated by moving kerosene lamps, and eerie, momentary shadows, gigantic, cast by passing cars against building walls: a darkness that rang with shouts and cackles and squeals of laughter. A little after sunset a drum would start rolling at the nearby Pombe Shop and the sounds of singing would add to the other sounds of the night. We would sit in the shop with two or three panels removed from the door to let in the night air; the adults would talk in low murmurs, while we children watched the teeming darkness outside and waited for what it would next summon at our doorstep.

There was Timbi Ayah the fat mama, Boy Manda Kodi the notorious loafer, Tembo Mbili Potea the mad Goan, Chapati Banyani the mad African. This latter would stand outside and sing:

Chapati Banyani, nani kula?
Shamsi, Shinashiri, Khoja, nai?
Akili potea kama ngombeeee!
Who eats the chapatis of the Banyanis?
Shamsis, Ithnashris, Khojas, no?
They lose their senses like cows!

He would peep inside at the cowering kids all huddled together, making wildly suggestive eyes, before stepping back into the darkness, into which his cackle then lost itself.

This was Dar es Salaam, frightening until you knew it, mysterious until you grew with it.

Before Kulsum's reminiscences, before Edward bin Hadith, before Ji Bai... there was my cousin Shamim. Small, dark, grubby Shamim, who was two years older than I, who seemed to be everywhere and knew everything. She was the daughter of Bahdur Uncle, Kulsum's younger brother, who was away in the interior trying his luck at business.

At the back of the shop was the large room where the majority of the family slept. From it, one door led to a small annexe where my grandmother slept, and another door led into the courtyard, which was a patch of beaten earth with odd bits of litter lying about. There was a large lorry tyre on which Shamim and I would sit for long, engrossing minutes deep in conversation. Shamim was my guide to the world of the Kariakoo shop, my protector and informant.

There were two darknesses that terrified me in Kariakoo: the darkness that lurked outside, that could stretch out its fingers and take you away, and the darkness that was hidden away inside, in the outhouse at the back, the hell that awaited you if you made a false move.

There were in the courtyard, besides the lorry tyre, a drum half-covered with a piece of wood and pieces of plank to step over wet patches where the sewage had leaked out and the rainwater not dried; on one side was an open shed that was the kitchen, and to the other was a crude structure of brick and cement with a raised metal roof that was the lavatory. This was the other darkness, and it reeked. The floor was of smooth cement but wet near the pit, which the light from the crack in the door barely illuminated. Everything surrounding the pit was in darkness, except near the raised roof, where basking in the sunshine large lizards lurked, ready to pounce on unfortunate victims. The roof creaked and banged violently sometimes and when it rained water fell on the occupant. The pit loomed large and menacing; large flies buzzed at its mouth and down below you could just see the shit stewing in its juices and the myriads of maggots crawling about on its surface. This was hell. This was where bad boys were thrown away, this was where unwanted babies landed. This *is* hell. How can there be a worse fate? What fires not more welcome than this acrid pit? I think of all the unwanted kids eating shit in a postnatal abortion. Even if there were suspicions, who would be willing to dig in the muck... They did that of course, one day, and the police later dragged out an African woman screaming her innocence, 'She fell in, she fell in, I tell you,' and the old shehes with their tasbihs rolling in their hands, throwing curses at her and expostulating to Allah, 'He only is the Giver, He only takes away...'

Shamim would take me there, waiting outside, holding the door half open, talking to me, periodically asking, 'Are you ready? You are taking awfully long today... is your stomach clean? We must talk to ma about that...' (Ma, the dispenser of purges every Sunday, holding you down on her lap, thumb and forefinger locking your nostrils, pouring homemade purgatives that themselves reeked, down your paralysed open mouth, leaving a residue that you washed down with a shudder: all ailments she could trace to an unclean gut.)

There are some instances we care not to remember, not to think about, and when they swim up to the surface we pretend that that's all there is, the vague shape... We dare not recall further, pull them up beyond the surface... except when we sit like this with our bag of wares and dig up the depths... In other words, Shehru the Kariakoo hag that dispenses memories with much more flourish and style than Hirbai dispensed purges, has no bourgeois qualms about the quality of her contents; all the hesitation is mine.

Sometimes in the morning, brushing our teeth on the stone step that led to the lavatory, Shamim and I would go in together, and Shamim at the door and myself near the pit, pass water. Once she produced a matchstick. 'Take,' she said. 'Now give me the burn.' The burn was more of a threat than a reality. It was what happened to little boys and girls in certain circumstances. A private punishment for a private crime. 'Where?' I asked eagerly. 'Here,' Shamim explained, taking my hand, 'where we pee from.' At this point Rehman Uncle walked in. 'Why, what are you doing in there together?' he asked, genuinely surprised. 'Ur-ur-ur...' he pressed his nostrils at us. We came out and he went in, confused. Uncle Rehman was quite a simpleton.

Timbi Ayah was the evil woman of Pombe Shop. At night as the drums of the shop started beating we would huddle together in Grandmother's home, in the big room behind the store, mentally tracking her, telling ourselves where the mad woman would be at that moment. 'She is outside Aunt Fatu's shop, now she is banging on Ali Rajan's door... she is chasing Chapati Banyani... Boy Manda has come out...' Timbi Ayah took away bad children. And what did she do with the children she took away? She made them work, Shamim said. They would feed the chickens, milk the cows, plough the field, sweep the yard, wash clothes and dishes... And when food was scarce, when she had eaten her chickens and the cow and the vegetables, she ate the children. Did no-one escape her then? No-one – except those who knew her name.

Timbi Ayah had a secret name. Listen. Once on a fine, sunny day a brother and sister were stolen away from their homes by big, fat Timbi Ayah. Their names were Janet and John. Every day Janet slaved away for Timbi and her little brother helped her. Timbi Ayah returned from the Pombe Shop every night and demanded food, which Janet brought for her. If she did not like the food or if she was very drunk, she beat them. Every night in secret, when Timbi was asleep and snoring, the brother and sister cried and prayed. One day when Janet was milking the cow and weeping with sorrow, the cow looked at her pitifully and said,

'Listen. You can escape from the Fat Evil One if you can find out her real name.'

'How can I find out her real name?' asked Janet.

'Ask the cat,' said the cow, 'she stays inside with the Fat Evil One at night. Perhaps the Fat Evil One has told her.'

So Janet went to look for the cat, whom she found near the tree, sunning himself, and asked him.

'Ask the dog,' said the cat, stretching himself. 'She talks to the dog. Me, she tells nothing.'

The dog was chasing crows. 'Ask the hyena,' he said, 'the hyena travels at night and he is wily. He hears things.'

So Janet waited the next night at a pile of bones she had collected, and when the hyena came by, she said, 'I know, I have not been considerate of you, Mr Hyena, and not kept bones for you, but if you do me this favour I will always remember you with the choicest food.'

'What is it you want, little girl?' asked the hyena.

'Tell me Timbi Ayah's name.'

'I know many names, little girl, but that one I don't know. Ask the owl. During his flights he must have heard it somewhere.'

But the owl only shook his head. 'Ask the rabbit,' he said, 'he is resourceful.'

But the rabbit, who is the cleverest of all creatures, cleverer even than the hyena or the lion, only scratched an ear. 'No, little girl, that one is a hard one.'

Finally, Janet gave up, and was very sad. There is no hope, she thought. We will have to wait until Timbi Ayah is dead. As she went to feed the chickens, she saw the cock, standing proud and handsome behind a fence, his feathers red and white and black and brown, all puffed up, his golden crown rising high, and he eyed the girl sternly.

'Why are you sad, little girl?' he asked.

'I would like to know the name of Timbi Ayah,' said Janet, 'no one knows.'

'Have you asked me?' asked the cock.

'Can you tell me, please?' The cock stretched himself further and he looked right and left. 'Who is the most beautiful of the animals?' asked the cock.

'You,' replied Janet.

'And who is the wisest?'

'You,' said Janet, 'please tell me, Bwanajogoo…'

'Hear this,' said the jogoo. And he puffed himself still more and he raised his proud head even higher, and he cried out: 'SHOKO-LOKO-BANGOSHAAAAAY!'

'So you shouldn't be afraid of her,' said Shamim, 'now that you know her name.'

My mother had four brothers. The oldest, Kassam, was upcountry, and so was Bahdur, Shamim's father. Hassan Uncle lived next door to Grandmother and Rehman Uncle, who was the youngest, lived with her. My grandfather Mitha Kanji had died some five years earlier.

Hassan Uncle and Zera Auntie, his wife, lived under the same roof on the other side of a corrugated iron partition. They had five children. Inside the shop there was a small, square hole in the partition, through which gifts sometimes fell to us, Kulsum's and Bahdur's dispossessed children. Zera Auntie was a compulsive giver. Were it not for Zera Mami, Hassan Uncle's brothers and sisters – all at the receiving end of the charity – all averred that their brother would have been a wealthy man. She would hover near the hole, in the evenings when the shops were closed and Hassan Uncle was inside, and as soon as she spotted one of us, she'd yell out, 'Hey, you! Come here, come here!' And we would go, hesitantly, expecting a chore but hoping for more, and lo! a half-shilling would be pressed in the hand, or a toy. They sold toys as well as clothes, and their children had plenty of both. Their son Mehboob was about the same age as Begum. He had a film projector, which he used to show films to the neighbouring children for ten cents, which his sister Parviz collected at the door. Once Sona and I, aware that a show was soon to start, went to their home and as we entered were accosted by his doorkeeper. 'The ticket is twenty cents for two,' she said. 'My mummy said I can go and watch,' I began. 'My mummy said—' she started in imitation, twisting her mouth and shaking her head.

'You!' came a shout from inside. It was Mehboob. Several of Zera Auntie's children had developed her habit of saying things twice in succession. 'Let them in, let them in, I say!' he commanded from behind the projector. 'They're poor, they're poor, don't you know their father is dead?'

Inside, a bunch of wide-eyed children sat cross-legged on the floor in expectation as Mehboob fiddled around with the projector. A white bedsheet hung from a wall in front of them. Finally, when everything was ready, the first clip was shakily reeled onto the screen. Charlie Chaplin in Kariakoo. The Chaleh. We were never quite sure if it was the quality of Mehboob's equipment that made Chaleh move in his peculiar way, but we all laughed, watching him fall all over the place, our heads moving side-to-side keeping time with him.

In the evenings Kulsum would put me and Sona to bed. We slept on the floor, eight or nine of us in parallel like tinned fish, in the room behind the store. I came first, on the side closest to the common wall, then Sona and then Kulsum. The two of us were put to bed early while the elder kids and other commoner kids, as Kulsum would have it, played hide and seek in the backyard, amidst the sounds of thumping feet and calls of 'Thapo!'

It was dark and gloomy on the side where I slept, cobwebby and dusty. There was a huge wooden closet on one side, always open and dark, and a pile of our baggage with clothes strewn on it close by. There was no ceiling in the room, just wooden cross-beams from which hung a single lantern.

'Why are we poor, Mummy?' I said. When she didn't reply, I started my well-rehearsed tantrum, which had never yet failed to get me what I wanted, and which usually created a minor turmoil in our bereaved family. 'I want Daddy!' I bawled.

Kulsum began to look a little helpless. And then I saw an ominous sign, a future portent: her lips pressed, the fingers on one hand come together, the hand stiff. 'Haram Zadah! You ill-begotten one, why do you make me cry, and him cry, and…'

A small incident, this. Perhaps. The smack across the cheek was well deserved or wasn't… what does it matter? But it marked the new Kulsum – the Kulsum of the pressed lips, the efficient business-minded Kulsum bringing up between five and eight children, the single mother of modern parlance. Daddy was relegated to the past, a memory, happy, something to look back to, to return to, while the more immediate problems of the world received attention from day to day. Sure, she despaired sometimes and remembered him and cried on the more happy occasions because he wasn't there to share them. And when Sona or I slept close to her and were locked in the tight embrace of her fleshy white arms hearing sweet nothings from her… who is to say she was not missing him then? But as the days wore on she toughened, became less sentimental – the flesh sagged, the bones thickened, the lips thinned, the lines on the face set permanently, the hair greyed – until she turned into the hardened, marmalade-guzzling old woman she is today.

A small incident, perhaps. A child crying for his father and the mother spanking him for disturbing the peace… and the dead, for the dead don't rest easy with children bawling for them.

Mchikichi Street was not far, a few shops from Grandmother's you turned right to Tandamti and came to the market and turned left. There in the mattress shop she was waiting, Ji Bai… resolutely… perhaps seeing my tantrum in her mind's eye, the witch, imposing her will upon me like a magnet, guiding me to that union with the past, while comforting me: 'Later, later…'

Now the dead speak, from the depths of the gunny sack, Shehrbanoo speaks.

I remember a beautiful Japanese fan. The vanes were threaded with a white silk ribbon and were themselves of imitation ivory, an intricate pattern cut three-fourths of the way up formed an arc of frieze when you opened them. At the closed end they were also threaded with silk, and there was a bob of silk thread there.

This fan was a gift from Jenny Auntie, and it fell into the way of darkness…

Rehman was my educated uncle. He had reached the Junior Cambridge level, although he failed the examination, like most boys who sat for it, and worked as a book-keeper downtown. He was engaged to Jenny Auntie. She was fair and pretty with short boycut hair, bright and chirpy, in smart clothes and high-heeled shoes. She lived downtown and was a typist. Everybody agreed that Rehman was lucky to get her. And everybody wondered exactly how she would fit in to the Kariakoo household. But she loved me, intensely and exclusively, for no other child in the house received the barest attention from her, even when they were thrown at her feet. Every time Rehman Uncle brought her home, I would run up to her sweet perfumed embrace, sit on her lap, stand pressed to her knees and receive gifts of sweets and boxes of chocolates.

One Sunday afternoon they took me to the seashore with them. We took the bus from Msimbazi, which dropped us outside the cathedral, and then we walked along the front lined with trees and filled with crowds of people. Vendors on foot hissed by with their peanuts and popcorns, others clinked coffee cups, still others sat in rows along the sidewalks calling out their wares – fleshy, yellow mangoes cut up enticingly and sprinkled liberally with red chilli powder, khungus and guavas and thope-thopes and oranges and jackfruits whose wild odours shouted promises of tastes out of this world... We walked past the cathedral, saw the famous Lutheran church, and the high court. There were ships anchored in the harbour, the tugboat racing gracefully but purposefully on the blue water, ngalawas bobbing up and down or pulled on shore, fishermen mending nets, yachts sailing out from the yacht club, the ferry inching its way to the opposite shore. This was Dar es Salaam on Sunday: hundreds of Indian families on foot, men leading the way, women bringing up the rear; men playing whist on sidewalks; boys and girls making houses and waterways in the sand; men in suits and women in white walking to church.

When we returned it was dark, the bus dropped us a little way before the Pombe Shop, and Jenny Auntie's reassuring forefinger pulled me along at a brisk pace on the side of the road as I strained my eyes to avoid pedestrians and potholes. We were late, and I could sense the urgency in her step and was almost running. There was the sound of drums, and a stench of brewing liquor, of woodsmoke, and roasting maize, meat and cassava. From time to time my eyes would fasten on the half-wall of the Pombe Shop from which the stench steamed out thickly and the drum-sound called. We reached the break in the wall, which was the entrance. Smoke filled the air inside, yellow flames rose up at the back, licking the sides of huge cauldrons, large shadows danced and people shouted.

At the entrance I saw her.

I knew her name but couldn't make myself say it. She was fat and immense, moving up and down to the rhythm of the drums, her huge belly jiggling against the khanga, her arms raised sideways, their flesh rippling with pleasure, her eyes gleaming. She jiggled forward and then backward, but all the time she kept approaching. My uncle and aunt had stopped, and stood there as if mesmerised by those drunken eyes approaching, and even when I cried and pulled at Jenny Auntie's finger, she did not move. And then Timbi Ayah was upon me, pulling me by my other hand, so that I was between her and my aunt in a tug of war which the black woman won as Jenny Auntie's tight grip slipped, and I was dragged screaming into the warm brewing darkness with its fires and dancing drunken people, its squeals and laughter...

I learnt that a man brought me out of that inferno.

Jenny Auntie was a witch. She tried to take poor, simple Rehman Uncle away from his mother. But Rehman was a good son and he was strong. So Jenny Auntie in revenge tried to take me away and give me to Timbi Ayah. But I knew Timbi Ayah's name even if I could not say it aloud. Perhaps that had saved me. Shamim and I on the lorry tyre debated over this long afterwards. And we took the beautiful fan and dropped it into the other blackness where maggots crawled in pungent juices of human excreta.

That Sunday evening, as we walked up and down the seashore several times, Jenny Auntie had given Rehman Uncle an ultimatum: either after marriage they lived in a separate flat, downtown, alone, or the engagement would be off.

I didn't see Jenny Auntie for a long time. Perhaps they kept me hidden from her, Kulsum and the rest. I never saw her, until I forgot what she looked like – except that she was slim and fair and pretty.

Breakfast was a prolonged, indefinite affair in that house. Early in the morning someone – my grandmother or my young aunt Zarina – set up the table. By the time the children had been dragged out of bed there was already a small circle of adults chatting and drinking tea around it. The shop was open, manned by Grandmother and the servant. At this time spirits were high and everybody talked loudly and called out. The dining area was the veranda, which opened into the backyard and was almost filled by the long, dark brown table and the chairs and bench. Two to three sufuriyas of tea were cooked on the coal stove, which was brought right into the yard so an eye could be kept on it. We breakfasted on loaves of soft, steaming white bread, washed down noisily with sweet, thick tea from porcelain mugs. Sometimes we had sweets bought from the African girls who vended them in the street outside, and occasionally my Aunt Zera would make a philanthropic swoop on our breakfast table, bringing jelebis and ladoos in oily brown paper bags. It was breakfast time also beyond the corrugated-iron wall that separated our yard from the African houses behind. Woodsmoke rose from that area and also the sound of African women and children. Grandmother knew them and sometimes ordered the maandazi from them. We breakfasted till way into mid-morning. The adults were up one by one within a few minutes of each other, starting to clean and sweep the rooms and dressing up, beginning their daily chores, and the children lingered on, clambering up the table, spilling tea and food on the floor. Flies droned with pleasure there, indulged by the sun, which lit the veranda in the early morning then would rise up and bring cool shade. We left this happy place only when the table was wiped clean, and my sister and cousins came armed with brooms and wet rags. The solid wooden table always carried with it the smell of breakfast, the stickiness of sweet and strong tea and evaporated milk from Holland.

It was from my cousin Shamim that I learnt we were finally to leave that house. She who told me about Red Riding Hood and Cinderella and Hansel and Gretel, and Timbi Ayah's real name, who would take me aside by the hand and say, 'Sit,' and sit down with me on the veranda step or the large tyre in the backyard, who when I got restless and began to stand up would keep my hand pressed down and raising a forefinger begin, 'Listen. Once upon a time,' in English and then mixed with Cutchi and Swahili tell me a story, said: 'Listen. Your family is moving to a new house.'

'Is it in Nairobi?' I asked.

'No. In Dar es Salaam.'

'Whereabouts, then?'

'Somewhere. In a new building. With a terrace. On the second floor.'

'Are you coming with us? I want you to come with us.'

'Then you must tell your mother.'

10 | *Habib Mansion*

Kulsum standing outside her shop every morning, eyes half closed over the tasbih, briskly threading her hands, whispering the sacred formula for good luck before she opens the first of several padlocks on the door, as the servant and the tailors wait nearby.

The beginning, the traditional beginning, *Kulsum's* beginning: always with the Bismillah, the Name, or the nad-e-Ali for more dire straits… for it is related that in the Battle of Khyber when the Prophet, on the verge of defeat and in despair, uttered this prayer, Imam Ali the Favourite appeared on his horse Dul Dul with his mighty three-edged sword Zulfikar, and he came and supported the bridge with his bare hands for the army of the righteous to cross over to victory.

So much on the strength of a prayer, a name.

Habib Mansion, into which we moved, was on the corner of Kichwele and Viongozi Streets, two blocks away from the no-man's land of the Mnazi Moja grounds. It was the newest two-storey concrete building on the Kariakoo side of Kichwele, having taken the place of the mud and limestone and corrugated-iron shop-house. A yellow corner building with a roof terrace, a symbol of patient acquisition of wealth, of squeezing a stone dry, as Hassan Uncle would later say. With Habib Mansion the development of the Kichwele/Viongozi intersection became complete: there were on the remaining three corners, Salama Building, and Anand Bhavan, and Mzee Pipa's Amin Mansion.

Kulsum had paid handsome goodwill money for the choice location, the corner store open on the two fronts to the two streets and a display window, a showcase, between them. Every store had a name, painted by Khaki (modest) or Rex (expensive) or an anonymous African (cheap) painter. Begum and the others were all for the name The Curiosity Shop, culled from some school book, but the voice of my uncle Hassan, Kulsum's adviser then and later on all matters relating to business, intervened impatiently. Hassan Uncle's long face became longer when it expressed contempt. The mouth stayed open, having said what he wanted to say, his eyes widened and his body arched backwards as if that was the only way he could get a proper perspective of your silliness.

'What curios? Where are the curios, eh? Choose something people can see. Okay, Bai, tell me. What will you sell?'

Kulsum had in mind the stores of Nairobi's Indian Bazaar, to which even the European ladies from the Highlands dropped in, where you could satisfy the most exacting requirements, from a needle with the tiniest eye to the freshest shipment of chiffon and nylon and georgette from England. 'Fancy goods, brother,' she said, 'I want to sell fancy goods.'

The signmaker was asked to paint over Curiosity, and The Fancy Shop it became, and Hassan Uncle rode away on his bicycle satisfied at his achievement.

Every family has a nickname, usually describing some member of the family, so you are so-and-so's brother or of the so-and-so family. But there are no strict rules about nicknames. You could get one for the oddest of reasons: for your looks, for what you said once, for what someone spoke about you, for your occupation: or for no apparent reason at all. A public blunder is sufficient to brand you for life and perhaps for the next generation too. When you move into a neighbourhood, you wish in your heart of hearts, above anything else save for good business in your shop, for a *nice* nickname.

Parmar Tailoring Mart was next door to the Fancy Shop. Parmar was simply Parmar; no nickname: a stranger, however familiar his face, who cycled in every morning from the Hindu village in Kisutu, where he probably already had a nickname. Next to him was Roshan Mattress, named after her shop and her body.

Of fat women, the expert lady-watchers of Kichwele and Viongozi all concurred there are those that are ugly-fat and those that are beautiful-fat. Roshan Mattress was of the latter sort. Plump really, rosy and fair, soft but not sagging flesh in all the right places, beautiful in the classical sense though obese (what a term!) in the modern, Westernised sense. When she flaunted those haunches, swinging her hips on her way to throw a taunt or two at Mzee Pipa, the more lewd bystanders would pick their crotches in muted satisfaction – for this was all they would get, the real thing was reserved for a certain police inspector, Kumar, no person to mess around with.

Mzee Pipa, Old Barrel, was the oldest resident on the corner. In Anand Bhavan was short, fiery Nuru Poni the pawnbroker who also wrote letters to the Editor; his store was next to Moonlight Restaurant, which belonged to an Arab. Salama Building boasted Daya's wife, the rumour-monger, and the Mawanis, whose son Snivelling Alnasir was my classmate.

Thus was constituted, in the main, the corner of Kichwele and Viongozi, also called the Pipa Corner after its most illustrious resident. You could miss knowing where Viongozi was, because all streets that took off from Kichwele looked alike, the downtown visitors insisted, but everyone knew the corner with its small 'keep left' where Mzee Pipa kept shop.

Mzee Pipa, Nurmohamed Pipa, would descend the stairs every morning to his shop, fat and weak-legged, leaning on the shoulder of a servant, wheezing and coughing all the while, suffering from some interminable disease which might just as well have been the condition he lived in. His was also a corner store and our entrances on Viongozi faced each other. All day long he would sit in a white singlet and a worn-out loincloth, perched on a car-seat atop a wooden crate, so that surrounded by all his wares, he looked on the two streets. Crates heaped with grain and spices formed an uneven chequerboard facing Kichwele on one side; a wood-topped counter with a fly-specked glass front, containing old yellowing items, closed off most of the other side, leaving a small passageway behind him. Tufts of grey hair jutted out from under his soft, fat arms. His uncovered chest was a jungle of grey hair, his layered chin had a white stubble, his white head was cropped close. He looked sweaty and dirty, a part of his shop; it seemed you could rub layers and layers of turmeric or coriander, or whatever else he sold, off his skin, he breathed in and breathed out nothing but musty air with the odour of grain and spice, gunny and cockroach egg. Inside, the store was dark and cool. A large and dirty green tarpaulin sheet hung from an awning on the Viongozi side. Behind him were stacks of old newspapers – *News of the World*, the *Illustrated London News*, the *Observer* – for sale by the pound to neighbouring stores. Behind the papers were gunny sacks filled with grain, and behind these, in the storeroom, was complete darkness, where no light, natural or electric, ever reached, where only the servant ventured. There were cupboards on the walls that had not been opened for years. On the door of one of them was a faded sign showing two pictures side by side: one, a man at his desk, holding his head in despair, his safe open and spilling over with useless scraps of paper and rats running amok among them, with the caption: 'I sold on credit'; the other, a smug gentleman counting money in a neat office: 'I sold for cash'. Both English gentlemen looked upon scruffy Mzee on his car-seat, selling for cash, not giving anything away. Scrooge in Kariakoo. His hands would be in continuous motion. He would put a handful of spice or gum on a piece of square paper, then fold it rapidly, twice, to make a cone, then a third time, and finally tuck the remaining edge in and throw the finished packet into a basket. It would fetch ten cents from some African woman out to buy the day's groceries. Ten cents collected in a rusty metal tray with a handle, and deposited into the wooden cashbox that stood under his eyes next to his stomach in front of him on a table. Drop by drop, they said, you can fill an ocean. With clink after patient clink of ten-cent coppers in the cashbox he had acquired his wealth, brick by brick Amin Mansion had gone up over the mud and lime dwelling on Kichwele and Viongozi, named after Amin the son who came after a curse of seven daughters patiently suffered through, all now married.

Oh yes. Our nickname. Pipa Corner was kind to us, we were new and had committed no great folly yet. We were all named after Begum, whom we ourselves sometimes called King George's daughter. They called Begum 'Nairobi'; and sometimes, for her imperious ways, 'Victoria'. In Kichwele they denoted more or less the same thing. Of course, any name can be used with a contemptuous twist. Instead of saying, She is like Victoria (a queen), they could (and did) say, She *thinks* she is Rani Victoria. Hunh.

There was a feud on in Pipa Corner, between Pipa's wife and Roshan Mattress, a quiet heat that remained of an old quarrel, which from time to time rekindled.

In the days before Habib Mansion and Amin Mansion and the other brick buildings went up on the Corner, Nurmohamed Pipa and Roshan's father had lived across from each other in their shop-houses. Roshan Mattress and Roshan Pipa, the eldest of the seven daughters, were bosom friends, what are called jedels, both fair and with ample bouncy bodies, both high spirited and friendly with all neighbours. They would do their lessons together and walk side by side and sometimes even hand in hand to school. The kind of friendship girls vow to keep for their lifetimes, husband or no husband. Then came a man. Nurdin Samji was fair and handsome, from a respectable downtown family, educated, and worked in a European firm. Sometimes in the late afternoons, when business in the shops was in the doldrums, he would come to Kariakoo collecting for the family firm. One day the word was abroad that the affluent Samjis of downtown had their eyes open for a prospective daughter-in-law. Which of the two Roshans would they pick? One afternoon two Samji matrons descended on Kichwele and Viongozi as it lay drenched in sunlight, barely awake. As soon as they had stepped out of the car and were sighted surveying the territory, a servant was dispatched from the mattress shop and duly brought the two ladies back with him. This was all observed from the produce shop, which was in confusion. By the time the Samji ladies emerged, a deal had been struck, and Roshan Pipa had lost. Even before the two Samji women had left the neighbourhood, the first quarrel had begun.

Now Roshan Mattress lived in Downtown and was dropped by car at her shop every morning by her husband. And Roshan Pipa, in a somewhat hasty face-saving move, had been married into a family whose fortunes were taking one tumble after another. Mrs Pipa had an endless supply of the choicest invective against her daughter's former best friend. The sight of Roshan Mattress burned up her insides. 'Eh, Haram Zadi, you bastard-bitch!' 'She's not satisfied with stealing one woman's man. She has the whole town going through her lap!'

Roshan Mattress had retaliated twice against the Pipas. One of the men Pipa's wife was alluding to was Virendra

Kumar, inspector in the CID. One afternoon at two, just after Mzee Pipa returned from lunch and nap, Inspector Kumar arrived with two askaris to search the place for stolen goods. The neighbourhood gossip went that just at that time Mzee Pipa had in his keep a stolen necklace. It was not only from patient acquisition of coppers that Amin Mansion had gone up. Well, Inspector Kumar wanted to search the dark storeroom behind Pipa's shop, and coughing, spluttering, wheezing Pipa obliged the inspector by sending the servant with the police and giving them a small wick lamp to light their way. The search was fruitless, of course. And they said that the necklace was hidden in the very lamp that the suave Punjabi officer took with him into the rat-infested interior. Mzee Pipa did not give something for nothing. The second time, Inspector Kumar was tipped off about some forged currency. Mzee Pipa had on him one such note when the police car parked outside. As the inspector ducked his balding head under the awning, the Queen's fair head was negotiating the throaty passage into Mzee Pipa's ample abdomen. Soon after the two fruitless swoops upon Pipa Store, handsome Inspector Kumar turned his efforts to something more fruitful: Roshan Mattress.

Our welcome into Habib Mansion. A lorry has brought our Nairobi furniture from the customs warehouse. Loud, impatient, sweating men are negotiating the bunk beds and the dining table inch by inch up the stairs, others down below are heaving the display counters into the shop. Elsewhere locks are being installed, a heavy dresser with thief-proof compartments awaits attention, a carpenter oblivious to the din around him patiently takes measurements for a sofa, trunks of clothes and kitchenware are carried inside the flat. And a harried Kulsum, having screamed herself hoarse, finally orders Mehroon to take Sona and me out of her hair, so the three of us go upstairs to the roof terrace. First we run around the pentagon area several times to get a feel for its dimensions, to imagine the numberless games that could be played here. Then we look over the walls at terraces of other two-storey buildings, we catch a glimpse of Hassam Punja's tallest building in town. Then we raise ourselves hesitantly over the wall and look down at Dar es Salaam; at the traffic below, the criss-crossing unpaved streets and squat African dwellings that make up most of Kariakoo up to Msimbazi, the long Kichwele Street running all the way from the Railway Station near the harbour to Illala beyond Msimbazi. Finally, using dressmaker's chalk, hesitantly – because it's a new building – we make hopscotch squares on the floor and prepare to play. We are still in sandals, in clean clothes, and Mehroon has a ribbon in her hair. All proper.

Thump-thump-thump, in comes a terrible threesome, all barefoot, the eldest a heavy-set girl in a rather short dress, with scraggly hair, thick lips and large mouth from which come hoarse nonsensical syllables the likes of which we have never heard, trailed by a boy and girl closer to my age and also making strange sounds with their mouths. We stand still in terror, while they thump along from wall to wall, as we ourselves had finished doing, before finally coming to a halt before us, the eldest with her arms akimbo. All the while hoarse syllables of meaningless sound falling topsy-turvy from their throats. But the message is clear: this is their territory. By rights we believe it is ours, since it is directly on our ceiling; they are standing on top of our flat. This day we let ourselves be bullied by this mute trio, we walk down the stairs frightened out of our wits; but we will claim it, this terrace, we pay rent, they don't.

This was our first sight of our neighbours the Bubus, the mutes, who lived below us in Habib Mansion. They were a family of five orphans, three of whom could not speak but let out loud horrifying howls when they quarrelled. In their saner moments they used gestures and made soft sounds that were almost a pleasure to hear. Then you could almost make out the words they struggled to dislodge so painfully from their mouths. To call them everyone simply hooted: 'Hoo!' and they responded. The eldest of the five was a girl, normal, and all neighbourhood complaints were directed to her. Then came fierce Varaa, who had terrorised us on the terrace. Her real name was Gulshan, but Varaa was her warcry, she was the loudest of the lot. She howled in sorrow and in anger, she could bring the whole building down with her cry, Varaa, Varaa, Varaa. Then came Ahmed, also normal, but a bully, two years older than I.

To go down to the shop from our flat we had to pass their floor, and when a fight was in progress we trod it with special care, even gingerly. There would be howls and screams, objects smashing, bodies falling. It would not have taken much provocation, it seemed, for the whole lot of them to stop fighting among themselves and fall on you like a pack of wild monkeys.

How memory makes monkeys out of our enemies… We thought of them only as howls of madness, of a family gone collectively berserk, but now I think of the sorrow, the frustration. Eh, Shehru – what, no better memories? Not a word of kindness or understanding? Only the bitterness, Ahmed sitting at the bottom of the staircase, legs stretched out, daring you to step over, the howls under the dark staircase, the ambushes on the stairs at night… and Kulsum would complain to their grandfather the landlord, to the numerous uncles and aunts. Periodically, the grandfather came to mete out punishment. He was a small, thin man in a crumpled white suit and a black fez. He brought with him a stick which he held firmly and with obvious purpose. When the doors closed behind him the howls became ferocious, interspersed with the old man's imprecations. It seemed then that the rest of Kichwele and Viongozi held their breath, throwing glances towards the bedlam, as if to say, What now?

No, the reconciliation came later, a truce really, and it had to be paid for, in cash.

My cousin Shamim, after a few months with Fatu Auntie who would scrub her body with Vim to make her whiter, came to stay with us. There were then six of us, with Kulsum, in the two rooms. There was Begum, of course. Then Mehroon and Yasmin who were my Aunt Gula's; and finally Shamim, Sona and I. Mehroon was now ours; but Yasmin by a family decision belonged to Bahdur Uncle, Shamim's father who was seeking a fortune in the interior.

In the sitting room, which was brightened with tube lights, was Kulsum's big double bed on which she would sit in the evenings cutting patterns from bolts of cloth for the next day's sewing. The radio would be on, turned low, and homeworks done in various corners. Sona and I would be sent to bed, and when the rest of the family turned in, the one of us whose turn it was would be taken to Kulsum's bed to sleep with her. The other would sleep with one of the older girls.

We fought, Sona and I, we fought, and cheated, and cried, to share our mother's bed, to feel her tight smothering embrace as she murmured endearments at us...

In the afternoon, after school, the girls helped in the store, while Sona and I were put to bed and locked in, upstairs. When we awoke after the nap, it would already be getting dark, most of the day was over, and in a panic we would rush to the window and cry for our release. Downstairs there would be more of us than customers, fighting over snacks of roasted cassava and corn and the occasional bottle of Coke, as the three tailors came in before closing time bringing their day's work, which would be tallied and noted down against their names in a big ledger and their thumb-prints or signatures taken against the entries. Hassan Uncle had advised Kulsum to take a signature for everything.

At the month's end, or in the days preceding the Eid, the store stayed open late and everyone was downstairs at once; all were needed, to show customers, to wrap, give change, or simply to watch out for the 420s. Kulsum always sat at the head of the store, behind the big centre display counter watching over the cashbox, on a high stool… and when business was slack she would be looking out, straight ahead, brooding, picking her chin…

The Fancy Shop never made much money, but from the beginning it stood apart from the other shops of the Corner. For one thing there was the number of children you would find helping to run it. Then there was the display window, large and prominent between the two doorways – you could not miss it from the street. Here Begum arranged her creations – inspired by Nairobi of course – of matching children's wear suspended over toyland still-life. Street scenes, drawing-room scenes, cottonwoolly, sequinned Christmases, at which African boys and girls would come and gaze for long mouth-watering minutes. The other stores started copying, their windows hitherto dark and boarded up were now lit, as Begum proudly noted. They could not keep up with her, and they did not like her, this arrogant Victoria of ours, but they couldn't help admiring her.

What shall we do with the drunken sailor?
What shall we do with the drunken sailor?
What shall we do with the drunken sailor earleye in the morning?

Miss Penny, not yet Mrs Gaunt, walks primly in front of us in high heels and dress suit. In a line of twos holding hands our class crawls forward, a brown-and-black millipede in khaki and white. She stops, turns, waits and inspects as the line moves past her, getting tighter as the stragglers catch on, picking up voice. Then she thrusts forward, tall and straight, slim and shapely, striding easily on her high heels as if she were floating, clean and sweatless. You could sing in front of Mrs Perera or Mrs Nanji until you got hoarse or they pleaded for you to stop, but how difficult, positively awkward, it was to sing before Miss Penny! Her voice was sharp and precisely defined, her syllables clipped, beside which our shapeless self-conscious phonemes proceeded higgledy-piggledy, running into each other in a mumble.

(There speaks a true colonial, the voice of a conquered one, says the gunny voice from the corner in its most radical tone.

Shush, Shehrbanoo. Wasn't I conquered, didn't she vanquish me? Tell me.)

'Miss—' A boy gets up from his place and gives her a yellow rose in full bloom, not overly ripe.

'Why, thank you!' says an appreciative Miss Penny with a smile just so and not overdone. She sniffs at it and puts it into her buttonhole. 'What's your name?'

'Alnasir, Miss.' Cheeky Bottoms to the boys. His accent is the closest to hers and he is of course a teacher's pet. He has an elder sister who coaches him in these tricks. They have to be done just right. Watch.

'Miss.' A shy voice, barely audible, which has to be repeated to be heard. A second rose is proffered, this one hardly in bloom yet, still half-covered by the green and brown calyx, and this one by the other Alnasir, the crier.

'Thank you. And what's your name?'

'Alnasir.'

'A second one! All right – now you, Alnasir, begin the song "Alouette".'

The obsequies over, Cheeky Bottoms starts the song and a hesitant chorus accompanies him. The snivelling Alnasir takes his seat on the ground with the rest, and the second rose stays in the hand. Miss Penny sits on a chair, legs crossed, the class in front of her, under a mango tree in the grove behind the school. It is the outing period.

Soon a boy comes running out of the back gate, starts walking and stops a few feet away from the class as at an imaginary door.

'Please-may-I-come-in?' he calls out in urgency, raising a hand and bending a little at the waist as if he's asking to go to the lavatory.

Miss Penny doesn't hear him. She is looking the other way, through the shady grove past the scrub and to the road beyond.

'Please-may-I-come-in?'

She turns to look. 'That's not a door, silly! Why are you late? Did you report to Mrs Schwering?'

'Yes, miss.'

'All right. Sit down.'

Permission granted, Hassam sits down.

He is the future teen idol: Elvis and Beatle, then Iblis. Small boys will want to emulate him, girls will flock to him, but there is no trace on him of that future renown and manner. There are in this class now, singing a song of sixpence, their potentials also hidden: a future motel-chain owner in California, a few smugglers, a thief, two pharmacists, two accountants, a nervous scientist, and a Lisbon bar owner... There is Shivji Shame who will never get past Standard IV, big, bluff, who always gets told off but never knows why. As Miss Penny looks left and right, reflecting, book in hand, and Cheeky Bottoms leads the song, others at the back play with toy cars in the sand, and some are already portioning out the mangoes in the tree.

I was admitted to school on my first day by Mr Menezes, a Goan neighbour whom Sona and I called Uncle Goa. His wife was a teacher in the Girls' School and we called her Madam. Uncle Goa worked at the East African Customs and Harbours, and every morning drove to work in his dirty green Morris, in civil servant's spotless white shirt, shorts and stockings and black, polished shoes. On this occasion he took me to school, before going on to work, and enrolled me.

'Grandfather's name first,' said the application form, and Uncle Goa asked me.

'Huseni,' I said, naming my renegade half-caste ancestor, and became Huseni Salim Juma for ever after.

The rest of my family ignored the whole question and became Dhanji, even the more classy Dhanjee, a name invoking wealth and respect, while I, under the auspices of Uncle Goa and Mrs Schwering's glaring eye, became: anybody. No trace of tribe, caste, colour, even continent of origin. How much in a name? Salim Juma, the name chose me, and it chose my future and this basement in which I hide myself with my gunny, where the clip-clop sounds of feet outside remind me of Miss Penny and the Boys' Primary School.

I joined school when there was a virtual reign of terror under Mrs Schwering. Every day after the morning prayers had been shouted out to God ('Give health, happiness and peace to our worthy teachers, parents and all our brethren, amen! Give us the divine guidance to make us worthy students of this school, amen!...'), Mrs Schwering, before dismissing the assembly, would swoop down on a class for a spot check: fierce Mrs Schwering with blond curls and loose, haltered dresses revealing a fiery red chest, with hands on her hips inspecting two lines of nervous students standing to attention conscious of every hidden blemish in their attire. And out, frayed collars, unironed clothes, dirty shoes: out, dirty fingernails, uncombed hair, dusty knees: and out, every time she inspected our class, big Shivji Shame with stained shorts, no underwear – looking unsymmetrical in front and pathetically threatening – and wearing brown, dusty Jumbo rubber shoes minus socks. Whining, oversized Shivji Shame who could not answer a proper word in English would be brought out in front of the assembly and a crowd of happy cheering boys would howl 'Shame,

shame, Shivji, shame!' After which he would be sent home; but he never went home, he would wait outside and come out to play during recess or when school was over.

Every day after school, I waited by the back gate near the outing area for my sister and cousins. School for the first two classes ended half an hour earlier. Cars, some with chauffeurs and others with fathers, waited in the shade of the trees. Vendors of mangoes, guavas, coconuts and potatoes with chutney sat in a row and called out. Some of my more seasoned classmates already started trudging home, others sat in cars, still others rode on servants' shoulders or waited as I did, drinking warm water from the tap which protruded from under the hedge. Then the bell would clang, a noise would erupt and the older children flowed out from all directions. There would be running and thumping, banging of doors and shouting. Scores mounted up during the morning were settled now and a circle of boys would form, cheering around two figures grappling in the dirt. Soon a father would emerge from a car, or a chauffeur or a teacher, and break up the fight.

Sometimes, just before the bell, the Coca Cola seller, a burly Indian, would arrive with some orderlies; as soon as they saw him the hawkers would gather up their money and run. This was the fujo. The boys would shout 'Fujo!' and scramble for the food. Sometimes even when the Coca Cola seller had not arrived, the bigger boys raised a false alarm. Everyone loved a good fujo, you got free khungus and potatoes and guavas, thope-thopes, kitales, mangoes... except that... you remembered for a long time the frightened face of the vendor who ran as if for his very life, particularly the new one, the youngest...

And throughout the arduous walk back home, avoiding potholes on Msimbazi Street, looking away from the glaring sun as from suspicious-looking characters, my fibre schoolbag with its slate and two broken halves of pen in my hand, there would be Begum's constant chatter, her running commentary on the day's events in her class. Begum our leader, the strict disciplinarian, mother's lieutenant at home: tall and thin, walking confidently on, ignoring catcalls, talking, talking and you dared not interrupt her. Her classroom leapt to life on the dusty road, a mirage in a hot desert. Zarina Alibhai, Farida Damji, Parviz Meghji… and others, I watched them grow up in these mirages and other images evoked for us by Begum; I know things about them they've long forgotten or care not to remember.

Behind the school was a large, overgrown, sunken piece of land which filled knee-high with water when the rains were severe. The girls stayed home on such days, unless they found a ride that would take them to and from the front gate of their school. I and other smaller boys would then go in a large pack headed by some bigger boys, and we would cross the lake, removing our shoes and socks and wading through the field, sometimes pushing paper boats or coconut branches in the water. The following day we would watch in dread for signs of jigger on our soles.

Once when the water subsided, an Indian woman's body was dragged out… rotting flesh, fragments of a sari, unclaimed, not missed… Suicide, they said, or murder; what matter? Perhaps she could not bear a child. Perhaps she did not bring a good enough dowry. Why this fragment, Shehru, this frayed remnant of a memory? A tribute, she says, to an unknown woman, a woman with her own memories and her own world.

One day during the outing period while Miss Penny looks in the distance, boys bring out toy cars and motorcycles and start playing in the sand, constructing roads and tunnels… and way at the back, against the tree trunk curly-headed Salim Juma shows something in the class reader to a group of friends, who look at one another and giggle, and look at Miss Penny and giggle.

'What are you playing with?'

The boys look up at Miss Penny now standing over them with her book and ruler.

'What was it, boy?'

The question is directed at the sniveller, Alnasir. Miss Penny bends over him and orders him to stand up, ruler raised threateningly.

'Salim, Miss—' A finger is pointed, the circle of boys loosens and I stand alone with my accuser and my judge.

'Yes, what did he do?'

'Like this, Miss.' Alnasir raises the book to his face and kisses the drawing of Roda captioned 'Roda goes to school.' Roda has a satchel in her hand, and Roda too is curly-headed.

'He kissed little Roda, did he now?'

'And he said, and he said—' Breathless, helpless, vulnerable Alnasir.

'And what did he say?'

'"Look, I kiss Miss Penny, I kiss Miss Penny!"'

'Stand up straight, boy!' This one to me, and as I stretch my legs, phat-phat-phat-phat-phat-phat, six of the best from Miss Penny's ruler on the calves. 'Where do you *come* from, you naughty boy?' And an order to stand in front of the class all day, every day, for the rest of the week, no recess.

On the third day, after recess which I did not get, in desperation: 'Miss... Miss... Please may I go to the lavatory?'

'Keep still!'

I keep still. I look at my feet, and then I look up shyly, at the grinning faces of my classmates. Handwriting period, the monitor hands out Marion Richardson texts, the boys bring out double-lined books.

'Miss. Please.'

This time, a terrifying look, and I freeze. Until a warm trickle goes down my leg and a boy raises the alarm: 'Miss!'

'Quick, boy, run!' she says, but what's the use, doesn't she know there's no stopping midway?

Africans had a ceremony for the little boy who wet himself. Older boys would carry him around the streets announcing the deed in a chant: 'Dumbe dumbe daria, he has wet himself!' And so it was with me for several days on the way home, the humiliating chant, until I stopped school for a few days.

I returned to school with a rose for Miss Penny, which Begum allowed me to take, just once, from her rose bush on our roof terrace. And so we reached a truce, Miss Penny and I. She learnt my name and wore a rose that I stole subsequently from Begum's plant. And she would choose me to read in class or during outing: 'Read,' she would exhort, 'read from the beginning, don't feel shy,' she would say, like the angel Jibrail commanding tongue-tied Muhammad in the cave, and I would read, until my humiliation was forgotten.

'She is my favourite teacher,' I would say. Not Mrs Lila or Mrs Velji, who favoured the rich kids, but Miss Penny who favoured me. One day she disappeared for a few weeks and returned Mrs Gaunt, and I watched from a distance with heavy heart as the man drove her in and stopped outside the main door, and the boys gathered around the car to watch him kiss her. 'But I kissed her first,' I would say to console myself.

11 | *God, Two Queens and the Famous Five*

Wisps of memory. Cotton balls gliding from the gunny sack, each a window to a world… Asynchronous images projected on multiple cinema screens… Time here is not the continuous coordinate of Mr Kabir (who knew all the theorems by heart and could tell you the page numbers in the maths book on which you could find them) but a collection of blots like Uncle Jim drew in the *Sunday Herald* for the children, except that Uncle Jim numbered the blots for you so you traced the picture of a dog or a horse when you followed them with a pencil… here you number your own blots and there is no end to them, and each lies in wait for you like a black hole from which you could never return—

The mosque was among the maze of streets in the heart of the old Indian quarter downtown. Twenty years old, and it looked ancient and imposing: grey stone, clock tower, iron gates, the gallery of rogues always sitting outside. Every evening at six you would see men and women traipsing by respectably, servants hurrying with a newspaper-covered plate of food on their last chore of the day, boys loafing, all along Kichwele Street towards the distant tower, where ten or twenty simultaneous marble games were winding up in the compound, marbles being stuffed into dirty pockets by dirty hands, food offerings being collected, and preparations made for the first prayer at quarter to seven. Mnazi Moja was a Central Park: you would cross it alone at night only at your own peril. We had hidden thief-proof pockets sewn into our shorts, but often it was just easier to part with the five-cent or ten-cent copper, hand it over to the shadowy African mugger who was no bigger than us.

The rogues' gallery, later called the Dirty Dozen, was an assortment of scruffy characters who all lived on the community's charity and hung about the mosque. General Juma in military uniform, who would do a solo march-past when mosque broke up, going left-right left-right up and down the compound until he spied Hassam Punja getting into his Mercedes, at which point he would do an 'Attention!' salute smartly and put out his beggar's hand. Squat, lame Bahdur, who moved like lightning up and down stairs, chasing after boys when the mosque was emptying. Hussein Chai always asking for tea money, accusing passersby of stealing his shoes, who would scrape a large blob of throaty phlegm from his tongue and hurl it at an offender. Fat Gulu who, grieving a lost love, at the stroke of midnight, at the end of festivities, would go up to the band and lead the cheer in its name, 'Hip-hip! Hurray! Hip-hip! Hurray!'

There was a Mshiri who had a cigarette store on Kichwele Street... a thin Arab in loin cloth and T-shirt, chappals flapping behind him as he took his long, ambling steps, rising and falling on his toes, body dipping with every step, long arms swinging, grinning sideways, looking for boys to show kindnesses to as one big hand brushed against their little bottoms.

* * *

The lids which covered like iron doors the manholes in the streets spoke of exotic places. One said 'Cape Town'. Did Cape Town then lie beyond that door, underneath? Check the world map, yes, Cape Town was directly under us. But no, said Shamim the wise, the world is round, haven't you heard of Columbus, yes, Christopher Columbus? *Australia* was under our feet, no matter what was written on the iron lid. Then, if you opened it, this lid sealed so securely, would you fall feet-first or head-first into Australia? Well, perhaps you did go through Cape Town…

The Famous Five of Kichwele and Viongozi: Shamim, Kala, Sona, Shiraz and Salma. The latter two, Shamim's brother and sister, new arrivals sent to Dar for schooling by my nimble-footed Bahdur Uncle, who moved from Kilosa to Shinyanga in search of better business. Shinyanga is close to the diamond mines, said Bahdur Uncle to Kulsum, only a few more years and I'll take them off your hands. My star is rising, over these diamond mines.

What do the Famous Five do? They make bandas on the terrace with planks of wood, sit under its shade and hatch plots involving gypsies and smugglers and desperately wish for moors and rolling plains for their imaginary caravans and to hike through. They study the Cub handbooks and know the components of the Union Jack off-pat. When the mood strikes them they help our grandmother cross the road, they never keep the money they pick up on the road, and they use a variant of the Cub promise. I-promise-to-do-my-best-to-do-my-duty-to-God-and-the-Queen: to-help-other-people-at-all-times… and to obey the Famous Five law! Dib dib dib. Dob dob dob.

PO Box 15037, Dar es Salaam, Tanganyika Territory (TT), British Empire. So Begum filled in the sender's address on the envelopes carrying letters to her pen-friend in Sarawak or to relatives in Kenya, KC, C for colony, before licking the stamp on which the Tanganyika giraffe faced the Queen. She stares out of other currency notes now, an older, grimmer version of the graceful young woman on horseback riding in some plush green English grounds, stopping and descending at a gate and turning to smile and wave briefly at her subjects standing to attention at a cinema house as the national anthem drew to a close.

'Where is the English woman?': Tarzan, pulling a respectable native hair lock. Steve Reeves as Hercules bringing the pillars of Greece (and the house) down in the noon-hour one-shilling-all-round show at the Azania (where the projector was so low you could raise your slipper and see its ugly image on the screen): every building in Dar had a Steve Reeves, we had Ahmed. And every building in the wake of Greek or Italian heroes who followed Hercules also had a Maciste – who was usually the same boy who was Steve Reeves. There were also many Zimbos in Kariakoo. Zimbo was the Indian Tarzan, Lila was his Jane, and Dada his monkey. The noon-hour show was packed with the fans of these heroes. There would be roars of delight and sighs of anticipation or disappointment. Audience participation at the Azania. Sona exhorting his heroes: 'Watch him! Aré baba, look behind you! Yes! Yes! Give him one! Give him two!' and in a frenzy: 'Pillau! Eat Pillau!'

Early in the morning on the day of the Queen's birthday the Famous Five set off to witness the march past at Government House… first to the Askari monument, the furthest reach of the Indian section, then further still through the tree-lined street past the old white-washed houses in which the Europeans lived, dogs barked, haughty servants and quiet ayahs looked on, as we scampered along beside the museum outside which stood two old cannons that had seen service in the First World War. The King's African Rifles would be at ease standing in array, waiting for the Governor. Then the waiting crowd would stir, before settling down to watch intently, as with a yelling and a screaming the red-faced European sergeant-major would give the order to attention and go pounding to the Governor, and the guard of honour would begin. The portly Sir Edward Twining, out of his usual baggy suit, looked formidable now in full regalia.

Sir Edward Twining, Sir Alan Lennox Boyd, Sir Evelyn Baring, Sir Patrick Renison… the list goes on. You will forget the faces and the contexts but you'll carry the jingle of those names to your grave… what's in a name, you ask… the sounds of power and authority, the awe and the glory. They will stir inside you, these sounds, when a small part of you in your heart of hearts holds back, holds back when they condemn her, when you should condemn her, a colonial power over Rhodesia… And when you scan the headlines for the fate of her warships… when she is no longer powerful and glorious but cynical… always, that small, that tiny part of you rooting for her, why deny it… you were vanquished, as you said…

Is it right, Shiraz who had come from Kilosa would ask, to press down a ten-cent copper into the ground and rub the crown into the dirt with your foot so as to brighten it… or to put the silver fifty-cent coin on a railway line to flatten it and let the Central Railway run its iron wheels over the Queen?

At home Begum was queen. Tall and thin, pony tail tight over her head: imperious as Victoria, fierce as Boadicea, wielding the cobweb broom like a sceptre. On Sundays she cleaned the house, had the floors scrubbed, the mattresses turned over or taken out to be sunned, laid traps for mice, went after cockroaches with the kitchen broom, sprinkled DDT in the cupboards. She was the talk of the neighbourhood, this girl who worked so hard and even went down on her knees. Every Sunday, inspection of the troops: drawers, for orderliness, nails and knees for grime, shoes to be polished in readiness for Monday, socks all paired off into fist-sized balls. Then we could go out. We were grouped into seniors and juniors, Blue House and Red House. The Famous Five, of course, were the juniors. For a few months Begum drew up a chart on which were chalked up our scores with black and silver and gold stars. At the end of the month scores were counted and prizes of handkerchiefs, colour pencils and Baby pens handed out. But this method of incentives proved too expensive for Kulsum and the more traditional one of threats and punishments prevailed.

An imposing Philips radio stood on the toy cabinet between Kulsum's bed and the sofa. A powerful oracle: if anything worthwhile was in the air it would grab it, from Cape Town to London, America to Bombay. All Sunday morning as Begum went on her knees and ordered the servant and baked in the heat of the charcoal fire, the radio stayed on and the world poured in. In martial Urdu or sing-song Hindi or BBC English, Connie Francis or Lata Mangeshkar, the children's programme on TBC, the request programme on KBC, Akashwani on All India Radio... It was for the radio she stayed upstairs. At about noontime the sweet odours of ghee and cinnamon and coriander wafted out from the open door. We would walk in nervously, wash our hands and feet and sit on the sofa. Shortly after one o'clock the grave tones of the Hindustani Service of the KBC turned positively funereal, as the voice said, 'Elan.' Brows furrowed with concentration, Begum would carefully note the death announcements for a familiar name that she could drop at the table for Kulsum's benefit. A false move here, a laugh or a loud sneeze, a fit of the giggles, and after the elan her long, hard fingers would close on a culprit's ear, and turn and turn then release it, bringing a deep red, followed by the pain, ringing inside the skull, coming in waves of dizzying magnitudes. The store closed and Kulsum and her helpers would arrive. Nine of us would crowd round the table for lunch, the only meal we all had together. It was half day for the servant, who would leave after washing the pans and dishes, and Kulsum would take her only afternoon nap of the week, and Sona, Shiraz and I would go outside and out of her earshot for a spot of cautious cricket.

The hazards of playing cricket in Habib Mansion: you could play on the little balcony at the landing, outside our door, but in that case you could only use a golf ball bought from Mzee Pipa, and the off slips were at neighbour Sharrifs door, so after a few cracks at it out would shoot the sleepy and furious Sharrifs arm and give the batsman a cuff. You could try our terrace, among the flowers, which could bring fierce Boadicea racing up: or the other terrace, which could bring a Sharrif more furious than before.

I started going home from school with other boys. I went with Jogo, whose father went about limping in the streets at four in the morning calling people to prayer, and with Alu Poni the pawnbroker's son. Sometimes a rickety old red Dodge pickup with an open body gave free rides from school. It was called 'Chama Chetu (Our Party) Namba Three' and belonged to a genial failure called Fateh, who had slid down from business to business and now was at rock bottom, selling coal. On the back of the pickup was another sign, 'Your old friend, Fateh the coalseller', in Gujarati. Every day after school a lookout was kept for Chama Chetu, and when it was sighted, racing up to the gate in a cloud of dust and smoke, cries of welcome greeted it: 'D-S-K-9-9-9!' which was the number on its licence plate. Packed brimful with boys and a few brave girls who could risk a mirror placed on the floor, with a smirking, slimy Ahmed standing in front of it, Fateh's pickup raced home, throwing jeers at passersby and slower vehicles, making two stops, one at Msimbazi and the final one outside the owner's home not far from our corner.

Alu Poni lived on the ground floor of Anand Bhavan, behind the pawn shop. Outside the pawn shop there was always a jostling crowd, behind which could be heard the pawnbroker's shouts. Their home opened at the back into an enclosed yard, about thirty by ten feet. Drawn on the far side on one of the walls, the ubiquitous stumps, in charcoal.

A clean bowl, grazed bails, flying stumps: they all had counterparts in the world of charcoal-drawn stumps. A thick black stripe across the rubber ball, a smudge, a gap in one of the stumps. How's that? came the appeal, and you all went to examine the evidence. Leg breaks took off wildly from a crack, and the off break – oh, the off break: there was an upward slope on the off side so that the ball would seem simply to come to a stop in mid-air. Zero velocity. It would stop there tantalisingly suspended, telling you: 'Hit me! Go on, go on, hit me.' And you would swing, for a chhako, a six against the far wall – which is what it was waiting for, because then it would take a dip and land on the stumps.

But even here it was not entirely safe. The outside wall, on the offside, was about eight feet high, and a missed catch could easily go over the wall and land among the huts beyond. Then would begin the begging and pleading. The three Ponis were fluent in Swahili and could reply word for word. We would climb on top of stones and crates to look over the wall where there was a bare patch among the broken glass, and Firoz would begin:

'Excuse me, mama! Excuse me. Aisei! Hodi!'

'What now?' an irate mama would show a face.

'Mama, if you could throw the ball... please.'

'Aaaah! What do you think? You can throw the ball here any time... and suppose it hits one of the children—' Now the whole mama would be visible.

'Polé, mama. Sorry. Forgive us.'

'Didn't you say polé the last time? And now again... you think this skin is made of stone, it doesn't hurt—'

'The last time, mama. It will not happen again. Truly, mama. By God.'

'No.'

'I beg you, mama, God will reward you.' Giggles behind him. 'Aa-aa!' No.

Then would begin the bargaining. Ten cents. Forty cents. A deal at twenty-five and the ball came flying across the wall.

There were two ways around paying the ransom. One was to keep quiet and try to retrieve the ball by using coal tongs tied to a long broom. Or Alu or I was lowered behind the wall and then pulled up with the ball. On the other side of the wall was a hut, with a narrow space in between. On one occasion however a mama must have heard my shuffling against the baked mud, for while I was picking my way among the debris a bristly broom-head landed against my own head. With barely stifled cackles, my companions' heads withdrew behind the wall and I was left alone to face a glaring broom-wielding mama. I took two steps back, emerged into an open space, and started running, chased by the screaming mama. 'Catch the Indian, the bastard...' Another mama emerged, her hair wet. I cut across the compound towards the outer door, the two mamas in hot pursuit. But then the wet-haired one tripped on her khanga, and for a fleeting instant I looked behind to see a naked, black body glistening in its wetness, before I emerged into the safety of the street.

'You saw her naked, Kala? Tell me what you saw – did you see her black black fuzz, her arse—'

'I don't know...'

'Oh God, he saw and he didn't know what he saw – Oh God,' Firoz walked off, violently scratching his crotch, eyes fastened skyward in despair.

The next day the two brothers had a plan for me. With the promise of a chance to play in their fictitious MCC, the

Msimbazi Cricket Club, I went back to the huts with a proposal. There I met a third fat mama.

'I want to see the young mama—' I began.

'Halima!' She screamed. 'An Indian boy asks for you!'

Halima came out. 'What? Again? You boys have no shame?'

'Mama... my brother sent me... my friend's brother... Do you want one shilling? Do you have the time, mama?'

I was chased all the way to the Poni home by the furious woman, and the five of us hid in the bedroom. Two mamas talked first to Alu's mother and then Nuru Poni came to hear them. 'They have no respect! They have no manners!' fumed the mamas. And Nuru Poni pacified them in his best Swahili: 'You are their mother, mama. True, true. I will punish them. If you want, I will let you punish them. Alu, come. Here, mama – do with him what you will.' They left convinced that justice would be done.

Meanwhile, cricket stumps and bats had been sent into hiding in the neighbour's home. But Nuru Poni, anticipating the measure, bought a cheap broom, threw away the head and used the handle on the backs of my friends, while Sona and I went home with unrequited guilt on our heads.

Nuru Poni, the philosopher-pawnbroker, who was not averse to using his fists against ruffians who sometimes mixed in with the crowd outside his shop. His were the only Asian boys who learnt to read the Quran, in the original. An African shehe called twice a week, and for an hour each time, the three boys chanted after him from the Juzu. From Nuru Poni came such jewels of wisdom as the adage 'Done is done, it cannot be undone, even if you go to London', and more down to earth advice such as what to do when called by nature at an inopportune moment. In this case you loosened your belt and rubbed your belly right to left; or perhaps it was left to right. That was the problem with this remedy, an error could be disastrous if you were caught, say, in the middle of Mnazi Moja.

Nuru Poni's actual name was A.A. Raghavji. He came from Zanzibar and was an old acquaintance of Kulsum's family. He had been – although his interests had now shifted to civics and politics – a pious young man, a lover of God, like Mad Mitha my mother's father. When Mad Mitha announced his doomsday vision for the island, Nuru Poni had been one of the first to take a boat out. An African customer once asked him what he hoped to see in the mosque at four in the morning, which he never missed. 'Nuru,' he had replied without blinking an eyelid, meaning God's light, and the cynics of Kariakoo found him his name.

Every evening Kulsum sat on her big bed, feet up, scissors in hand, biting into it night after night, making callouses to last a lifetime: scissors in hand and measuring tape round her neck. Snip, tear... Bend, beend, hold. Snip-snip-snip-sniiiiiip, snippet. Cloth diminished, bolts from Osaka, which carried when new pictures of pretty Japanese ladies or Fujiyama, became thinner and the pile of cutting for the next day's sewing rose higher. It was family hour. On Mondays and Fridays the Philips oracle held attention, high on the glass case which enclosed the memorabilia from my father's days. It announced listeners' requests and throbbed young hearts with the sounds of Pat Boone, Elvis and Cliff. Bedsprings were not insured against the wilder improvisations of rock 'n' roll, when 'Jailhouse Rock' was played, until finally it seemed that the song was altogether banned from the programmes.

Sometimes the BBC told stories... which we rarely listened to, we had storytellers of our own...

Begum on prime time, standing next to the radio, better than the BBC...

Kulsum supplied us with our daily chapati, but Begum sold us our dreams. Her stories were for the benefit of all but directed at Kulsum. She sat like a goddess on her couch, Kulsum, a few feet away from anyone, surrounded by colourful cloth, measuring tape for garland – and scissors for weapon? She would listen quietly, and there would be something like a faint smile on her lips, except that we knew it was not a smile but a thought: what thought? what ghostly memory? On the second floor of Habib Mansion as the street below emptied of people and sound, and every building and every lighted flat in it belonged more and more to the surrounding night than to the society of each other, we took lesson and hope from the stories. Wellington and Nelson rode in triumph under our tube light, Portia leant against the toy cabinet in a lawyerly pose smirking at Shylock, and Captain Scott wrote down the words 'We must go on,' before going down in an Antarctic blizzard.

Kulsum would have something for our edification, a story from the mythology... How the five Pandava brothers, once having given their word to their mother to share everything, went on to share their wife. How Tara Rani would steal into the night to pray to her Lord against her husband's wishes, until one day he found her out and with sword in hand waited for her, only to see the evidence in her hand, the meat, turn into grapes and ladoos into oranges. 'Rani, show me this path,' he pleaded...

And sometimes, after much cajoling... loading her with a plate of pawpaw and a glass of hot milk... promises of pressing her aching feet and aching head... she would relent and part with a bit of her own past.

Shamim still plied me with fairytales, with Ali Baba and Aladdin... and when she played the Sphinx in a school production, on whom could she practise her lines but me...

And, at the bottom of the stairs, sat one Edward bin Hadith, fundi, tailor. An improbable name, a mixture of English and Arabic, 'Edward, son of Story', but he insisted on its correctness, and at the end of the month he would make an Arabic-looking scrawl in the long black ledger book and take whatever remained of his earnings. He came from a village near Mombasa and occasionally went home and sent letters there. He had been banished under the stairs by Kulsum because out in front he never ceased chatting (kuru-kuru-kuru-kuru, as she put it) and would not let the customers be heard; or, worse, he would involve them in long convoluted conversations, until, inevitably, they beat a retreat, seeking refuge in the street. In the alcove, the only catch in his wicked snare was I, whom she could spare.

Sometimes, even there, he would call out to a passing woman, 'Shoga, do you know the time?'

'As if I carry a watch. Are you a fool or what?'

And he would break into a joyful cackle, thumping on the wooden stand of the sewing machine, at having drawn notice.

'Salum, come here. Come here, come here,' he would wave me over as I came down the stairs.

'What? I want to go.'

'Come here, I tell you. What's your hurry?'

'So?'

'Listen carefully now at how Abunawas conned his neighbour into exchanging a small saucepan for a huge cauldron.'

'But you've told me that already!'

'Okay, then. Do you know why dogs sniff at people's arses?'

He would relate with gusto, waving his arms, thumping the machine, taking time to vent his cackle, and I stood spellbound, or simply detained forcefully by his hand on my arm. By the time he had finished and wiped tears from his eyes, a pack of African boys and girls would be gathered behind me outside the doorway.

* * *

Of the three tailors, Edward took away the least money at the end of the month. Beside him in the alcove sat the master fundi, Omari, who would laugh at Edward's jokes and chat with him, but never set aside his work. Kulsum gave him the hardest but the most lucrative assignments: men's shorts, school uniforms on contract, clothes for Sona and me.

Efficient Omari, dreaming Edward. Sometimes in the afternoon Idi, Mzee Pipa's chauffeur, would drop in for a chat, sitting at the bottom of the stairs, having brought boys from school – Pipa's own Amin, and others whose fathers could afford to pay. Idi and Omari went home together, smartly groomed, newspapers under their arms: two men of the world who knew what they wanted, leaving Edward to finish his work.

But every Friday Idi had an errand to run before he left. He drove to mosque with two plates of food; one, rich and fresh, for God, and the other, stale and hard, for Mzee Pipa's sister, a pauper who sat outside the mosque with a white enamel plate and a begging bowl. One Friday Idi had a joke at the expense of God and switched the two plates, as Mzee Pipa found out when he got the chit that Idi brought with him from the mosque while announcing that he had found a new job. It was with the new Labour Union on Viongozi Street a few blocks away.

If you wanted to point out the meanness of the Pipas, you would point a finger to the old man's sister, a pauper to whom her brother sent charity in the form of stale chappatis and a fifty-cent coin every Friday, the day when all the twisted-mouthed, the lame, the elephant-headed and -footed, the pock-faced, the noseless, the sightless and others paraded the streets with begging bowls and got theirs too. Yet Idi's act was considered generally not as charity towards the sister but as a crime against God. The only person who lauded his act was the Pipas' old enemy Roshan Mattress. But this woman was carrying on an affair in broad daylight with a Punjabi policeman, what could she have to say about good and evil?

What then, did Idi and Omari want? Idi and Omari belonged to the Party… whose office was on Viongozi next to the Labour Union's and was mysteriously lifeless except in the evenings… the Party which the coalseller celebrated on his rickety Dodge that brought us from school, we who could not afford Pipa's gleaming green Ford Taunus… the Party with which – as we later realised – Nuru Poni also sympathised. But then, under the two queens, it was only an irritation – it did not like you calling the servants 'boy', or 'golo' – not to be heard, anyway.

The window. It looked down on Kichwele and Viongozi and up at the stars. It had iron bars painted silver that felt cold when I pressed my temples against them. Half-curtains hung from a slack spring.

From this window you could look straight down into the first-floor flat once occupied by the Mawanis and now by a Goan family. As soon as they moved in, Mrs Daya announced there was something funny about them. They came with a secret to hide. There were five of them, the mother and father, and two girls and a boy. The eldest was Alzira, in her mid-twenties, and she soon won a place in our hearts and a reserved seat on the bench in our shop. Tall and gangly Alzira, with a large mouth and short, straight hair, her long, faded dress hanging loosely on her frame. She was a dressmaker. In the late afternoons she would walk in, with a piece of cloth and a threaded needle in her hands, a large grin on her face, and sit on the bench, chatting with Kulsum, exchanging banter and gossip with the girls when they were around.

But in her home it was all different. No laughter there. The father was a retired civil servant who emerged, it seemed, only to track down a newspaper or a bottle of beer. The mother appeared even less frequently. The brother and sister, Peter and Viviana, had a life outside Kichwele and Viongozi, in the world of the Goan Institute and parties and dances, and were rarely home. But Alzira... Alzira was ours. From my window I could see into all their three rooms, all facing Kichwele, all with large uncurtained windows, all enclosing an unbearable gloom. It was like watching a silent film, an adult film society movie without dialogue where the pain and hurt are screaming through the silence, scene after scene of meaningless, forced activity that I saw from my second-storey perch, temples pressed against the cool metal bars.

To this window I would be drawn at four in the morning, when the air felt cool and unspent and the street below was deadly still and the street lamps burned with a steady glow like breaths of life suspended in the darkness... the deadest time of night, when only the gods could be abroad, and those seeking the gods. A little before four, Jogo's father approached, limping on the street, calling on people to wake up and remember the Eternal, except that his voice grated so much and what it spoke was so ridiculous, it reminded you of anything but the Eternal. A little after four-thirty came a shuffling sound from a long way off on the street, accompanied by murmurs. This was the gang of Kulsa Thauki, all women, except for the watchman in a blanket leading the troop, that left somewhere from Msimbazi and marched in the middle of the street all the way to the mosque, picking up more of the faithful on the way. There was a time when Kulsum was hit with the meditation bug, then the troop would shuffle to a stop right below the window and Kulsa Thauki would yell, not too loudly, 'Kulsum Bai, are you coming?' If I was at the window, I would shout, 'Wait!' and if not, Kulsum would get out of bed shouting, 'Yes! Yes! Wait a little while!'

By the time the pack had left, something had been lost from the night's mystery...

* * *

The scissors. I see Mehroon chasing her sister Yasmin with the scissors, through the bedroom, the sitting room, the dining room, round and round through the three doors. There were times when all order broke down: tears, screams, warnings and threats. And Kulsum tearful —

Go on, Shehru. There's no holding back, now.

Kulsum would be in tears—

Shehru!

She too broke down… at the end of her tether, she would give a whimper… and then… one-two-three she would beat her white chest with her hands, she would beat it until it was a painful, smarting dull-red and say – 'I give you my life, I give you my life, I give you my life' – and weep uncontrollably.

Then the imprecations would begin, 'No, Mummy! Please, Auntie. We are sorry. Never again. No, Mummy!'

And peace would return.

Thank you, Shehru.

12 | *Forbidden Fruit*

Five years – half a lifetime – passed, gradually the memory of my father, Juma, was receding behind the overgrowth of fresh memories that were appearing with the density and vigour of a jungle. He became part of a glorious, idyllic past framed for us in his picture on the wall, stored for us in the locked glass cabinet that housed our former toys. Beside Kulsum's bed was another glass case, long and rectangular on a round table, in which stood a rust-red and black, two-feet-long model steamer given him by a shipping agent for some service. It looked so real, this SS *Nairobi* as we called it for want of a better name, its four-blade propeller and its rudder heading it straight towards the heart of Kariakoo – we would look at it admiringly, every time discovering something new and delightful about it: three lifeboats suspended on either side, decks protected by railings, the exquisite little cabin doors and ladders and cargo hatches that opened. No guest left without being suitably impressed. But no-one knew what ship it was, its *real* name. At the seashore our eyes became used to fruitless searches among the numerous cargo liners that hooted their way in and out of the harbour, jostled by one of the two tugboats. Only once, on my own, I thought I saw the real thing – rust and black, long with white cabins, three lifeboats on each side… it was so much like the model in our sitting room. I ran home in great excitement to report the discovery. There were many believers.

I was chided for not having thought to look for its name, and the next afternoon after school Mehroon and Yasmin and I were sent off to the seashore on a mission to confirm my find. It was as though we were in some sense going back to the past... or if not actually going back then touching it in some way. All the way to the shore Mehroon and Yasmin would talk of nothing but the old days in Desai Road, of which they of course remembered much.

But there was no ship of that description in the harbour... nothing rust and black... in fact nothing but a white passenger liner, like a plastic toy ship with holes punched at the windows. My ship had sailed away...

We should have known – we knew it – but what's wrong with hoping... in case Time makes a false move... it doesn't, of course. The past is just this much beyond reach, you can reconstruct it only through the paraphernalia it leaves behind in your gunny sack... and then who would deny that what you manufacture is only a model...

At first the SS *Nairobi* was kept locked in its case and treated with extreme care. It was the star show in our sitting room. Kulsum sometimes hid banknotes behind the ship. But then one day the key got lost, the hundred-shilling note behind the ship was urgently needed, and the lock had to be forced. After that, important pieces of paper like electric and water bills found shelter behind the ship, and then in front, and sometimes on the funnel. Some time later the glue inevitably came off a cowl and it toppled; then the cable supporting a lifeboat broke; a ladder slipped; the main antenna broke, a cargo boom became detached and hung from a mere pulley thread... until finally we had a capsized ship, a memory burdened by day-to-day worries like unpaid bills and unanswered letters...

Among the toys in the toy cabinet was a chubby, red plastic doll in a round frame on which it rolled with a tinkle. It was my baby-show prize. One December Begum brought it out, gave it a cotton-wool beard, put a red cap on it and put the finished Father Christmas in our shop window. It drew crowds of kids for two Decembers, before it too bit the dust, dented, punctured, fly-specked.

… The clutter of memory that eventually finds its way into a… gunny sack. She smiles, Shehrbanoo. And throws out three knives.

Oh yes, there were the three Kashmiri daggers, of course, whose blades were now rusted. No-one knew what to do with them, where to put them. And there was a sword with a red scabbard. My father Juma a closet pirate? And what about the six rugby balls? Juma, a fence? But, six *rugby* balls, for God's sake!

One day Kulsum had a dream. She saw Juma in his grey cashmere suit returning home from a night out. 'He walked in and then seemed to recede, approaching and receding, and I said, "Aré, listen, where have you been? The children have been crying for you, they want to go out for ice-cream at night and here in Kichwele there's no-one to take them, there's no-one to relieve me in the shop and sometimes when I want to go for pee or water I ask Parmar to wait there and I go up…" and he said, "Don't complain, Kulsum. I would so much like to eat an apple," and he sat down on the chair and I went to bring him an apple, but the next instant, when I had returned, there was no-one on the chair, it was empty. I woke up with my heart beating thur thur like a fan.' The solution was clear. Begum and Mehroon concurred: apples had to be sought.

You found apples mostly in story books, where they hung from trees in leafy orchards and sandy-haired boys in shorts and stockings and pretty girls in blue frocks climbed to retrieve them. The apple was the prince of fruits, second only perhaps to that fruit which Roman princesses with soft undulating bodies like Elizabeth Taylor's in soft silky gowns indulged in while lying lazily at a pool or on a raft: a bunch of grapes. It was difficult to find these fruits in Nairobi, how much more so in hot, humid, Dar! In Dar you could buy apples and grapes and chocolates at the Lushoto Garden Store downtown, frequented by the pretty and smart mothers of those sandy-haired children whom we saw on our way to Government House to celebrate the Queen's birthday.

Idd was approaching, it was Ramadhan. The best part of Ramadhan was that shops stayed open late and we could play on the sidewalks way after dusk. The best time to play hide-and-seek is after dark on the street when there are spots of light and many shadows to hide in. The nice thing about hide-and-seek is that boys and girls, old and young, can play. Inside the shops about this time stocks were running low and cashboxes feeling solid. My father up there had perhaps realised that it was the time of year when he could expect a treat from his loved ones on ground and had put in a request.

On the supposed last day of the fast, Begum and Mehroon went to Lushoto Garden Store to buy some apples. It was not as easy as they had thought. You have to *order* apples, they were scornfully told. How many do you want? Four, they said, not a little intimidated. Hunh. Not only did the Europeans have their orders; it turned out that my father was not the only one in the spiritual domain who loved apples. After much pleading and repetition of Kulsum's dream, it was decided to deprive some European children of their share. Begum and Mehroon returned with four large apples.

These four large apples, not quite as red as in story books, but with shades of green and orange and yellow and purple that gave them more character, more mystery, were placed on a plate on the dresser in our bedroom, beside the customary plate of sweet, fried vermicelli to be taken to mosque the following morning: only if the moon was sighted before then. But the moon was not sighted that night, Idd was delayed another day, the vermicelli was taken away and distributed for breakfast, and the four apples stood enigmatically on their plate, high up on the dresser, sending out a glorious aroma.

What must Eve have suffered as she watched the forbidden apples hanging temptingly in front of her... It is not simply the taste... it is also the mystery... the *knowledge*!

At ten that morning the coast was clear, Begum was in the kitchen, Mehroon in the store. Without a conscious thought in my head, like a hawk, I picked up an apple and raced out of the bedroom, through the dining room and up to Sharrif's roof where I ate it in breathless large bites, core and all. And when I'd eaten it I sat there, still breathing loud gulps of air, watching the charcoaled stumps on one of the walls. Tears of guilt fell down my cheeks.

Between four apples and three apples, there is a quantum of difference – that of a crime committed. Between three apples and two apples, the difference is not as great. Slowly I got up, dusted myself, and walked down to the flat. The coast was still clear, the crime undetected. I took the three remaining apples and this time walked to the roof and ate them all.

Inevitably, it was Begum who detected the crime, saw the empty plate, and gave a scream of rage. Immediately Ali was fetched, but the servant indignantly denied the crime and was believed. He did not even know what this new-fangled fruit was. That left four juniors, Shamim being presumed innocent, and Begum Sherlock got to work. It was right up her line.

The four of us were lined up in the bedroom, in front of the empty plate. All acknowledged the gravity of the crime, against God and the Dead, all denied having committed it. But she was nobody's fool. 'Confess now,' she said, 'and you'll be forgiven. At least you were honest.' Silence. 'This is your last chance, I am warning you. Then I'll show no mercy. Mummy will write a letter to your teacher. You'll be put to shame before the whole school!' Still, silence. 'All right, I'll show you who's clever!' She had already told us the story of the short straw, how the thief broke his in half for fear that it would grow. So what could she do now? Plenty. She illustrated with another story.

'One day a king wanted to test his three sons. He showed them an apple and told them, "This is a magic apple. Whoever eats it will succeed me to the throne and live for ever. But I don't want you to touch it until I tell you to." He left the apple on a table. In the morning it was missing. When the king asked the sons about it, they all denied eating it. So what do you think the king did? I'll tell you. He asked each one of them to drink a glass of *ve-ry* salty water. The water was so salty it made them vomit. And from the vomit he found out who was guilty.'

'Who?' asked Sona, a legitimate question, but he narrowly missed a slap for his impudence.

Salma was the prime suspect. Salma, who wet her bed sometimes and was the root cause of bedbugs in the home against which Begum valiantly and constantly battled. Bravely Salma went forward and downed a gulp of brine. Her stomach gave a violent spasm, 'Aargh,' even Begum looked a little startled, and the contents of her stomach came out in contraction after contraction of yellow, slimy liquid with floating debris of the day's ingestion, mainly peanuts and peas, but no apple as a stern Begum went to confirm. Salma stood there, her face a horrible grimace, a thin stream of sticky saliva joining her mouth to her fingers in front of her, and she gave a loud howl.

Begum's eyes fell on me next and there extracted the truth. 'It was I,' I sobbed in terror, 'I don't want to drink the—'

'So!' In one lightning move, first a backhand slap on the face then thumb and forefinger closed on an ear in a tight grip that only she could manage, twist, twist, twist, this way and that, and by my now red, swollen ear I was taken down one agonising flight of stairs then another and another to be presented to Kulsum. She said nothing. All afternoon I sat behind the glass counter, out of sight of customers, crying,

'I am sorry, Mummy, I'll never do it again.' Only Edward, who had seen me dragged down the stairs, would come periodically and ask her, 'What is the matter? What did he do? Surely, mama, it cannot be that bad if he is crying.'

That night her hand came down upon me again, as it had on that fateful day when I was instrumental in spilling the milk, and a rain of slippers fell on my buttocks, my thighs, my arms. 'You Shaytaan, you Daitya Kalinga, even in death, even in death,' she sobbed, 'you'll steal from him.'

Red chillies were stuffed into my mouth and I was locked in the terror of the dark bathroom, there to suffer with burning eyes and burning mouth, standing howling on its rough, wet and sticky floor, the laundry lying in a large heap in a corner, clothes hanging like ghosts behind the door and cockroaches running around with loud rustlings.

That night it was my turn to sleep with my mother. But in tears I fell asleep in that little hell, and was not claimed, and Sona took my place beside her.

A little before dawn, just after the old Jogo had passed by our building calling the faithful to prayer, I was woken up by Shamim. She released the bolt slowly, turned the light on, and shook me awake. Then she gave me a glass of milk, and without a word took me by the hand to sit at the windowsill where we waited in silence for Kulsa Thauki's gang to come shuffling by on their way to mosque.

When you steal from the dead, whose death you're partly responsible for (although not knowingly); when you've eaten the forbidden fruit, not one, which could be forgiven as childish temptation, but the whole lot, and you can only blame it on the devil; when the living don't understand, and God does not reply to your entreaties: you can talk directly to the dead.

There lived in Kariakoo a certain Zanzibari of evil reputation.

His name was Kassim Kuiji. It was said that Kassim Kuiji claimed to be a prophet. He had a coterie of followers, the chief among whom was my vociferous Aunt Fatu. For problems or wishes Kassim Kuiji gave you a prayer to recite. It was guaranteed to work, but there was a catch twenty-two. It had to be said the right way at the right time, and it had to be kept secret. Evil befell anyone who divulged his secret. Kassim Kurji in his red fez and white drill suit haunted him in various forms and drove him insane. They said that the great man muttered in his sleep and his bed shook from his power. To some he was the fallen angel Azazil. He controlled numerous djinns. He meditated for hours, sitting rigidly erect, without moving a muscle, without twitching an eyelid. Once Fatu Auntie had suggested that Kulsum visit Kassim Kuiji. No, said Kulsum firmly, I have my own tasbihs, thank you. But Shamim, who had stayed a few months with Fatu Auntie, knew more. Kassim Kurji could call back the dead.

Try telling that to your mother. The dead, she will say, go directly to God, unless they have done evil. In that case their souls flit about restlessly like mosquitoes, looking for mischief such as trying to communicate with the living. Did we think Daddy was a bad person? No. Then why should he be sent back? We would all meet him when we also went to God. Sona and I were given a prayer each to recite before going to bed. 'It will make him happy.'

We preferred Daddy a little evil so he could come back. On a Sunday morning the Famous Five at last found an adventure worthy of their name: Five Call on the Dead. We went trooping towards the Kariakoo post office, ostensibly to check the post. Upstairs we had not passed muster yet and Begum, listening to her favourite hits and chasing after cockroaches, had been given the slip. On the way we stopped at Uncle Hassan's New Medical Store, where he prescribed pills and mixtures for his African customers, to pick up the postbox key. Aunt Zera was there and as usual could not resist her philanthropic drive, and gave us a fifty-cent coin each, thus bringing good luck on the enterprise from the start. We walked past the market to the post office, checked our box, found it empty, and carried on towards the destined store. Anyone who saw us walking noisily past the post office could not have told that we were on our way to talk to the dead. But if he had some instrument that detected beats, he would have heard five hearts thumping loudly. It was a corner grocery store serving an African clientele at which we stopped. I would have preferred Shamim to do the talking. Failing that, her brother Shiraz. But it was my father we had come for, it was my responsibility. My brother and my cousins gave me the signal and I moved a little forward. There was a big, middle-aged woman sitting at the till. 'What do you want?' she yelled sourly as we stood below on the street. She had a large white bosom and her hair was tied in a bun.

'We want to talk to Uncle,' I began.

'Henh?' again the yell. 'Which uncle?'

'Kassim Kurji Uncle!'

The die was cast. The woman was nonplussed. The old man himself came out. It was as we had pictured him. Red fez, white drill suit. He was short and thin with a dark brown face, the skin old yet unwrinkled: like dry leather.

'The children came to see you,' said the woman, adjusting a strap of her bodice. She was now standing up, tall, taller than her husband, and imposing, hands on hips.

'What do you want?' said Kassim Kurji in a soft voice.

'Bapa,' I addressed the old man, 'can you bring my father back?'

He looked at the woman. She gave him a reference, which was completely lost on us, ending with a nod towards me: 'This boy's mother was given in marriage in Nairobi and his father is dead.'

'Come inside,' said Kassim Kurji and turned to go back in.

We hesitated and looked at each other in fear. 'Go, now,' said the woman, and I took the first step. A long corridor led inside, it was dark and felt cool and damp and had rooms to either side. What does the house of Satan look like? What lies in the shadows that lurk there, who lives in the rooms? We passed three such rooms, doorways leading to dark, sparsely furnished interiors. Djinns, they say, live simply. This was Kassim Kurji who commanded djinns, whose bed trembled with his terrible powers. In front of us he looked straight ahead, gliding smoothly in small, easy steps. Behind us escape was already blocked by the broad figure of the woman. Sona gave a sob and clung to me by my forefinger, I stopped to wait for him and Shiraz was forced to pass me, for which he never forgave me. Finally Kassim Kurji turned into a room, Shiraz almost fell in after him as he missed a step, and Shamim gave a yelp and Salma whimpered.

We all went in. The room was empty, save for an African-style bed strung with fibre, on which were a blanket and a shawl, and beside it on the side of the door was a prayer mat. Kassim Kurji went and sat on the mat on his haunches. The woman brought a glowing coal brazier and sprinkled some incense on it. The room began to fill with thick, sweet fumes through which we watched the red coals and the glowing face of the man near them. He bent down and kissed the mat three times, then he sat erect, eyes lightly closed, hands in front of him loose and relaxed. He started muttering in Arabic something incomprehensible and guttural, his voice stiff but musical, so that it seemed that if the djinns could be evoked, it must surely be through this mysterious tongue. We watched and listened, unconscious of everything else but this small man in white drill and red cap who sat before us on the mat, from whose mouth which opened into a small black hole hard syllables of mysterious and wonderful words escaped. He stopped abruptly and took some long, easy breaths with his eyes closed. Then he kissed the ground three times as before. He opened his eyes and after a short while said, 'The djinns say that the man was a big soul. He cannot be called. He is with God.' The brazier was now quiescent and the fumes had dispersed. There was a stillness in the room. 'Go now,' said the man, still on the floor. The woman was not in sight. Shiraz gave me a nudge and we slowly filed out through the corridor and into the bright sunshine of Kariakoo.

A little way from Kassim Kuiji's shop on the way to the post office was 'the store with two lions'. It sold fishermen's nets and the name board over the doorway showed a lion trapped inside a red net. On one of the walls was a metal poster showing a lion trying unsuccessfully to catch up with a rider on a Raleigh bicycle. Then came another poster showing Stanley Matthews dribbling a football. After Stanley Matthews was a mattress shop, and it was here that we saw the woman from Kassim Kurji's shop, standing with an old woman, watching us trot by on our way past the post office and Hassan Uncle's New Medical Store all the way to Kichwele.

I never saw Kassim Kurji again, and when he died a few years later his reputation had gone down somewhat. But there was something about that mattress shop. On our trip to the post office we would sometimes walk past it to take a look: at the old woman sitting at the sewing machine by the doorway, the young man at the till inside, the African sitting outside on the sidewalk working on a mattress with needle and thread.

One day as I hurried by, alone, the old woman called out: 'Ay, boy. Come here.' She was standing inside, holding a brass measuring rod. I went in and she put the rod down on the counter and came back to face me. She was short and thin, in a long grey frock of the soft material that old women favour. Reddish-grey henna-dyed hair on her almost tiny head was tied at the back in a bun the size of a golf ball. The face was wrinkled, the eyes shone brightly.

'What's your name?'

'Salim Juma.'

'Juma... Juma... so you went looking for your father—'

I said nothing, what can you say to a strange old woman who's cornered you, I looked around me discomfortedly, as if for a chance to escape, or for help. I looked at the young man watching me from behind the counter, then at the African who looked up from a mattress, and felt reassured —

'Well, listen, son of Juma, you listen to me and I shall give you your father Juma and *his* father Huseni and his father...'

Sweet knowledge. Ji Bai spoke and I listened.

There are those who go to their graves not knowing where they came from... who hurtled into the future even as the present was yet not over... for whom history was a contemptible record of a shameful past. In short, those who closed their ears when the old men and women spoke. But the future will demand a reckoning. We will not forgive those who forgot, the new generation of the Sabrinas and the Fairuzes and the Farahs will say.

Ji Bai opened a small window into that dark past for me. She took me past the overgrowth into the other jungle. And a whole world flew in, a world of my great-grandfather who left India and my great-grandmother who was African, the world of Matamu where India and Africa met and the mixture exploded in the person of my half-caste grandfather Huseni who disappeared into the forest one day and never returned, the world of a changing Africa where Europe and Africa also met and the result was even more explosive, not only in the lives of men but also in the life of the continent.

I remember my first view of Shehrbanoo... a dumpy gunny sack enclosing a broken world, the debris of lives lived... slumped in the inner room beside Ji Bai's bed, her mouth closed with a sisal twine. Ji Bai untied the loose knot, instantly a smile appeared on the gunny where there was a grimace before, and that laughing mouth was never shut again. Eh, Shehru, but for me in my grey shorts and flip-flop chappals where would you be now?

The first things Ji Bai brought out from that bottomless depth were the three books.

There were, of course, Ji Bai, Gulam, and Ma the squint-eyed mother whose authority was on the decline. And there were Ji Bai's four remaining children, little Mongi having died at Rukanga, and Gulam's brother Nasser who never left them. Abdulla, the other brother and friend of Germany, never left Rukanga, he married there and he died there. He had one son, Kaiser, named after the deposed Great One, and several grandsons, of whom Aziz became Ji Bai's travelling companion...

After school, between two and four when all senses were dulled by the heat, I would steal away with the postbox key, my ready excuse, to the mattress shop. Just to see the happiness on her face as I came in was worth the trip. Seated on the bench, frosty Coke bottle in hand, I would let myself be pampered and loved and told stories to, while the African sewing the mattress would look up with satisfaction, and her grandson Shamshu at the till would interrupt her with suggestions. 'Tell him about the march to Rukanga, Ma.' '... and the roars of the lions, Ma!' 'Tell him about Bibi Wasi – what did she look like?' (Ji Bai: 'Oh, she was prim and pretty, with an umbrella and white frock and her face would be all red...') And once in a while the trip to the inside of the house, to sit on her old bed, and see what Shehru came up with...

Kulsum had never mentioned this side of our history, what point was there in letting her into the secret? But of course, she found out. For Shamshu was the favourite customer of Hemani the secondhand bookdealer; he had acquired from Hemani a roomful of books, walls lined with Famous Five and Secret Seven, Perry Mason and Hercule Poirot, stacks of Kit Carson and Kansas Kid and Buck Jones and Davy Crockett. And Shamshu, who himself did not read his books but would look upon them with the care and tenderness others reserve for their pet children or their pregnant wives, showed a greatness of heart in lending me select titles from his precious shelves.

A Famous Five or Secret Seven book without the rubber stamp of the library on every alternate page, ex libris Shamshudin Gulam Dhanji Hasham, or words to that effect!

'Unless you have stolen it…' said Kulsum, 'tell me how you got it.'

They opened a stall on Bagamoyo Road far away from the town, deep inside the African district, selling pili-pili-bizari: chilli and turmeric, a clove of garlic here and there, sugar by the packet, flour and grain by the kibaba-cup, kerosene by the jigger. And they were known in town, even though the family name had been changed to Hasham, there were people who could point their finger at them and say, 'There walks the house of Dhanji Govindji, who stole from God,' and cross the street and walk on the other side.

During the hartal of 1923, the strike called by Indian shopkeepers to protest against the Government's requirement that accounts be kept in English, they had to close the stall even when they could ill afford to, they didn't have a shilling in the house. They had to sell through the back door, the compound, where the mamas knocked and pleaded for groceries and brought vitumbua and barazi for them.

Through the 20s and into the 30s, the years of boom, when the big mosque with the clock tower went up, all in stone, with huge wooden doors and iron gates, when the Indian population swelled and Dar grew and grew, they carried the shame, afraid to look people in the eye, to get into an argument, for fear of a taunt.

There was one incident Ji Bai never forgot. Her son Kassim, ten years old, was playing in the street with other boys. She sat minding the store, looking out over the groceries, it was a dull humid afternoon right after a brief rainfall, the ground was wet on the surface although the sand underneath was dry... A sudden commotion woke her up from her reverie: Kassim was racing furiously towards her, bare feet thumping on the ground, kicking up dust, chased with even greater thumps of larger bare feet by a grown woman: Sheru Bai of the Indian shop across the road. Kassim raced inside, panting loudly, and looked at his mother in relief. No sanctuary. Sheru Bai without losing the slightest speed raced right into the store, caught hold of the boy by the hair, shook him a few times and slapped him twice. Then without a word or a look at his mother she stomped off.

A kid's fight, perhaps. But wasn't I, the boy's mother, the proper authority to be told? Kher. Never mind. We survived this and other insults. The people forgot, but it took them twenty, twenty-five years to do so. Sheru Bai and I are friends now. We've both seen hardships.

In the 1930s Gulam became a missionary. He joined a group of young men, many of them freshly off the boat from Bombay, who went on car trips to the interior to keep their brethren in line and to teach the faith to the African. In the first purpose they were phenomenally successful: few intermarriages, fewer concubines or multiple wives, mosques and schools going up everywhere. In the second, they proved a miserable failure: instead of promising rewards both here and in the hereafter, instead of providing education (which they couldn't, themselves having none) or hospitals or shoes and clothes, they spoke of punishment: Every grain of sin the Lord will carefully weigh: bongo ya kichwa itatokea sikioni they translated freely – the brain of the head will pour out from your ears. And no-one was willing to buy that, even as insurance. In 1938, one day on the road from Morogoro to Iringa (later to be known as the Hell Run), their car skidded into a ravine. All the five young missionaries inside died on the spot. And became instant martyrs. At first the bodies were to be brought back to Dar. But that was decided against and they were buried at a roadside grave close to the spot where they were killed, with inscriptions in stone commemorating the event in three languages. Until recently, said Ji Bai, cars and lorries on the highway slowed down in deference to the five martyrs who died there, and those that raced past did so at their own peril.

Thus Gulam saved the family name. And slowly the family began to prosper – there was food on the table, creditors left satisfied if not jubilant, children went to school, there were clothes to wear. But there was nothing like the old glory.

All the while, she watched Juma in her crystal ball, she knew when he was married, and she grieved when he died, and one day it told her that Juma's family had arrived in Dar. How to contact them? How to speak to this stern young woman Kulsum, who had lived in the home of the great Hassam Pirbhai, and what to tell her? Of the shame – the *double* shame of sin against community and sin against God?

Then Providence played its part. It was Juma himself who brought about the meeting – follow the train of events: the dream, the forbidden fruit, the sin, the lapse, the search for redemption, and history bloomed, knowledge was victorious.

Kulsum, of course, would have none of this. 'The budhi is demented,' was her verdict.

'Aré, Ma, the boys' father comes from a good family,' she told Ji Bai impatiently over a cup of tea, the one and only time she went to see the old woman. 'The Merchants in Pakistan are his uncles—'

'Precisely so, Beta,' affirmed Ji Bai, 'the same family…'

'Even so,' Kulsum would later say, 'the past is done with. Who can say what really happened, what the budhi is not making up… Think of the future…'

But I was given a new look, the carbuncle in the family, vague evidence of a long-ago temptation.

Ji Bai triumphant.

This was when Kulsum was at her lowest point since her husband's death, she could not have survived the tragedy that loomed overhead, when the milkman was told simply to keep away and I kept in the background lest Providence select me as an agent for one of its unpleasant deeds.

Mrs Pipa came on a call of sympathy and left, her blackened pachedi and all, a portent of death and disaster.

Kulsum never forgave Mrs Pipa that call.

First, the Pipas. One son, Amin, after a long curse of seven daughters, when the couple were well past middle age. Amin had nieces and nephews much older than him. All except one or two daughters were unhappy in marriage, none got along with their mother. Some were married into poverty, one was married to a milksop, and Roshan was married off in haste to a drunkard. The problem with being married to a drunkard is that he spends all the money and he beats you. The whole community knows your story, and the more you try to hide your shame and disappointment, the more difficult it is to think of divorce, the beatings get worse, your eyes puff up, your hair turns grey, your face takes on a haggard look, your body loses shape, and he beats you like a drum, you tell your parents, but they send you away with prayers for remedies, the beatings continue until there is only one way out...

Amin, the delicate child, obviously, for whom the light green Ford Taunus was bought and the chauffeur hired, to take him to school, who liked to hang out with tough boys who took from him not only marbles and shillings but something else as well. Of the goings-on in the small space behind the Pipas' courtyard, we found out from Ahmed downstairs. Ahmed sold information and thrills. This was the payoff, his price to stop harassment in the streets and under staircases. For that shilling you also got the most titillating pieces of information, something you hadn't even dreamt of. For example, the sight of Roshan Mattress and the inspector in action in the back room behind her store – all you did was to climb onto the sewer pipe from the Bubus' balcony, walk along it against the wall, a twenty-foot drop under you, to the storeroom roof in the building courtyard, and then climb down to the courtyard floor and peep in through the iron bars to watch the fat lady offer her milk-white behind to the inspector. This opportunity was declined because the storeroom roof was layered with broken glass against just such an intrusion, and who wanted to be caught with his back against the wall, standing on a sewer pipe, with wrathful Boadicea watching from the top? To see Amin's sin was easier, you had to go to the Pipas' courtyard with your guide Ahmed, climb on some crates soundlessly, hold your breath, and watch. Which is what we did, Alu and Shiraz and I, our hearts pounding: raw flesh, raw sin, buggery in a cubicle reeking of urine and bird droppings and rotting pawpaws.

One night a single scream pierced the silence outside, after which normality returned, with the elder Jogo hobbling along with his call to prayer and Kulsa Thauki's gang shuffling along on their way to prayer. In the morning we heard that Amin had been taken to the hospital at night with a fever.

Within a few days he was dead from a mysterious illness, and then the screams and weeping and sobbing were continuous for a few nights: Mrs Pipa and the seven sisters.

From that time onwards, the Pipas' lives were more or less over. When a few months later their daughter Roshan jumped to her death from a second-storey window of a friend's flat, God, as far as the old couple were concerned, was flogging a dead horse. Amin Mansion stood like a mausoleum over Pipa Store, and old Mzee Pipa counted away his hours throwing package after package of spice into the basket in front of him, like grains of sand. But the green Ford Taunus continued to take boys to school every day and brought them back, fifteen shillings a month for each boy, and every Friday two stale chapatis and a fifty-cent thumuni landed in front of Pipa's sister who sat with begging bowl outside the mosque.

When Sona's fever would not go away and his eyeballs and nails turned an ominous yellow and he passed brown water, Kulsum took him to Dr Vellani, who put her in a taxi and sent her home, promising to come himself to give the injections every day. But Sona would not get better. Kulsum bribed the gods and promised more bribes, but the heavens remained silent. Dr Vellani started bringing on his rounds his Madrasi wife, who was also a renowned doctor. Kulsum sat up all night on a mat beside her large bed on which Sona lay comatose, her tasbih rattling impatiently and her mouth whispering urgent prayers... and finally her two elder sisters joined her in the vigil. It was then that the neighbours started coming, Mrs Daya, Uncle Goa and Madam, Alzira, Nuru Poni, and finally Mrs Pipa, who, as she left, said, 'My son Amin had the same illness.' It was for this remark, which so cut her to the quick, that Kulsum never forgave Mrs Pipa.

* * *

At this point the situation resembled, although somewhat imperfectly, the scenario of many a massala movie from Bombay, as they are called, in which a poor innocent lies dying on spotless white sheets, attached to a blood transfusion device, while somewhere a bearded Musulman is saying 'Allah, Allah' to the click of beads, a Catholic woman (nurse) is crying in front of a crucifix, and a woman in a sari plays a sitar to a Hindu god reposing on his cushion. The sheets were soiled, the room was dark and there was no transfusion device pumping away. But Alzira had promised to pray to her God, and the three sisters were clicking beads and moving their mouths in a mixture of Hindu and Muslim prayers. Fatu Auntie started the first few bars of a hymn, which Kulsum immediately put to a stop with a sharp 'Stop these sad songs. There will be plenty of time to forgive sins...'

(Fatu Auntie, a born tragedienne of the Zanzibari school, never missed a dramatic opportunity. When she arrived, she had taken Kulsum in a tight, tearful embrace accompanied by an audible sob, thus lowering the cloud of gloom even further on our household. When my grandmother Hirbai had died, several months before, and the men were taking away the body for burial, Fatu Auntie, who had not got along with her mother for the last ten years or so, had let out a terrifying shriek, 'Oh, villains you, where do you take my beloved mother—' To the cemetery, of course, Fatu Masi, but the men, frozen in mid-stride with the coffin bearing down heavily on their shoulders, could not of course say this.)

Thus Fatu Auntie, who sat back smarting from her younger sister's sharp retort.

When enter Ji Bai, leaning on my shoulder, having greeted Mrs Pipa on the staircase. I had in one hand a small bundle tied up with a piece of cloth. Ji Bai threw one long look at Kulsum on the floor, then at Sona on the bed, and proceeded with her work. She opened the bundle and took out a small brass bowl, the kind used by barbers, and handed it to me: 'Water. About half full.' I brought the water. Meanwhile Ji Bai had found some sewing needles. She sat beside Sona and felt his body. 'How are you, my boy?' she muttered. She pressed his hot forehead, all his limbs, and finally his stomach, in a kneading motion, with one hand. Then she took a needle from the other hand, and in one sweeping but slow motion moved it along one arm, from the shoulder down, whispering something, and dropped it into the bowl. This she repeated with the other arm and the legs. Finally she ran a needle from his forehead down to the back of his head. Every day she came to inspect the five needles lying under water in the brass bowl. Slowly the water turned yellow, and Sona's fever came down.

Now you may say that it was only the rust from the needles that turned the water yellow, that what she did was all mumbo jumbo. But admit it – deep inside, you know that it just might be possible, that it was her medicine that had worked. Would you take a chance – that all the people who swore by her medicine were a superstitious lot and misguided?

Ji Bai said that she had learnt her art of healing from her sister-in-law in her hometown, when she was still a girl. It was a woman's art, handed down from woman to woman on the eve of Hindu Diwali… yet the prayers were all ayats from the Quran, she insisted: sort it out, you purists.

One afternoon, while Begum and the rest were downstairs in the shop, entertaining and being entertained by Alzira, sharing the meagre portions of roasted steaming white mhogo, Shamim and I went upstairs to conduct an experiment. 'Let's find out if you are a man yet.'

I lay on my belly on the lower half of a bunk bed, her bed,

and standing on the floor beside me she goaded: 'Rub, Kala, rub. Harder, and it will come out if you are a man—' I rubbed and I rubbed, a fly button came in the way, yet I rubbed – 'It's not coming, are you sure?' 'Rub, Kala, rub—' 'But it's not coming, I tell you… it's hurting, this stupid button—' 'Maybe in a few months more…' And then release, sweet sticky discharge. 'You're a man, Kala!' And who should turn up then: 'SALAAA!' Boadicea.

Kulsum knew better than to rail against nature. She pretended she did not know of the event. But that night she wrote to her brother Bahdur: 'My boys are now getting to that age, and I think it advisable that you take your daughters in your care…'

This time Bahdur Uncle did not dither. In two months he had sold his store and arrived in Dar, as penniless as when he left it, and took Shamim, Shiraz, Salma and Yasmin with him. He opened a small pili-pili-bizari store opposite the market.

13 | *Cricket and Elections*

The scene: the Gymkhana cricket ground on a sunny Sunday afternoon just after tea break, one team battling valiantly and with almost certain futility against the century and a quarter piled against it, jeers pour in plentifully from one jubilant side of the spectator area and tempers are short on the other. Batting are Hindu Sports Club, against the Challengers XI. The bowler is Gumji, short and affectionate for Gulamali Manji, better known for his century against the touring Indian team two years ago, when he would stylishly clip Desai's bumpers between gully and third man for repeated fours. For that amazing feat, even when Tanganyika lost by an innings against India, Gumji became the *Herald*'s Sportsman of the Year. Gumji became a legend but never scored another century, instead he started to bowl his own fast bumpers.

Gumji rubs the ball against his trousers, gives his famous squint in the sun and comes running against Tapu.

'Come on! Come on, Gumji, come on, Trueman, break his stumps!'

'Aré Trueman your arse, watch the chakas fly.'

'Shut up, cuntface!'

Tapu is a nervous batsman, short, muscular and dark. And he taps the bat nervously, once, twice, as Gumji approaches, and as the ball flies towards him he gives a wild swing.

'How's that?' the wicket keeper shouts as the ball smacks into his gloves, and the umpire plays deaf.

'Change the umpire!' shouts a segment of the crowd. 'Ay, Fernandes, go and eat fish!' The umpire, obviously, is a Goan.

Nervous Tapu is known for his wild swings. Always, he either scores a six or nothing. And recently Tapu has scored many sixes. In fact, six sixes in an over. But this time, as he swings the second time to an angry full-pitch from Gumji, the stumps go flying. As the disappointed batsman reaches the gate, a spectator on the grass croons at him: 'Ay, Tapu… maja avi? Ay, was that fun?' The angry Tapu swings his bat at him, and the fight begins.

'Ay, Banya, pick someone your own size!'

'Shamsi, Khamsi, khamosh! Quiet!'

Fist fights and stick fights get under way at several places. Coconut branches are appropriated for the battle, as are mangoes and Coke bottles. Fiery Gumji has reached the spectator area, has climbed on a car rooftop, saying, 'Come on,' fists raised, ready to take on the world. Some spectators discreetly walk away, the clubhouse is over-run and the uniformed African barman closes shop and disappears, the European snooker players slip out of the back way and into their cars.

'Dengu! Dal-eaters! Your Gandhi went around in diapers! Your Nehru goes around in pyjamas!'

'Jinnah the bone pie!'

A song gets under way:

Banyani ganga!
Pili pili manga!
Choroni kula!
Kitanda lala!

'Go back to Pakistan!' 'You go to India! Shit eaters!' scream the young men.

News of the ruckus reaches the settlements in Kisutu and Upanga and Kariakoo and Downtown and boxbodies filled with rowdy enthusiasts of the respective communities leave for the Gymkhana Club.

But happily the fight is settled by those who first started it. The two teams, now in their blazers and sweaters, make up and shake hands in the best tradition of cricket. 'We are one,' they say, 'we Asians must stay together.' Tapu goes to apologise to the Challenger fans and stoically accepts a slap on the face from a screaming middle-aged man and presents the boy whom he had previously hit with the weapon, his own Donald Bradman bat. 'We are one,' goes the cry. The match will be replayed, the field empties of the crowd, and the Europeans return to their snooker and beer.

The reason for the animus between communities is the impending election to the Tanganyika Legislative Council, the first election of any consequence in the country. Every man or woman to vote for one European, one Asian, one African, for a multiracial Legco. Not democratic, said TANU: five representatives for 20,000 Europeans, five for 80,000 Asians, and five for 8 million Africans: divide and see for yourselves! But TANU went along.

But where TANU, the Governor, the Africans, in short everyone else, saw 'Asian', the Asians saw Shamsi, Bohra, Ismaili, Hindu, Sikh, Memon, Ithnashri. One seat in each polling district, seven or more competing communities.

The captain of the Hindu Sports Club was P.K. Patel, or PK, a clerk in the East African Railways and Harbours. His brother RK was a lawyer and leading member of the Asian Association. RK's wife Radha was the TANU-supported candidate for Dar. Her strongest opponent was Dr Habib Kara, supported by the UTP (the Governor's party, some said) and the Shamsi community. RK was educated in Bombay, and Kara in Poona. Both had then gone to England, from where Kara brought home an English wife, and RK brought back Radha. Both had children studying in England.

This was the first election anyone had ever seen where you could send a representative right to the top, to the Governor's council, to speak for you. This was only the beginning – if they did not know that, they certainly sensed it. The stakes were high. On every pillar and lamppost in Kichwele and Msimbazi, outside every Asian shop, were the signs exhorting 'Vote for Kara!' and 'Vote for Patel!' and displaying the candidates' sombre faces and their symbols. Radha Patel's symbol was the wheel, representing progress. The fact that it resembled Asoka's wheel on the Indian flag was missed by her enemies. Dr Kara was represented by the lofty torch, throwing its rays skywards. 'It represents knowledge,' he said proudly. But Dr Kara's light was more mystical than political. He came to our shop and shook Kulsum's hand. Of course, we all knew him. The first doctor in the community. A Mombasa boy. Chubby and fair in a light bush shirt. Kulsum had been his patient, briefly, and given him up, as she had a dozen others. He had been treating my grandmother when she died, and although negligence on his part was always claimed by her family, this did not come in the way of how they voted. He came to our shop just to make sure, and went away reassured by Kulsum.

Against the lofty light and the steady wheel ran the fragile rabbit. The rabbit, Edward bin Hadith would tell you, is a cunning animal, as cunning as Abunuwas. In fact Abunuwas looks just like a rabbit. The rabbit outwits the hyena and leaves the lion shaking its head in despair. Watch out for the rabbit. The rabbit was the symbol of Fateh the Coalseller. It was a mystery why Fateh ran for the election. He had the support of no community or party. When Dr Kara walked the blocks of Kichwele Street with his lieutenants, all in bush shirts, when Radha Patel alighted from her car in her afternoon sari accompanied by her son or daughter, Fateh would sometimes draw them to a challenge. 'What is your platform? Which people will you represent?' Dr Kara, who wore black-framed spectacles and looked like a studious schoolboy, would smile genially. 'Knowledge. Education,' he would say. Mrs Patel's line was also straightforward. African country. Races living in harmony (Oh yes, Dr Kara would echo when he was around, all equal, no differences) we are all Tanganyikans now. Dada Hodari, Fateh called her contemptuously. She has a mpishi at home, and a gardener, and a houseboy, he would tell the Africans, you think she will abandon them? And this Daktari. His children are studying in England. What will he do for you? Fateh threw his challenges in Swahili, he was answered in English. Whatever Swahili Dr Kara had spoken in Mombasa, now eluded him. Mrs Patel, it was said, was acquiring the language and could read her speeches in it. But Fateh did not know English. In other words, he was not educated. He had been to school only to take other people's children there. He was scruffy-looking, often unshaven, and in not the cleanest clothes, as befitted his profession. 'Wey, Fateh,' the TANU supporters would tease him, 'eti, what will you say to the Governor at a tea party if you are elected? Don't forget to wash your hands! His Excellency wears the whitest gloves!'

Fateh was supported by kindred spirits. Drifters and dreamers. Idealists. Edward could not help but support the rabbit, whose praises he had sung for so long. It was more of an aesthetic choice. The underdog rabbit against the torch and the wheel; it was irresistible. And Bahdur Uncle, who had known Fateh since childhood, was drawn quite naturally into the excitement and rhetoric of the campaign. He had the bearing and the habits that others, more responsible (Hassan Uncle for one), disliked: he liked to have fun. He was rather stylish, sometimes in white shorts and shirt, holding a cigarette in the style of Gary Cooper. His wife Dolu was not unlike him. The fact that she sported a beret on some occasions is indication enough. They both loved to see films, and when they enjoyed a film, they saw it again and again – even when they were broke.

Fateh did not have enough money to have flyers printed, and the 500 shillings he had to deposit to register his candidacy he asked to borrow from Bahdur Uncle. Bahdur Uncle of course did not have 500 shillings, and came to Kulsum with some story, taking the money from her emergency fund, money reserved for the Downtown wholesalers. Thus was Fateh the Coalseller's campaign financed, at least to a good extent, and my mother never forgave her brother. The next time he came to her for emergency funds she refused, as did the rest of the family, and he spent a month in debtors' prison.

On the day before the election Fateh rented a loudspeaker from Rajan Radio and he and Bahdur Uncle drove the streets of Kariakoo exhorting people to vote for the rabbit.

Kimbia na sungura
Fateh ukimchagua
Ataleta mbio na furaha
CHAGUA FATEH! CHAGUA SUNGURA!

Run with the rabbit
If you choose Fateh
He'll bring speed and pleasure
CHOOSE FATEH! CHOOSE THE RABBIT!

It brought smiles, his manner, his familiarity, his slogans echoing from the building walls. Children ran after the Chama Chetu, running with the rabbit. Old men in kanzus, who had known him since he was a boy, would look in pleasure as he passed, as if to say, Our own Fateh! But so what? The rabbit is fast and clever, as Edward would say, but what can he do for you? The rabbit is kind-hearted, he takes children to school free of charge, while Mzee Pipa extorts 15 shillings from poor families who have no choice. But can he talk to the Governor? Or to the reporters who come from England and America? He has style, but it is the style of a Kariakoo loafer. He is not a gentleman.

On election day of course he offered rides to the polling booths to his supporters. A few mamas who had giggled at his carefree manner went. A few old men went. Children ran after him. But most of the people on Kichwele and Viongozi went in TANU cars or on foot or, as did Kulsum, in one of Dr Kara's rides.

After the voting Bahdur Uncle went with Fateh as his counting agent. The two, one holding a cigarette in his best Gary Cooper manner, the other carefree in the Raj Kapoor manner, walked among the working teams at Arnautoglu Hall like a pair of foremen, watching them carefully put a cross over a name on a graph paper for every vote counted, seeing their opponents' tolls rising higher and higher, finally coming to terms with the fact that the steady wheel had snuffed out the lofty light and run over the crafty rabbit.

The election had been multiracial, each race to be represented in the Legco, but the winner was TANU, only TANU was represented. For in the past months Julius Nyerere had gone from village to village asking young men to leave aside loafing and join TANU; he had patiently followed the old men who would take him to the very spots where their tribesmen had been hanged by the Mdachis, and they had asked him, could he really get rid of these people who had defeated the Mdachis, and he had said yes, follow me. And even as our own Queen Begum was confidently telling Kulsum, 'Do you think the people who defeated Napoleon, and Hitler, who hanged Kimathi and put Kenyatta away, will just pack their bags and leave?' – TANU's strength was growing. And after the election, which TANU won for the Africans, Asian started telling Asian, We must change, we must diversify. The duka is doomed. We must go into industry, into the professions, into farming, we must move into other economic sectors. Wait and see, said others, the British have not left yet.

When Sir Richard Turnbull was announced as the new Governor, we said, Oh *him*? The District Commissioner – the one who was in Moyale in the NFD and in Isiolo, who was in Nairobi during Mau Mau? Oh, *he* knew our daddy! We did not write to him, or to his daughter, reminding them of the fact, but the thought did cross our minds. Reminded of her past glory, of five, six, ten years ago, Kulsum was not willing even to listen to the stories I brought from Ji Bai. Stories from a remote past, from a village on the coast, stories of black ancestry and a murder…

Taratibu, taratibu. Patience, patience. Don't cry, my beloved, said a Swahili love song to the tune of a Hindi film melody. Song to a black Radha, coming from the blaring loudspeakers of the Kariakoo market, reminding me of my great-grandfather, the fair Govindji, who got her for cold nights. I would see her in every black woman I laid eyes on, looked up and down upon. The modest but by no means docile Swahili draped in black buibui and exuding the sticky fragrance of halud; the short and fair Chagga, the shy Makonde… I had visions of Sabini our night watchman, bringing his wife to say goodbye… Did she look like her, my great-grandmother Taratibu – a shy Makonde woman with a face marked by stripes and a large black button on her upper lip? Her mouth stayed open, and she had large teeth, and she just said yes or no, looking at the ground in front of her. Sabini left to become a church minister in his home town south… At night I would stay awake thinking of her, of what she had looked like. I would say her name forwards and backwards, backwards and forwards… Tara-tibu, tibu-tara, tara-tibu, tibu-tara, conjuring that name from the past until I felt hot and tired and Jogo's father drew nearer…'Man's mind is fickle… the world is a fair…' in clumsy Swahili to an even clumsier tune.

A slave woman kept by an Indian trader in a small town. Think about it, about her. Perhaps she always hated his guts, hated it when he touched her, undraped her, screwed her… or perhaps she liked him a little, or even a lot… her name was Taratibu, she was not incapable of love… and he risked damnation for their son.

Black ancestry was not something you advertised. Kulsum had two girls' marriage prospects to think of. A whiff of African blood from the family tree would be like an Arctic blast, it would bring the mercury of social standing racing down to unacceptable levels.

'Do you want to see a festival?' asked Edward one day. 'Yes,' I replied, and off we walked to the bus stand and caught a bus to Illala.

We got off at a shopping area, rather dead at this time of day, with two dry-goods stores side by side in a squat, yellow brick building called Rupia House, a few men sitting on the cement floor outside, doing nothing… A sound of drums came from the interior, behind Rupia House; we took a side street and made another turn into a long narrow alley, past mud houses in various states of completion, and joined the current of men, women and children hurrying along it. All around us, women in buibui, the scent of halud and Bint-el-Sudan and Jasmin, men in clean, pressed trousers, long white kanzus… The sound of drums was drawing nearer, the beat was taking a shape, the jingle of tambourines was now audible, the current of people poured into a clearing beside a house frame, and men, women, children hurried towards the festival of the Prophet's birthday behind the house and beyond a mound of earth. The square enclosing the band was five deep and we craned our necks to see inside, between black-buibui-clad female and white-kanzu-clad male figures. Like other boys and girls I pushed my way in through a group of women to the front, and watched. The band was beating a constant, tireless rhythm to one side, nearby the elders stood in a line moving to the rhythm of the drum, holding up ceremonial walking sticks, and in the centre two males improvised a sword dance with sticks, parrying, jabbing, hopping away in a circle and returning, and a third person, a tolerated lunatic, was doing a solo. Men from the crowd, elderly men usually, stepped inside the square to relieve a dancer, challenge a foe, exchange parries... Edward went in, cutting a striking but incongruous figure in his bright green shirt and white trousers, refusing a challenge but moving gracefully away in a circle, doing some kind of a shake, stick held vertically in his hand. Behind me, around me, as I watched my friend dancing, the crowd pressed in, black bodies I'd never been so close to, scent of soap, of perfume, of sweat, flaps of buibui fanning my hot dusty face, soft warm curves of women pressing through filmy buibui, enveloping, inviting, absorbing as I stood there senseless in the heat, the flying dust, the odours, all the while my dukawallah hand clutching the hard silver shilling in my pocket that would take me home. After the dance the square broke up and we drank sherbet, he a bright orange one and I a red one, and we ate peanuts and like experts we stood discussing the performance. People now noticed me, boys ran by mischievously close, provoking, shoving...

Kulsum had gone frantic with worry. The servant Ali had been sent to the school grounds to search for me, Sona was dispatched to Alu Poni's, Jogo's, and various other households. As the afternoon drew to a close, Uncle Goa's help was sought. In his green Morris he first went to the school grounds, then he went up and down the main streets and alleys, questioning boys playing in the streets. He tried the Khalsa, Goan, Patel

Brotherhood, and Gymkhana cricket grounds to check if I had stayed to watch a late practice. He was returning from the police station when I stepped off the bus, and he drove me the rest of the way home. The store was open and filled with family, not a customer in sight, a stern and worried-looking Kulsum, perched on her high stool at the counter.

'Here he is,' said Uncle Goa genially in Swahili, with a flourish of his hand. 'All safe and sound!'

'Where were you?' cried the chorus.

'We were worried sick.'

'Look at his feet! His clothes! His hair!'

'What have you been up to?'

Uncle Goa had slipped away.

'I went to see a Maulidi with Edward.'

Pandemonium. 'The rascal!' 'What made you go with him?' 'Don't you know you could be robbed or killed?' 'Wait till he comes tomorrow!' 'Fire him!' 'There are djinns and ghosts there!' 'Drunkards too!' 'Beta, don't you like our company that you go away without telling us?'

Poor Edward. He knew what awaited him, for he came late the next morning and suffered Kulsum's lecture in silence. But the next few nights they all watched me with amusement as I demonstrated to them the sword dance with my father's rusty sword from the red scabbard...

With an elected majority of supporters in Legco, TANU demanded more and more. The new Governor had placed an open tray before it and asked: What do you want? And TANU, Nyerere, with an eye on the whole tray politely asked for one thing then another. And Sir Richard, with all the intention of giving the whole tray away, offering one thing and holding back another, just to see how badly they wanted the whole works.

The key word, of course, was self-government. Not yet

independence. Everyone was cautious. Ask for everything at once, and you'll look greedy, uncivilised.

What do we want? asked Nyerere. What we want in this country, sir, is that anyone, irrespective of his race, as long as he owes allegiance to Tanganyika, is a complete and equal citizen as anyone else. Hear hear! Hey... hmmm. The background sounds of approval in Legco. How avidly the proceedings were followed. It is not every day you watch history being made, and know what you're watching is history in the making. The *Herald* was euphoric, the *Ngurumo* roared approval, as the Legco members, one and all, said Equality, equality of the races. A reasonable chap, people said, a gentleman, a statesman!

On Mnazi Moja ground, behind Arnautoglu Hall, they enacted a little skit.

'Nipe coffee,' says the man (barefooted, shirt-tails hanging out, but trying to look tall and imposing) who is playing the European boss, to his servant in stiff accented Swahili. The servant is alarmed. 'But, Bwana,' he says nervously, 'to give you a kofi... how can I do it? You are the boss, I am the servant...' 'Nipe coffee,' says the boss impatiently, 'haraka.' Quick. 'Please, Bwana, don't ask me to give you a kofi, tafadhali, ask someone else... the Mhindi's servant, he is a cad... the taxi driver—' He trembles. 'Mimi nataka coffee! Haraka! Coffee *moto. Moto sana!*' Hot coffee. 'Haya, Bwana,' says the servant finally, in resignation. 'You asked for it. Moto moto.' And he gives the boss a resounding slap on the face, a kofi. The crowd is hilarious.

Matchbox tops began showing TANU flags and jembes and torches and political slogans instead of Swedish steamers and clippers. People from the Labour Union and TANU and the women's union kept coming and took the fundis and servants to a side and whispered with them... Watch the green colour, advised Hassan Uncle to Kulsum, in his cryptic way, there lies safety. Buy flags, buy badges, pay the fundis day to day, make them sign for everything.

'What do I want?' asked Omari our expert tailor, the fundi. 'What I want, madam, is backpay for six years according to Labour salaries... what I want is vacation pay for six years and what I want is end of term bonus.' The fundi Omari and his friend Idi, who now worked at the Union headquarters, and sometimes wore 'Release Jomo Kenyatta' shirts, estimated that when he was paid the arrears Omari could just walk into the shop and own it. Omari bided his time and calculated, ready to pounce with the backing of the Labour Union. And Kulsum, in an exact literal translation, was scared shitless.

We would like, said Nyerere, to light a candle and place it on top of Mount Kilimanjaro, to shine beyond our borders, giving hope where there was despair, love where there was hate, dignity where there was only humiliation...

Spoken like a statesman, sir. A Tanganyikan emblem of liberty... fair, flaming Kilimanjaro rising from the plains in place of fair Columbia with the torch... Why not? We also have dreams we would like to share, and worthy ideals, and hopes not only for ourselves but for everyone... if they will let us.

Miss Castelinho, with the wide sexy mouth and the beauty spot, usually walks to school from teacher's quarters holding a parasol against the sun. Sometimes Mr Ramji gives her a ride on his scooter and they are seen disappearing into the bushes to do what the boys, rightly or wrongly, speculate graphically about. Miss Castelinho is the class teacher of Standard VIA, now collectively undergoing the pubescent itch: excitement at the sight of a kiss, excitement at the mention of a kiss, excitement at the thought of a kiss. What was once the outing period is now used for singing. Out are 'Sing a Song of Sixpence' and

'There Was a Little Nut Tree'. In are Elvis and Cliff and Neil Sedaka and Pat Boone.

Consider a typical period.

Hassam, *the* Hassam, Elvis, later Iblis, is singing and Castelinho is beaming proudly.

'When the moon takes its place… of the sun in the sky…I'll call for my girlie, we'll go walking by…'

The beaming Castelinho walks to the door, chats with another teacher. 'He's a good singer, isn't he? This one's brother. He's handsome. Smart too. How the girls will fall for him!'

Behind her, Hassam continues, '… we will make love—' and the class sings in chorus solemnly after him, 'We will make love!'

'Oh yes,' Jogo thumps his desk in joyful affirmation, but not understanding what he is singing, '*We will make love!*'

That year, Miss Penny Mrs Gaunt was leaving for England, and Miss Castelinho organised a goodbye event for her: eleven boys dressed as fairies holding up cards, singing Bing Crosby's 'May the Good Lord Bless and Keep You'. The class groaned. It was not the attire that the boys objected to but the song. 'Oh, that budha,' groaned Hassam. To which Miss Castelinho responded a pert: 'Who says Bing is old?' and stood there redfaced, her weakness exposed, answered by whistles and catcalls. Bing! Hey, Bing! What a first name, Bing! Ping! Ding! Bing Bang! Bang Bang Bang!

Eleven pretty boys were chosen, but of course none of the coarse breed from Kariakoo. The Kariakoo boy stands out. The shirt is faded and the collar sometimes frayed. The shorts have the requisite creases but they don't stand out, as in newer, freshly laundered garments. The shoes are cobbler-made, the chequered designs on the socks scream 'Hong Kong!' He carries a kikapu, not a Japanese-made plastic satchel or a little trunk. And when his mouth opens – we kumamako, stop it you motherfucker! – venom in three languages. Every third or fourth word is a swear word, observers have noted. Thus stands catalogued the Kariakoo boy. But someone must have whispered into Miss Castelinho's ear, Better take this Juma boy, Mrs Gaunt likes him. How else can one explain why Snivelling Alnasir was chucked out and yours truly asked to replace him? Even when Snivelling Alnasir cried and sniffed all afternoon? But his family were not nobodys, they owned a fleet of lorries, had moved out from Kariakoo into a brand-new bungalow, and his elder sisters were by no means the snivelling sort. They came, two of them, and khus-khus-khus, whispers in the corridor with Miss Castelinho. Alnasir was reinstated and I was chucked out, after only two practices. 'You don't want to take part, do you?' she said. I looked at her in bewilderment. 'Do you want to take part?' she asked impatiently, as if talking to an idiot. 'Yes, yes, Miss!' Here goes Alnasir, I thought. But no. She kept quiet. Some time later Mr Ramji came in. 'Eh budhu, come here.' I went. Two cool fingers caught hold of my ear. He played with it, tenderly at first... how cool and delicious they felt, those fingers! Then he started twisting it, this way and that, and like a scrap from the *Daily Herald*, it caught fire, it felt burning hot, and oh, it hurt. It hurt like iodine on a wound, red chillies on the tongue, a kick in the groin. But now I was smart to their game, and I kept mum.

The next day a furious Kulsum came to school and almost slapped Mr Ramji on the face. 'Is he your son, you bastard? Don't you ever touch him again.' Mr Ramji stood red-faced in the compound, looked on by Miss Penny Mrs Gaunt and the servants. 'No Cutchi,' he feigned, and the servants pacified Kulsum.

Miss Castelinho (who had hidden herself during the confrontation) had a brilliant idea. She would use twelve fairies. When the performance was given and we sang 'May the Good Lord Bless and Keep You', holding our cardboards in front of us, tears were seen in Miss Penny Mrs Gaunt's eyes. And when we turned the white cardboards in our hands she read the words 'God Bless You!' across the stage, and she definitely looked away, she could not contain herself. I was that bright beaming exclamation mark on the stage, Miss Castelinho's brilliant afterthought.

She left us a gift. The 400th anniversary of the birth of William Shakespeare is drawing nearer, she said. I want to leave you a gift of a book… *Alice in Wonderland*. Because it was truly wonderland for me, this place… On her last day, it was recess, the car came to fetch her, again he kissed her. The car drove away slowly, followed by a crowd of running cheering waving shouting boys. Goodbye, Miss Penny! Goodbye, Mrs Gaunt! Goodbye, Miss Penny!… Mrs Gaunt!

It was December 1959. The school year was over and Miss Penny Mrs Gaunt was gone. In the evenings, TBC's request programme *Dial a Disc* was under way, collecting charity for the Christmas season. At Karimjee Hall, on the 15th, the Legislative Council sat for an important session. The public gallery was packed. Thousands waited patiently outside. Acacia Avenue was lined with people carrying green TANU cards. Taxis and private cars were bedecked with flowers and greenery. Movie cameras were in sight, the world was watching.

The speaker was A. Y. A. Karimjee, descendant of the great Karimjee family of traders. At some point the House adjourned and awaited the arrival of the Governor, Sir Richard Turnbull. The Governor was escorted in and read a long address from the throne. When he had finished there was applause from the members, which grew in strength, louder and louder, until at home our ancient Philips radio could not contain the thump-thump-thump of joy and emitted loud static. A shout of joy went up at Moonlight Restaurant, and a procession took off to meet the bigger one emerging from Karimjee Hall bearing Nyerere on shoulders. Thus Dar received the news of madaraka, self government.

'Godspeed,' said the Colonial Secretary Iain Macleod, wishing the country a happy journey.

Independence was painless. A man's colour is no sin in Tanganyika, said Nyerere. Those hooligans who go about making wild statements that the events of Congo would be repeated in Tanganyika should be severely reprimanded, scolded the *Herald*. Tanganyika is not Congo, where nuns were raped and hundreds murdered and shops looted.

A few weeks before the great day, PWD lorries appeared in our street at night and left behind wide, stocky pipes edgewise in the centre of the road. Soon large, colourful canopies went up from these pipes, colourful lights and banners appeared, and at night Kichwele Street looked bright and glorious, like a street from toyland, and those with cars drove all over town to compare the decorations and to speculate which public display would win the first prize.

There were some doubts and more serious speculations; Kakar the lecherous grocer in Mrs Daya's building stockpiled corned beef tins and rice and potatoes in his store, and some would ask the Ismailis what the Aga Khan had advised them to do, but the Ismailis were smiling, not saying, and simply joining in the celebration.

Independence was painless. Prince Philip came to give the country away, but in Kichwele we stayed home and followed the events in the newspapers and on the radio. And on independence day, at midnight, zero hour, while the decorated street below was empty of man or motor vehicle, sitting silent, neglected, like a bride not picked up on the fateful day: upstairs, sitting quietly around the ancient Philips oracle, we saw in our mind's eye the lights turn off at the National Stadium, the

Union Jack quietly come down and the lights turn on again to reveal the new green and black and gold national flag flying; we heard the thunderous applause in our sitting room, carried by radio waves, and again, we all swore, far away at the National Stadium, carried this time by the wind.

14 | Boyschool and Independence

When the new Shamsi Boys' Secondary School was built, it was so far from the nearest habitation that it was still a picnic spot. Hassan Uncle estimated it on his bicycle odometer to be five miles from our shop, and 'five miles' it remained, it being risky to question the stony expression that could elongate in an instant into a look of contempt. It took forty minutes of brisk walking on Viongozi and United Nations to get there. Touring expeditions of large, extended families took off from Downtown, Kariakoo and Upanga for the new school every Sunday afternoon before it officially opened. Each batch of pilgrims brought news about its wonders. The light-brown stucco and blue painted exterior, the neatly cut hedges, the garden alive with red bougainvillaea and hibiscus and khungu trees. Every classroom had a side of French windows facing a neatly cultivated patch of garden. There were individual desks and chairs with rubber shoes, instead of the barely movable bulky desk-benches of previous times. There were the cricket and football fields, the tennis and basketball courts. All that was lacking was a swimming pool. When Kulsum returned from her journey her varicose veins acted up and her legs had to be massaged. 'All around... jungle,' she sighed with pleasure as Sona's hands kneaded her calves and feet, 'we thought there might be lions around.' But the lions had left some years before, and when the school opened monkeys were occasionally caught in the trees.

The two-storey school building partly enclosed a square that was a rock garden and housed the bell. Every hour a servant in khaki, conscious of a hundred pairs of eyes pinning him from all directions, would walk over to it and ring it, twice for ordinary sessions and a long peal for recess and end of day...

The Boys' School. Boyschool, or BOSS. It was the pride of the community. Everything about it, its architecture and construction, its location away from Downtown, its expanded curriculum and emphasis on English, pointed to new vistas. Its motto: Labor Omnia Vincit. Its symbol: a blazing torch, Promethean fire. Its uniform: khaki and white. Before it moved into these premises, it produced barely literate shopkeepers, their highest achievement a failed Junior Cambridge. Now like a rocket launchpad it was on its way to meet the world... really meet the world, as witness Alu and Sona, or even Jogo in his own crooked way...

To belong to it brought privilege and status. It was to be one of the big boys, the next educated generation; it was to belong with Solanki, Kara, Goani, the test cricketers who played for Tanganyika, with the genius Kassam whose brilliance even the teachers feared, the actors Peera and Jaffer, the hero Ali who gave his life saving a drowning girl, as the plaque outside the front gate testified. In the December holidays prior to my admission there, Solanki had scored a century against Lindi Secondary School and led the school to victory in the annual Christopher Cup match. On the second day of school, crusty old Mrs Silver the acting headmistress held up the trophy in assembly, shook Solanki's hand, and amidst loud cheers declared the day a holiday. This is the way it should be, we thought, Jogo, Alu and I, grinning all the way home to surprised parents, this is Boyschool!

When we came, the headmaster was Mr Green, one of the new batch of teachers who came after independence. He replaced the legendary Mr Smart who had been there for more than a decade. Of the original group of English teachers only Mr Gregory remained. He stayed on in school, and when he retired, as Chinua Achebe and Wole Soyinka replaced Charles Dickens and John Buchan in the curriculum, he stayed on in Dar, and now he lies buried in the Anglican cemetery, which is only fitting for someone who taught Shakespeare to a whole generation of schoolboys there. The Indian teachers stayed on. They watched one generation go by and waited for the next. 'You, baboons!' said Mr Haji to Form IB one day. 'I have taught your fathers before you!' 'Did you also teach our grandfathers, sir?' asked Jogo in all innocence, and then pulled in his neck like a tortoise and waited in resignation for Mr Haji's wrath to land on him. Which it did, on his back, a brief pummelling of blows. Mr Haji was big and fat, stuttered, and had balls the size of coconuts. He came pouncing on you, stuttering oaths and invectives, a steamroller hissing and puffing. It was said by the senior boys that the momentum of those pendulous gonads was so great when he came rolling along that he had to apply brakes, which he did, and stopped suddenly with a jerk. The flywheel effect.

Mr Haji taught biology. He had his own museum, which housed a specimen of a human foetus, and on parents' day the fathers and mothers, uncles or sisters, filed by respectfully before it. Boyschool meant that we were done with cockroaches and butterflies, sunflowers and pollination. On the first day Mr Haji introduced the seven systems of the human body, from the lowly digestive to the lofty nervous. 'I know which one you want to do first, last and always,' he wagged his finger. 'For this you come to Boyschool? For *that* you have to wait until Form IV! What, "Aaaah!" Tell me. You groan! Do you know this, eh, do you know it...' And our mouths opened in amazement, Did he really do it, that gesture, he is really something, the lecher. He was a sly customer. He started with the digestive system.

They never reached the reproductive system. For that you had to consult the *Nurses' Book of Anatomy and Physiology*, which you borrowed, and there you saw it, in full glory, to the last pubic hair, the female genitalia, and you would look at it in the afternoon, upstairs, while the rest of them were downstairs in the shop, and you kept the book hidden, hoping that Mehroon or Begum would not discover it, until you discovered one day the books *they* kept hidden, books like *Introduction to Marriage*, and *How To Keep Him Happy*, which did not resort to the abstraction of drawings but gave you photographs, and you sweated and you swore to yourself that you would never do *that thing* again, for as Mr Azad had taught, you would never then be able to satisfy your wife...

There were two religion teachers, Mr Rahim and Mr Azad. Mr Rahim, portly Rahim Master who was approaching retirement, was of the old guard, his method exhortation and the whip, a veritable terror, particularly for those who had no sense of a melody. He expected you to know entire hymns by heart and to be able to recite a verse or two when called upon. He would start from the first desk on the first row: an arbitrary verse, and then, if you didn't know the whole hymn and thought you could predict your verse, by simply counting to your seat and learning it quickly: wrong! Rahim Master could read the heart of a cheater. 'Your mark E, and write the whole hymn fifty times.' A thump or two on the back, and 'Stand on your chair!' Rahim Master had a squad of Monitors, who went around each evening searching the lavatories of Empress and Empire and Avalon and Odeon Cinemas for truants from mosque, and reported them the following day. They could come into any class in session, be it that of Mr Siddiqui or Mr Gregory, read from their list and take away the trembling miscreants to receive their due punishment: usually a couple of strokes from Rahim Master's cane. This was of course at the height of his powers, which declined gradually after independence. Even then, it was he who dismissed the daily assembly after the headmaster had finished. 'School,' Rahim Master would say, not having lost an ounce of his former composure, 'School, 'shun. Dismiss.'

Of Mr Azad, what can one say... Younger than Rahim Master by a generation. He had been to London: 'A milkman leaves a bottle of milk at your doorstep. A newsboy leaves a newspaper. Two hours later, they are still there, untouched. How long do you think they would last here, eh, Jogo? It is not for nothing they ruled the world.' He gave us notes on *The True Faith*, a mystical treatise, with promises of explanations. At the end, we discover, we have copied the book word by word. Only his lecture on masturbation was original.

It is Rahim Master they remember, old dying Rahim Master: 'He taught us. At least he taught us. Name a hymn – I can recite it, even now...'

At the same time as Mr Green and the British teachers came a new breed of local boys now become teachers. Mr Datoo, who took our maths, was called 'Guy'. He was tall with crew-cut hair and had girlfriends among the new teachers at the Girls' School. Mr Datoo's teaching methods were a novelty. While Mr Kabir of the old guard remembered theorems by heart and expected you to do the same, Mr Datoo would demonstrate them. To teach Pythagoras' Theorem he took the whole class to the cricket field and proved it by measurement. In midyear he left for America. He returned several years later on vacation with his American wife, and was followed round town like the Pied Piper by many of his former pupils. He took them to the USIS library and showed them the university catalogues.

That year also Cheeky Bottoms left to study in England, never to return. Snivelling Alnasir also left for England. Some years later he called up Mr Datoo in Connecticut. Mr Datoo was amazed. 'Alnasir, do you have any idea how much this call will cost you?' he asked. 'Don't worry, sir,' came the sleepy reply. 'I have free access.' My former neighbour and classmate was a night clerk in a hotel in Earls Court. This was before he owned this and other hotels, of course...

We greeted Sekou Touré of Guinea, Tubman of Liberia, Olympio of Togo, and we wondered when the great Kwame Nkrumah would come. The Japanese trade ship *Sakura Maru* anchored at the harbour for several weeks and gave away much-prized advertisements; for many it was like a gift ship from a friendly people... BOAC advertised 'Good Night Nairobi, Good Morning London!' on the Comet 4, which one day Begum and Mehroon went to see with Alzira and from which they brought back plastic forks and knives, which were also much prized. Circus Brazil came. A motorcyclist from the Seychelles set up a Wall of Death in Mnazi Moja; people paid a shilling at the door, climbed the stairs to a circular balcony and watched the man ride his motorcycle round and round up and along the wall.

What is this thing called Independence? We woke up one morning, the green and black and gold flew instead of the red, white and blue... and we were one nation among many... A brotherhood of nations? No, said some. Think about it. See all those boundaries on the map? Soldiers on every one. Customs. Immigration. You need a passport simply to go to the toilet. (Hassan Uncle's words.) Only the Masai can travel freely these days. Soon they'll need a passport. And their cows will need a passport… (Aside:… meanwhile we can use them to smuggle goods and currency to Nairobi and abroad.)

Then there were of course the demagogues out to provoke reaction against the Asians. 'The Asians are not integrating enough!' thundered one. 'If you want to stay in Africa, you must learn to live with Africans… the days of your dukas are numbered!'

'Foul!' murmured the gathering of shopkeepers at Diamond Jubilee Hall. 'Didn't we only recently give a gift of four sewing machines to the women's movement?'

'They have their eyes on our daughters, mind you,' Hassan Uncle gravely muttered.

'This flag,' roared the commissioner, 'it has the colours of Africa! This black and green and yellow flag – what does the black signify, eh jamani?' He held up his arm and pinched his black skin for all to see. 'This. And the green is the beautiful land of Africa. Eh? And what is this yellow stripe in the middle? Eh?'

'The Indians! The Mhindis!' shouts an unknown voice.

Uproar. Laughter. Gleeful self-congratulation. And an angry commissioner. How to pacify a furious commissioner? 'E e TANU ya jenga nchi…' someone started. Everyone joined in, clapping hands, 'E e TANU ya jenga nchi…'

The commissioner was escorted to his car.

'Never invite him again. First he eats our food, then he lambasts us!'

Dear Sir. In this newly free and democratic country of ours there are certain rights and privileges due to its citizens, i.e. a respect for privacy and consideration for the majority. I would like to use this space in your esteemed newspaper to lodge a complaint about a disturbance that has been going around in my street at an ungodly hour when the respectable and working population of this country sleeps. I talk not of the anopheles mosquito, of which there are plenty in my street, nor of djinns, of which there may or may not be in the same. I draw attention to a certain person who goes about the streets at four in the morning making incomprehensible utterances to wake people up to go and pray. Now those who wish to go and pray at this hour may prefer to be shouted at from the street, but what, I pray, is the fault of the majority who wish not to be disturbed? I have proof that from the twenty buildings surrounding mine, only two people get up and follow this person to the mosque. This is a clear breach of democratic principles, and I beg the authorities to persuade the person concerned to cease his disturbance immediately. A.A. Raghavji.

A. A. Raghavji – Nuru Poni – who in his younger days had been one of the first to wake up and walk to mosque at four, as his nickname 'Nuru' attested, now preferred to sleep through the night, having been taken over – relatively speaking – by an agnostic phase not unrelated to the changes taking place in the country.

Every morning A.A. Raghavji's son, Alu Poni, waited for Sona and me outside the Moonlight Restaurant which blared Arab music and rattled with tea cups. The three of us would then begin the first part of our trek to Boys' School, along potholed, dusty Viongozi Street. It was cool, at seven in the morning, the sun still behind the white-washed mud houses on the right. There would be a steady trickle of business at the Arab corner stores.

Exactly halfway on our journey, just before Viongozi Street opened into sun-drenched Morogoro Road and joined former Cameron (now United Nations) Road, we stopped to pick up Jogo. Sitting at the front, in the store that was more a stall outside a mudhouse, sat Jogo's father, the subject of A. A. Raghavji's letter, his meagre goods within easy reach of him. He would be perched on his seat at the till, serving jiggers of kerosene to his African customers, or packets of tea and sugar or matches. Occasionally he would yawn loudly and sigh, 'Oh God, make me good!' He had a dirty, unshaven face and wore thick glasses that magnified his eyes. Ever since the letter appeared in the *Herald*, he had begun to be called 'The Disturbance'. What he shouted in the morning were not 'incomprehensible utterances', as A.A. Raghavji well knew. He began with Arabic verses in his old and croaky voice, horribly mispronouncing, and then, perhaps bored of saying words he did not understand, made up prayers and poetry first in Gujarati, and recently in Swahili. But A.A. Raghavji, as his son reported, could not sleep. He woke up and waited for the first utterances in the distance to begin, and thenceforth agonised as they approached, relentless until they reached a peak under his window and then receded. After which he could not go back to sleep. His letter's notoriety and its fame spread. It was said, especially by those who could not read English, that he had called old Jogo a machar, a mosquito, and a djinn. Neighbours refused to sign his petition, and he became short-tempered and testy.

'He is brushing his teeth, he'll be out in a moment,' Jogo's mother would announce when we asked for him in the morning, and shout, 'Abdul! Your friends are here!' Politely we would decline the offer of breakfast, and when the wait got too long, accepted a drink of water. Finally Jogo would emerge, grinning, swinging his school bag, his wet hair hastily combed, with gummy eyes. He was watched by his fat mother. He was solid, round and dirty. Except on Mondays, his shorts were never clean or pressed, his collars were always frayed, his shoes, when he wore them, dirty. He set the pace for the rest of our journey, telling bawdy jokes and inventing stories. He was our educator in sex. To learn from him was to hear dialogues among insects and fruits that had visited wonderful and hair-raising places in the anatomy, and had lived to tell the tale.

They were earth and ether, Jogo and Alu, but their fathers' quarrel had not rubbed off on them.

My friend Alu, I would have to coax him to come to films with me whenever I could wrestle a permission out of Kulsum… He was tall and frail. With puberty he became awkward and bespectacled, sweating from his palms and back. He carried a handkerchief in his hand when he wrote, which he also used to sniff with. When he shook hands, which he rarely did, he pocketed the drenched hankie and proffered a limp hand. In those days, with an Elvis hairstyle kept in place with a ready comb, his one dream was to be able to play the guitar and sing. From somewhere he obtained the specs for an electric guitar and had a piece of wood cut to shape by a carpenter. For a few weeks he bored us with talk of frets and bridges and keys as he waited for the equipment to arrive at the music shop. It never arrived, and he refused to consider another instrument. The wood with the bridge stuck on it lay near his bed while he waited, until gradually he gave up the project. An image of dead seriousness clung to him. A wraith. Awkward and gawking, giving off a faint odour of damp garlic, but obstinately persistent: a future professor, yes, but Elvis, no.

We were treated to our first and last tea at the house of our neighbour Uncle Goa. He brought the invitation shyly one day, a message from Madam.

'A birthday?' smiled Kulsum knowingly.

'No. Goodbye,' he smiled back from the doorway.

'The world has changed too rapidly for us,' he said when we were there that Sunday. 'We have decided to go to Lourenço Marques.'

'We cannot watch our servants turning around and throwing

insults at us.' Madam spoke as she stiffly brought the tea and accessories on a large tray, which she proceeded to unload on the centre table. She was a big woman, bigger than Uncle Goa, and a little exertion left her breathless. Kulsum watched with interest as she placed the faded beer mats on the quarter-circle serving stools and brought the cups one by one, aided by her son Brian. (Brian with the blue-green eyes, who was not allowed to play with us.)

'But we have nowhere to go,' said Kulsum. 'We were all born here.'

'Yes, yes,' Uncle Goa said hastily. 'For you it's different.'

Gentle Uncle Goa. Kulsum had called upon him only rarely, in emergencies, but then he served with devotion, single-mindedly. He had taken me to school on my first day, when there was no one else to do it. (And together we had bungled my last name.) On the day I went with Edward on our Maulidi excursion at Illala he had driven all over town for a few hours looking for me. He recalled the incident. 'Don't run off again and worry your mother!'

(Well, Uncle Goa, if only you could see me now... from wherever you are...)

'So,' said Madam. 'I am asking fifty shillings for all the kitchenware and one hundred and fifty for the Singer. The fridge I am selling to someone else.' Kulsum agreed. She had already made other arrangements with Uncle Goa.

... I sit in the shop, behind Kulsum, tinkering with Kulsum's 'zigzag', hidden from view by the raised cabinet cover, the bobbin case open in front of me. Kulsum sits on her high stool behind the counter, commanding the two doorways. At this languorous afternoon hour Uncle Goa comes in, in his best uniform, white shorts and shirt and stockings, and black shoes.

'Well, Mrs Junta,' he says awkwardly. 'I have come to say goodbye.' There is a pause, and they shake hands.

'Give my regards to Madam,' says Kulsum. 'And remember us sometimes.'

'Thank you.'

'And thank you for all the help you have given me.'

'Ah, it was nothing…' He takes two steps, stops and turns around hesitantly. 'Mrs Juma… I have developed a deep respect for you—'

'I am only a woman, but I do my best…'

'Something I find hard to say…'

'Thank you for what you've done.'

'I just wanted you to know.'

'I know.'

'Then… goodbye, Mrs Juma. Give my regards to your children.'

'Goodbye, Mr Menezes.'

'It's done!' I shout. 'The bobbin is fixed!'

To see your mother from a distance… Past forty, the body is thickening, bitter experience etched in those furrows on her forehead, visited by several illnesses that would never leave her, her medicine box getting more crowded every year with jostling pill bottles, the pills gradually eroding her grief and memory. Think of all those wooers, those men Hassan Uncle would bring during those initial years on some pretext. The first one was surely Mahmed Bhai, the book-keeper, into whose hairy ears we would poke thin long strands from the bathroom broom for fun. Why else would he stand this punishment… perhaps *we* drove him away. And the others, big and small, thin and fat, mostly it seemed from the interior, they would come, sit for some time, have tea and leave. She accepted no offers, memory was her husband. But she knew how fragile was the reputation of a widow, and she never went to town without either Sona or me with her… long walks to the Downtown wholesalers which we both hated, because there was no reward in them.

* * *

Sir Richard Turnbull, then Governor General, left; a torch was lit on the summit of Mount Kilimanjaro as promised, but its light not as glorious. The country was poor, we were told, and we have waved mother England goodbye. Per capita incomes were thrown about for comparison in political speeches, in the newspapers and finally in school. The enemies of the country were identified. Poverty, illiteracy and disease. Freedom from Hunger! Uhuru na kazi! Self-help schemes went under way.

Every Sunday a lorry would stop at Kichwele and Viongozi to pick up volunteers from our corner, and people who had never wielded a spade before, Nuru Poni, Ramzan Daya, Nurdin Samji, went happily to build schools and housing schemes wearing khanga shirts and singing "E e TANU ya jenga nchi!"

Those who had waited for Uhuru to throw riches at their feet were frustrated. Hassam Punja still owned his ten or more buildings, new bungalows were going up in Upanga, the new buildings going up on Msimbazi and Kichwele were mostly Indian... and Indian girls were still not forthcoming. The judges were Europeans, the managers of the big companies were Europeans, the headmasters in the schools were also Europeans. What had changed?

There will be those who remember the three kofias, who gained a brief notoriety at the time of Chief Abdalla's trial. The Swahili daily, *Ngurumo*, showed a picture of one of them, with his hand in a peanut vendor's basket. This was at the rally in support of the chief, outside the High Court. 'Is this what they think the kofia is for?' asked the caption. Who else but Jogo? He discovered the photograph himself (who else among us flipped the pages of *Ngurumo*?) and showed it around, even to the teachers.

The kofia episode began with a haircut, inspired by Ji Bai's revelations and the euphoria of Uhuru...

One afternoon I went to Madhu Bhai's shop and asked him to cut my hair short, to the scalp. A short koché-koché.

'What! A new hairstyle this? What new actor or actress dictates this fashion now? Elvis is going bald?'

'No, no, I just want it short.'

'Aré – when it grows back, you will look like a real kalidas. Already it is colour you have lack of!'

'Please cut it, now!'

'Have you asked Ba?'

'Yes. She sent me.'

'Acha. Could be a matter of religion. But you don't have lice, now? If so, first put kerosene and then come back!'

'No, no! I don't have any lice!'

Madhu Bhai began humming and selecting scissors while I watched myself front and back in the infinite images of the two facing mirrors.

Madhu Bhai was introduced to Kulsum by Hassan Uncle as a reasonable barber. He first cut my hair on the sidewalk outside my grandmother's shop in Msimbazi. Then he still went around on foot with his leather case and in 'barber's uniform' of white bush shirt over white trousers, and black cap. You could spot a barber a good half a mile off in his uniform, patiently trudging along or pushing a bicycle, and if you had rather not sit still for half an hour and experience a burning hairline afterwards, you disappeared. Barbers knew when the month was up for their charges and came to remind and set appointments. Then they came looking for you under the staircase or on the roof terrace or wherever it was you were seeking asylum. Madhu Bhai promised his old discounts when he opened his New Empire Hairdressing Saloon. Here we could read old issues of *Filmfare* and the *Illustrated London News*. And Madhu Bhai still entertained, with Gujarati bhajans and proverbs and his phenomenal double fart. 'Bosch!' he would exclaim in mild surprise at the first release, and then greet the second one with a satisfied 'Red Cross!'

'There,' he said, when he finished. 'Fresh as a hot chapati! It will soon grow back. Next time you come, my son Ashok will be here. I am leaving.'

'You are going? Where?'

'Bharat! Desh! The old country!'

'Do you own many buildings there, Madhu Bhai?'

'Lots. Plenty. But don't forget to look me up when you come there! My son will tell you where I am.'

The young Ashok, whom I had never seen before, never had any news from Madhu Bhai, except to say, 'He's well!' He was soon joined by a partner. It was Kulsum who said with a smile, much later, 'You know, eh Kala, that Ashok is as much Madhu Bhai's son as you are!'

Alu, Jogo and I started wearing kofias, which were taken from the unredeemed stock at A.A. Raghavji's pawn shop. Kulsum did not object too much, her father had worn a fez, and some old men from our community still wore them, and the neighbours said it's a good thing for the boys to integrate a little. But she looked at Begum and Mehroon and said, 'The next thing, you two will come home wearing buibuis!'

Mehroon and Begum had finished secondary school and were working as machine operators, one at TANESCO and the other at the main branch of Barclays Bank. Mehroon had acquired a string of admirers and now travelled in style. Every morning a young man picked her up in a Peugeot and in the evening another one dropped her in his Volkswagen. The curtains in Mrs Daya's apartment would start fluttering excitedly at these hours. She called the two men Ashak and Mohbat, lover and friend, although which was which she could never say with consistency. The Volkswagen owner, Alnoor, was the favoured contestant, and Mrs Daya already saw the day when Kulsum would go nowhere except in the 'Volksie'. 'Give us a ride now and then,' she would tell Kulsum, 'don't go waving at us like Queen Victoria!'

Alnoor was bandylegged and chatty, a former opening batsman of the Boys' School. He wore loose white shirts with sleeves partly rolled and two buttons open, revealing a hairy chest, very much the sportsman. He would leave the car and come in to greet Kulsum, putting back his comb as he entered, with, 'So how are you keeping, Auntie? Did you have your vitamins? The legs all right?' Mrs Daya, having spied him, would sometimes walk in with a pretext ('I have misplaced my needle') and start bantering with him. 'Well, cricketer, how many sixes did you hit on Sunday?' It was a switch to his motor. 'Aré, Auntie, this time a clean bowl! All stumps down. Solanki threw a fast bowl, I never even saw it coming! Clean bowl! I tell you Auntie – I'll have to shape up!' 'And this without even being married, you! Your back should be strong, yet!' Mrs Daya would say. 'But Auntie, it's not the back – that's still strong, God be praised – it's the eyes!' 'Ah, you're blinded! With what, now I wonder!' Her only regret was that her daughter was not old enough yet. 'Kulsum,' she said. 'If your Mehroon doesn't like him, tell her to hold on to him until my daughter is ready. But don't give me the spare tyre. You keep him!'

The spare tyre was Amin, with the Peugeot, well dressed and proper, with a crisp, narrow moustache. Every morning he waited patiently in his car for Mehroon to come down, reading the *Herald*. Mrs Daya reported on his movements. The day he first met her, he gravely shook her hand and immediately earned her lasting contempt.

The expert fundi, Omari, showed no intention of leaving, still accumulating in his mind the thousands due to him in arrears, and Kulsum still dreaded the day of reckoning. And when he started asking about the rent of the store, she knew the end was near. 'What business is it of yours?' she asked in annoyance, and he merely grinned. Idi, Pipa's former chauffeur, still came around occasionally, and one day his uniform was sewn on our machine. With this provocation the situation reached a head and Kulsum sent for Edward. 'Ask him how much he wants. I'll give him five hundred.' Half of what she had put away for this eventuality. Edward went away, and after work stayed behind. 'He says he wants the shop.' She said seven hundred, Omari said no. She said one thousand and no more, he said he would wait.

One afternoon when Alnoor came to drop Mehroon, Kulsum got in the car with him and they drove to the Labour Union offices, which were in a two-storey concrete structure that had sprung up in a block of African mud houses off Viongozi Street. With her she took all the long, black ledger books, the red tapes wearing off at the binding, containing the tailors' accounts for the ten years. Under each name, for every working day, the day's work, the amount earned. At each month-end, the accounts cleared, with a signature in Roman or Arabic, a blunt cross or an inked thumbprint, and the date. A combined lesson from husband and brother: don't trust anyone, a signature for everything. The Union officer looked at her books and told Kulsum: 'Mama, you don't owe them a cent. We told them to join up, not to work piecemeal, they laughed at us. Send him to us now.'

'I don't need your work from tomorrow,' Kulsum told Omari.

'I will want my rights.'

'I have been to the Union office. What you were paid is enough.'

'We shall see.'

He came back the next day and pleaded. 'Please, mama.' 'No,' she told him, 'my children are still in school, and we don't have enough.' 'Please,' he said, 'I would like to buy my own machine and work from home. Please help me. Your daughters work. You have enough.' 'They will soon be married, and I will have no-one then. The boys must finish school.' 'Please, mama.' He would not leave. She gave him three hundred shillings.

It was a triumph for Kulsum. 'And Idi, the one with the big head, the educated one with the newspaper: he just stood there, silent. You know what work he does there? He is a driver!'

A postcard came from Uncle Goa, not from Lourenço Marques but from London. It was addressed to Kulsum, and said, 'Our plans changed. Regards to the family, Mrs Daya, Parmar, Mama Roshan (Mattress), and others.' Kulsum beamed at the picture of Big Ben. It was the first postcard she had received in her life.

My cousin Yasmin, who had spent eight years with us before going to live with Bahdur Uncle, was admitted for a nursing course in London, and we all took her to the airport. She sat with Mehroon and Begum in Alnoor's Volksie and they cried all the way. I sat with Alnoor in front, both of us with the grave looks of those driving in a funeral procession. Occasionally we exchanged masculine looks of understanding. Kulsum and Sona came in Amin's Peugeot, and Bahdur Uncle drove his family in Fateh the Coalseller's Chama Chetu.

Yasmin had her hair set and wore everything new. She carried a sweater and had a BOAC bag slung around her shoulders, very much a picture of the seasoned traveller. We stood in a circle around her, making small talk as we waited for departure time. Other travellers, students, were similarly the centres of family attention, dispersed all over the big room. Hearts were heavy, the families eyed each other over the distances with curiosity, and acquaintances only nodded at each other. There were Europeans going back: with what feelings? They all converged on the bar, it seemed so easy for them. Finally Alnoor set the farewell process in motion.

'So,' he spoke jovially to Yasmin, 'think about us now and then. Don't forget us little people completely. When you return, don't walk around with your nose up in the air!'

Yasmin laughed. 'Do I look like that kind of girl?'

Gentle Yasmin, with the plain but very white face and the very tight ponytail, how much we loved her, who bathed us when we were young, and set the food on the table, and sheltered us from Begum's wrath. It was only Mehroon, her sister, she fought with…

'She will be a London-returned,' Bahdur Uncle said, his voice breaking and lower lip trembling. Aunt Dolu was being brave.

'Take care,' said Kulsum, stepping forward, and pressed a folded currency note into Yasmin's hand.

Then the tears started to roll. First Mehroon, then Begum, then Shamim. Bahdur Uncle wiped his eyes. Kulsum and Aunt Dolu both looked stern, not a tear between them. The rest of us looked appropriately serious and went to shake hands. Yasmin laughed at this formality. Then Alnoor became frantic. 'Photos! Photos!' he came forward with his camera. 'We've not taken photos.' Photographs were then taken. Yasmin with Bahdur Uncle and Dolu Auntie, her official guardians. Yasmin with Mehroon and Begum: the original trio who had worn pinafores and ribbons and frolicked in Nairobi's City Park, and then taken care of five children in Kichwele. Yasmin with the whole family. Yasmin and Kulsum. More goodbyes and tears, and finally a ruffled Alnoor: 'Goodbye, eh,' with a small choke. 'All the best': Amin, shaking hands. Yasmin brought out her ticket and joined the queue towards Customs, the family waved till she disappeared and some more in case she still saw us, until Alnoor said: 'Okay. She's gone. Goodbye, Dar, good morning, London. She'll be there in the morning.'

15 | *Red Skies and Western Eyes*

In January 1963, the president announced the introduction of a one-party system of government, with special powers. Beware! at once warned the *Herald* in its editorial: beware of the fate that befell Sylvanus Olympio of Togo! Sylvanus Olympio, once regaled in Dar from Kichwele to Independence Avenue as the nation's first official visitor, had been assassinated only a few days before. But our Julius stood firm. The translator of *Julius Caesar* would yet outlive his opponents… and in the following months and years these fled to London from where they dispatched feeble pamphlets to be dropped on Dar from feeble two-seaters, or they cooled their heels in icy Sumbawanga on the border with Zambia until they had learnt their lessons. As Mr Gregory was heard to remark, the Brutuses to our Julius were not made of the same stuff. Our republic was only one year old.

November 23, 1963. Dates become important: you realise now why they invented the calendar – to turn events into dates, the artefacts, the knicknacks of yesterday that you store away in your gunny somewhere… November 23, 1963 – who, having seen it, can forget it? At 2 am the president summoned his ministers to the State House and issued a statement. 'He trod faithfully in the footsteps of Lincoln, with him he is now linked in death…' That morning Nuru Poni's shop did not open, Alu Poni on the way to school told us why. 'KENNEDY SHOT DEAD!' Nairobi's tabloid the *Daily Reporter* screamed, 'Africa loses a champion.' We all loved Kennedy – who didn't love Kennedy? – we knew the names of his children and we simply adored his lovely wife... There were many photos of Kennedy in Dar, the biggest perhaps in the display window at the USIS library, with the caption, 'Ask not what your country can do for you...' and others in many of the dukas with our own president... and a coloured photo, small but prominent, in Nuru Poni's shop, taken from the cover of *Newsweek* and framed, because among his many heroes, handsome Kennedy was the pawnbroker's favourite. So we knew our Kennedy, and the news of his death hit us hard. The following Saturday all government offices, all businesses and industries remained closed in a national day of mourning, a special High Mass was broadcast to the nation, all flags except the Chinese flew at half mast.

(How naive we were... even as nations we looked for heroes...only to learn later that in politics, history, there are no heroes. Were we conned, Shehrbanoo, by the greatest con artists of all, the packagers of Madison Avenue...)

In December of that year, Kenya and Zanzibar became independent. And, as naively, we looked forward to that long-forecast event, a federation – the United States of East Africa – and even betted on which of the three leaders would head it.

In January of the new year a local Sheikh formed the United Democratic Party and called on the president to announce new elections or resign in favour of Chief Abdalla. 'Let us remove Cliff and Elvis from our walls and put on them Chief Abdalla instead.' To which a British columnist in the *Herald*, quipped, 'Does the pious Sheikh have on his wall a picture of Elvis the Pelvis instead of the Kaaba? What next?' The chief, who had been previously tried for accepting bribery, whose acquittal

Alu, Jogo and I had celebrated outside the courthouse (where Jogo had been caught by the *Ngurumo*'s camera with his hand in a peanut basket), later rejoined the party. The British journalist, who had also a few months before derided a member of Parliament for enquiring about mermaids in the Indian Ocean, and who later called visiting Stokely Carmichael 'Stocky Carbuncle', was sent packing and was last heard of from Australia. The Sheikh became a prominent astrologer, with a column in the *Daily Reporter*.

At 7 am on 12 January those who were in the habit of listening to Zanzibar Radio in the morning, the patrons of Moonlight Restaurant, for example, and therefore – without choice because the radio blared right through their walls – neighbours like Nuru Poni, heard the announcement: 'I am Field Marshal Okello! Wake up, you imperialists, there is no longer an imperialist government on this island. This is now the government of the Freedom Fighters.'

So we woke up to the presence of John Okello and his periodic pronouncements on the radio. Radio Zanzibar of course became popular, everybody wanted to listen to this field marshal. Arab-owned Moonlight Restaurant stayed closed for a week, while blood flowed in Zanzibar in the revenge of those whose ancestors had arrived in chains and filled the coffers of the merchants and the princes with their heartbreaks and sorrows.

I recall a Zanzibar girl... Wait, don't tell me about her, Shehru – not yet – tell me about the revolution, tell me what she said... 'Even before we heard the announcement on the radio we heard the sounds of shots... not that we hadn't heard them before, there had been several riots... bloody riots before, how could we not have seen this?... but this time we knew it was the real thing, the big one. It wasn't surprising really, it was in the air, ask anyone, they smelt the revolution twelve hours before it came, those who had been out on walks or drives, or observed strange behaviour in their servants... the servants had been sworn to secrecy, you see. Mother immediately started stuffing jewellery into her bosom and father looked at me and trembled... I did not realise why just then... girls bear a responsibility to their fathers which boys just do not have... but we all know that, don't we, except not in those terrible terms... There was a big Arab door in the front of our store, father closed this and kept the others open (this was so the looters would not be angered), and we went to the back section of the house. It faced a street that always voted ASP, so we were always safe from the backside. We stayed there for five days... there was a tap, but no bathroom, no toilet. On two of the nights mother and I tiptoed to the front section, and in great hurry cooked rice and eggs and potatoes. The looters came, certainly, several times. They combed the whole street on the frontside. They broke down the big front door, fired several shots and took everything in the shop. They stopped outside the door to the back section each time, a flimsy door behind which we were hiding and praying, trembling and weeping, father had me and my sisters under the bed... for we had all heard the screaming and crying from the Arab quarters. Why those revolutionaries – or looters, whoever they were – why they did not break open that door, God alone knows... perhaps they thought it was the back entrance to a house on the ASP street, but so what, they could have checked... and why the smell of cooking in the kitchen didn't rouse their suspicions... We knew that the Government was taken. There was an opening under the roof in one of the walls, from which standing on a chair, you could see outside... we could see people we knew walking to the mosque, both their arms up, their fingers making the "V" signal for victory, to show which side they were on (the winning side, of course), sometimes goaded on by the militia, but we were too frightened to come out then… and Mahmoud saw, on the first day, Jena Bai following her two boys to the mosque, at a trot, and as they neared the gate, a militia man ordered them to stop – Jena Bai, you see, was a poor widow on welfare – Jena Bai stopped but the two boys, sixteen and seventeen, began to run and the man shot them down… The Sultan and his family had escaped, and the Prime Minister was in jail. We huddled in the inside room and waited. From time to time we heard screams in the distance and we knew something horrible was happening. Men and women screaming, our eyes would widen, our hearts would thump, and we simply awaited our fate. Father would get up to look outside from the hole. Mahmoud, usually brave and rowdy, now whimpered beside mother as she sat on a stool. The rest of us sat on beds or the floor. Finally our time came, after five days, at about eight in the morning the door came crashing down and two Africans stood on top of it, guns in their hands, and held their noses in disgust. It was not the food smell that betrayed us. But nothing happened, we were walked to the mosque like the rest… when we entered it the first person we saw was Jena Bai weeping, weeping inconsolably, but we heard no-one else from the community had been killed… only two people, the only two people Jena Bai had in this world. We had been given up for dead.'

A few days later they started arriving by boat, refugees from Zanzibar, with horror stories about the revolution. The idyllic isle of cloves jolted into bloody reality. Thirteen thousand dead, mostly Arabs. They brought nothing with them, these Asian refugees, except what escaped the notice of the soldiers of the revolution, still green behind the ears and unused to searching: the moist interiors of bhajias studded with diamonds, kebabs clutching earrings in their spicy insides, gold bangles sunk in greasy curries. Family heirlooms, lives' earnings and investments, most of which was plundered, a little crossed the ocean in ignominy. Thus we got little Miss Ahuja with a figure that threatened to break hearts and burst pants, and we got Shirazi, nicknamed Unguja, among the numerous refugees in school. We heard of rape and pillage, the revenge on the Arabs. They fought back, shot themselves or set themselves and their families on fire in their homes. 'We had duriani in the morning, biriani for lunch, and Arabiani at night,' the hapless Zanzibari refugees would boast. 'Never in any situation rape women whose husbands have been killed or detained,' John Okello had warned his freedom fighters, 'no soldier may rape or even touch a virgin girl.' All else was halal meat. But our Unguja had not had any Arabiani yet, that we knew. He drifted in our school from class to class with his compatriots, trying to learn as much as he could while the authorities were deciding what to do with the Unguja refugees. Finally, after a year, they settled down, but not without occasional calls to the headmaster's office to confirm their status.

The week following the Zanzibar revolution, Dar was rife with rumours: that the army would take over, the British would return, Cubans had been sighted in Zanzibar. A few grocers had quietly delivered gunnies of rice, onions and potatoes to the mosques. Mukhis were in consultation. In Zanzibar it was at the big mosque that the Shamsis had sought refuge during the revolution. Beware! the *Herald* had warned: now rumblings were heard from all corners of the town. Who would be the Brutus to our Julius? Kambona, some whispered.

On 19 January the field marshal from Zanzibar came to Dar es Salaam in a Government plane and was welcomed at the airport by Kambona.

At six-thirty the next day, Monday morning, Hassan Uncle pounded on our door.

'Aré wake up all of you, are you still sleeping?' he shouted irritably. A little before, the alarm had rung on our made-in-England Classic silver clock as it had reliably done for many years now. Begum, the first to get up, had set a pan of water and tea leaves to boil and entered the toilet. When Hassan Uncle's fist struck on our door, Sona and I were awake too and brushing our teeth side by side at the washbasin, yellowish black liquid from the coal powder paste dribbling down to our elbows from our mouths. At that moment Begum used the flush. Mehroon, entering the scene, after some hesitation lifted the crossbar from the door and unlocked it. Kulsum walked in from the sitting room, and the door opened to let in the cool fresh air from outside and the irate Hassan Uncle. We surrounded him.

'My bicycle,' he said frantically, pointing to the door, 'I've left it downstairs. I must hurry.'

'Why, brother, is Zera sick?' asked Kulsum calmly. My mother's hair was dishevelled, she was barefoot and didn't have her glasses on and looked rather like a witch.

'Zera?' Hassan Uncle shouted with impatience bordering on customary scorn. 'Aré, don't you know, it has started. Lock the door, don't let the servant in. Lock the door, you hear, and don't let the servant in. Don't... let... anyone... in.'

'What has started?' Kulsum asked, a little stupidly.

'Riots. Like Zanzibar. Do you understand? *Like Zanzibar.* That's all I am saying. My bicycle is downstairs, I must run. Lock the door!'

'But wait! Don't we have to go to the mosque?'

'When the time comes. Meanwhile lock the door and pray. Don't look out of the windows. Keep the kids away from the windows!'

As soon as the crossbar was put in place behind him, we rushed to the windows. The street below was strangely, ominously quiet. Those portents of life in the city, the green and beige DMT buses, were not hurtling their way on the street this morning. There were no pedestrians and only a few cars and bicycles. The street remained quiet even when the cool of the morning was invaded by the heat, and the streets and buildings acquired a glare when viewed from the windows. At about nine Kakar the lecherous grocer – so called because he made eyes at Begum, Mehroon and Yasmin – casually cycled up towards his store in Mrs Daya's building. He put a key to a padlock and hesitated. Then he looked around and behind, removed the key and walked slowly to the street and looked up at the windows. He saw faces peering down at him through window bars. Then Mrs Daya yelled down at him, 'Eh Kakar Bhai! Go home! Haven't you heard? Hasn't the news reached your area? It has started!' Kakar did not hesitate. He ran for his bicycle and swiftly pedalled away the way he had come.

Kulsum prayed. She sat on her bed saying tasbih, Begum was slumped on the sofa reading, Mehroon peeped outside between the curtains. Sona and I stood on our knees on the windowsill, our foreheads pressed against the metal bars. It was too quiet outside in the street for Kulsum's occasional but frantic warnings to sound convincing. From the building across, Mrs Daya and her daughter peeped between their curtains. Inside, the radio was quiet. It had been quiet all morning. In the street below a few Africans had wandered out from the side streets and occasionally looked up. We looked back fearlessly; we did not know yet what was going on in the minds of our mother and sisters.

Presently an army lorry filled with soldiers came speeding down the road, followed by another. The soldiers raised their guns and the pedestrians who had gathered to see cheered them. Sona and I were yanked down by Mehroon and Begum and we peered between the curtains, now terribly frightened. A Land Rover came speeding by. In all minds Hassan Uncle's ominous words: Like Zanzibar, like Zanzibar, like Zanzibar... *what* like Zanzibar, for God's sake? We had heard it, we had read it, even imagined it... it is one thing to enjoy vicarious excitement through the radio, or the articles in the Nairobi tabloids... but Zanzibar repeated here... the horrors knew no bounds. The Tanganyika Rifles, formerly the King's African Rifles whom we had watched smartly parading on the Queen's birthday when Sir Edward Twining was Governor, now transformed into a force of terror.

Congo and Zanzibar. Nuns raped. Duriani, biriyani, Arabiani: I chuckled even as I trembled. What to do if they attacked my sister or mother? There is a trick your mind plays on such occasions, a kind, parently trick – she does not *picture* the word *attack* when she pictures Kulsum and Begum and Mehroon... or when she pictures *attack* she does not see your mother and sister and cousin. Arabs had died defending their women. I would do the same. But then, what? Would they have the sense to commit suicide? If only Kulsum had not turned in my father's pistol. How handy it would have been! But there were Ali Chacha's Kashmiri daggers, their blades rusting and neglected no doubt, but better than nothing.

... a mob rushing up the stairs, led by Omari the tailor, eyes red with rage, seething with revenge. 'Now I will have the shop. The Fancy Store, now all mine!' His head kept getting bigger and bigger as he ascended, bent forward, arms swinging in front of him until at the head of the stairs there was nothing but the head, big, black, puffed up, eyes red and gleaming... it passed through me, this head, and behind it was Edward bin Hadith my friend, standing behind the crowd, apologetic, in his bush shirt and trousers and sandals, his hands down but held together in front of him, as at a prayer. All around me was the sound of the black mob, screaming, yelling, heckling, ascending the stairs in waves, coming at me and going through me... Then they were breaking down the doors, there was the pounding of bodies and rocks on wood, and I stood behind with my father's pistol in my hand, arm raised and ready to shoot, I watched the doors slowly giving way, the thick wooden crossbar not breaking but the brackets that held it giving way and falling backwards, limply, the stopper coming off with a snap, the rattling doors gradually yielding at the hinges and the locks… the locks gave way first, the doors swung open, partly falling away at the top hinges, and the crowd went pouring in…

There were shouts from the streets, the sounds of bare feet thumping on the Tarmac, and inside Kulsum was standing in the middle of the room looking intently towards the window as if from that distance she could see down from it. In one hand the tasbih was speeding through her fingers. Sona and I, peering through the curtains, saw the looting of shops in progress.

Men and women – no children – running up from the sidestreets empty-handed, running back arms full of goods – ready-made shirts and singlets, shoes, harmonicas, radios – joyfully recalling the name of the bountiful Japanese ship (from which they had got nothing): '*Sakura Maru! Sakura Maru!*' What they could not carry they dropped on the road, and they returned, not to pick things up but to go to the source of the fountain itself, a newly broken-into store. Some undressed right in the shops, and ran home half buttoned up carrying armfuls. A man speeding along with a brand new, shiny red Italian-made accordion stopped in his tracks, wavered for a moment, then threw down his heavy burden with disdain on the sidewalk, picked up some shirts and singlets instead and sped on. The accordion I had lusted after, every time I passed the show window of African Bazaar, was picked up by the next runner. In our area it was the large, expensive shops with lighted display windows that enticed passersby and were looted. Iron grilles had not come in then and the glass came out easily with the throw of a rock and a charge.

It was a jubilee that lasted a few hours. None of the runners on the street had thought of climbing the stairs to the flats above. Early in the afternoon the army mutiny, as it had been, was over and soldiers descended on the sidestreets, searching African houses, looking for looters and loot. Faces were slapped, dwellings ransacked, dirty-looking hastily worn clothes were torn off to reveal milk-white singlets, crisp new shirts, starched drill shorts.

In the evening the radio promised that quiet reigned in the country once more. Kambona came over the radio. 'This is your Minister of Foreign Affairs,' he said. 'The Tanganyika Rifles and the police are still loyal to the Government.' But where was Julius? No mention was made of the President. An uneasy, quiet night followed.

The next morning the sun poured in as usual, through the east window, over the half curtains. Buses thundered on Kichwele, and government workers rode, pedalled and walked to their offices. At seven the servant knocked on the door and was uneasily let in. There was no bread and he was sent to Moonlight Restaurant to fetch maandazi. The radio in the restaurant crooned in Arabic to an absent Mustafa. Yet people watched from their windows for signs of disturbances. Soon the lecher Kakar arrived on his bicycle and opened shop. The bread cart followed, pulled by one man and pushed by another, and was converged upon on all four sides by boys and servants. Then Parmar cycled in to his tailoring shop, and all the other stores in the area opened too.

A crowd stood in a semicircle outside African Bazaar, watching. The fashionable store, the size of four normal shops, was empty of goods and the owners were clearing the debris of glass, cardboard and straw. A European-looking mannequin torso lay on its side with its neck twisted. It was the store with the most enticements to offer on our block, calling the passerby to come and watch and desire.

That day we stayed away from school. It was a day buzzing with gossip, news and tall tales. Servants hailed each other to tell stories of how the day had passed in Magomeni, Buguruni, Temeke. The Bohoras had put up a most spirited performance in their block of shops downtown, the men defending the area with clubs and sticks, shouting 'Ao, eh mader chod, ao,' come you bastards, to the mob that was beginning to form. An Arab refugee from Zanzibar shot down two policemen and two civilians and his whole family except a boy were massacred. Mrs Daya came down from her apartment with the juiciest story. A certain reputable Downtown family had ventured out in the afternoon in their car and been stopped and searched by the soldiers. Mrs Daya told the story in a pious, injured tone, as if to imply: The thought of it! 'Any guns here?' the soldiers had asked, feeling the breasts of the women. Mrs Daya and Kulsum held their sides, giggling silently.

On her way back Mrs Daya repeated the story to Roshan Mattress, who guffawed. 'Serve them right! Didn't the askaris feel anywhere else?' she sniffed and set about her work, efficient as always, pulling kapok and sisal mattresses into place, leaving a path to walk between them. Later that day Inspector Kumar came. The President's whereabouts were still a mystery. There were of course many opinions, announced with great certainty and authority by government types and rebuffed with equal certainty and greater joy and merriment, not to mention contempt, by the fundis and servants at Kichwele and Viongozi. Eti, our Julius, Mwalimu himself, hidden in an old State House German-built tunnel, sitting there like an old woman – like his mother! – shivering under a blanket! Perish the thought! What foolhardiness. Swam half-way to Zanzibar and picked up by a British manuari? Possible, but not likely. It was all a plan, a great plan, Mwalimu wanted to see who were his real supporters and who would betray him. Edward put a twist to this theory. He had seen someone, someone who looked very much like our Julius but dressed up like a pauper, and Mwalimu must therefore be going around in disguise assessing the attitudes of the populace. Like Haroun al Rashid in Baghdad. When Kumar was on his way Edward boldly walked up to his car and enquired about the President. But the Inspector just smiled and smacked his cane lightly against his thigh. Keep guessing!

The story that the ladies of a certain house had had their breasts squeezed spread among the women, causing irrepressible fits of giggles. They wiped their eyes, held their sides, and put their hands to their heaving chests, while at the same time managing to look shameful. Early in the afternoon Zera Auntie, on her way to the medical store, came by to enquire after everybody's continuing good health and parted with: 'Did you hear? What a shame—' She showed her tongue to indicate the shame. Kulsum looked blank. 'You know, so-and-so,' said Zera Auntie. 'They have their clothing store in the town—' 'Yes, yes, I heard,' Kulsum said, 'the soldiers stopped them.' 'Yes, and they felt them here—' said my aunt squeezing her own breast and sticking out her tongue to indicate the shame of it all. 'Hai hai.'

At four in the afternoon the rumour spread that a disturbance had begun in an African sector. Kakar closed shop and sped away on his bicycle. Parmar lingered awhile before following suit. The rest of the shops then closed and the servants were sent away. Nothing happened. Mehroon and Begum returned from work some time later and once more we heard the story of the squeezed breasts.

That night we crowded round the radio in silence and heard Baba wa Taifa, father of the nation, our Julius assuring us that the trouble was over, exhorting us to remain calm, to act grownup, not to spread rumours and panic.

The following day he toured the city, visiting the looted stores, reassuring traders, exchanging banter. Followed by a barefooted crowd, surrounded by policemen, himself in sandals, bush shirt, loose trousers and swinging his stick, he came to African Bazaar. He did the entire block on foot and paused outside the mattress shop to inquire in jest, 'Mama, did they leave your mattresses?' At that point Roshan Mattress did something she had never done before, she revealed a side to her character that would dominate her activities from now on. Taking a deep breath, one arm to her waist, she raised the other to her mouth and let out a tremendous vigegele – beh-beh-beh-beh... and the African women in khanga and buibui and frocks all followed suit in a jubilant ululation. A loud, female expression of happiness rang out, the crowd tightened in excitement behind the policemen, and the President strode on, beaming.

Three days later, early in the morning, eight helicopters and a handful of Royal Marines succeeded in disarming and capturing the First Battalion of the Tanganyika Rifles, which had mutinied. The former KAR had proved a joke at the hands of its mentors. 'What did I tell you, sister?' said an elated Hassan Uncle dismounting from his bicycle. 'The British have not left us!'

The mutineers were sent to their villages, or awaited trial in prison; tall Nigerian soldiers in green fatigues arrived to keep peace and paraded the streets with their black and white flag (they can't eat ugali, said a rumour); the Royal Marines departed, feeling rather sad about leaving the stray dogs they had adopted; and Awadh, young Awadh...

Staring at the camera, a bandage round his head, in new shorts and shirt, clinging to a black Red Cross nurse, clutching a toy car with one hand... sole survivor of the Arab family blasted away during the mutiny. That look at the camera... and the heads crowded round the newspaper photo in front of Kulsum at the counter... to stare and stare and drink in that look that no one could describe but stirred you to your depths... so that you will never forget young Awadh... What will your future be, young Awadh... will you grow up angry and vengeful like those Arabs on the island and do something brash and useless and terrible with your life – as did your father who took shots at the mutinous soldiers? Above all, how will you *forget*, Awadh?

The patriotic fires kindled in Roshan's ample bosom took her towards organising. She became a leader in the Women's Movement. When the women of the capital congregated at Party Headquarters for a march in support of the President, Roshan took Mrs Daya with her. They marched, they ran, they sang, with nuns, teachers, prostitutes, shopkeepers and politicians; they lost their shoes and they got blisters. The next day Mrs Daya was bedridden with sores and pains and vowed never again to go with Roshan. But Roshan was her same old self, pushing and pulling piles of mattresses, bouncy, jocular and sour at once.

The men and boys of Kichwele and Viongozi marched behind Nuru Poni, Alu's father. We wore kitenge and khanga shirts, we took with us the President's picture, we carried banners proclaiming our loyalty and we sang and danced. And when we reached State House, Nuru Poni made a speech in Swahili that did us proud.

'Chou-en-Lai! Nyerere! Chou-en-Lai! Nyerere! Chou-en-Lai! Nyerere!' We chanted, lined up in school uniforms on Uhuru – formerly Kichwele – Street, this time outside Kakar's, opposite our own Fancy Store, to welcome the Chinese premier. Altogether now, boys and girls, holding Chinese flags, Chou-en-Lai! Nyerere! You and I! Nyerere! You and I! Nyerere!

Beware this Chinese, some said. Remember when Nehru went to China? 'Hind-Chin bhai bhai.' We are brothers. And when Chou-en-Lai showed Nehru a map of the world, lo! *there* was a little bit of India written over by Chinese characters!

Africa is ripe for revolution, said Mr Chou-en-Lai, denouncing the imperialist running dogs.

> The four seas are seething
> clouds lowering and waters raging
> the five continents are rocked by
> storm and thunders!

The Kenya tabloids fretted, American ambassadors fretted. Keep the cold war out of Africa! Why Tanganyika turns East. The red and the blacks. And so on. The tabloids said that Nyerere had even started wearing Chinese-style shirts – but Kulsum could have told them that her father sold precisely the same style of shirts, made of Marikani, not Teteron, in Membeni. Two Americans were expelled. Documents, involving the Western countries, were discovered, with plans to overthrow the country. Cheap forgeries, said the Americans. A book, purportedly printed in Albania, calling for the overthrow of the three big East African countries, was distributed. Cheap forgeries, said the Chinese.

East African federation had become more and more remote, the pictures of the three Presidents with the caption 'Who will be the boss?' irrelevant, and a few months before Nyerere had announced a federation with Zanzibar. We must do what we can. 'How Nyerere solved his Cuban crisis', wrote an American reporter. A competition was announced for naming the new union, and sixteen people pocketed 12.50 shillings for suggesting the new name. Tanzania.

At a Diwali celebration, the Prime Minister of Zanzibar said that Asians must intermarry with Africans. To which Hassan Uncle retorted in the privacy of our store, 'What did I tell you?' And a letter in the *Herald*, written by a Mr White, unfortunate name under the circumstances, said, 'Do wildebeest and zebra mate? Do giraffes mate with elephants, or lions with leopards?' and concluded with a quotation from Kipling. To this, our tireless letter-writer A.A. Raghavji, a.k.a. Nuru Poni, replied: 'When wildebeest and zebra, or any of the other pairs mentioned by Mr White mate, nothing happens, but when people of two races combine, beautiful children are born with the virtues of both races and the prejudices of neither, one must hope.' Eh, did you hear this, Kulsum Bai, he is willing to give away his daughters, so far has he gone.

Was Mzee Pipa, counting out the minutes, hours and days with his little ten-cent packets of spice in Pipa Store, as evil as he was made out to be? That must remain a mystery, as the secret of Alzira and her family, which they would take with them to Goa...

It was all planned, said those who considered themselves knowledgeable – among whom one must count Mrs Daya and Roshan (who was biased, of course), and Nuru Poni's wife, and Edward bin Hadith. It all started with the arrival of Mzee Pipa's niece Nasim from Mafia. A drab girl, this Nasim, with big legs, wearing beltless, loose dresses with *large* flower patterns or checks, and ribbons of an awful colour. She stayed not with the Pipas (who could stay with Mrs Pipa?) but as a boarder a little way off on Kichwele. Not educated beyond Standard Eight, she wanted to be a typist. But her English was Standard Eight, and a Mafia Standard Eight at that.

With Africanisation under way in the civil service, Roshan's husband Nurdin Samji followed the path taken by many Asians and retired, with the prospect of a pension from the British government. Nurdin Samji was not a very welcome helper at his wife's mattress shop, where the handsome Inspector Kumar could pop in any time. He had to be sent on many errands, and he also had the sense to keep away for extended periods. He would visit the neighbouring shops and stay for chats, shopkeepers entertained him and he them. He did not go to visit his brothers Downtown for an obvious reason: Do something, you milksop, they would tell him. He was often sighted on the sidewalks, a good-natured man who did not know what to do with himself or his time.

'Why don't you teach English to my niece?' Mzee Pipa asked him one day. 'And you could also teach her how a European office is run. Give her some of your know-how, your experience.'

Why not, thought Nurdin. A good deed, to be stored away somewhere in the karma account books of the gods.

'I will pay you,' added Mzee Pipa.

'We'll see,' said Nurdin.

He drove the Mafia lass to typing class and back and gave tuitions at Mzee Pipa's, upstairs. And lo! (al hamdulillah! said Edward) Beauty and the Beast in reverse. A bad taste in dress can be changed; the hairstyle of a hag, even that can be changed! Big legs, but look, they are proportionate with the body – and look what you've got: a young beauty not plumper than Roshan. Nurdin walked proudly beside her, and he started to give her driving lessons. Many a romance in Dar has reached its proper maturity in driving lessons. It is not from anyone that a girl will consent to take driving lessons. Driving lessons are taken in lonely places, early in the morning or on Sundays.

Kichwele and Viongozi held its breath: no-one had any sympathy for Roshan Mattress, but how would the she-devil, the tigress, respond?

'Hmph,' said Roshan Mattress. 'Big deal. I know precisely what that lalu is capable of: a little holding hands, driving around, talking under street lights, but nothing else, he doesn't have it in him: then the girl will find a boy, a proper marad who can satisfy her, and my Nurdin will come running back to his big Roshan.'

Inspector Kumar still visited.

But Roshan miscalculated. On two counts. Inspector Kumar's post was also Africanised. That was, after all, part of the demands of the mutineers and many of the politicians now wringing hands in exile in London. Inspector Kumar, a foreign national, had expected this fate. He had a family. One afternoon he came for the last time. He parked his car outside, with his wife and two children inside, went into the mattress shop, and emerged after two minutes. Roshan Mattress followed. Hands on her haunches, she watched his car drive away and stood watching long after it had disappeared.

Nurdin and Nasim's romance blossomed, and it went public. Within a few weeks Roshan Mattress closed her shop and went to live in Upanga. Nurdin married his second wife and lived in Downtown, and Roshan, still his first wife, concentrated on the Women's Movement. Occasionally she would lecture the Asian women, explaining the Government's policy in some detail. From time to time, after major processions, her photograph would appear in the papers.

16 | *These Dreams, Ready Made and Gone*

The most memorable part of the wedding is the farewell and last ceremony. You remember it when she comes back after the first fight, and you remember it when she bears the first child. You remember it when he begins to beat her, and you remember it when her hips grow bigger, her face looks plainer, her manner preoccupied. And the parting that once was a mere formality is a deep schism, permanent and hopelessly cruel. And you realise, one day, why there were tears then even though it rained flowers; why every step of the happy way was paved with good-luck portents and disguised prayers.

On the afternoon following the official wedding, the registration and blessings by the mukhi, the afternoon after the reception and the first night spent at the Sea View, the couple are escorted by the bridesmaid and the best man to Kichwele and Viongozi, where they slowly make their way up to the roof terrace of Habib Mansion, laid with mats. Mehroon enters like a goddess, a blushing queen looking elevated and larger than life – in her wedding white, a dress made by Alzira of the most expensive brocade available in town (the groom paying), in high-heeled shoes and with her long hair set in a style known as the birdnest. As they enter the doorway they step with a little excessive vigour, just in case, on auspicious clay saucers, the camera clicking away, and walk over to the sofa which is the centre piece of the terrace. After lunch, the groom's youngest sister appears and takes hold of Mehroon's dress and doesn't let go until she is paid a sum approved by her family. Sona then hides the groom's shoes and doesn't return them until he is paid a sum approved by his family, in other words, Begum. Patience is wearing thin by now, the bridesmaid and the best man get up, and Mrs Daya takes the cue and shakes Mehroon's hand and gives her a big hug, sobbing. Then Mehroon's friends appear to wish her goodbye, and the other neighbours, Alzira, Roshan, even Mrs Pipa. Finally comes the turn of the family, beginning with Ji Bai, who's won her way in but just. And then Sona and I go to shake Mehroon's hand, shyly, because we've never shaken hands with her before, this cousin-sister who has bathed us and spanked us and taken us to school. Then weeping Begum comes and gives Mehroon a big hug, followed by Kulsum. Tough Kulsum, without a tear in her eye, shakes Mehroon's hand, slips some money in her hand... at this point she is supposed to tell Mehroon not to return except with her husband, she is no longer a daughter but a wife with a home of her own, but then she breaks down. Mrs Daya pulls her back, the bride and groom leave, the bride throwing rice behind her, to the left and right, her abandoned rights in the home of her parents, and without looking back she descends the three flights of stairs to be greeted by a bevy of chattering, excited African girls murmuring, admiringly as young girls do on such occasions, 'Mhindi ame owawa,' the Asian girl has wedded, and passes through them to the waiting car whose trunk is now filled with her belongings, the doors slam shut and the car drives over two small coconuts for more good luck and takes the bride away.

A tearful, distraught Kulsum looking beseechingly at the departing car, as at a hearse...

Mehroon played it safe, and married not the cricketer Alnoor, but the serious, the prosaic, Amin with the Peugeot, whose family owned business in Tanga, to where the car was soon speeding after the farewell. The cricketer would be in Kinondoni or at the Gymkhana with his friends every Sunday, he was still a child and would have to be tamed. But Amin was all ready, waiting to marry, join the family business and start a family. Mehroon was nineteen.

'To spend so much on them, to give them so much, to expect so much from them, and then to give away to these men and their families this dream, ready made,' Kulsum would say. 'But why did you agree to the wedding, then?' Sona and I would ask in exasperation. To which she would give a look that said: Better this than the curse of an unmarried daughter. 'Don't worry, Mummy,' Begum had told her, 'I have no intention of getting married as yet.' Until, that is, Sona wanted to hear good things about himself, and begged Begum to visit the Parents' Day at the Boys' School.

Sona remembers. A whim, a chance thought. No one had ever been to enquire about him at any Parents' Day. Everybody else's parents did... well, everybody who counted. Adil Mawji's father never missed one, neither did Zahur Meghji's parents. At every Parents' Day, to which Sona himself went to demonstrate some experiment, show some scientific wizardry to the awestruck parents – colours changing in a test tube, sparks flying from a point – the teachers would throw meaningful, questioning looks at him. Who are his parents, from whence this golden genius, why doesn't someone claim him? This time Begum did. She toured all the labs and saw all our teachers.

On her way from Mr Haji's museum, where she duly saw the famous foetus in bottled solution, she heard a strain of piano music. There was a big piano in the assembly hall, across from the museum, which was used mostly by the expatriate European teachers. Begum saw Mr Harris playing and walked over and stood behind him, watching over his shoulder.

Mr Harris was the physics teacher. Bearded, serious, solid, one of the new group that had arrived from Britain with Mr Green. Only recently had he begun to show signs of having a life and opinions outside of physics. The whites in Rhodesia had given themselves independence, Ian Smith was the hateword all over black Africa, and Tanzania had broken off relations with Britain. The Union Jack flying outside the British High Commission on Independence Avenue had been burnt by university students. Every day dozens of lorries, with owners from all over East Africa, rushed oil supplies from Dar to Lusaka (now a household word), bringing back copper, risking lives and property over the treacherous Hell Run on the road from Morogoro to Iringa (where Ji Bai's husband Gulam had met his death many years before with four other missionaries). Among these lorries that raced to Lusaka and back in four days were two Leylands, with Somali drivers and local turn boys, belonging to my brother-in-law Amin, which could be seen sometimes undergoing repairs at Kichwele and Viongozi. Kulsum declined putting her savings into the venture and later regretted that, because Amin added a Fiat to his small fleet, this being the prestigious make of lorry. Mr Harris, at last showing signs of life and opinions outside of physics, asked the class, 'How would you solve the Rhodesian crisis?' To which we replied, to a man, 'Fight!' Mr Harris shook his head and said, 'Do you really believe violence and bloodshed would solve it?'

Thus, Mr Harris, who was playing the piano in the hall as Begum stood behind him to watch.

Begum, if she had been a daughter in a rich family, would have learnt to play the piano... she would have driven a car and she would have been to London, and like the London-returneds, learnt to speak – English, Swahili or Cutchi – with that uppity accent they put on... With all due respect to Alzira, her clothes would have been mostly imported... and her hair... her hair would have been short. She would wear pants and tweed skirts and she would tie a bright-coloured scarf at the neck... She would know the piano and she would know how to waltz and tango and limbo and twist... Her children, to whom she would teach the piano, would be pretty if girls and handsome if boys and go to an exclusive school like the International School, and she would talk to them in English.

'Any requests?' asked Mr Harris, and smiled.

'Petit Fleur,' she said.

'That's for trumpet—' he said, 'but—' and tried a few notes.

'Theme from a Summer Place,' she said, and he obliged with a few more notes.

'Please Don't Treat Me Like a Child,' she said, and he looked up startled.

'What?'

'By Helen Shapiro, you know—'

He didn't, because he had run away from it, and other things like it, but he played her something else.

It was said sometimes, all in good fun, that you kept an elaichi, a cardomom, in your mouth to kill the breath of cigarette. Oh, they added, you smoked because you drank... you know, the company and so on. And drinking obviously was a prerequisite for gambling and whoring. So it all began with an elaichi in the mouth. When a girl got married her family wanted to know two things about the boy (besides how much money he made): Is he from the community, the comm, and Does he keep elaichi in the mouth. With a white man, there was double jeopardy, plus the added penalty that he ate pork. You could do worse, but not by much, by marrying an African or a Sikh Punjabi.

How did she manage it, this liaison? The school was out of consideration as a rendezvous, both Sona and I were there every day. And he would be spotted in Kichwele from a mile off. But on Saturdays Begum came home late, at three o'clock, because the girls at the office, she said, went out on a little lunch. It must have been then. A two-hour date every week for a few months, at the restaurant in Sea View Hotel perhaps.

One evening Begum broke the news to mother. 'Sona and Kala's teacher wants to marry me.' 'Who is he?' 'He is a European.' 'Over my dead body. Do you want to murder me? Take a knife, go on, take a knife, take these scissors, I'll give you my soul!' There followed a scene such as we had not witnessed for several years. But Begum had prepared for just this eventuality.

The next day Begum did not return from work. Her friend Shamim Jadavji brought home a note, addressed to me:

'I have gone to London with Mr Harris, your physics teacher. There we'll get married. Forgive me, please, both Sona and Kala, I did not intend to get married so soon, but I could not have kept my affair with Peter secret for long. The rest I cannot explain… your time will come. Look after Mummy. When enough time has passed perhaps she will find it in her to forgive me too. Love and kisses.'

She had taken away a small suitcase, with a few clothes. A few other things were missing; some books, photographs, her old doll.

A week later Kulsum gave away the store. Edward and another fundi took home orders, which when completed she delivered to a few stores downtown. There were three of us now, all in a daze, in the flat upstairs at Habib Mansion, and sometimes when she was especially depressed and brooding, Sona and I would find time from our schoolwork to play with her the card game two-three-five, a variation of whist for three desperate and lonely people. Whenever she heard the drumbeat at nine o'clock announcing the news, she would look up involuntarily, at the Philips on the glass cabinet, catching herself doing it, fighting something deep inside her.

Part Three

Amina

17 | Big Black Trunk

I think of you, Amina. I remember you on the front page of the *Herald*, a small African figure among large athletic Americans in Afros, tiny fist raised in protest outside a public building. 'Students occupy university building', read the caption. How proud we were then, our own Amina raising hell in New York. 'Free Amina!' we said exultantly, closing our own fists, but ours was a call not to free Amina but in praise of a free Amina...

We would see them sometimes, Alu Poni, Sona and I, as we trekked to school on Viongozi Street. Three girls would appear across the street from us, in complete uniforms, green and white skirt-blouse, black shoes and white socks. One Arab and two Coast Africans, all with short little pigtails, walking self-consciously in close formation, giggling and talking, keeping eyes averted from lecherous bystanders. Before the three of us reached Jogo's block, these three had disappeared into a sidestreet, a short cut to the girls' school.

How many times must I have seen her, for how many years I cannot recall. She was part of my scenery as I was part of hers, one of the many people on the road, walking or cycling to work, sitting outside a house on the step or on a stone bench. At some point I stopped taking notice when I saw them, but

I recognised her instantly when I saw her again, fully grown, a student servicewoman, witnessing my ritual humiliation as I reported for duty at Camp Uhuru.

The National Service grew up on the ashes of the King's African Rifles, in the wake of Tanganyika's 'day of shame', when the navy of the former rulers had to be called in to disarm the mutinous guardians of the country, which it did in a trice. The National Service was set up, with the aid of the Israelis, to provide military training, political awareness and literacy for motivated youth with a right head on their shoulders, from whose ranks the Tanganyika People's Defence Forces were to be recruited. Young men volunteered in the hundreds. So far, so good.

When the Government announced compulsory national service for high school and university leavers, the students were up in arms. After having gone through the territorial high school entrance exams, the Cambridge School Certificate Exams, the Cambridge Higher School Certificate Exams, O levels and A levels, Alternative N and Alternative T syllabuses, having taken three exams every year for fourteen years, all to be successful in life, and now to be subjected to the ignominy of tilling the fields and chanting slogans and marching for six months, and after that to go to work in uniform and give sixty per cent of your salary to the government for eighteen months! The students marched in protest. 'Colonialism was better!' they chanted. 'Student power!' Dar was humming with excitement. Student power! The crème de la crème standing up to Mwalimu himself! First it had been the army in revolt. Now it was the students – not so easy to extricate from this one – who would he call for assistance this time? Expatriate teachers nodded wisely to themselves: this was something they all knew at least a little about. This was something governments in the West all dreaded – student mobilisation. The President invited the protesters to come and meet him at State House. In the grounds outside, seated with his ministers, patiently he heard them speak and saw them wave their fists in the air. Then he spoke. Colonialism is better, you say? Go home. Yes, go home, the lot of you, to your towns and villages. The University is not for you. The University was closed, the unions banned, including our Boyschool's own parliamentary-style COPS, the Council of Pupils.

When the President said go home, he was meaning business. The students, in the State House grounds, saw themselves surrounded by the army. The new army. Every student there had his name taken, every student, boy or girl, was escorted to their residence at the University where they meekly packed their belongings and left for their hometown to report to the local authorities.

To say that colonialism was better! Eti. They had no sympathisers in the streets, these boys and girls who went to school and university free of charge and were given pocket money and travel expenses on top of that!

Every year Asian students, after completing school or university, joined their African counterparts to go and build the nation at camp, to learn to defend its borders. Every year at Camp Ruvu, each Sunday Indian mothers would arrive with servants bearing sufuriyas and tins, laden with curries and mithais and chevdo to last their daughters until the following Sunday, and leave the camp gates tearfully with their empty vessels, as if returning from the very gates of Hades. 'Your girls are treated well,' said a minister to a meeting of concerned women, but who would listen? It was all right if you gave them ugali and beans day in, day out; but when they had to bite rocks when they chewed rice, when they got bones the size of their heads to gnaw, when maggots floated in the stews... it was all too much, said the mothers.

It was because of these concerns, expressed a little too loudly, that the Asian boys and girls were not selected for the most out-of-the-way places. But if you have a name like Salim Juma Huseni...

When I turned the front page of the *Herald* to find out which camp I had been selected for, and who was coming with me, I found my name not at nearby Ruvu, or at Makutopora near Dodoma or Mafinga near Iringa or at Oljoro near Arusha. It was a new camp called 'Uhuru' some distance north from Bukoba, near the town of Kaboya on Lake Victoria: in other words, the furthest possible place, along with Tamim, Umbulla, Mbogo, Raphael, but no Manji, Samji, Bhimji, Kanji – no other Asian.

'A mistake!'

'Definitely a mistake!'

'I tell you, you will not survive! People die of malaria there!'

'What if something happens to you out there in the jungle?'

'Do something, yar!'

'Baboo!'

This last was whispered by someone in Kulsum's ear. Baboo was then one of the richest men in Dar. He drove a Mercedes and lived in Salamat Villa, a luxurious home in Upanga that made the nearby embassies look like hostels, with an exquisite garden full of pink, yellow and red roses, bougainvillaea, hibiscus, champeli, jasmines and immaculate hedges, all tended by a resident gardener. Baboo was known for his charity. So was his father, who at his deathbed had had his life extended by ten years by a holy man, so it was widely rumoured. This much-publicised private event earned the old man his nickname of Baboo ben Adhem. The ten years had expired recently.

Like a little boy I accompanied Kulsum to Baboo's scrap

and hardware store Downtown, where he sat, humble and softspoken, in his blue Kaunda suit.

'I have never been parted from him,' said Kulsum emotionally. 'I have brought him up without a father, I've given my all to him, and I don't want anything to happen to him.' Just the right touch. If Baboo had the power to change my fate, he couldn't refuse.

'None of my friends is going to this camp,' I added for good measure.

Baboo looked at me sceptically, but picked up the phone. Such is the power of wealth, I thought. He spoke straight to the Police Commissioner.

'Baboo here. Jambo, Commissioner, how are you? Al hamdu lillah, I don't have a problem. But I have a boy here, perhaps you can help. Do you know anyone in National Service?... He's from your tribe? Good. I'll send the boy over.'

It is my day to see the great, I thought. How easy it was... And how fortunate that the Baboos and the Punjas and the Premjis were there to serve you, to ease life through its difficult passages. Kulsum went on her errands, I went to Police Headquarters. Once I notified the desk who was expecting me, I was escorted straight to the personage.

How humble are the great, I thought. First Baboo, now him. The Commissioner was a short thick man also in a Kaunda suit, sweating profusely behind a desk loaded with papers and large ring binders, pencils, pens and an ink bottle... An old upright fan whirred from a stand in a corner. No uniform and cap, no belt or gun, not even a moustache!

'Yes? What can I do for you?'

'Mr Baboo sent me.'

'Then what can I do for you?'

'It is about National Service. I have been sent far – Camp Uhuru, near Kaboya... Lake Victoria. You see, recently I had an infection of the knee. The doctor said it was tuberculosis of the knee… the whole knee was swollen, I couldn't walk… I have to come for checkup…'

The Commissioner looked at me as if he had something bitter in his mouth but had to pretend it was not there. But his voice was kind when he spoke. 'Here,' he said, writing me a chit. 'Do you know where National Service headquarters are? Ask for Lieutenant Colonel Henry.'

Lieutenant Colonel Henry was in dark green army fatigues and a brown feathered hat of the type officers of the King's African Rifles used to wear at the marchpast at Government House on Queen's Birthday. He was looking out of the window at the garden being watered, and I could have been watching a film, so striking, so out-of-the-world he looked. His uniform was impeccable, gleaming with starchy stiffness, his trouser legs jutted out in two knife-edged creases and were stuffed in at the spotless boots. The man was almost white, slim and not very tall, with sharp grey eyes.

'Yes?' he said, going to his desk.

I knew the game was up. 'Police Commissioner Shabani has given this,' I almost stammered and extended the note. Halfway through my account about my sick knee, he got up and I stopped. 'Go,' he said curtly, pointing to the door. I took a step back. Then he blew his top. 'Do you think we are running a kitchen? Don't you think we have doctors here? Who told you to come here? Out!'

The Lieutenant Colonel's last question was repeated to me by Alu Poni that afternoon. 'Fool! You should have gone to Bhatia. He arranges such things. Baboo—' he gave me a look of contempt that could have come straight from the face of Hassan Uncle.

'His children don't do National Service!' I protested, defending my choice.

'They go to Bhatia.'

* * *

I see this somewhat silly episode (an example of shirking civic responsibility – but let's not judge it out of context: the chain of influence from Baboo to Commissioner to Lieutenant Colonel was real: and neither the kindly Baboo nor the phlegmatic Commissioner did after all decline assistance) – I see this comedy now as an attempt to foil the workings of fate: how else to explain, what else to call, the irrevocable relentless chain of events that unfolded... how else to recall the overwhelming logic of what actually happened, compare it with the flighty fancifulness of what might have been. Somewhere in the government bureaucracy a moving finger wrote, the *Herald*'s presses rolled in assent, and nothing could change the destiny that was sealed.

You were told (by those, and there were many, who claimed to be in the know) before embarking on your journey to camp to take with you a large, iron trunk. In it to put away some of life's exigencies that could come in handy: a suit and some decent clothes for the times when you would go to town, canned food, such as corned beef and beans, not to forget chevdo and gathia and ladoos... and, oh yes, toilet paper: a must – what they gave you was more like sandpaper. You were told to lock the contents inside this trunk with a heavy-duty steel padlock. And it should be so heavy, this trunk, it should not be easy to walk away with.

I took the big, black trunk that lay under Kulsum's bed all these years, my father Juma's trunk constructed by some long-forgotten Bohra tinsmith in Mombasa at the turn of the century, that had travelled with him from Kibwezi to Nairobi and later carried his bride Kulsum's belongings from Mombasa... then loaned to Ali Chacha for his home-leave to India on the SS *Amra*, for which service my father received the three Kashmiri daggers. Under Kulsum's bed it contained all sorts of knickknacks: a corset we would sometimes open without saying a word, a brassiere pad, soft and spongy we would put our cheeks and nose to, a compact, a moth-eaten velvet clutch purse, a Taj Mahal with its columns broken, the sword, a piece of tarpaulin, a khaki cap probably a police officer's, not unlike the one Inspector Kumar had worn. All these were hastily poured into a suitcase and room made for my safari inland.

To go to Camp Uhuru you first took the crawling Central Railway Line to Mwanza. Peace Corps teachers would joke that the train was so slow you could step off it and go out for a stroll, and when you had finished you had to wait for the train to catch up. You saw the blackest of black nights, cooler than the nights of Dar, fought mosquitoes, and looked out of the windows at those sparse dots of light in the jungle, sparser than the stars in the sky, and you wondered what they were doing, these people in their small huts in the jungle with their kerosene lamps… who they were, what they did, what they thought… and when the morning came, the sweetest and clearest of mornings with its yet tender warmth and an ever so slight caress of a breeze, you saw them squatting, chewing on their mswakis, wondering who you were and where you were going… You reach Mwanza and are sent to the bus station, where you wait all night for the next bus to Kaboya. All day the next day, the bus groans and whines and breaks down, is pushed by the passengers, and starts again as it climbs up protesting towards Kaboya.

In forty-eight hours I saw the vegetation change from the coastal coconut palms and sisal to the grassland and shrubbery of the plains and into the thick, tropical forest at the lake. I saw Lake Victoria, vast, tranquil and mysterious… for in the background lurked the Nile and Sudan and Cairo. History reflected from that shimmering vastness: what matter if the mind cautioned you to take that history, its white man's romance, with a grain of salt?... the mind has many sides that do not talk to each other... meanwhile how can I help thinking of Speke and Burton, Livingstone and Stanley, catching the excitement and missing my breath at seeing Lake Victoria for the first time and seeing in my mind's eye the River Nile pouring out from it in a great gush and flowing all the way to the land of the pyramids and pharaohs and Cairo the northernmost tip of Africa... In pitch darkness, after two breakdowns, the bus stopped on the road at the top of a hill. Passengers were woken up by commotion at the door and the sounds of feet on the roof. A few young men speaking the high school lingo of Swahili mixed with English were getting off. The word 'camp' was mentioned incessantly and I looked around nervously.

'Do you have a lot of luggage?' asked my neighbour, an African padre.

'Yes. Iron. It's on the roof.'

'Better wait till we get into town. You can come back in the morning.'

Camp Uhuru was a good three miles from the road. One of the boys outside produced a torch and they disappeared into the jungle, their torchlight flitting to and fro like a firefly. The bus engine, reeking of gasoline, roared and spluttered into life, an existence that violated the purity and mystery of the forest all the way to Kaboya and left behind a trail of exhaust.

The bus stop was outside a local hotel. The padre waited for my trunk to be lowered from the roof and took me to the desk. He asked for separate rooms, and as we parted outside our doors, told me, 'Lock your door. A National Service vehicle comes to pick up provisions every morning at the market. They'll take you to camp.'

* * *

How to explain the numbness, the loneliness, the total paralysis of memory, the glazing over of reality, at finding myself in the interior of Africa not knowing a soul, not knowing what to expect... as I sat on the springy bed with clean if stale-smelling linen, the locked door in front of me, the only furniture a locally made chair and dresser, on the wall a black-and-white calendar from the local cooperative with a photograph of men lugging sacks... at such moments you wonder if someone is watching you all the while, from a hole somewhere perhaps, and if that someone came in and cut your throat in the night whether you would ever be found by those who cared...

... Strange black men chasing me through a thick, palpable darkness, carrying raised flaming torches and uttering strange oaths... I ran through thick bushes, stumbled over protruding roots and fallen stems, slipped on fallen wet leaves and bark, brushed against thorny branches that cut the skin and drew blood in thin streams... All the while the sounds drew closer, from all directions, the strange oaths, incessant drumming, branches crackling, feet thudding. Tall trees stood silently on either side, like hooded men, menacingly watching my progress into the jungle. I was on a beaten path, and this path was like a tunnel cut into the forest, and at the end of it was a light, the red flickering light of flaming torches against a pitch-black background, and the sounds of strange oaths, of drumming, of branches crackling, feet thumping the ground. As I hurtled towards it, it felt warm, this red flickering light of many torches, and it began to turn yellow and feel hot, and was blinding me as it streaked in through the window in radiant sunbeams, roasting me where I lay perspiring...

Downstairs the town was awake, the market bustling, the bus stop busy...

'I bring you a guest,' said the driver of the vehicle to the sentry at the guard house. From behind the open Land Rover, among sacks of rice, maize flour and red beans, I surveyed the scenery around me. We had driven up a red dirt road through the forest, crossed a stream and climbed up the side of a shallow valley. On the other side some huts were visible. The camp, on this side, consisted of a few large khaki tents and some whitewashed buildings.

My iron trunk was in front of me, painted black, my name prominent in white letters, secured with a heavy padlock.

The sentry, a thin bony-faced Mangati youth, came to take a peek at me and grinned. Here was a man from the interior. I looked back at a set of wild-looking front teeth, the deep forehead, a scar at the side of the head. He was deep, properly black: what we call mweusi. I grinned back.

He let out a shriek, almost doubling up in a show of anger and hurt.

'Shuka-shuka-shuka – get out! Who do you think you are? Are you a minister? Do you think you are an ambassador, a balozi? The Queen of England...'

Calmly and sure of myself I pushed my trunk behind me, jumped down and dragged it after me. Then I placed it on a shoulder, supported by one hand, the other at my side, as if to say: 'All ready for service! Uhuru na kazi!'

The Land Rover drove off kicking up a trail of dust and gravel, leaving me to my fate.

The sentry looked at me with bloodshot eyes. His khaki stood up with starch and his boots shone. But his face somehow gave the impression of having just woken up.

'I,' he pointed to his chest, coming close, 'am an

NSP: National Service Police – understand? Repeat after me: National Service Police.'

'National Service Police.'

'If you misbehave, you are brought to me for punishment. Now, did you understand?'

I stood dumbfounded.

'Say yes, you!' He screamed, stamping a foot.

'Yes.'

'"Yes, Afande" you head-full-of-water!'

'Yes, Afande!'

'Now. When you come here, your books and your learning you leave outside at the gate.' Stiffly and with ceremony he walked up to the gate and stooped to beat a post with his stick. 'Here. Mother and father and uncles and aunts you leave here. Brothers you leave here. Sisters—' He paused to reflect on the lewd thought. 'What do you have in the trunk? Dal? Chevdo? Biriyani?'

The trunk now stood stiffly near me like a companion.

'No. No, Afande!'

'Pick it up and run. Come on, run. Run-run-run.'

'With the trunk?' I cried out in disbelief.

'Bagalas maguy! You talk too much. Put the trunk on your head. Now run.'

Up and down the hill I ran like an unstable donkey, a pregnant camel, my eyes on my feet lest I tripped or stumbled, the trunk bearing down on me, and unknown to me a spectacle for the rest of the camp. Twice it came down, this big black trunk, came crashing down at my feet, each time I picked it up, put it on my head, then on my shoulders and then back when my skull threatened to open up under the weight. And at my side the berserk NSP, goading me with 'Reft-light, reft-light, heet-ha, heet-ha,' beating the ground at my feet with his stick, letting out an agonised shriek every time I took a wrong turn, as if I had seriously wounded his feelings. Oh how I cursed you Nathoo and Bandali and Alu Poni, you who had advised me to take the trunk when all I needed was a small rucksack!

Finally, as I was later told, one of the regular afandes showed mercy on me and sent word to the NSP to stop my ordeal. I was brought to a halt before Afande Ali, who then instructed someone to lend me his mess tin. It was there that I saw her again, Amina, under a tree with other fresh recruits from the schools.

'If there is a hell on earth,' somewhat emotionally I wrote to Alu Poni that night under the light of a kerosene lamp, 'this is it.'

A few weeks later, with new insight gained, with the help of a metaphor: 'We Indians have barged into Africa with our big black trunk, and every time it comes in our way. Do we need it? I should have come with a small bag, a rucksack. Instead I came with ladoos, jelebis, chevdo. Toilet paper. A woollen suit. And I carried them on my head like a fool.'

To which Alu Poni, Mr Swahili himself, the superpatriot, replied: 'What happened to your hell on earth? You are getting brainwashed, my friend. We should be allowed our ladoos and jelebis. What's wrong with them? If you were made to look like a fool, don't blame yourself... Go to town on Sundays. Just walk into any Asian store and tell them you're from the National Service. They'll feed you.'

Thus began a parting of ways.

The songs of the National Service. When those months became a faded memory, when the names of favourite afandes were forgotten... when the names of the guns had slipped the mind... and a quarter-mile jog left them once more helpless... the songs remained, clear, every nuance in place, all improvisations at instant recall... on picnics, on Sunday afternoon family gatherings, there would be someone who would recall the song to the kinate. Kinate? Kinanguruma, it roars! Kinate kinanguruma! Ho-ye ho-ye, kinate kinanguruma! Tunakwenda! Kinate kinanguruma! Kula wali… Kinate kinanguruma! We go to eat rice in our mess tins, and the kinate roars. We put Blue Band margarine on our breads… the kinate roars! oh how it roars! Even when political or economic pressures had driven these former recruits across the seas, the kinate never ceased to roar. In a living room or kitchen in London or New York, in an office in Mysore or Karachi those songs were hummed. An ode to the President or the Land Rover, or even those inane lines taught by some cynical British or Israeli officer to his trainee afandes: How many days in a week? All together now: Seven days, seven days, seven days!

Early in the morning we trotted to the main road wishing death on the enemies. Chaka-mchaka? Chinja! Kill! The Portuguese? Chinja! Salazar? Chinja! The South Africans? Chinja! And Ian Smith? Chinja! And Verwoerd? Chinja! And Kambona? Chinja! The straws? Cut! The pipes, all? Cut! As the Mwalimu had taught, the capitalists had long straws with which they sucked. And the bigger capitalists, the man in the street added, used pipes. Africa is ripe for revolution, Chou-en-Lai had said, and the National Service was in the forefront. Who is building our nation, eh mama? Not the Americans, mama, no, not the Americans!

A quarter-mile down the valley from where the Mangati kept watch at the gate, the tiny Umoja River gurgled through on its way to Lake Victoria. Here after work we washed in its icy clutches and waited around on its banks like lizards on stones, while our clothes dried. From upstream came the tantalising sounds of the girls doing the same. But the Umoja had a bend where we dipped our bodies and you had to wade a good distance upstream among stones and through a curtain of brambles and branches to catch sight of the frolicking nymphs. Further downstream the villagers from across the river washed. At the narrowest the river was a few stepping stones wide. To go to town you had to cross it, they said. An Arab called Bakari ran a transportation four miles further up from Denge, the village across. You had to find Bakari, they said.

Denge was eight huts, three on either side of the path and two flung away in the jungle, each with a plot of garden, a goat or two and some children. Corn, banana and pineapple grew in profusion. We'll take you to Bakari, said the children, and they ran in front of and behind me. Occasionally they disappeared behind a hut or a large bush and watched my progress, peering out and laughing. We're taking you to Bakari, they assured me. The road was deserted save for a couple of women on their way back from the store with kerosene, and a steady female chatter in school Swahili that stayed unembodied and behind me all the way, making wisecracks about the Asian David Livingstone.

We came to a largish village. Some of the houses were layered with cement. A large tree stood almost in our way in the centre of the village, giving shade to a large area. Here my little band of escorts turned left and stopped at a whitewashed house. A Coca Cola sign hanging out from the door said, 'Prop. Abu Bakar Muhammed'. The door was closed, on it the ubiquitous Raleigh ad, man fleeing lion on the bike, and Stanley Matthews dribbling for Sloan's liniment. A blue Volkswagen van was parked outside.

Covered in sweat and dust, I banged impatiently on the door. A black woman answered.

'Is Bakari there, mama? I want to go to town.'

She went inside, leaving the door ajar. To my right, at a little window, came sounds of girls chatting excitedly, and I saw that I was being watched, the subject of amused curiosity. Meanwhile the three girls from the camp caught up and stood behind me, leaning against the van, all in pretty, light frocks and looking as fresh as ever. The one in the middle was Amina.

Bakari came to the door, from a very private moment, it seemed, in a white T-shirt and a green loincloth.

'Jambo, Bwana Bakari,' I said.

'Jambo, jambo. Yes? You come from the camp, do you?'

'Yes. I want to go to town. Can you take me?'

'I am closed today. Come tomorrow.'

'What now? Do you think they'll let us out tomorrow? Eti, this man thinks we are on holiday here!'

'Come on, take us to town, Bwana Bakari. And this Indian hasn't seen his fellows in two weeks. Have pity on him!'

A lewd grin came upon the Arab's face. His hand brushed lightly across his crotch. 'You girls want to make some money while you're here?'

'Shut up, Arab, let's go.'

Abu Bakar Muhammed actually did not run a regular bus service but used the van to transport goods and took an occasional passenger. With me he made an exception. The Africans and this Arab, seeing this sole, lost Indian in their midst, felt obligated to put him in touch with his kind. He looked at me as if he had no choice: 'Let's go.'

'And we,' said the girls. 'We're coming too.'

'Please let me screw you,' begged Bakari, making his lewd gesture again, and all the way to Kaboya he tried to convince them of the benefits they would obtain by satisfying this, his one wish.

He dropped us at the market and promised to be back at six.

I looked around me at downtown Kaboya and wondered in which direction to start walking. There was a smell of ripe pineapples and bananas, lake fish were on display, a bus was being loaded.

'Hey, Indian,' she called out after me, and all three came

up. 'Be sure you're here at six. We don't want to go with that Arab alone.'

We were Indian, Arab, African. What were names for? They meant nothing to us, part of privacies we did not let each other into, had no desire to intrude into…

'All right.'

The town of Kaboya was built around the market. Streets went around it in squares, and other streets cut across them, so that the whole effect was that of a maze. The streets closest to the centre were paved. One street withered into a path that ended at the lake. Across from me was the hotel, the place where I had spent my first night in these parts. It now greeted me like an old friend, a familiar neighbourhood place. I went in and ordered tea. And I did what my ancestor Dhanji Govindji had once done at Matamu, I enquired about the local mukhi.

I walked on the sidewalk, to the inner side of a dry, littered gutter, and looked for a decent-looking Indian face inside a shop. A man stood haggling with a fish vendor on the steps of the third store I passed and I walked up to him. 'God bless, Uncle. I am from the National Service. Can you tell me where the mukhi's shop is?'

The man eyed me, scratching a beard that was beginning to turn white. He was in white pyjamas with a large shirt hanging out. 'The mukhi, henh? Haya basi,' he said to the vendor, concluding the deal, 'take them upstairs. Saidi!' this to the servant, 'stand here and keep watch!' Without another word to me, as if it was quite normal for a strange boy to ask for the mukhi, he hurried inside, where a door led into a courtyard.

The store was filled to capacity, not a shelf in any birij empty, every wall covered, the customary President's photo prominently displayed, a calendar with English, Arabic and Hindu dates, with Hanuman, Ganesh or Rama covered over with a photo of the Kaaba, and two fundis sewing outside, facing each other from opposite sides of the doorway, the customary guardian angels. A rich store... not a customer in sight, but obviously they came in season, handling wads of crisp new 'masais' with the facility of bankers... A boy ran in from the courtyard then back out as if he had taken the wrong way. Two girls peeped in, and then giggled. One was about my age, the other younger. And I thought, How sweet the sight! One takes the sweetness of Indian girls for granted – the playful, even mocking, innocence that evokes tender feelings inside you and you forget how possessive you feel towards them – only when you've not seen one for some time do you realise that... It seemed ages since I had left home, it was two weeks. I stood there waiting, reflecting on the sweet innocence of Indian girls among other things, a spectacle for those inside and outside. People gawked from the sidewalk, shamelessly retracing steps to take a second look. The informality that comes from familiarity. They too felt possessive.

After about ten minutes, the man appeared, eating something. 'Come,' he said. 'I'll take you to the mukhi.'

A staircase went up from the courtyard. Boys and girls lined up at the foot to watch me. We went up, past the kitchen, where two women stood at the door to see me, from behind them coming the sweet smell of Sunday fare, hot ghee, frying saffron and cloves and cinnamon. We went inside to the sitting room, where a bald man of at least seventy, with a white beard, sat beside a stately Philips radio.

'Bapa,' said the man who had brought me in. 'Our guest.'

'Aah!' said the Bapa, 'come, come. Sit beside me. Tell me your name, whose son?'

A chair was brought for me and I sat beside the old man.

'Now tell me. Your name?'

'Salim Juma.'

'Aah! But Juma can't be your family name. What's your family name?'

'I don't know – Huseni is my grandfather's name. His father's name was Dhanji Govindji.'

Bapa was excited. 'Now you are talking! But that's still not a family name. Never mind. There was one Dhanji Govindji at Matamu. Not the same one?'

Give them a name and they'll give you a place.

'The same one.'

'Hm. You will stay for lunch, na? Of course, you will! Do you want to wash?'

One side of the flat opened into a large and wide balcony closed off with a wire mesh, overlooking a courtyard. This was the dining room area and the whole family had lunch here at a long table. The old man had four sons. Lateef had brought me in. Kutub was the second one, younger. The other two were away. The two women simultaneously served and ate. Bapa's wife, Jena, was dead, but a picture of her sombre self hung on the wall in the dining room. (How seriously the old folks sat to have their photos taken… as if they wanted their inner selves to be captured, left behind, not a smiling facade.) The rest of the family were the eight children of Lateef and Kutub. The older one of the two girls who had peeped inside the shop to take a look at me was Zainab. She never looked up that day.

It was two o'clock in the afternoon and the mesh cast a shadowy net on the table. They fed me like a king. I sat next to the old man and he fed me the choicest morsels himself ('Eat. Eat for the whole week!') and the titbits of information about himself. 'I am Jaffer Meghji. But like you, the children don't use the old name. They use Jaffer. I have the honour of naming future generations!' I learnt that one son was in Dar, and the youngest studying in England. One daughter was married in town and four others in different parts of the country.

Later I took a nap on a soft, cool bed with white, spotless sheets smelling deliciously of home, whose springs did not lower you to the floor as the camp beds always threatened to do. And then after tea, promising to return every Sunday if not more often, I took off for the bus stop to wait for Bakari. From a window in the flat, Zainab watched me go.

(After National Service all the Asian boys agreed upon at least one observation.

'These blacks, bana, they had such long ones, dangling there like anything—'

'Yes, like a donkey's or something—'

'And we sitting there with our shrivelled little peanuts of cocks—'

'Aré, even the cold water wouldn't make a difference to their sizes!'

'That's the point, yar! That's precisely the point! These long dangling things don't have stretchability. Young's modulus zero. They are already at their maximum lengths. While these peanuts, these little jugus grow and grow like there's no end. They grow into fighting bananas and they still want to grow!'

'Girls prefer them, yes?'

Such our insecurities. And later, an observation from Sona at college: 'Indian boys studiously avoiding each other at the showers, but (I swear!) all the while throwing casual glances at each other's members as if to ask: Hindu or Muslim, Muslim or Hindu?')

She was sitting under a tree halfway up the hill from the river to the camp, on a bright red khanga with a cashew motif in black and white. Book on lap a flagrantly incongruous sight, besides violating the Mangati NSP's injunction to leave scholarship at the main gate.

'Come, Indian, don't feel shy. No need to change your course.'

'I have a name, you know. What – preparing for university already?'

'Don't be silly, Indian.' She dropped the book on the ground and slyly watched me read the cover.

Amina as she sat there… In PT shorts of the female variety with elastic at the legs, and T-shirt… small and attractive, fair and African. With a twig she flicked a black ant off her thigh. A smooth, coffee-coloured thigh…

'Abdel Latif Kodi – *Songs of Captivity*. You are reading poetry.'

'Yes, Indian. Poetry of my kinsman, in my own language. But what do *you* do to pass your time, Indian? Have you had a Mhaya girl yet? You can afford the best of them—'

'Perhaps I should tell you I'm not that sort of a person—'

'What, a prude! Isn't that what you boys talk about in your tents? Come payday and you'll have yourself a Mhaya girl and get drunk. How can they refuse, poor peasant girls, the attraction of real money? But I forget, you are a modest sort – the story is around that you don't remove all your clothes at the river. A clothed Indian among naked Africans.'

'Some of us have a different sense of propriety.'

'Some of us are Indians, and some of us are Africans.'

A black girl lying on a red khanga in a green forest, near a stream. She would sit there under the tree with her book, everytime weaving new strands to her web, headlong I would fall in.

'Why do you call me "Indian"? I too am an African. I was born here. My father was born here – even my grandfather!'

'And then? Beyond that? What did they come to do, these ancestors of yours? Can you tell me? Perhaps you don't know.

Perhaps you conveniently forgot – they financed the slave trade!'

'Not all of them—'

'Enough of them!'

... And what of *your* Swahili ancestors, Amina? If mine financed the slave trade, yours ran it. It was your people who took guns and whips and burnt villages in the interior, who brought back boys and girls in chains to Bagamoyo. Not all, you too will say...

It was not only you who were brought up with a sense of modesty, Indian. My mother never showed her face outside, she went about in a buibui. Your mother, you say, runs a store wearing a dress... Perhaps they have met.

Do you know what it was like to be an African in colonial times, Indian? It was to be told that no matter what you achieved, you were ultimately a servant. Miss Logan our headmistress once took me aside and told me, 'Amina, my ayah has gone away, could you help me for a few hours today?' My ayah has gone away... After all this, what of self respect? How many years before we regain it? I look at an Indian or a European, and I wonder, 'What *really* does he think of me?' How can one *not* be militant?

Abdel Latif Kodi is a poet from Lamu. He was jailed for suggesting that independence in his country has benefited only a few, the new capitalists-cum-politicians in their pin-striped suits and Mercedes...

* * *

What of Zainab? I imagine her with her bearded husband and two rowdy kids on a walk outside the New Naaz on Sundays, in hijab, with pyjama and kurta, looking very Iranian… But that was not so, no it was not to be.

She was so soft and beautiful, so fair, so tender. She would be downstairs in the store, with Fatima her younger sister, every time I came. We would banter for a while, the three of us, then I would go up. At lunch she would be looking at her plate, but afterwards would bring me my tea. On my third visit Zainab and Fatima were out on a walk and passed me while I waited for Bakari to pick me up. And so it happened every Sunday thenceforth. They wanted to know more about me, about Dar. Did boys and girls go to the same school, could they talk in public, how many cinemas in Dar, had I seen the Comet 4 plane, did I go to see Cliff in Nairobi… Zainab had finished school and had no intention of going to university. 'I will get married.'

'Do you have a boyfriend?'

Blushes and giggles, no answer. Then the next time, 'There are not many boys here, you know!'

'But *all* girls in Dar want to go to university. You should, too. You're wasting your life!'

'My father is very old-fashioned. Even if he sees me talking to you like this, he will eat me up whole!'

'Alive,' concurred her sister.

'Whole, and alive.'

One night, a little after one at the camp, a lot of noise was heard coming from the front gate area: the sounds of trucks, men, luggage falling. Not one person from the servicemen's tents bothered to peep outside. At three-thirty an emergency whistle sounded for assembly. At the circle, afandes, carrying lamps and stamping their feet in the cold, waited like angry wolves.

'You cows, you pigs! The camp is filled with sounds of strange men, of trucks, and not *one* of you takes a peep outside? *Eti*, this is an army? These old women will fight the Wabeberu? They will take on Salazar's boys? Do you know how many hours they go without sleeping in Mozambique? Chuchuma! Chuchuma! Chuchuma! On your haunches!'

It was a new voice. Military service proper had started. Hitherto the work had been farming, mostly, tilling the fields, weeding the banana plantations, digging rocks, and building brick by brick the afandes' new permanent quarters: sullen faces periodically looking up at the sun for some indication of the time of day: then a whistle would blow to fall in for the march to food: happy faces once more, calling the kinate. This morning we were visited by six new afandes from Leaders' Training at Mafinga, to initiate military training. It began with strange voices goading us on in the darkness, to jump like frogs for an hour, heedless of pleas, medical excuses, tears.

The next morning the camp was buzzing with rumours about the Indian afande, who was responsible for the punishment. With every sore muscle that cried out, a heap of abuses was hurled at our new tormentor. He was like an elephant, they said, tall and fat. He did not walk but stomped, this tembo. He would crush your feet into jelly. He could walk all day and night. He had been to Mozambique. At Ruvu he had chased a lion.

But the new afande failed to appear that day.

The camp had two corrugated-iron outhouses for the recruits, outside which long lines of ill-humoured men and women, toothbrushes or mswakis in their mouths, formed every morning. The two sheds stood behind the tents, their two open doorways looking out over the valley. You approached them from behind and you gave a polite little cough as you approached. If that failed to get a response, you waited at the side and gave a louder cough from deep inside the throat and waited for the answering grunt. Then you tried your best to convince the occupant to hurry up.

'Come on, now, come out – you think you're the only one here?'

'Allah! I've not even started yet!'

'There are three of us waiting here, and you sit there like a king. You think this is your home, now?'

'Go away. I have diarrhoea. You think I like this stinking hole?'

'If you're not coming out, I'm coming in—'

A tinkle of the coveted National Service belt, and out he came, in full uniform, stomping, not looking up, and marched past us to the camp. I looked at him astounded, not believing my eyes.

'Even he finds it strange,' said the person behind me. 'Are you going in or not?'

'You know him, eh, this afande?' he asked me when I was in.

'Yes, I know him.'

'He's vicious, eh?'

'Yes, he's truly vicious.'

If I had been allowed to pick a thousand names for this new afande, I would not have picked his. Big, bluff, now vicious, Shivji Shame!

On Saturday afternoon the squint-eyed Afande Ufinyo came looking for me in my tent. 'Where's the Indian? Wey Mhindi, come with me. And bring your pack of cards!'

'Afande Shivji wants to speak with you,' he said, when I came out, taking the cards from me.

The afandes lived in barracks behind the front gate. Shivji sat on a folding chair outside a hut, doodling on the ground with a stick.

'Ah, Juma! Of all the places, to meet here!'

'Yes, bana. But when did you join National Service? And *why*?'

'It's a long story. You know, Juma, out here we are not equals. See these stripes – I am a sergeant. Soon I'll have scissors here – major. You're a recruit. You are in my power. But I am your friend. And you know why, Juma, I am your friend? Because when I stood in front of the class and when Mrs Schwering or Mrs Lila would tell everyone to say "Shame! Shivji Shame!" there was only one person there who was not yelling "shame", and it was you. I remember that. That is why I am your friend.'

They dreaded the Terror of Mafinga, Shivji the Tembo, Shivji the Simba. When he took his company on exercises they crawled over rock and mud in areas infested with snakes and scorpions, and spent the remainder of the day scrubbing and starching. His routemarches inevitably stretched into the following day. But he also taught them well. That was one company, Chaleh Coy or Charlie Company, that could have walked straight into battle, that sang of Mozambique and Rhodesia with gusto, and set the pace for the rest. They could dismantle and assemble their automatic weapons in the dark. When they came to attention, it was at once, to a man, without the slightest shuffle. And his punishments were savage, similar, as he said, to those he had once received. Only on weekends, between two pm on Saturday and six pm on Sunday, did his iron rule relent. Then he was not to be seen. Other afandes could be seen going for a drink, or washing or ironing or even playing cards… but not Shivji. He stayed to himself. They said he smoked bhang, that's what gave him his madness.

On Saturdays Amina and I met under our tree and we talked. We never stopped parrying… if we did not banter and challenge, how could we relate, come close over the chasm that separated us…

The tree was behind a bush a few yards away from the road. The guardpost was visible from behind the bush. On Saturday afternoons servicemen went to a village further down the road, where they got drunk on konyagi made of pineapple juice and stumbled back retching to the camp late at night. One afternoon Shivji stumbled towards us, mildly drunk, with a wrapped bottle in his hand.

'Relationships between men and women are forbidden in the Service,' he said as he sat down heavily.

'But friendship is all right,' quipped Amina, and I heartily agreed, not to be outdone in denial.

'Excessive friendship is dangerous,' said Shivji, wisely. He unwrapped the bottle and passed it around. Amina got up and announced, 'You men get drunk, I'm leaving.'

When she had left, Shivji grinned and wrapped up the bottle once more. 'That gets rid of her. I bought this for tonight.

'You know, Juma,' he said, 'it's a wonder. Who would have thought, so many miles away from home – you and I… it's destiny.'

'I still wonder, Shivji. Why you joined.'

He glared at me. 'You don't think I'm better off? What was I back in Dar? Selling oil door to door. "Uncle, have you bought your oil for the month? The latest shipment of ghee from Musoma. Better than KCC. Here, taste it – " That's what the likes of you would have wished on me… while you go and get yourselves educated.'

He brought out a tin box of 555 and took out a twig of marungi and chewed it.

'I am the master of my world here! For the first time in my life. People look up to me. I am a leader. I command them, I can make them laugh and I can make them cry.'

'I've had a tough life, Juma. No mother-father, brought up by grandmother. We had no money, and many nights I went to bed hungry. I would beg in the shops. Every month a woman would bring us a little money. What can I tell you – I was big but I was a coward. Boys would beat me up and I would cry. Even the younger boys would threaten me: Eti: "Weh Shivji, meet me outside." And I would tremble. People would pat my arse. Why, even when I was older, when I had left school and was ferrying oil – little Arab boys ran after me. There was this African who went around with me, carrying a tin of oil. One day he said to me in anger: "Weh Musa, you fag! Hanisi. What are you? What are you afraid of? Give one of them a good thumping, such that he'll recall his blessed grandmother. That's how you'll get respect." That's exactly what I did, Juma. But I was so nervous. There was this thin, wiry Arab called Faisal with a squeaky voice. "You," I said, that's all I could manage, "You," and I stepped towards him. He stood there firm, confident, mocking me. All I could come out with was a timid backhand. But I tell you, Juma, it sent him reeling! Oh, the joy of it! He was crying, holding his head, I felt exhilarated! There is no thrill like power... I have tasted it, I am addicted to it! You remember I met you once on the road, and I said if you needed anything? It was then, soon afterwards.

'Then, when Chou-en-Lai came, when I saw the National Service and TPDF marching... the power in their arms, their legs... I decided to join, to become a man. I was sent to Ruvu for training. But I had not conquered my fear yet. I had not learnt the extent of my strength. It was all right to fell a bonepie like Faisal Sefu, but the African... that was another story. I was scared of the blacks. And they saw this Paado, this Fatty Matimbwa, who could not last long in their midst and they wanted their fun. They would steal my things. Within one week they had exchanged their old stuff for mine. I would spend hours starching my clothes, polishing my boots, and as soon as I turned my back on them I found them exchanged. Then I would be punished. I could not mix with them. I would feel lonesome and many nights I would cry in my bed. One day I took hold of myself. After starching my things I wrote my name on the inside of my shirt and the belt of my pants, Musa Shivji. I suspected who this person was, who always exchanged my clean clothes for his dirty ones. It was a tall African, as tall as I but thinner. They called him Twiga. Well, as soon as I saw the dust-covered shirt and pants folded carelessly on my blanket where my clean, starched ones had been, I walked up to his bed and looked at the inside collar of the shirt lying there. Musa Shivji. I went to my platoon commander and reported. "You have proof?" he said. "You Mhindis think all Africans are thieves." "Come and see," I said. Well, my friend Twiga got extra drill. But it was nothing – half an hour of running with his kitbag – wait till you hear what happened to me.

'When this man had finished his punishment (it was Sunday afternoon, a little before roll call) this man comes up to me and gives me a shove. You know, like he was looking for a fight. He shoved me a few times and I did nothing. I was paralysed with fear. But this man, I thank him for it, he did not relent. He kept shoving me and I kept moving back, and the other members of the tent cheered him on. Finally I was against one of the ropes and I couldn't move back any farther. I told you he didn't relent and I thank him. He shoved, and in desperation I returned a shove in good nature, saying, "Cut it out!" Someone shouted, "Weh Twiga, you have an opponent!" Twiga started coming at me like a wild animal, and blindly I took a swipe at him with my right hand – a terrific swipe that landed at the side of his head. Mama, what joy, what jubilation, the crunch I heard, he looked at me like I was Satan and went down! Juma, by God, I tell you, the man went down! The other fellows slunk away. That night I was a giant, a dumé, simba! But only for the night.

'This man, I had broken his jaw. He was taken to the hospital and word got around. And I was punished. I was punished for being a fat Indian who had won, because I had humiliated the whole lot of them, from then onwards none of them dared face me one to one again. What I went through at Ruvu, Juma, it made me what I am today. I was sent into confinement, with one NSP to guard me and keep me busy.

'On the first day I was asked to fill a drum with water. The drum was on top of a hill near the kitchen, and the tap was some distance away downhill. I had to carry the water in a mess tin, little by little. I don't know how many trips I made – fifty, sixty, a hundred – before I collapsed. The next day he told me, this dog of an NSP, to stand in the sun with a brick in each hand, raised over the shoulders. And when he felt like it, he made me run with them. I had to fetch his food and wash up when he finished. I washed his clothes. I won't tell you what else I had to do... They would have killed me if I'd let them. The camp commanders must have known what was up. They would pass by with amused looks in their Land Rovers. They must have known: everyone knew: an Indian who volunteers for National Service has no-one, no friend, no kin. Isn't it true, I ask you Juma?

'The following day he took me, this Masai NSP, to break stones at the river. All morning he lounged about on the bank sunning himself, as I broke stones and carried them to a pile. Towards noontime he brought some food. He went for a swim. Then naked he started eating. "Afande, I'm hungry," I said. "How dare you talk to me while I eat!" he roared. I went on with my work and we eyed each other. When he finished, he got up.

'He had brought two mess tins of food, now he held mine in his hand. "Indian!" he said. I went up to him. He poured the food at his feet. "Eat." There it lay, the brown beans frothing and the solid lump of ugali, and over it his dick erect. At that moment, my fuse up here, it blew. I gave a roar and jumped at him. "This time I will kill you," I said. He went down and I on top of him, and I had his arm behind his back and started squeezing his throat. When his feet stopped thrashing, I released him. He was still breathing, then he started to moan. "Have mercy!" "Report a word of this, and I swear by my God, by my Mhindi God that I will kill you. Now where is my food?" That evening and the next two days I was served. He washed the mess tins. He washed and starched my clothes. We played cards. That, my friend Juma, is called Power.

'I was called simba. Only a lion, they say, can tame a Masai. Funny thing is, the more my reputation grew, the more I was expected to do things, to show off my bravery. When some real lions came close to the camp (we could hear them roaring at night) I was expected to lead the chase.'

'Did you?'

'Yes, but I was scared! But there were Africans who were willing to come with me, and I couldn't show them how frightened I was!... No, I haven't been to South Africa. But I was sent to the Mozambique border. It was nothing really, some men were needed to carry provisions and build facilities and a few servicemen were chosen. But we came with all sorts of stories, how we fought the Portuguese, and so on.'

Thus Shivji Shame, now the terrible Afande Shivji. He looked the same but he was different. The uniform was starched and proper, the boots polished, but here was no handsome, impeccable Lieutenant Colonel Henry, just Shivji. What had changed, what struck terror in his new recruits, was the person Shivji. We became friends, this new Shivji and I, despite his initial admonition, and every Saturday he would come to the tree where Amina and I sat, lower his ample body on the grass and make a few wisecracks, after which Amina left and we would idly chat. An angry man, without anything in the world, just the army, and his ambitions of making it there.

* * *

Bapa, old Jaffer Meghji, what did he know of Dhanji Govindji, my ancestor and mukhi of Matamu? Did he know of the sin, and the murder? There is nothing about Jaffer Meghji in Dhanji Govindji's accounts of transactions. Yet he knew something, this old man whose eyes lit up at the name, but he never let on…

Zainab! What young, pretty Shamsi girl has an ancient name like that? We had progressed to… Yasmin, Shamim, yes, flowers… Nur Jahan, the light of the world. But Zainab… Lateef, Kutub, Faruq, we left these archaisms a long time ago how could I have missed? Where was the Karim, the Amin, the Alnoor? The names should have told me (and the beards, yes!) but blindly I walked in, into a nest of – not Shamsis but rivals.

Take the name Yusufali Adamjee, outside the small store that sells stationery (among other things) in Kaboya. A name that immediately identifies a Gujarati Muslim of a certain sect from Surat, who traces his ancestry in Arabia. The cloth cap, the shirt, the white beard, a sure confirmation. 'Eh Chokra,' he calls out as I pass with Amina, outside his store. I stop in my tracks, look in, and he motions to me. 'Come inside.'

'See you at the Land Rover,' says Amina and goes off.

'John,' shouts Adamjee, 'two teas!'

'What is your name, boy?' he asks.

'Salim Juma.'

'Shamsi?'

'Yes.'

'There is not a single Shamsi family in the town! Not since 1920!' He eyes me. 'Do you understand?'

'Bapa—'

'Bapa!' he says contemptuously. 'So the bastard has already worked his spell on you. The next time you come here, eh ulu, you'll walk straight into a wedding procession. Yours!'

'What?'

'Yes. You, Bapa's darling adopted son, you are going to

marry his granddaughter Zainab! That I have heard from the old man's mouth, with my own ears. Do you plan to marry her?'

'No. No, no. There is nothing between us. You can tell them from me. I have no intention of marrying Zainab. I am going to university. Tell them I'll never go to their house again! How dare they assume I want to marry their daughter! And tell them this from me. They should send Zainab to university. They should not force her to get married!'

'Oho. Oho. So the spell has at least partly worked! I see. That sweet-sweet tea that she brought you in the afternoons? And the pendas, did she give you a sweet-sweet penda to eat before you boarded Bakari's bus? And that soft-soft pillow you napped on smelling the sweet-sweet fragrance of jasmine from her hair? That, my friend, is what contained the spell. Two more weeks and your mind would have completely turned – they would have given you a shop in Kaboya, my friend! And you would have borne them an Abbas or a Hamza. That's what happened to their other son-in-law. He came from Mwanza. And he's never left!'

'How do you know all this, Mr Adamjee?'

'I know. There is not a single Shamsi family in Kaboya. All the others left or converted, became Sadiqis. I am a Dawoodi. And I am leaving soon. Come on, have tea. It's pure – all my daughters are already married, subhanallah!'

Yusufali Adamjee drank his tea from the saucer and watched me do the same. Then he winked at me. 'This black girl with you – she gives, eh?'

The feud in the community at the turn of the century, the murders in Bombay, the splintering of the Shamsis into Hindus and Muslims, progressives, fundamentalists and mystics: one of the sects was fundamentalist Sadiqi, with its dress code and the Prophet's beard, its imposed modesty for women. (Interestingly, the old photograph of Jena, the old man's wife, did not show her in veil: a convert?) Of the remaining Shamsis some disappeared into various mainstreams, and there was left a single, still eclectic and little confused Shamsi community. The remaining Shamsis and the Sadiqis could not live together; in many towns and villages, the minority either converted or left. That had all been a long time ago, a feud that sometimes got bloody, and for many years even when the actual conflicts ceased and the two communities lived in the same town, their members would not eat at the same table. In Matamu there had been no splinter groups, and the Matamu Shamsis had later dispersed. In Dar, all that remained of the conflict was a slight hesitation, a questioning pause, before the boys answered it for themselves and sat down to lunch together. But here, in Kaboya, a backwater in the middle of nowhere, there remained a bastion of the old conservatism, a memory of the bloody conflicts and the losses suffered.

That was our first visit, Amina's and mine, to Kaboya together on official business. There would be one more. I never went to the Jaffer household again.

On Thursdays at camp, during the hours before lunch, Amina was asked to give lectures on politics and culture. She decided she would read to her class. First she gave them Abdel Latif Kodi, then Shaban Robert. She translated excerpts from Chinua Achebe. She read Nyerere, Nkrumah, Lincoln, Martin Luther King, Lenin and Marx. I was enlisted as assistant and the two of us were excused regular duty and never learnt to fight with weapons. On our first trip to Kaboya we went in search of *The Merchant of Venice* at the local school library. This turned out to be one cupboard in the staff room, with no Shakespeare.

Two weeks later we returned, in search of former high school students who had been educated elsewhere and might still have a copy of the play with them. We found one at the house of Ali Ramzan, former student of Shakespeare in Dar, now shopkeeper. It was lunchtime, and Mr Ramzan, a bearded Indian, made us sit down to eat with him. His wife did not appear from the kitchen and a servant brought the food. After lunch, Mr Ramzan, after reminiscing about his Shakespeare days at Dar, parted a little hesitantly with the book, as if with a little of his life. His name was scrawled in ink on the first page, Ali Mohamed Ramzan, Standard XIB.

On our way back, on the lonely road that came up from the lake, Amina was looking for Shylock's famous defence, when a noisy truck full of Indian boys celebrating a victory drove in front of us on a crossroad and stopped. Out came rowdy adolescents looking for fun and ran straight for Amina. 'Come on, dada! Give us some, too!' The usually fiery Amina looked at me in terror: 'What do we *do*, Indian?' And she started screaming, running down the hill. The boys then came at me. From their midst, Zainab's brother Faruq stepped out. 'Listen,' he shouted as if at a mosque gathering. 'This ill-begotten half-caste son of a dog has spoken ill of my sister after eating from our house. What shall we do with him?'

'Kill him!'

There is one thing I have always dreaded, an irrational perhaps primal fear for the safety of my cranium, the very thought of which makes me cringe... a solid-wood made-in-England cricket bat aimed at my head. The hysterical Faruq now screamed, cricket bat raised...

She told me she had fetched Mr Ali Ramzan and the two had run up the hill to save me. The boys ran off, leaving me bruised and bleeding.

* * *

Faruq had called me a half-caste, so obviously he knew of my background. What else did Jaffer Meghji know… did he meet Dhanji Govindji on his travels or the other way round… I never got around to asking (the slippery old man only skirted the subject)… and then it was too late. So much information simply hoarded for years and now lost… And the gunny sack is reduced to silence on the subject.

… The back of a Land Rover on a bumpy road, Amina still clutching *The Merchant of Venice*. 'Listen,' she says. 'Here it is. "If you prick us do we not bleed? If you—"'

'Yeah, we bleed, we bleed all right. Can't you see I'm dying?'

'Why don't you lie down, Salum? Rest.'

'On this?' I point to the grooved metal floor in disbelief. 'And split my skull completely? If you hit our skulls – aah – don't they crack…'

'Here. Put your head on my leg and lie down.' She stretches her legs out and straightens her skirt. 'Here.'

There. I put my head where she indicated. Above the knee. The clouds overhead throw down a wicked glare and I turn my head. 'It's hard here.' I move my head up and into the warm embrace, the sweet enclosure of her lap.

'Hey, Indian,' she says. 'Watch out. You're no better than the others.'

'If you tempt us, don't we fall…'

'Weh Amina,' chuckles the driver in front. 'He's got you now!'

I heaved and embraced her waist, pressing deeper… I'd got her… and her legs moved apart ever so slightly to receive me.

And I swear that the Kaboya skies that never rain after noon rained some to celebrate.

I fell asleep.

18 | *Dar, Massachusetts, New York, and the Moon*

The bush telegraph, they say, is slower than the electric, but it is more thorough. It begins as a whisper in the air. Carelessly, easily it travels, then it grows, acquires and gathers momentum, a current of whispers, then a murmur in motion. It delivers not one cryptic line in a khaki envelope but a resonance: mass of fact, opinion, speculation and pure fabrication. The news is in the air: Did you hear about Kala, the so-and-so who did the such-and-such… How did they know about us, Amina and me, in Dar? The message buzzed in Kaboya from man to man and woman to woman until it could not be contained, and from thence via bus and railway and lake steamer, through couriers, Post Office, and word of mouth to Kulsum.

Edward met me at the railway station. An older-looking Edward in the usual bush shirt and sandals, fatter, and because fatter looking taller and a little dissipated. He almost missed me, not recognising me in military uniform and moustache. We shook hands and walked to the taxi he had reserved.

Edward was Kulsum's envoy.

'What's this I hear? You have an African girl?'

'Sort of…' I grinned. 'Yes…'

'It's true, then! Salum, weh! now why do you have to go and do a thing like that? First Begum, now you—' He was angry. Not angry to hurt me but angry to be hurt, disappointed.

'Why do you object?'

'It's not proper, Salum, it's not time yet... Africans and Asians are different... it's like the story of—'

Edward propounding his theory of separate development of the races.

'You talk like Verwoerd! Like Smith! Salazar! It's because of people like you that the Africans are screwed in South Africa...'

'Ah Salum, weh! Stop it.'

A few months later, that August, Alu Poni left for Massachusetts to study engineering. His departure was kept secret until the last few days because he was leaving without permission of the Ministry of Education. Someone could always go to the Ministry and say, 'But so-and-so is going to America, why can't my daughter go?' 'Which so-and-so?' the officer would ask. 'That so-and-so.' 'We will not let him.'

The National Service turned Alu Poni into an avowed anti-Communist. Perhaps it merely affirmed a tendency in him... and the change I saw in him was partly a mirror image of how I myself had deviated. The six months in Service, away from our families and normal ways, changed all of us, not only into boys who could now easily run a few miles or grow a moustache, but also into boys who asserted themselves and their ideas, boys who thought about the world. The world came to the Poni household via *Newsweek* now. The Vietnam war was raging. America was bracing for a presidential election, and the race to the moon was on... One Sunday, a few days before he left, Alu's mother invited all his friends to lunch, to wish him goodbye. There were Jogo and me, his bosom buddies, Hassam, of the rock group Iblis, Walji who had got a place in Dar to study law, Nathoo and Bandali who were going to Nairobi to study engineering.

From the head of the dining table Alu gave us his vision of

the world which he would be taking with him to America. The Domino Theory: if Vietnam goes, so will Cambodia and the rest of Indochina, and there would be one huge Communist menace in the East, ready to pounce upon the rest of the world. There was a certain personage, he said, learned in the books, who had definite proof from the scriptures that the last great battle between God and Satan would be the coming Third World War. The Devil will rise from the East, he said. 'And which great power is rising from the East?' he asked. 'China! The Devil will have an army of six-point-six million men, it is said – and which country could possibly have that many people? China!' China, he said, and therefore Communism and its godlessness were the dreaded Daitya.

Daitya, by which name Kulsum would curse at Sona and me sometimes. Alias Azazil, Iblis. His coming would mark the climax of Kali Yuga… he would raise the dead, make bread from air to feed a starving world… and the people would flock to him in error and abandon God… The Kali Yuga was already upon us, said Alu. Soon we would be faced with the great war between the powers, the forces of good and evil.

'But where will this great war be fought? In Africa? The Middle East?'

'It could be anywhere, bana! Even in space…'

All this while his mother served samosas and lapsi and biriyani. Discomfited, Nuru Poni simply grinned from the side of the table, showing his teeth, at the sight of the apocalyptic Alu. Nuru Poni, who by Government decree could no longer do business as a pawnbroker, but a staunch party member who happily sold Chinese polyester suiting, drank tea from a pink Chinese thermos and wrote with a Chinese Parker pen look-alike.

Nuru Poni had kept up with the times. In slow sure steps he had progressed and departed from traditional beliefs, becoming more rational and political, so that he admired Mao and

Tito, Nkrumah and Nehru. A progressive man in a progressive country. But that day, a lonely man: an Asian, out of step with his community. His two older sons had aspired to nothing more than Kariakoo shops and Kariakoo brides immediately after high school, and now his favourite and brightest son was going off to America thinking that the CIA were God's emissaries.

We sat at the table, all envious of Alu. He was so sure of himself, going out into the big world to fight big problems, to join the forces of good against the forces of evil, while we remained here in a small country fighting our small problems. We saw him in America making rockets, at Cape Kennedy, at the Jet Propulsion Laboratory.

Alu Poni, he was simply pulled into another orbit and never came back.

After lunch, Hassam, former Elvis and now Beatle fan, sang us some songs. To bring us back from the apocalyptic mood he sang with a grin 'May the Good Lord Bless and Keep You', with which we had wished Miss Penny Mrs Gaunt goodbye, and now we sang it for our friend, not as fairies but as young men recently returned from service. After which Hassam went into a Beatle medley, refusing to sing Elvis or Jim Reeves, but agreeing to end with 'Kwa Heri'.

It was a month after Alu Poni had left. A Monday morning. At five o'clock people found themselves looking out from their windows. What had woken them up? The sound of voices this early, of doors opening or shutting, of too many vehicles on the road, a scream perhaps. Outside the Ponis' store were parked four Land Rovers. The voices were low and all activity was hidden behind the shadows of the vehicles. No-one went back to sleep and sufuriyas of tea were put to boil.

The next morning word was abroad about the 'passport detentions'. Eighteen people had been taken into preventive detention for frauds involving the immigration office. That morning the Ponis' store remained closed, as if somebody had died in their home. But Nuru Poni's detention was a mistake, as everyone on our corner could have sworn. That afternoon a little after lunchtime he wearily stepped off a bus, in his crumpled white drill pants and white shirt and opened his store. The keys, it seemed, were with him.

When Nuru Poni returned he found that his own son Firoz was in detention. Firoz was married and had his store a little down the road on Kichwele. Under his bed were found blank passports already signed and endorsed by the immigration office, which he could simply make out in the names of whoever could pay him. The fee was 200 shillings. Alu Poni probably left carrying one such passport.

The greatest thrill of being young and at university is the discovery of your own mind and thoughts, the limitless possibilities; and the belief that what you think matters. We thought the country was listening, Africa needed us. We formed SNAFU, Students for a New Africa. Every Friday this think tank met in the Nkrumah Room. We considered papers, examined the week's news, issued communiqués, organised debates and seminars, published bulletins. Yes, we did stir up the campus while we lasted, and the membership reflected a cross section that would encourage anyone who had hopes in the new Africa.

Aloysius Mbogo, chairman. He played Mr Turton in *A Passage to India*, when it was produced at Boyschool with black actors playing the whites and Indians playing Indians. His one love was to preside. 'Gentlemen, gentlemen! Now this is a serious matter. We will settle it by consensus.' And settle it he did.

Amina Saidi, chief thinker. The fiery Amina of Kaboya fame, whose anti-imperialist and humanist ideas were now steeped in the colours of Marxist-Leninist theory. Amina called the shots: scrutinised the politics of suggested speakers, quizzed the speakers after they spoke, especially when she was disappointed, wrote the draft editorial for the newsletter: in short, the life of the organisation. She skirted rather dangerous territory sometimes, even then: 'Is African Socialism all romantic hot air without theoretical (i.e. scientific) underpinnings?' This debate drew a huge crowd, including local officials, and she was not quite ready to go all-out in support of the motion ('It is said that all peasant societies have some form of joint ownership in theory, but in fact—'). The motion was soundly defeated. 'Industry or Agriculture?' was the heading of one editorial. Her vision then was of a modern, small industrialised African nation along the lines of one of the Soviet satellites.

Geoffrey Umbulla, a thin wiry fellow, a self-styled party watchdog. He came in the full Youth League uniform, a mannequin in green and black drill shirt and pants, and yellow scarf and beret. His name appeared prominently in our communiqués, in case anyone doubted our loyalty. But he was opposed to the concept of a public debate, which was a 'foreign import'. Quietly disliked. Several years later he was detained for seditious activity, distributing Kambona leaflets at the university: he was also in a hurry, as we of course knew.

Ali Tamim, also called 'Shehe', who came in kanzu and cap because we met on Fridays, wise in human affairs, who made the final peace whenever a meeting broke up into squabbling factions.

Salim Juma, one-eighth African. I was made treasurer and business manager (talk of stereotyping) of *The Voice* and before every issue toured the Indian dukas for donations, taking a 100 per cent African with me, and never failed to raise enough money. Also in charge of raising membership, which was lagging.

Zuleika Kassam, from Zanzibar, who came to Dar after the revolution. Of whom more later...

These, and a few others – Ogwell, Raphael, Walji, Washington – out to influence the world.

Amina and Ji Bai. They simply fell in love. They met twice, when I took Amina with me on the rounds of the Indian dukas. Old, bony Ji Bai could match Amina word for word. Among her friends were more Africans than Asians… old men in kanzus would stop for a chat, women would go inside with her to tell her secrets, boys would shout a greeting… sitting at the sewing machine all day, except for a few trips inside, was how she passed her time. 'Nyerere is my son,' she once told us. 'We Mswahili, nini?' Amina asked, another time, to which she said, 'Yes, I am Swahili… and Indian and Arab… and European,' at which point she walked stiffly up and down as she thought the Europeans did, and sat down giggling. 'Taratibu,' she once told Amina, 'taratibu,' carefully. But Amina had heard the story from me. 'Oh no,' she said, misunderstanding (but only partly, she later conceded), 'no taratibu for me.' And Ji Bai, looking closely at her all the while, as at a specimen, simply said, 'Live. Live, first, then start hurrying to wherever you are going.'

One day Amina asked her about the Maji Maji war. 'Oh, the Germans,' she said, 'bad, bad. For a small mistake, khamsa shirin, faap, faap. A bigger mistake, fifty strokes. Or a hundred. A thousand or more strokes given in a day… One day there was a revolt.'

She went outside and brought back a twig from a weed growing at the steps. She held it to her forehead and with the long reach stick held like a spear she started dancing and chanting 'Maji maji, maji maji, maji maji, maji maji…' Amina of course joined her and the two did some 'maji maji' before a few young men joined in from outside, and the whole shop was going maji maji…

* * *

To have met in the jungle and fallen in love there, among people we did not know, on the banks of a stream, under a tree, how easy it was. No sooner were we back in the city than we started carrying the burdens of our races. In the dead of night, when no eyes could see, Asian or African, I would go quietly to her room. Or, sometimes on Saturday afternoons, when the others were in bars or in town, we would meet behind the football field, chewing grass, talking, trying to remain intimate.

But our world was pulling us apart.

To uproot a healthy young shoot – a lively sapling with a lot of energy and promising many new things – and transplant it in an uncaring soil... that is what returning to Dar meant. For me, it was simply to be doing the unthinkable; to be the subject of discussion for anyone in the community, from the precocious ten-year-olds to the senile: *the children, religion, the differences, it's not easy, nothing to do with racism, of course...* And what words did Dar say to her... to have fallen in love with one of the exploiter class, a dukawallah, mere agents of the British, these oily slimy cowardly Asians, what future did they have... the world had so much to offer a bright young African girl.

Kulsum eyed me suspiciously every time I returned home, as if I had come with hands soiled by the vilest deed, so that she would purify me by inviting people over, by observing special rites for my father, by taking me to watch Indian films at the drive-in with her friend Mrs Daya, by talking about the past when there were Begum, Mehroon, Yasmin, Shamim, Shiraz and Salma with us, when times were hard but there was a real closeness, a bonding, among us.

One day Edward went to see Amina at the University. 'Weh Amina,' he said, 'listen. You have it in your power to kill another woman.'

Amina did not know who he was and gave a characteristic

reply: 'Are you telling my future? You are a mchawi? You gaze at stars?'

'If you go ahead and marry this boy Salum—'

'Who said anything about marriage? And what business is it of yours?'

'This woman's husband died when she was young—'

'Weh mpumbavu, nini? You fool, do you think one can turn off love for an expediency?'

'It is possible to control it.'

For Edward love was something you could give and take at will. Even if you had it inside you.

'What do you know of love? You who have slaved away your life at a Singer telling stories—'

'I have known love but I have controlled it.'

'What love, you... working for an Indian woman and telling stories to her son!'

'I have known love but I have controlled it.'

She told me her mouth opened to hurl another contemptuous epithet at this fundi, but then his words clicked. Amina's eyes opened with new respect... pity perhaps. 'You know, Salum,' she told me. 'There were others before us.'

'You're telling me...'

To get back to Dhanji Govindji. Did he know love, before those missives started coming from Junapur urging his good sense, and the mukhi sent him to Zanzibar? Did he tell Bibi Taratibu before he sent her away, This won't work, our worlds are too far apart, they won't let us? And Bibi Taratibu, the Gentle One who later ran a tea shop at the end of the village, watching her half-caste son grow up into a loafer, did she love, or did she simply put up with the pawing of this lonely Indian? And my grandfather Huseni escaped from this intolerant world but left behind a pining woman... did he also love and control, as Edward would have it? But whom, another woman, or the pining Moti? There was Uncle Goa, who in another scenario would have run away with my mother and now, as Amina told me, Edward... unrequited loves, because we catch the world unprepared for us.

She announced one day she was going to New York on a scholarship. It was a chance too good to miss. The two years would fly, she said, meanwhile we'd test our commitment and let the world get used to the idea. To see her off came two West African professors and one British, some American friends, black and white, and her local friends. SNAFU was put in abeyance, except on the day we saw her picture in the *Herald* and there was talk of having regular meetings once again. She wrote a few times, long descriptive letters full of her experiences, the exuberance of black power and the student movements against the American involvement in Vietnam, the fight for the third world. Things are happening here, she said, there is a feeling that you can really change the world, the numbers are on your side... can this be real? When Martin Luther King was shot I stopped hearing from her altogether.

But when she left, I thought she would come back to me. By then the world, moving at breakneck speed, would be ready for our revolution... when the evidence before my eyes since childhood had always told me, a journey overseas changed you indelibly. In that hour of grief in America, what could I have offered her, what did I possess which could hold her... She was in another world, and I knew I had lost her.

The Bee Gees were singing 'Massachusetts', from all the radios on Kichwele on Sunday mornings, and Alu Poni's few cryptic notes from Boston sounded as distant as those from the moon.

He knew, of course, of his brother's arrest, and assumed his letters were being read.

Try explaining gravity to Edward bin Hadith. The news of the moon landing thrilled him, although he did at first put forward the hypothesis that all the pictures had been taken on earth and the Americans were simply fooling the world. But the news bombardments and the colour photos outside the USIS library were simply overwhelming, Quran- and Bible-thumping traditionalists notwithstanding. But then, how do the rockets leave the earth? Here, I braced myself to explain Newton's laws. To which Edward's response was a sungura story, with the sungura-rabbit playing football against the hyena. But the sungura was on the moon and could use its low gravity to give a whamming kick, a mkwaju like the ones the legendary Ali Kajo and Kadenge from Mombasa had never seen... Try protesting on the side of science against a gleeful, orbiting deaf Edward bin Hadith, for whom the moon is only a stepping stone...

19 | Britannia's Children

We were living in Upanga, in the cooperative flat on Upanga Road that comprised Kulsum's second investment, using half of her husband's insurance money, the first half having gone towards key money for the defunct The Fancy Store, now replaced by a very ordinary Kariakoo shop, its showcase that once drew crowds to watch the Father Christmas display in December now simply a storage area for excess stock. The flat had a long history of defaulting tenants, one after the other, whom the lawyer Kulsum hired could not evict because he was working for both plaintiff and defendant, a fact that emerged when the police went looking for him one day and he escaped to India. The one tenant she could successfully get evicted was her own brother Bahdur...

Bahdur Uncle had to vacate his Kariakoo shop opposite the market to make way for a two-storey building and bus-stop. Kulsum had a flat available, but she did not trust him. So she took a signed statement from him to the effect that he would vacate after a year. Twelve months later Bahdur Uncle would not leave and Kulsum got a court order. Bahdur Uncle, when the police arrived with the order, moved to a slum in the same general area, slated for demolition, and then Kulsum, Sona and I went to live in the Upanga flat.

(Shamim, my cousin... the image simply intrudes itself... she had become fat, but attractive-fat, with short hair, a younger

Roshan Mattress with a reputation for excessive flirtation… but history does not repeat itself, not yet. She was studying in Uganda at Makerere and Bahdur Uncle was anxiously waiting for her to return and lift him out of his misery.)

Kulsum sitting at her zig-zag sewing machine, staring ahead of her, at infinity, picking her chin, brooding.

The zig-zag of course came with us from Kichwele, as did much of the furniture from the flat upstairs. The ship SS *Nairobi*, the toy cabinet, the Philips. A bookcase was a new addition, with some *Reader's Digest* Condensed Books, assorted Oxford dictionaries, Ian Fleming, *Prester John*, Lobsang Rampa. The same photographs on the walls, with one addition: the family portrait at Mehroon's wedding. This hung a little to one side, as if leaving place for another, twin photograph: the absent, Begum's never-to-be wedding family portrait…

After Kichwele – that dominating artery now called Uhuru Street, with its bicycles and cars and buses, its dust and its people and the buildings that appeared ancient after only ten years – Upanga nights were lonely, its maghrab more oppressive… the skies were open, when children cried they did so against the universe… couples walking on the sidewalk, you saw their heads and shoulders over the hedge, walking and murmuring, their thoughts ever so serious, weighing down on them, as if so much was at stake, so much depended on the right decision… Peeping pawpaw trees casting ominous, twisted shadows outside gardens, looming coconut trees rustling overhead, gutters tracing dark lines on the streets. All against a background sound of chirping crickets. What was it about Upanga that gave it such gravity at night?

Sometimes a lonely trumpet would sound, a practising band musician, playing of all things ancient 'Swanee River'…

Kulsum sitting at her zig-zag, brooding, picking at her chin: what is she thinking about? About Sona's coming departure.

* * *

Sona was one of the boys whom former Boyschool teacher Mr Datoo influenced when he returned from America on a visit. On a fateful afternoon in Dar, Mr Datoo went about town like the Pied Piper followed by a train of adulating boys, the procession ending at the United States Information Service library on Independence Avenue, university catalogue section. 'You can make it,' Mr Datoo had told the boys.

Catalogues started arriving at home, glossy affairs promising exciting academic opportunities ('A first-hand look at the moon's rocks, can you beat that?'), with tantalising photos depicting student life in Arcadia: playing tennis barechested, under lights; the glee club in session; making a snowman in the shadow of an imposing statue; and that favourite of all catalogues: boy or girl reading under a tree (even if it's the only tree on campus, as Sona would later joke).

Kulsum did not pay much attention, if at all she pooh-poohed the whole project. No money, not possible, was what she firmly believed. Edward and another fundi took piecemeal orders from her and these she delivered Downtown. A few more years to go, she said.

Then one day Sona brought home a thick envelope, Abraham Lincoln stamps on the outside. It spoke not only of admission but also of a scholarship. The letter was signed 'Gene': Foreign Student Counsellor. We were sitting at four o'clock tea, it was Sunday, I was home from University. Kulsum looked flustered, angry, searching for an answer, knowing she would soon find it, and that would be that.

'What's wrong with the University here?'
'It doesn't teach what I want to study.'
'What do you want to study?'
'History – of our community.'

'And what job will you do studying the history of our community?'

'I will teach.'

'Why don't you become a teacher here, and study the history of our community at the side?'

Would he have left if she had refused permission? But for someone like Sona, the case is always a clincher. All signs point to the same direction, the path opens of its own accord...

Sona the golden boy, how much she had loved him, we all had loved him... the youngest, the darling... even the meanest of his pranks, offences, were laced with mischief and laughter. The golden mean, he took no sides, hurt no-one, and had no strong beliefs: above all else, did he, does he, then love only himself? For that is what you expect from everybody's darling.

In the next week Kulsum had two visitors. The first one was Mr Blunt the Form VI counsellor, followed by Brother Augustine, a Quebec Jesuit who lived in a house behind our block of flats.

Brother Augustine lived with a few other Jesuit brothers, how many no-one quite knew. He was the kind of white man who takes a tengo of chickens with him inside a bus and then clumsily runs after one if it escapes, returning triumphant – red-faced, smiling, sweating – to everyone's delight. A studied idiosyncrasy this, perhaps, but he was by no means trivial. He would sit with Sona on the wall that bordered the house – Sona never saw the inside of it, even when he knocked to enquire about Brother Augustine he was asked to stand outside, by whichever of the Jesuits that answered: CIA agents? we speculated – and the two would talk. It was Brother Augustine who convinced Sona of his vocation – the study and love of antiquity: old alphabets and scripts, crumbling manuscripts: the 'history and mystery' of sects, in medieval Europe and India and – Sona's later interest – Coastal East Africa.

Brother Augustine wrote an additional special recommendation for Sona.

Kulsum always stuck to an old maxim: nothing comes before education. Be it month-end at the shop and 420s hovering at its doors like vultures over a dying body, say you want to study and Kulsum would leave you alone. After the visits of Mr Blunt and Brother Augustine, after being told that not everyone's son or daughter gets admitted to a university like that, and with a scholarship, even in Europe or America:

Kulsum made her biggest sacrifice by letting Sona go.

Kulsum's commandments to Sona: Don't marry a white girl. Don't smoke or drink. Don't eat pork. Don't turn your back on your faith and your community. Don't forget your family.

And so Sona left: no government sponsorship, no picture in the *Herald*, but like Alu, quietly. With him he took a box of old printed books, tattered, torn, yellowing, relinquished to him by amused old ladies. A treasure, he said.

Only Kulsum and I went to the airport to leave him. Kulsum waved and waved, even when he had disappeared behind a door, her four fingers folding and unfolding in a mechanical, absent-minded, outward goodbye that was a mere form for the torment she felt inside.

Sona's first letter was from London:

> *Kala: Everything they said about it is true! It is glorious, it is magnificent, I don't know how to describe it. Even from the plane, before landing, the miles and miles of cultivated, ordered land, then blocks of paved streets, stretching endlessly, the staid row houses, the cars parked neatly outside, the streets like endless ribbons and traffic snaking its way through them, the tall buildings, the parks, the river. The first thought that strikes you when you take this all in (after you've said, how clean, how great, how beautiful!) is, how*

many of our Dars could fit into this world of a city. And inside *London – the Parliament buildings, Nelson's Column, Westminster Abbey, Big Ben – good old Big Ben, I wanted to go and hug it – and Buckingham Palace – it's all here – repeat –* it's all here! *And I don't mind telling you, I saw the Queen leaving Buckingham Palace and I waved at her. That's what I wanted to do for a long time, didn't you?*

When you walk past these great structures rising up, when you see the craftsmanship that went into the smallest details in them, when you sense the weight of history these magnificent structures support – when you find yourself reciting the names of people and events they remind you of – when you experience the pomp and pageantry, the purity of sound and the tradition behind a simple boys' choir (which I did on television)... when you walk the halls and corridors, see the rooms, feel with your hands a solid wooden desk – where Newton, Shakespeare, Milton conceived their universes...you wonder. Is it surprising they behaved the way they did when they came to our countries, these Englishmen? Sure, we too have a history, and old traditions, but they are undefined, uncelebrated, and sometimes as confusing as a cauldron of witches' brew, don't you think? There lies the difference between our histories...

And how does Britannia treat her offspring who come from all over the world to pay respects?

At the airport, lines, long lines: coloured, white, coloured, white... A coincidence? Hardly. First class and second class British subjects. You look at the others in your line, and you wonder, Am I one of these? Why do they look so strange... and dark? You ask yourself, Why do these Indian women always travel with bedding, for God's sake? You want to move away from them, then you check yourself. It could be your mother. You smile. Kidhar se ate ho? Amritsar. Ap? Tanzania. *You wait for minutes on end, watch them endlessly quizzing those ahead of you, as the other lines beside yours swiftly diminish and passengers from other, European, flights join them. Then my turn came. But it came in a special way. Alau was ahead of me. I was called before they had finished with him, and we were taken to see some officer. Then we were questioned, in separate rooms.*

'Why do you want to stop over?'

'I want to see London. Like the pussy cat.' No smile.

'What's your destination?'

'Boston. It says so on the ticket.'

'Then why do you want to stop over?'

'To see London.'

'For how long?'

'Two weeks.'

'Do you know anyone here?'

'Yes. Lots of friends. My sister lives in Cambridge.'

He searches me, brings out my black book of addresses, copies out names and addresses. Brings my bag, searches it. Leaves with the black book. And so on, once more the questions.

'You've completed school.'

'Yes, that's why I'm going to university.'

'You don't want a job in London, for instance?'

'Why would I want a job here when I've got a scholarship to study in America?'

'This scholarship. They just gave it to you?' (Is he jealous?)

'Yes.'

'Anyone can apply?' (Not you, if you're so dense.)

Finally, after several hours, he let me through, but Alau, as you probably know by now, wasn't let in. I wasn't even allowed to go and wish him goodbye. Poor, sad crestfallen Alau watching me go to London.

I stayed at Palace Inn on Gloucester Road, and it's a zoo of a place. There are three very springy iron beds in each room, and many of the occupants there are permanent. You can hear the Beatles here, but I confess tearful Talat Mahmood songs are probably more appropriate, the place looks so gloomy. It is run by a Mr Toto, who welcomes all the lost children of Britannia who find their way here, never turning anyone away even if he has to put them up in his own rooms. Breakfast is in the basement, and you can get eggs in three styles — omelette, sunny-side up, and over — and tea in Indian or English, and the Kariakoo boy who takes orders also gives you tips about possible part-time openings and how to get visas. 'Didn't we play marbles together?' I asked him as he put my omelette and chai on the table. 'Excuse me,' he said, without looking up, and stiffly walked past to take another order. He might even have sniffed... Jeeves, I said to myself. Girls are looking for secretarial positions and boys for articleships here. Come evening and they return, exhausted on their platform shoes (the boys), in the tailor-made Teteron trousers you can recognise anywhere, carrying briefcases full of O Level and A Level certificates, real and fake letters regarding previous experience, to compare notes and pore over newspaper advertisements for the next day's enquiries. There are many sad and tired faces, many tears shed in the night. I met your friend Jiwan: he was overjoyed to find out that I was sleeping in the same bed in Number 1 where he had shed so many tears. Someone should talk to those sheets... Those, like Jiwan, who find what they are looking for of course leave to look for better accommodation. Some have simply given up hope of becoming CAs and go to work in factories, returning late in the night with grimy faces. Some have simply turned into cranks. There is one person from Dar who goes around showing a photograph of himself taken (he says) with a professor at the University of London.

I am at Begum's now. They are doing quite well, but sometimes there is talk of going back to Dar (to teach) or some other place. The full names of the two children are: Peter Juma Harris ('P.J.') and Sara Kulsum Harris. There goes the next generation.

Yours: Sona.

20 | *Deluge and a New Saviour*

How to recall a storm, the actual downpour, the continuous pelting, in this case, of events that battered at the old world and brought down the shaky structures which had lost their foundations? Wiped clean was one prevailing image, exaggerated and too personal, applying perhaps to the bankbook, for a storm wrought by human hands does not wipe clean but leaves debris behind. Broken hopes, broken families, above all, broken faith washed away by the torrents into time's flooding gutters, to be replaced by a new cynicism: every man for himself and God against all.

In the Parliament of Tanzania the Uniform Law of Marriage was passed: Marriage shall be entered into only with the free and full consent of the intending spouses. No crib marriages, when parents betrothed infants while still rocking them to sleep in their cribs, and boys and girls could remember being married all their lives… but that custom was long gone, only to be joked about every time a child was born; and going but not completely gone was the custom of *giving* a girl in marriage – now the Indian movies and film songs and *Filmfare* magazine all preached 'love marriage', it was only a question of whether kisses could be allowed on the screen, swimming costumes and fat female thighs being all right – and in the soft light of the evenings the shades of mango trees in Upanga could be seen occupied by couples in clandestine meetings. Why clandestine? Because the message was Love, if you want to love, but love in secret, otherwise get married. Ah, the thrill and the sweet agony of those rendezvous! You go with beating heart every time, you don't want to be seen, yet you don't want complete privacy, for the world must know or guess and suggest, part of the thrill is simply the speculation and the teasing. Months can go by without that sacred word spoken. *Love*. For once it's spoken the wind catches it and whispers it around and it gets conjoined with its mate, *marriage*. And as long as no obvious bounds are broken, the parents simply go along with this sweet flirtation-exploration, hearts overflowing with joy, there are few things as satisfying as a child getting married properly.

Tell that to the parents of four Zanzibari girls.

One Sunday morning four girls of Persian descent, ages fourteen to eighteen, were taken before a full meeting of the Revolutionary Council and asked to choose husbands. The girls refused and were sent to prison. 'Better prison than...' said Kulsum. But hear this: a few days later the girls were taken to the homes of their Council-chosen husbands. Old bearded shehes, two to three times their ages, married previously: the flower of youth, the apple of dad's eye trampled in the mud.

In Dar, some Muslims sent a petition written in blood to the President, angry letters were sent to the *Herald*, a flood of marriages took place; a call to the Shah of Iran was made, to send gunboats; and in the United States a court granted Alu Poni permanent residence on the basis of these reports, faithfully included by Nuru Poni in the weekly batch of news clippings he sent his son.

At this time also Amina arrived with a boyfriend, and we joked, 'Weh Amina, were you too scared to come alone?'

* * *

In January 1971 former KAR sergeant Idi Amin, star pupil of his British mentors, who had hunted with them the Mau Mau in the Aberdares, took over as President of Uganda, hours after Milton Obote ordered his arrest by telephone from the Commonwealth conference in Singapore. It was also at this conference that the British Prime Minister's clairvoyant powers came to light, for he had quipped that some of the Commonwealth leaders might not have a country to return to at the end of the meeting. A few days later Obote came to Dar.

Long before Mawingu House reached for the clouds behind Ocean Road to become the tallest building in Dar, by which families with cars would drive on Sundays before stopping at the Naaz, before the Standard Bank and the IPS buildings similarly took off upwards, there was Hassam Punja's building: not a concrete block of air-conditioned offices for overseas firms and overseas-educated professionals, but a pyramidal structure broad at the base, narrowing to the top, an imposing landmark overlooking Mnazi Moja from the downtown side, where families lived and scruffy children ran around, in which cricket and marbles were played, where a bar called the 'Roof Top' thrived emitting strains of Bosco and Satchmo music into the air and ejecting drunken sailors back into the streets, and where at least one prostitute was permanently stationed.

Hassam Punja was in some ways like Mzee Pipa. But he operated at a higher level: a businessman rather than a shopkeeper. Legend had it that he too had acquired his wealth through hard work, starting off in the humblest of professions, a boy selling peanuts. From this he had risen to acquire a large number of buildings and a soap factory. Like Mzee Pipa he had to be escorted around, but he rode in a Mercedes. He also suffered from ailments and did a peculiar thing: all the time, whether sitting or on his feet, he rolled from side to side, oscillated very much like the rotund red dancing doll I had won as a healthy baby once. There were all sorts of stories that boys concocted about Hassam Punja's escapades, which all boiled down to one fact: because of his sideways roll he could not be shot, or hit with a boxing punch, rolling away just in time to dodge it. This made him invincible.

When the Arusha Declaration was announced – when the nation chose the socialist path and banks were nationalised and the state took over the importation and exportation of key items and the distribution of produce, and strong foreign exchange rules were put in place; when men, women and schoolchildren in the thousands marched in the streets in support of the event; when groups of people took off by foot from the smaller towns for Dar to show support; when Asian boys hitch-hiked across the country and visited the villages and said, 'We are also ungaing mkono' this Declaration, and were then welcomed by the elders and fed – during a rally not far from Mnazi Moja a government leader pointed to the yellow pyramid-building that towered in the distance and laughed: 'Tell him not to worry. We won't take his buildings!'

Not that anyone cared. The rich have few friends except the rich. And not many were as rich as Hassam Punja.

Four years later all of Hassam Punja's buildings were taken, to which event everyone attributed the heart attack from which he died. This blow he could not avoid, they said of our dancing millionaire as they pored over the newspaper pages to see who else had been hit, and how badly. None of the big commercial buildings were spared: from the lofty IPS building which the President himself had opened a few months before, to Hassam Punja's pyramid built from peanuts, to Hassan Uncle's modest Ushirika House built from medicines.

It was Hassan Uncle who brought the news to our home.

Bringing his bike to a tottering halt outside and leaning it against the wall, he stumbled in.

'Did you hear? Washed out!'

Kulsum was at her sewing machine, deep in thought. She simply looked at him.

'Did you hear? Washed out, I said. We are washed out—'

'Washed out what, brother?'

'Aré, in which world do you all live? Haven't you heard? Our buildings, our property, our houses, all gone. Saaf! Clean! Nationalised. Mali ya uma. Property of the masses. He's betrayed us, this stick-wielder, Naranbhai, Kalidas—'

Hassan Uncle having listed the Indian nicknames of our president, sat down and buried his head in his hands. It was the closest he could come to sobbing. Kulsum got up and went to him.

One day in Membeni in Mombasa Hassan Uncle, tired of the hopeless poverty in his father's home, due in part to his father's ridiculous business sense and lack of worldly ambition, went to him and said, 'I want to go to Dar es Salaam. I will look for a job.' My grandfather Mitha Kanji put his hand inside the cashbox and gave him money for a third class fare to Dar on a steamer. Hassan Uncle tried his hand at several businesses. He first worked for his father's brother, a wholesaler, as a salesman, then he opened his own piece-goods store in Msimbazi. Later, for a brief period, he opened a pawnshop, which was a mistake, for the only successful pawnbrokers in Dar were Nuru Poni and his brothers, a family of pawnbrokers. Who all had to change trades when a new law closed down the pawnshops. One day Hassan Uncle went to the dispensary on Swahili Street to be treated for a septic foot. The dispenser, Ramzani, as he was dressing Hassan Uncle's foot asked him in Cutchi, which he spoke fluently, for a loan. Hassan Uncle gave him ten shillings. From there grew a lasting and lucrative friendship. For Ramzani knew all the prescriptions that had come his way by heart. APC for fever, Paludrine for malaria, Galloway's cough mixture (which could be diluted), iodine, 'lotion', MB for dressing wounds, belladonna, Zambuk for backaches, insulin injections for diabetes. Ramzani became the consultant for Hassan Uncle's Ushirika Medical Store, which opened close by. And when Ramzani went freelance, a travelling pharmacist on a bicycle, dispensing to all his previous patients, Hassan Uncle supplied his medicines.

Hassan Uncle treated African patients, Ramzani treated Asian grandmothers. Every day Africans from the neighbourhood flocked to Hassan Uncle's store, holding their sides in agony, their heads with pain, pointing to stubbed toes and ingrown nails, rubbing their stomachs, coughing and sneezing, carrying screaming infants and holding weeping pubescent girls… and went away with a remedy. Thus had gone up Ushirika House.

My uncle Hassan, no Albert Schweitzer or Mother Teresa; but, 'Ask how many people I treated, how many miseries I took away…'

Wait, Shehrbanoo. You who know as much about the Kariakoo mind – to use modern parlance – as anyone. How much did a bottle of Galloway's cost? Two shillings? Two-fifty? And how many bottles would they make out of one? Four, five?

– Yes, but hold your smug socialism there: they did not sell these diluted medicines at the price of the full bottles.

Still, one shilling? That's still more than two hundred per cent, not counting profit on the original bottle –

– Which is ten per cent. But how much profit did Mr Galloway make in London, to support his lifestyle? Or the makers of Toyota and Ford? At ten per cent where would he have been, like Mad Mitha his father, from whom he escaped...

Where is Ramzani, his mentor?

— No-one knows, the last Ji Bai saw of him was when he came to pick up her urine sample, and his foot was swollen. His profit margin was low.

In Kichwele, Mzee Pipa, who didn't even own a bank account, was heard to say, quite nonchalantly, 'What else now? Let him take me too,' referring not to Naranbhai, as many called our leader, the President, but to God. God heard him, because Mzee Pipa died a few months later, followed in a matter of weeks by his wife. After the second funeral, lights burned in Mzee Pipa's second-storey flat up until the wee hours of the morning, but no sounds came, no sign of a squabble – which neighbours, spending a sleepless night, had prepared to hear – from the six daughters who were closeted there, presumably occupied with the treasure hunt and dividing the spoils. There must have been enough for all. For, as the sign in Mzee Pipa's store had said, 'I sold for cash'.

It must have been the same God, on a rampage, who spoke a few months later to Uganda's Idi Amin in a dream. Allah told him that the Asians were sabotaging the economy, hoarding to create shortages, smuggling sugar, coffee and currency, not paying taxes... and they were not integrating, not allowing their daughters to marry Africans. Therefore, Allah concluded, the Asians must go.

Ugandan passports were confiscated from the Asians. Lines grew outside the British High Commission and the Canadian and American embassies in Kampala, stretching as far as the eye could see, men and women holding their valid or defunct blue British passports, birth certificates, letters from relatives, evidence of assets, affidavits, diplomas for sewing, plumbing and hairdressing... anything to make themselves more attractive, well-dressed prettified orphans queueing in sun and rain, waiting to be adopted.

Do we want these Asians? No, said a majority of the British public in a poll. No, said newspaper articles and a certain MP whose pronouncements on such matters have made his name a household and dreaded word among Asians in East Africa. If Amin can do this, some said in England, then so can we. The *Nigerian Star*, quoted by Nairobi's *Daily Reporter*, lauded Amin's 'final solution'.

This beautiful fertile country, let it become the America of the Hindu, a British governor had pronounced at the turn of the century. He had invited Indian dukawallahs to help open up the interior for trade, to buy African cotton for British ginneries and sell British-made cloth and shirts back to the African. This pearl of the African crown, as we later found out, became an inferno, a butchery from which the Asians were lucky to escape in time...

They left ignominiously, and in a hurry. The last three months had been terrifying. The army knew that goods were being liquidated, money being collected for the getaway – hidden in cupboards, cookers, attics, car chassis and buried in the ground until the time of departure – and troops descended upon the dukas to loot, kidnap and extort. Girls had been kidnapped, never to be seen again. It was this, more than anything else, they feared... a cowering bunch of dukawallahs with prayers on their mouths, against an army let loose in the name of God. They left penniless, except for what they could hide on their bodies without discovery. There was an inordinate number of women in period, Red Cross reported.

A few weeks after Amin's dream, a few hours before the first plane load of Asians was scheduled to depart, an East

African Airways plane was hijacked from Dar airport and left for Kilimanjaro Airport to pick up Obote's troops on their way to Entebbe. But the Ugandan pilot – a slacker in flying class, witnesses were quick to testify in retrospect – broke one of the cardinal rules taught to the EAA pilots: he slammed the brakes too hard and crashed. At the same time more of Obote's soldiers were on their way to Uganda by land. One half of this contingent, it was said, consisted more of politicians – former students – than soldiers, who first started to convert Amin's soldiers instead of shooting. It was as if Amina's intellectuals had gone to fight. It returned, badly mauled. Gaddafi sent 'tough Libyan commandoes' to Uganda; they never reached there; and Idi Amin bombed Mwanza, Musoma, Bukoba, Kaboya… and at home went on a blood-spree of revenge against his enemies.

In Dar, at Amina's house, we said Tanzania is different, its Asians more truly African. Indians have been on the coast for centuries, and they speak English – Amina attested, having come from abroad – *quite* differently from Indian Indians. There is a distinct Swahili-ness to their English. And ask them, she exhorted, the Indian term for bakuli, or machungwa, or ndizi, and you'll catch them at a loss. As for their brand of Swahili: first, there are several brands, from the bad (kuja-*ne*! or kuja-*to*!) to the good – which if you want to hear, go and talk to Mama Ji-Ji opposite the market; and second, have you heard the Swahili the Africans speak in Nairobi (eti, kula maji! or: mutu mubaya!)? And who would deny that a chapati, or a samosa or a curry were not Coastal food? Even biriyani. And have you seen the furniture of a traditional Swahili home? There you'll see Indian influence. And have you heard a Zanzibari taarabu? Hum it for an Indian and he'll give you the words in Hindi. There.

Thank you, Amina, I said.

In Zanzibar, Vice President Karume had been assassinated while playing cards... an Arab's revenge, or an insurance for his daughter?

... and there were sighs of relief from many corners, which the air blew away and kept secret... A twin-engine plane flew low over Dar one day, scattering pamphlets calling for the President's overthrow... Kambona, people said, who had flown to exile in London, whom Idi Amin had invited to begin operations in Uganda, who had not liked the Asians.

The Asians trembled. I never owned a building in my life, Ji Bai – Mama Ji-Ji, as Amina called her – said, what do I care? Nationalisation of commercial property; its rationale – making money and not working – made sense to her. The simple socialism of the folk: it's all ours, what's there to quibble about? As for Uganda – Ask anyone, she said, take anyone from the street, go on, and ask him, does this mama belong here or not? And she demonstrated, calling out, Weh Nassoro! Njo hapa! Come here. Nassoro came, a young man working in the vicinity, a black and yellow scarf tied stylishly round his neck, a grin on his face and obviously in a hurry. Am I not your mother? she asked. No, said Nassoro, my grandmother! and ran off, she giving the chase.

But elsewhere, where there was money, a new language had developed.

'How much is a hundred?' meaning, the masai, the hundred-shilling note.

'Depends. Where?'

'Kenya.'

'Sixty. Sixty-for-a-hundred!'

'And Ibrahim Bhai? What does he go for?'

'Forty.' For the dollar, the code name referring to Lincoln's picture on it.

'Sterling?' The pound.

'Sixty.'

Even a child could tell you the rates.

There are those who made their fortunes on them, and others who lost theirs, trusting too much, relying on a code that no longer existed. Into this uncertain climate happened the SS *Shree Dhana*, named auspiciously, for wealth, which it would have carried, nicknamed SS *Mowlana*, 'Saviour'.

But first: it could not have happened, this tragicomedy, without the Uganda expulsion, the 'exodus', which cracked our world open like an egg. There was a world, outside this egg, that you could escape to. Previously, even less than a year ago, going there was like going to the moon: only a few brave souls went to its alien loneliness and survived precariously. Only a few months ago the pious would tell you of the moral degeneracy of the West. Now there were Ugandan Asians in India and Pakistan, UK, US, Canada and Australia.

It started with a rumour. There is a certain ship. It can take you to Pakistan. And, with the proper bribery, all your goods and assets. The rumour circulated and soon became fact, passages on this mysterious saviour of a ship were sold like lottery tickets, through private agents and a certain travel agent. Over a few days, old heavy furniture, closets, refrigerators, radios, even TVs from Nairobi, were lowered into the ship. Hassan Uncle and Zera Auntie came to say goodbye. Where will you go? Karachi. Do you know anyone there? No. Will you be all right there? God willing... our people are there. From where this blind trust? 'Our people' were certainly there, many of them ready to scalp these African Asians who, they had always believed, were rich and proud. But this contingent did not make it. One day before departure, at about eleven in the morning, an old Ignis refrigerator hung suspended from a crane making its way into the hold of the saviour ship. But some silly passenger had secured the door of the fridge with a tape... which snapped at one point and then rapidly at several others and the door swung open. Out dropped manna for the dock workers below, notes in several currencies, and jewellery. The police were called, impounded the ship and found: fridges overflowing with currency, iceboxes stashed with dollars and pounds and rupees, butter and cheese compartments containing jewellery. Come and claim your property, said the police.

It was now, not before, when Ushirika House was nationalised, that Hassan Uncle was wiped out. Not completely, shopkeepers are indomitable, Hassan Uncle had other assets, but positively his last. He had five children, three of them overseas, including Mehboob, who had shown Charlie Chaplin films on their bedroom linen in Msimbazi so many years ago, for ten cents a show per person. Mehboob, after several false starts in Toronto, had rediscovered his vocation; he showed Indian films, first in school halls on weekends, and later in a full-fledged cinema house. And with the new name of Mehboob Khan, he came to claim his parents, one of whom, my uncle, had suffered a nervous breakdown.

The last time I saw Hassan Uncle.

The family had come to say goodbye. The sitting room was almost empty, except for two rows of chairs which had formed from a broken circle, and a table with tea and snacks. It was after the tea, Fatu Auntie had been going on and on about her life in Zanzibar forty years ago, and everyone was now in the mood for discussing the past. Hassan Uncle was silent, listening with a long serious face, arms folded. He wore, as always, a long-sleeved shirt with tails hanging out. Then Kulsum started talking about her Kariakoo shop, and naturally Hassan Uncle's name came up, and his face lit up with a smile and he joined in. He got up and said, 'Remember, I would go on my bicycle from Msimbazi to Kichwele like this...' And standing up, he went around the room, and then between the rows of chairs in figures of eight, his two hands in front of him as if he were walking the bicycle, which he had often done instead of riding it. At which point Mehboob Khan got up and brought his father back to his chair, and the goodbyes and the tears started, the loudest and the most prolonged naturally from Fatu Auntie.

Zera Auntie went around making elaborate goodbyes, telling long stories, and slipping hundred-shilling notes into hands and bosoms, in a last extravagant act of charity. She looked rather odd, in fact aged and toothless. There was a simple reason for this. Zera Auntie had been due for several fillings and a couple of extractions. Mehboob Khan came up with a simple, one-stroke money-saving solution: since all the teeth would go some day, anyway, and dentures being expensive in Canada, why not have the dentures fitted before departure? At the time of goodbye, poor pink-gummed philanthropic Zera Auntie, her hair in curls, was still waiting for her dentures.

As I was leaving, and he stood at the door shaking hands and giving hugs, Hassan Uncle said, in his usual cryptic fashion:

'Like the king.'

'What king, Hassan Uncle?' I asked, half expecting: Aré, what world are you all living in? and a contemptuous glare from the stony face. But he was kinder.

'Bruce... Bruce! The king with the spider!'

The tube light clicked on, as they say. 'Yes, yes, King Bruce!'

'Like him, we'll make it.'

Shamas Pir had promised the Shamsis a saviour from the west, and they had waited for hundreds of years. Now it seemed to some that he had come, not a pir, but a Pierre, Trudeau of Canada, promising a cold Eldorado to the north. He will take us, they said, as he took the Ugandans, leave it to Pierre True-do! And they, who had renounced the Queen's rule for a new future, abandoned hope and returned to her, still close but separated by an ocean.

21 | *Marriage of Minds: Alliances*

Sona left, and Amina returned. A triumphant Amina, full of the world: a sober, mature Amina, a feminist Amina, still a Marxist-Leninist; a bigger, heavier Amina, hamburgers and chips had gone well with her, but for that a more imposing Amina, Amina who came with a man, and note this, not a black but a white American, Mark, of slight build and full red beard, the same politics, soft spoken and very attentive and caring. They had come via Cuba.

Amina attracted neophytes, men and women to sit at her feet and learn about the reality and all-pervasiveness of politics. Life without politics was an illusion; so was commitment without activism, for this woman who had been through peace marches and campus occupations. She gave two lectures when she came; one on politics and the African novel, the other on feminism and Africa. So radical she looked, so eclectic was her knowledge, so much authority was exuded by the kitenge maxi dresses and the Afro hairstyle – immediately, she established a following.

She took a job as a teacher at Jangwani, and set up house on Viongozi Street, not far from where Jogo used to live. (Jogo, of course, had moved up, to Upanga.) The house became famous, and was filled with visitors. In the reception room books lined the walls and newspapers lay on the floor, where also Amina sat, on one of the pillows. It was impossible to go there without meeting someone coming out or preparing to leave after an audience. The outside door – old, wooden, discoloured and twisted by the ravages of alternate rain and sun – opened into a long corridor on each side of which, almost immediately you stepped in, were two large bedrooms with very small windows. At the end of the corridor was the sitting-reception room.

Here came all kinds of people, the original SNAFU, and recently the poet Abdel Latif Kodi, and some overseas students. The poet was quiet and looked rather ordinary, and only with some difficulty could one induce him to recite any verses. It was only with the Zanzibari Zuleika, now a Swahili teacher, that he really sat down to talk seriously. It seemed that there was another existence that he lived, where he was quite eloquent, for in his country he had been in prison for his views… an existence that Amina obviously shared. Then there was Beverley St George, also a teacher at Jangwani, a short Canadian girl with a rather freckled round face, who let herself be the butt of jokes sometimes, but who could hold her own quite well; and the Caribbean Indian student and poet Alex Ramdas, and Rashid and Layla, and Brother Zahir.

Rashid was born in Durban and brought up in Glasgow, taught political economy at the University, and never failed to rouse wonder in his listeners when, from his dark brown face and gold-toothed mouth, emerged an impeccably precise English accent, which earned him the title of 'Call Me Bwana'. Layla was his English wife, a red-pigtailed girl in long, dumpy skirts, rather like the picture of a maid on a Danish biscuit tin. But appearances were deceptive: she was a volatile feminist, whose reason for her peculiar dressing, beside the evident comfort, was to drown in them the leery eyes of men. Layla was a social anthropologist, and one day she read what she had observed and concluded about our mixed-race group, with the result that she was almost beaten up.

Alex, the Caribbean poet, had a strange habit of reading – from a paper or book in his left hand, the right hand held up in front of the audience, executing a circular motion, like a strange little machine spewing forth words. A poor reader, who is to say how good a poet? One poem everybody definitely considered bad: it had 'Ujamaa' appearing seven times, but it brought him opportunities to read at several University functions.

Then our own Brother Zahir, bespectacled, small and professorial – who, years before, would intercept us (Sona, Alu, Jogo and I) on United Nations Road on our way to school, emerging from behind a bush (for everybody avoided him) and asking, 'Brother, did you say your prayers today?' This had earned him the nickname. He had, by way of Moral Rearmament and Gandhiism, now arrived at a cold-blooded theoretical Marxism, throwing every historical event to the cogs of a class struggle machinery, letting it churn out the conclusion. Thus Idi Amin, whose bloody deeds came splattered regularly in the news reports, was simply a monster produced by the structures left behind by colonialism. How could one disagree with such generalities? And what good were they to those who were literally battered to death? To Brother Zahir and Amina (and the two could go on for ages, talking of case histories like doctors), the political economist Rashid, interminably reading Durrell, was a mere romantic: he loved everybody, good or bad, and laughed at and with them, and at himself. He was most like the 'Shehe', Ali Tamim, and the two were planning a book on the life and economy of Kilwa when the Portuguese came.

Of course, it was not only for politics that they came to sit at her feet – these teachers, lecturers and students. There were always two sides to Amina – the theoretician scholar to whom the government measures seemed non-vigorous, slow, half-baked, its socialist vocabulary lacking commitment and real meaning; and the person, the warm, passionate and even fragile Amina, who needed people, who could lure them unawares to her causes as she had once lured me in Kaboya. Without her that group was nothing. She provided the place, the atmosphere and the agenda. For most of us that place on Viongozi was more – a club for like-minded people, always open, always hospitable.

And every evening a gang of noisy young boys waited expectantly outside this bustling house, then Mark would emerge in his shorts and colourful T-shirt and they would follow him at a distance as he jogged on Morogoro Road, in the direction of Morogoro, down the hill and then back up again, the only American to have lived this side of Mnazi Moja.

I taught at BOSS, my old school, where once the only important things were to get first grade in Senior Cambridge, for the school to win the Christopher Cup in cricket and the Youth Drama Festival trophy. Like other schools we now had a farm, to which every afternoon a few classes were assigned. Mr Kabir, Mr Khan, Mr Sardar, once respective heads of departments, now you could see carrying the odd panga or jembe, desperately waiting for their retirement dates. None of them lasted till then, they went on to Zambia, these men who had simply come to teach but then had nowhere to go, who belonged nowhere. (Sona traced another of our Indian teachers in New York, Mr Patwekar, who lived in a single room and taught maths in a ghetto school.) At BOSS the basketball court was overgrown, the tennis racquets were taken away by the last tennis captain, the cricket ground was becoming a Serengeti without lions. Perhaps this was how it had looked when the school was not built and there *were* lions in the area. (Looking out of the door of Form IA I would imagine sometimes a maize field there… and the ghosts of past cricketers Gumji Junior, Goani, Abuani Solanki running through it, picking maize… or slashing at the grass with their bats.) Jangwani was not far and I would sometimes have lunch there with Amina and Mark (who taught biology there); their house was a further five minutes away. At Zanaki, the former Agakhan Girls' School, Zuleika Kassam, quiet SNAFU member, taught literature and Swahili. She also lived in Upanga. On two occasions we returned together rather late from Amina's house. The second time her mother was waiting for her. She spoke the Zanzibari Cutchi-Swahili mix.

'Weh Zuli, mbona umerudi so late-late, basi?'

'Mummy, I was at a meeting.'

'Ah!' She was visibly vexed. 'Why didn't you tell me, then?'

'I didn't know it would be so late, Mummy.'

The occasion had been the Uganda expulsion, its announcement, and the debate at Amina's was heated.

'To come this late, and walking tena, and with a man in the dark... ah-ah-ah... I could have sent Mahmoud...'

'But he's only Kulsum Bai's son!'

'Which Kulsum Bai?'

She came to peer at me, I was still in the garden, Zuleika was at the door defending her virtue.

'Hebu, basi. Kulsum Dhanji?'

'Yes,' I said.

'Whose son is in America and writes to her in Gujarati?'

'Yes, my brother.'

'It is true, eti? In Gujarati? They teach that there?'

'Yes.'

He had only learnt the script, which Kulsum had written down for him. The language of course he spoke!

'Come in. You will have tea?'

'No, I must go. My mother must be worrying.' I watched her go back in: like most Indian women her age she had a roll to her walk from unduly large hips, a result of successive child deliveries.

* * *

The union was obvious to the most casual observer. Two teachers. Same interests. Friendly to each other. No competitors in sight. While I smarted from Amina's betrayal and suffered Mark's exaggerated courtesies, the two of them plotted to keep us late so we could go home together. While I dutifully escorted Zuleika to her home after dusk, her mother waited up for her and formed ideas, and boys and girls in Upanga East, from Red Cross to the Chinese Embassy, from Upanga to United Nations, started gossiping. Someone whispered the gossip into Kulsum's ears. Kulsum promised two or three bribes to the gods, I don't know what she put into my tea, and she got to work.

A teacher. Same interests as mine. Pretty and lively. What was I waiting for? I said yes.

She said yes, and the engagement was announced.

Weddings are fun. Begum writes a tearful letter and Kulsum relents. 'Dear daughter Begum, to whom God grant etc. I am a widow and it is not appropriate for me to preside over the wedding of a son, to put on a colourful pachedi and welcome the bride home, this would be inauspicious and in bad taste. You being the eldest and married it is only appropriate that you should take over the task of the mother, you who brought them up while I was in the shop downstairs…' And Begum arrives fat but jolly with all kinds of luxurious gifts that she has spent a considerable part of her savings to buy, and bringing with her two enchanting, beautiful children with whom Kulsum cannot communicate except through gestures and broken English. And there are tears of joy, joy too much to contain, 'I wish he were here,' Kulsum sobs, remembering him, he whose name she never uttered, he who was and is always *he*, he whom she addressed simply with, 'Listen…': her husband.

Weddings are fun, they bathe you in milk and anoint you

with saffron and shower you with rice while they sing folksy songs in hoarse voices... they fuss over you and they tease you (Will you forget them when she comes?) and make sexual innuendoes that you don't know how to respond to... and finally you emerge, in your best suit from My Tailor and braced with Old Spice and put yourself in the hands of the best man, who accompanies you to the mosque... and she comes shy and tense in her white dress and glittering with jewels, her hair set high, hands painted with henna, tottering on her high heels, looking down... all afternoon having sat in front of a brazier being saturated in halud vapour, so that by the time you get her alone in the room at the Kilimanjaro, the family friends having left after examining the marriage bed for springiness and softness and taking that inane picture with your arm around her which you once swore you would never have taken, you can hardly wait and she can hardly wait but she lies down stiff and expectant, hard and full and fragrant as a ripe mango ready to burst, waiting with a fluttering heart for you to claim her.

Weddings are fun.

The morality campaign was on, Green Guard cadres went about town with a morality meter: this was a simple device, nothing more than a king-size Coca Cola bottle, which had to be able to pass through your trouser legs before they could be pronounced decent. Thus the fight against 'drainpipe' pants and jeans. There were many quarrels and near fights. Officials were not willing to stand by and let their wives' skirts be measured. And girls and boys out on Independence Avenue simply ducked into a store or restaurant when they saw a cadre approaching; and the tourists and expatriates simply ignored these guardians of public morality.

At about this time – Hassan Uncle had left a few months before – there came a visitor to Dar called Nasir Bunzai, from the mountainous district of Bunza in the north of Pakistan. Ever since the *Daily Reporter* of Nairobi did a series on the enchanting land of Bunza a few years before, the Shamsis in East Africa stood in awe of anything Bunzai. Bunza, it was said, was a land where people routinely lived up to more than a hundred years eating yogurt and nuts, breathing fresh mountain air, and possessed such a high degree of spirituality that they would wrap a newborn infant in fur and roll it down a mountain to test its sturdiness and spiritual power. Nasir was a Sufi from Bunza, a small man with a round face and thick spectacles, among whose feats was a night spent in a Chinese jail. He soon acquired a following, primarily among the women, chief among whom was Kulsum's sister Fatu.

My Fatu Auntie, who would have made an excellent tragedienne, was in a spiritual phase, having elevated her father Mitha Kanji, who had predicted the fall of Zanzibar in the 1920s, to the level of a pir. In this she was joined by several women whose fathers or grandfathers had followed my grandfather, then called Mad Mitha, out of Zanzibar to Mombasa and Dar. This group then embraced Nasir the Sufi, still keeping their loyalty to Mitha Kanji (whose photograph, showing him in a turban, had been produced). From Nasir they learnt the science of meditation, or dhikr, the Bunza way. At eight every evening they met at my aunt's, they sat in a circle on a mat, with Nasir at the head, and they held hands and chanted 'Allah! Allah!' Overcome with emotion and exuberance, several of the participants would weep.

Needless to say, there were many who viewed the whole affair with disapproval, to the point of casting doubt on the Sufi's moral integrity and on Bunza's spiritual pre-eminence. He too left, soon thereafter, to serve the more needy souls in Canada.

This left Fatu Auntie with Mad Mitha. What future for this fledgling sect? That remains to be seen.

* * *

The last time I saw Amina…

Across the street from Amina's house was a barber's shop, with the sign

MATUMBI
the champion HAIR
DRESSING & CATTING
saloon

where two barbers worked. I don't know if it ever changed hands, but I remember always seeing it, from the very first days I started taking that route to school. Next to the Matumbi was a nameless tea kiosk. Here one morning a neatly dressed man in a grey Kaunda suit, after impressing his credentials upon the owner, took a seat with a bunch of newspapers and began drinking tea, a procedure he followed for several days thereafter.

It was evening, after a reading by Abdel Latif Kodi at Jangwani. As I stepped into the dark corridor of the house I bumped into a stomach.

'Watch it,' I murmured in irritation, 'you're not looking where you're going!'

'Weh, Juma!'

Shivji Shame in mufti.

'What are you doing here at this time – you're a married man!'

'Yes.'

'And you are a father. What's the child's name?'

'Amina.'

'Aah! A girl.'

'What are *you* doing here? Without uniform—'

'Visiting. We want her to give a lecture. In camp.'

Shivji Shame was now in the army, but had not earned his mkasis yet, the major's scissors. He was still a sergeant. He brought his head close to mine and whispered, forefinger raised: 'You watch me, I'll make it yet. I've been to Uganda.' Out he stomped into the dark night.

Amina was in the sitting room, sitting on a pillow on the mat, back against the wall, feet stretched in front of her, hands in her lap... Abdel Latif Kodi likewise against the opposite wall. A resigned, almost serene look on both faces, as if they had left everything in the hands of some higher authority, of fate, chance whatever. What did they know?

'Our conscience,' smiled Amina, bidding me sit. The poet smiled graciously. 'No,' I said, '*there's* our conscience,' and pointed to him.

'A stifled conscience,' she said.

The poet left soon afterwards.

'Where is everyone else? I thought they were coming here.'

'Dancing. Drinking. Whoring, for all I know.'

'I was passing by—'

'It's late, Salum. Your wife can't keep you?'

'Where's Mark?'

I, too, had heard rumours.

'He's left. For Nairobi and Lamu. There are enough hippies there. We have work to do here.'

We sat and talked late into the night. No banter and baiting this time. What had come between us before was now no longer there: too much had passed. Now a mellow Amina and a mellow Salim, unburdened of the pure rough-edged ideals of youth, the cockiness of the youth of a youthful country. Man and woman, we had known closeness before, we slipped easily into its embraces, a tremor to our voices, a tremble in our taut bodies, infinitely happy at this rediscovery. We loved that night but did not make love. And when I got up to go, that exchange of looks, What will happen now, and the barest brush of her arm against mine. 'Be careful,' she said.

Oh sweet love, if only you didn't hurt as much...

At the end of the street, at Morogoro Road, a GT Land Rover was parked. A policeman got out and I nervously looked up.

'Jambo.'

'Jambo.'

'Where to, at this hour?'

'Home. I was visiting a friend.'

'A girlfriend, no doubt! You should be careful at this hour.'

'Yes. Asante.'

'Kwa heri.'

I took the lighted United Nations Road, then crossed into Upanga on Malik Road. Soundlessly I unlocked the door and tiptoed to bed on the sofa.

Anatomy of a marriage.

She never forgave me Amina. Amina the girl and Amina the name. When Beverley St George the Crazy Canadian said something about her being married on the rebound, the foreign phrase stayed on her mind, undigested, before it finally sank in with the bite of an acid. Hell hath no fury like a woman scorned. Zuleika took control with a vengeance. Within weeks Kulsum had fled to Tanga, to Mehroon. And then slowly came the attack... if not I, then everything I stood for... the very lifestyle, the commitment that had brought us together in the first place, the semi-bohemian simplicity and denial of everything foreign, the carefree intellectual existence free from the shackles of family and community...

But then, she had not *really* belonged, she had been more a sympathetic figure who belonged nowhere really, neither with the wives of the dukas, nor with those of the new mercenaries, she did not want to go abroad… and of our Viongozi group, she did not take it seriously (except Abdel Latif Kodi): Mbogo chasing Bev St George, Rashid and Tamim forever planning their book but not getting anywhere, Layla fighting windmills (all men, except a handful), Alex reading like a windmill, and Amina: what was she *doing*, sitting there like a queen bee at the end of the hive? And I, she said, I went there only to see Amina and to impress her…

When the child was born, she would have her be named by a local religious personage (the same one who had prophesied to Alu Poni), who besides foretelling the coming apocalypse could successfully split hairs over the differences between Aisha, Asha and Ashia (outside whose house, which was guarded by a dog, boys had recently changed the sign to read: Beware of God), who cast a horoscope and pronounced: A name with an 'm' in it – what better music to the ears than the gentle pleasing sound of the name of the Prophet's mother? Amina. Zuleika looked up in disbelief, turned to me for the dissenting voice to escape my usually sceptical lips. An alternative name could have been requested, but I accepted Amina almost too readily, in the process admitting to the guilt she made me pay for. Of course, she could have accepted the name happily, and let the new Amina, kicking and screaming with fresh energy overshadow the old one. But no. Such philosophical patience was not forthcoming, and I offer it only in hindsight.

She was the woman twice scorned. Hatred seething below the surface at every domestic function. My every visit to that house on Viongozi would end with a quarrel which would destabilise us for the next forty-eight hours. Chained to a volcano, I would whisper to myself, sleeping with a land mine. At dinner, we were at each other's throats like alley cats while little Amina looked in wonder from her imported high chair before joining in with her own screams.

* * *

The next evening, at nine, a lull in the hostilities at home, and in the activities outside – the nearby mosque had emptied – Zuleika was putting the little Amina to bed, and I sat with the *Herald* and a cup of tea, thinking periodically of the other Amina – what to *do*? – when there came a pounding on the door. A soft pounding made by a large fist. Shivji Shame simply pushed his way in as soon as the locks were unbolted. Again, without uniform.

'Ah, Juma. What news? I was passing by, I thought I should come and meet you.'

'Good of you to come, Shivji.'

'Fanta?' he asked.

His armpits were stained with sweat, there were beads of perspiration on his face. But it was the same Shivji, a little weatherbeaten, perhaps.

'No,' I said. 'Water.'

'All right. Then tea, please. Sweet, army tea.'

He had been to Uganda, he said when he was relaxed and slurping the tea. One of the rebel forces on their way to Uganda from Tanzania had passed by Kaboya, in the dead of night, in fact the Kaboya men had assisted it. But then the excitement was too much for them to bear, who for several years now had carried weapons and sang of fighting, and some of them simply joined the Ugandan force on its way to Masaka. 'When the shooting started – we were faced with tanks and a prepared army – aaiiiiii! we were scared... it was the first time we had seen any real fighting... killing... I tell you Juma, we were happy when the order came for retreat.'

'And when Kaboya was bombed – you were there?'

He looked at me. He asked for more tea. We waited.

'So?' I asked. 'How did it go? Not many died, I gather.'

'You don't know?' He looked up. 'About Zainab?'

'No,' I said. 'What about Zainab?'

The first time the bombs fell, they fell smack in the middle of the market, which was the centre of the town. Right across from the hotel I had stayed in, I recalled. Outside it was the bus stop, where Bakari had dropped me, with the three girls, and where Amina first spoke to me... People ran screaming out from the market, Shivji said, men, women and children, straight for the edge of town. Some went to the lake and waited, wading in the water or sitting in boats. That was when twelve people died. A big crater was left in the market. No one went to it again. But business must continue, the next day they lined outside, on the perimeter of the market, with their bananas and pineapples, fish and meat. The National Service was there to assist – to evacuate, if the need arose. Then news came that Bukoba had been hit again, Idi Amin was threatening to march into Tanzania, straight up to Tanga, and no-one was willing to wait. In cars, buses, taxis, bicycles, on pushcarts and on foot they started to leave the town, to go south, as far from the border as possible. People parted with their wealth just for a taxi ride, or gave one half away to carry the other half in a push cart. The Meghjis travelled in two vehicles, their own car and a taxi. Some ten miles after the side road departs for Uhuru Camp, the road rises steeply before falling again, and narrows for about a quarter of a mile, allowing only one vehicle to pass. To the right is a treacherous fall into a deep ravine bedded with bushes, trees and rocks. Before continuing on this stretch you have to make sure there is no car or bus coming from the opposite direction. Buses in fact let their passengers walk that distance. If you look down into the ravine, you can see the rusting bodies of vehicles. It was on this stretch that the Meghji car broke down. The driver got out to repair it, and the passengers came out to watch and stretch their legs: Zainab, her husband, her parents and Faruq. The rest of the family was a car and a bus behind, in the taxi. As the driver tinkered with the engine, behind them started a ruckus, no-one wanted to sit in the middle of the road in the sun, a ready target for the planes of Idi Amin if they arrived. Move, they said, impatiently, we don't have all day. Haraka, basi! They threw up their hands in disgust. Of all the times and all the places, and all the people!... But the car would not start. The driver of the Meghji car went to converse with the bus driver. Then some passengers, after shouting at him, got out of the bus, and with the encouragement of the driver of the car behind them, heave-ho! harambee! tia mate! songa mbele! they lifted the car at one side and pushed it into the ravine, before the family quite knew what had happened. But then, Zainab turned and gave a loud shriek, then a wail of grief... her two children, three and one-and-a-half years old had been sleeping in the car. Wailing and shrieking, her hands to her ears, she ran in the direction of the car and her children, and before anyone got to her she flung herself into the ravine, behind them.

'She wanted four kids, she would say. Oh God—'

'I'm sorry, Juma.'

It was said in some of the papers that in order to initiate a four-year-old into the practice of murder, Amin would have a soldier tied down and let the boy hack through his neck with a panga...

After this, what complaint?

The next day I received the news in the staff room that Amina Binti Saidi, Miss Saidi of Jangwani, had been detained. With her, Abdel Latif Kodi. And some soldiers, including an Asian.

If I had stayed a little longer... if I had gone again the next night as I had been tempted to do while reading the *Herald* listlessly, would I have been in detention too? Or if they had come for Shivji while he was with me... perhaps he had given them the slip then. How deeply was Amina involved? I did not really know, I did not belong to that inner circle of hard-core theoreticians. Like most, I came for the atmosphere, and because of Amina. It is too dramatic to think of a plotting, revolutionary Amina, a mastermind using the likes of me, Rashid, Layla and Alex as a harmless front for her activities. Most likely the initiative came from disgruntled army officers looking for educated mouthpieces and political planners. And how could Amina and her rigorous friends, sitting in the sidelights, forego this one possibility of power, of putting their words into action? It came too easily, they should have been wiser. It turned out, in the end, to be a student exercise run wild. I had of course asked Amina about Shivji leaving the house. 'Oh,' she said, 'he came with an invitation.' 'Will you go?' I asked. 'I am not sure.' What invitation: to speak or to join? I think they both knew the game was up when I last saw them, Amina, that night in her home; Shivji the following night in mine.

And then two weeks later, a request to see me in the staff room from an old woman in a buibui waiting outside... looking withered and rather pitiful, bags under her eyes.

'Jambo, teacher.'

'Jambo, mama. Your child in trouble?'

'E-eh.'

We were both quiet.

'She's taken away,' she said in anguish.

'You're her mother—' I spoke slowly. 'Come, mama, njo. Sit, mama. I am so sorry. What can be done?'

'Perhaps you can do something... a bad child, why did she have to do such things...'

Perhaps I could bribe someone. Or see a lawyer. Or had a friend in government. Being Asian, she thought, I had access to more influence. I said I would try. I tried to detain her, this woman who was part of Amina, to see Amina in her, to get to know her... but having stated her request she wanted to leave.

I never saw her again, never had the opportunity to do what I had promised. For that night Jogo knocked on the door with Abdalla.

A few years ago in Nairobi: Down the Ngara hill and opposite the road from Globe Cinema with its huge, coloured posters of Hindi films past, present and future (badly drawn film stars, male and female, with thickly painted red lips), there was an empty warehouse, boarded up. It used to be a furniture store; a trading licence had been refused to the Asian British subject owner. One day a pretty young woman in sari ran screaming from this warehouse, crossed the road, which is quite wide there, bringing the bustling traffic to a temporary disarray, and entered one of the small furniture dukas facing the cinema. Thus came to light a sickening extortion racket. Respectable Indian women, wives of doctors and lawyers, were lured from their homes to this empty godown by a telephone call that informed them in urgent tones that their husbands were hurt. But, top secret: certain local politicians were involved. The women, when they entered the dust-filled and cobwebby hall breathless and flushed in a frenzy of anxiety, were faced with four leering men leaning against a table, looking like the film star Pran at his worst (said the *Daily Reporter*), all Indian, who raped them, took photographs, and subsequently blackmailed them. One woman committed suicide, rather than pay, the only traditional alternative. The one who escaped was brave twice over.

Among the four men, one was a Tanzanian, not caught. Meet Jogo: the practical joker, caught with his hand in a peanut-seller's basket once, who would relate to us sexual fantasia all the way down United Nations Road to school, whose father limped all the way from the end of Msimbazi to Nuru Poni's shop in Kichwele at four in the morning calling people to prayer: innocent, deprived Jogo, turned pervert: the new man after the flood, mercenary, cut-throat, preying on fears. But mere extortion of housewives, however rich, is not the way to phenomenal wealth, empire. Jogo had turned international. While Idi Amin was ranting away in Kampala, calling Nyerere an old woman, lorries took off in the dead of night for Kenya, full of stolen coffee beans for export by local merchants. Shivji had been to Uganda: unbelievable as it seems, so had Jogo.

Reports of such deeds do not stay hidden. The bush telegraph whispers them around. They are essential, they lend to the image and propagate it. The wonder is (then, perhaps not) that the authorities are helpless.

When I opened the door Jogo stepped in and Abdalla waited outside. There is a certain bearing, an apparent tallness, that power and wellbeing give. He had it. He wore a white Kaunda suit and carried a carved ebony walking cane.

'You are a friend of Amina Bind Saidi,' he said, after the preliminary greetings.

The same Jogo in manner of speech, his familiarity, sharing a common background, time spent together playing cricket, organising teams and going to school. You begin to wonder, are we all like him?

'Yes, I am.'

'You know she has been detained for conspiracy to overthrow the Government.'

'I say, Jogo, can you find out where she is – her mother is frantic, bana.'

He ignored my outburst. 'You were seen leaving her house the night before she was picked up.' There was now a shade more authority in his manner of speaking, enough when you knew his reputation.

'So?'

'So you are under suspicion. Your turn has come.'

'Don't be silly! I don't even know what conspiracy—'

'I'm simply telling you. You'll be picked up any time. Outside,' he said in a low voice, indicating the door. 'Abdalla. He is not your friend. He works for Security now.'

Abdalla was in our school for some years. He was from a very influential family, a very private person in our Asian school, who one day had had an altercation with Sona, with the result that both were caned by the African headmaster (this was after independence), after which he changed schools.

Preventive Detention. A Land Rover arrives in the middle of the night and takes you away. No-one knows where you're taken or for how long, no-one mentions your name aloud, and when you return you've been silenced. What goes on there? What kind of jailers run these places and what would the likes of Abdalla, Asian hater, do to the likes of me?

Jogo offered a simple way out and I grabbed it. Too fast. I was a child in his hands, what with my own domestic predicament, and I swallowed everything he told me. Greedily. I did not even know if Abdalla was really in Security. I held a small conference with Zuleika, and then we both turned to face him.

'Do you have a passport-sized photograph?'

'Only one.'

'Enough. Pack your clothes. No-one knows where you're going.'

Another conference, then again we turned to look at him, helplessly.

'Coming?' he asked.

'Where?' Zuleika asked.

'Yes, where?'

'Trust me. I am Jogo, your friend.'

I looked at her, she nodded, dumbly.

I kissed the sleeping child, and I hugged her, my wife. I tried to miss her but I couldn't. 'I'll send for you,' I lied; she didn't reply.

As we reached the airport, I told him: 'I say, Jogo. Thanks for all this.'

'No problem.' He gave me the ticket. 'Destination Lisbon,' he said. '... Walji runs a bar there. And take this.' He slipped a package into my coat pocket. 'Give this to him.'

In Lisbon Walji, former lawyer and classmate, ran the Vitoria Pub, with his entire family, and I helped him, dispensing dreams of victory and early return to the Portuguese soldiers we had both decried in National Service. There was also a brisk trade in Iranian carpets, with a branch office in London. The family was waiting for Canadian immigrant visas. My own visitor's visa to the United States arrived much sooner, and I left for Boston. There to live off Sona's scholarship, in a dissipated, depressed existence, sharing his room, watching television, doing nothing, until in exasperation he said one day: 'Do something, dammit!' Which I did, taking the bus and coming here... He was terribly sorry, and frantic with worry, but he was right, I had no business infecting him with my depression. He was so happy, immersed in his books, revelling in a scholar's life, it was sinful to disturb him.

Jogo offered release, but into what? I think I ran away from the marriage, an impossible domestic situation... like my grandfather, Huseni... and even his father Dhanji Govindji who went to look for him. The irony isn't lost on me. But is it destiny that is ironical, or is it the ironical in us, a predisposition, that makes us go after a certain fate, a certain pattern – poetry being more real than reality, as Rashid would sometimes quote. Something of both, I suspect.

22 | And the Final Night

Memory, Ji Bai said, is this gunny sack...
I can put it all back and shake it and churn it and sift it and start again, re-order memory, draw a new set of lines through those blots, except that each of them is like a black hole, a doorway to a universe... It can last for ever, this game, the past has no end – but no, Shehrbanoo, you will not snare me like that, let it end today, let this your last night.

One day Ji Bai said to her family, quite casually, I want to go to Bajupur. Bajupur! They were stunned. Does it still exist? Who is there, in Bajupur? My sister, she said, you know one of them still lives, and their sons and daughters, they even write sometimes... But they are in Bombay, and in Poona, and in Karachi! Even so, she said, they will take me to Bajupur. What *is* there in Bajupur? I want to go to the mela there, Hazrat Ali's mela. One more time, before I die... I saw it once before when I was a child, now I want to see it again.

Once, it is said, in the villages around Bajupur, the Prophet's favourite, Hazrat Ali, came to Gujarat on his horse Dul Dul, at a place which is thirty miles from Bajupur, and as proof of this blessed event, there is a hoof mark from the horse preserved in clay. Every year a mela is held there and villagers come from miles around. They sing verses in praise of Hazrat Ali and they pray to him.

Ji Bai left with her adopted grandnephew Aziz. They met her

sisters and nieces and nephews and their children in Bombay and went to Bajupur by train. From Bajupur to the site of the mela is an hour's drive by taxi. Ji Bai recalled that it used to take them two days by bullock cart. They used to spend the nights in makeshift sheds, now there were comfortable rest houses set up for just this event. And she found the heat oppressive, Dar was so much cooler in comparison. In Bajupur itself most of the Shamsis had left, for Bombay, Poona, Bangalore, Delhi, and Karachi. Only the poorest remained. And the house… the stone house in which she had frolicked as a little girl, which even in those days had an upper storey, she proudly recalled, her heart beating thur thur – was still there, intact, and there were marks on the walls made by children just as she had imagined (remembered?) them to be all these years. Who owned it now? Unsteady and weak on her feet, 'Hold my hand,' she said to Aziz and went forward and touched a wall. A rough surface; she ran her old, bony hand over it, the veins showing like little ridges. Then, dislodging the other hand from Aziz's, she put both hands against that beloved wall, went closer to it, and softly beat her head against it, once, twice, thrice and she wept.

Later she told Aziz; now to see him, Salim. So they came, and she brought the gunny sack.

A letter from Amina.

Salum.

Surprised? I am in New York now. Older, perhaps not wiser (!) but careful, working for the United Nations, on diplomatic passport and all that. No smug remarks! What else can I tell you, where to begin? Your family is all right, which of course you know. Little Amina is truly wonderful and can talk now. I went to get your address, and guess whom I saw. Staring from the doorway of the

> *kitchen, as I was playing with the child, your mother! What big eyes she has! She just looked. I took the address and fled. What else? Shivji is out too, and I believe, reinstated. Abdel Latif is back in Lamu, desperately trying to avoid German tourists from Mombasa. But he is working with the museum there. And your friend (fiend) Jogo: he's in. For smuggling diamonds out of the country, and other things. Why don't you come to New York? There is so much to talk about, which I can't write here. (All the* details*!)*
>
> *Amina.*

And a letter from Amina.

> *Baba weh!*
>
> *It's been many months since you went, without saying goodbye. I hope your business there is soon finished. Mummy is giving tuitions in English, and I am helping her. In January I will start nursery school. Since you are a teacher, I hope you will teach me some things. Upesi.*
>
> *Wako Amina. (Transcribed by her mother.)*

Sona writes.

> *Kola.*
>
> *Are you there? This is the third letter... Anyway, about Books II and III, as I wrote before, II apparently contains old bhajans. 'DG's Favourites', in a sense. Do you know if he sang? I'm getting confused. I swear he's made up some verses – a case of genuine interpolation from DG! Now III. This one begins with a string of prayers, in Arabic, for different occasions. Perhaps illnesses. But it also has what sounds like a version of the Gita. Now why would the old man write his own version of the Gita? He was probably recording it – the language seems too archaic: imitation Sanskrit, and so on. (These*

types of forms are known, from other communities.) If so, why don't we know of other versions? Can you shed some light, from what she said to you? Why did the old woman have to die before leaving this? And also, some of the pages have not been copied well. Surely you noticed? Perhaps the writing is fading... there are ways of preserving it, you know. I am so excited, I wake up dreaming about these damn books!

Sona.

Perhaps, Dhanji Govindji, as he sat at the doorstep outside his shop listening to the ocean, in between his sporadic journeys in search for his son, *would* hum these bhajans. And if he did interpolate, what did he have to say about the sin of stealing from the community? What horrible punishments befell you and on those who came after you —

She lies on the floor, crumpled, her throat cut, guts spilled, blood on the floor. Dark crimson blood of a forgotten murder caked on the muslin shirt which Ji Bai preserved for so long, reminder of the tragic sin. On the table, the three fragile books, the originals with writing fading perhaps, packed to be sent away, their secrets unlocked but by no means uncovered. A gift for Sona. To lie anaesthetised in some locked cupboard, these dreams and hopes, these sins and prayers of a bygone generation – for the peckings of academia. The shirt, to be burnt, the rest to be discarded or preserved individually. Thus the disposition of the past. To be remembered and acknowledged, if only partly understood, without the baggage of paraphernalia.

The running must stop now, Amina. The cycle of escape and rebirth, uprooting and regeneration, must cease in me. Let this be the last runaway, returned, with one last, quixotic dream. Yes, perhaps here lies redemption, a faith in the future, even if it means for now to embrace the banal present, to pick up the pieces of our wounded selves, our wounded dreams, and pretend they're still there intact, without splints, because from our wounded selves flowers still grow. We had our dreams, Little One, we dreamt the world, which was large and beautiful and exciting, and it came to us this world, even though it was more than we bargained for, it came in large soaking waves and wrecked us, but we are thankful, for to have dreamt was enough. And so, dream, Little Flower...

Glossary

Note: Swahili words are denoted (S), the other words are Cutchi-Gujarati. The last vowel is always pronounced.

afande (S)	officer, of any rank; also: Sir! as a response
aisei (S)	from English: I say!
akida (S)	local leader or Government representative
al hamdulillah (S)	from Arabic: praised be God!
alishaan	luxurious
an-fata-ha-tin… (S)	mnemonic device for teaching to read an, in, un… from the Arabic reader
aré	an exclamation: what! etc
asante (S)	thank you
askari (S)	policeman; soldier
aulaad	progeny
ayat	from Arabic: verse
baba (S)	father
badmaash	evil
bahu	daughter-in-law
bakuli (S)	bowl
bana	Indianised form of bwana, used as 'man', etc
banda (S)	shed
band-waja	band

bao (S)	a board game common on the Coast
bapa	a respectful term for an old man; father, grandfather
baraza (S)	meeting
barazi (S)	a bean
bas	Indianised form of basi
basi (S)	enough
beta	child
Bhadalas	an Indian community in East Africa
bhajan	a religious song (hymn)
bhajia	a fried food
bhang	a narcotic
bhut	ghost
boma (S)	administrative or government office; stockade; fort
budha, budhi	old man or woman
budhu	fool
buibui (S)	a thin black garment used as veil, usually worn over dress and head
bungalas	bungalows; used of separate-standing houses
bwana (S)	sir
Chaleh	Charlie Chaplin; any funny person; comic
chevdo	a mixture of nuts, dais, rice fried with spice
chakas	plural of chako
chako	a six in cricket
chokra	boy
chuchuma! (S)	on your haunches!
crore	10 million
dada (S)	sister
daku	bandit; the villain in movies
dengu (S)	dal

dtika (S)	shop
dukan	shop
dumé (S)	man, with emphasis on manhood and bigness; a big man
duriani (S)	a fruit much loved in Zanzibar
elan	notice
eti (S)	an expletive used in many senses: what, I say, as if, etc
fujo (S)	disorder; used for the free-for-all that follows when a vendor runs away upon sight (or threat) of the police
fundi (S)	used of any craftsman or workman; in the shops, used of a tailor
gadi	wheeled vehicle; motor car
garba	a dance in which men and women perform in a circle
gathia	a fried snack
geet	song
goli	(male: golo) slave, servant
gopi	cowgirls: Krishna used to tease them
Govind	used of Krishna
hai hai!	an exclamation to show one's embarrassment
halud	a perfume
hanisi (S)	impotent
haraka (S)	quick
hartal	strike
haya, basi (S)	okay, then
hebu (S)	please (if I may; move; etc)
hijab	veil
hodi! (S)	knock!; may I come in? etc
homa (S)	rallying cry of maji maji warriors
hundi	promissory note
Idd	a Muslim festival

jamani (S)	folks
jambo (S)	how are you?
jedel	girl friend (of another girl)
jelebi	a sweetmeat
jemadari (S)	a local leader
jembe (S)	spade
jhannam	hell
joshi	fortune-teller
jugu	Indianised form of njugu: peanut
jumbe (S)	a local leader
juth bolte ho!	you are lying!
Juzu (S)	a first Arabic reader used in coastal East Africa
kalidas	servant of Kali; a commonly used (Hindu) man's name; used to denote Africans sometimes
Kali Yuga	the age of Kali
kaniki (S)	a black cloth used by women, in colonial times, now abandoned
kanzu (S)	a long garment of light cotton, usually white, worn by Muslim men
karibu (S)	welcome, come in
khamsa ishrin (S)	from Arabic, meaning 25 and used to denote the punishment of 25 strokes of a whip
khandaan	dignity, respectability, etc
khanga (S)	a colourful cloth worn by women to wrap around the body; usually has a proverb written on it as part of the design
khungu	Indianised form of kungu, a fruit considered wild
kibaba (S)	a cup measure, standardised to the commonly-used milk can

kidhar se ate ho?	Hindi: where do you come from?
kikapu (S)	basket
kikoi (S)	a piece of cloth with its own distinct design
kinate (S)	belly
kitale (S)	a coconut with no cream but an inside that can be eaten
kitenge (S)	a colourful cloth
kofi (S)	a beating
kofia (S)	a cap or hat
koni	Indianised form of kwa ni, used in the sense of: as if; and now
konyagi (S)	an alcoholic drink
kuja-ne, kuja-to	a Swahili word kuja = to come, with Cutchi ending
kula wali (S)	to eat rice
kumbe (S)	So; I see; etc
kuni (S)	firewood
kwa heri (S)	good bye
kweli (S)	true
ladoo	a sweetmeat
lalu	derogatory term used in the sense of: a good-for-nothing
maandazi (S)	a sweet, fried bread
machar	mosquito
machela (S)	a litter
machungwa (S)	oranges
maghrab	dusk
maji (S)	water
malai	cream
manuari (S)	from English man o'war
marad	a man; he-man
marungi (S)	a leaf chewed for its mild narcotic effect
massala	spice

mbona umerudi (S)	why have you returned?
mbuyu (S)	a baobab tree
mchawi (S)	a witchdoctor, magician, etc
Mdachi (S)	German person (cf. 'Deutsch')
mela	a fair
Mhindi	Indian
mhogo (S)	cassava
mimi (S)	I
mithai	sweetmeats
mnyama (S)	beast
mohor	a settlement negotiated for the bride before the marriage ceremony takes place
moto (S)	hot
mpishi (S)	cook
Mshiris (S)	an Arab community
msuri (S)	a cloth used by men on the Coast to wrap around the waist; often worn in place of trousers
mswaki (S)	a toothbrush, or branch used to brush teeth
mukhi	religious leader of a local community; head man
murshid	disciple
mutu mubaya (S)	a way of saying mtu mbaya (bad person)
mwalimu (S)	teacher; used for Julius Nyerere of Tanzania
mweupe (S)	white
mweusi (S)	black
mzee (S)	respectful term for an old man
naam! (S)	Yes!
nataka (S)	I want
ndizi (S)	a banana

ngalawa (S)	a dug-out boat
niani	a female; a ritual meal in which girls are invited
nipe (S)	give me
njo (S)	come
pachedi	a light cloth worn round the shoulders and head
panga (S)	a machete
penda	a sweetmeat
pili-pili-bizari (S)	spices
pir	a holy man, usually with followers
pisha (S)	move
polé (S)	sorry
rasa	a dance in which one or more persons go around in circles clapping hands and clicking fingers to a beat
salaalé! (S)	an exclamation
sana (S)	very
sanyasi	a man, in the last of the four Hindu stages of life, in which he renounces home and possessions to practise religion
Shahada (S)	the Muslim creed
Sharriffu (S)	an honorific title with religious (Islamic) connotations, used loosely
shehe (S)	same as sheikh
sheth	boss, master
shoga (S)	a woman's (woman) friend; also: a male homosexual
siasa (S)	politics
simba (S)	lion
starehe (S)	relax, take it easy, don't trouble yourself
subhanallah	Arabic: God is perfect
sufuriya (S)	a deep pan

taarabu (S)	a Swahili song set to the tune of an Indian film song
tafadhali (S)	please
TANU yajenga nchi (S)	TANU builds the nation
tasbih (S)	prayer beads
tembo (S)	elephant
tena (S)	again
tengo	Indianised form of mtengo: a portable coop or container made of light sticks
thapo	a game of hide-and-seek
thumuni (S)	the fifty-cent coin
tuna kwenda (S)	we are going
ugali (S)	maizemeal
ujamaa (S)	socialism; Tanzania's official policy of socialism
ulu	fool
unga mkono (S)	join hands; support
upesi (S)	quickly
vigegele (S)	ululation
mtumbua (S)	sweet, fried delicacy of the Coast
wako (S)	yours
wé, weh, wey (S)	you!
yar	friend
zanana show	ladies' show

Acknowledgements

My thanks to Zulfikar Ghose, Reshard Gool, Peter Nazareth for encouragement; Kulsum Bai Hasham for conversations; Vicky Unwin and AWS for being there; the Ontario Arts Council and Multiculturalism Directorate (Canada) for assistance; David Rowe for kindness. Also to Jane Harley for her patience with the gunny and Susheila Nasta for an exhaustive reading of it, and to Nizar Ebrahim for hospitality. I am indebted to Mzee Salum Majutu and Baraka Hamisi for a pointer on vocabulary.

About the Author

M.G. VASSANJI is one of Canada's most celebrated and prominent writers. Born in Kenya in 1950, Vassanji was raised in Tanzania and arrived in Canada in 1978.

He studied theoretical nuclear phyisics at MIT and the University of Pennsylvania before becoming a postdoctoral fellow at the Atomic Energy of Canada. From 1980 to 1989, he was a research associate at the University of Toronto. During this period he co-founded and edited a literary magazine, *The Toronto Review of Contemporary Writing Abroad*, and began writing stories.

In 1989, with the publication of his first novel, *The Gunny Sack*, he was invited to spend a season at the International Writing Program of the University of Iowa. He is currently the author of nine novels, two collections of short stories, and three non-fiction works. He is a two-time winner of the Giller Prize and a member of the Order of Canada. In 2016, he received the Canada Council Molson Prize for the Arts for his outstanding career achievements.

He now lives in Toronto with his wife and two sons, and visits Africa and India often. To find out more visit: www.mgvassanji.com.